A Friend of Mr. Lincoln

A
FRIEND
of
MR. LINCOLN

◆◆◆

Stephen Harrigan

 Alfred A. Knopf, New York, 2016

THIS IS A BORZOI BOOK PUBLISHED BY ALFRED A. KNOPF

Copyright © 2016 by Stephen Harrigan
FEB 1 2 2016
All rights reserved. Published in the United States by Alfred A. Knopf,
a division of Penguin Random House LLC, New York, and distributed in Canada by
Random House of Canada, a division of Penguin Random House Canada Ltd., Toronto.

www.aaknopf.com

Knopf, Borzoi Books, and the colophon are registered trademarks of
Penguin Random House LLC.

Library of Congress Cataloging-in-Publication Data
Harrigan, Stephen, [date]
A friend of Mr. Lincoln : a novel / Stephen Harrigan.
pages cm
ISBN 978-0-307-70067-4 (hardback)—ISBN 978-1-101-94686-2 (eBook)
1. Lincoln, Abraham, 1809–1865—Friends and associates—Fiction. I. Title.
PS3558.A626F85 2016
813'.54—dc23   2015015853

Jacket images: (left to right) © Lee Avison / Arcangel Images; © Susan Fox / Trevillion
Images; (background) Print by John W. Hill / The NYPL / Art Resource, N.Y.
Jacket design by Joe Montgomery

Manufactured in the United States of America
First Edition

FOR MAISIE AND ROMY

1865

ONE

◆◆◆

THE LINE TO SEE THE PRESIDENT moved slowly, stuporously, six citizens abreast. It began somewhere in the disordered crowd that had jammed the city square and inched past uniformed guards to the wrought-iron fence surrounding the statehouse. Micajah Weatherby shuffled forward with the rest, thinking he might be greeted at any moment by a friendly, astonished voice. "Cage Weatherby! By God, you're in Springfield? What are you doing waiting in this line with everyone else? Come with me at once. Why, of all the people he wouldn't want standing out here in the heat!"

He doubted, though, that anyone would recognize him. He was fifty-four, rather portly now, though only a few years earlier he had been as athletically trim as when he and the rest of the young blades of Springfield used to play fives against the brick walls behind the square. But the violent loss of his left arm had given him a disinclination to take exercise at a time when the driving purpose of his middle-aged body was to accumulate mass. So he was incognito: forgotten, fat, one-armed, his face hidden beneath the bushy whiskers of the age.

The odds were not certain that he would recognize anyone in return: all those once familiar faces, clean-shaven in the long ago but now doubtless also obscured by beards, and fleshy or slack with age. His old friends, unseen for so many years, would have missing teeth, thinning hair, stooped and tired stances. Perhaps one of them was standing within arm's reach—Joshua Speed, or Ashbel Merritt. No, if they were here they would not be waiting in line with all the barbers and storekeepers and mechanics. They would be inside already, in a special room set aside for them.

3

Although they began letting the crowd in at midmorning, it was noon before Cage was finally inside the statehouse and upstairs in the Hall of Representatives. There the line that had been moving so sluggishly was parted in two by the guards and suddenly accelerated, flowing around the catafalque with a disorienting swiftness. Perhaps that was for the best, because when Cage finally saw the face in the coffin he had to fight back the instinct to shut his eyes and shove his way back down the stairs.

He was on more familiar terms with death than most, even in those terrible years. But this was Abraham Lincoln, and this was death in a new register: more profound, more final, as bewildering to him as if he were encountering the unthinkable phenomenon for the first time. It was strangely silent in that venerable public place. Everyone was too stunned to weep. Nevertheless, he could feel his composure eroding. He was glad the procession had not been any slower. He did not want to look at that face a moment more.

He was too unsettled to see it clearly. He just had the impression of something truly and obscenely dead, dead for weeks and now, for all the grim majesty of the surroundings, cheaply and shockingly displayed. It was obvious the body should have been long underground. The banks of flowers and evergreens were meant to hide the scent of putrefaction, but they only made it more obvious. His face—could that really be, have been, his friend Lincoln's face?—was a moldering mess, collapsing in on itself beneath a glaring white shell of chalk and rouge.

When Cage looked up from the coffin he met the eyes of some poor girl from the Philharmonic Society. She looked stricken as she lent her voice to the choir's soothing hymn, trying to keep from fainting in the crowded, close room, the windows draped, the gas lit, the mourners passing by in their unending multitudes, glancing down one by one with the same expression of solemn horror. He felt sorry for her, imprisoned in this hothouse with a corroding corpse, under the press of an entire nation's sorrow.

He filed out with the others beneath various mottoes that had been put up among the greenery and the black droopers. "Washington the Father, Lincoln the Saviour." "Though dead, he yet speaketh." He made his way downstairs through the south door and into the blessed May air, where the smell of the lilac blossoms was unforced and no longer in service as a fragrant assault on decay. The whole square, the whole city, was covered in black. The massive columns of the county courthouse across Sixth Street had been turned into funereal barber poles with their swirling bands of black and white.

The people who were not in line to see the body, or who were not standing about aimlessly on the streets, were walking en masse from one place to the next where Lincoln had lived, where he had worked, to see the things that his now-sacred hands had touched. Cage walked with them, just another stranger in town, another grieving curious tourist, and found himself at the house at Eighth and Jackson that Lincoln and Mary had bought back in the forties, not long before they had mostly vanished from his life. The house had only one story back then. It had soon enough been turned into a capacious two-level dwelling of a prosperous man of the law. Cage had never seen it from the inside—never invited, thanks to Mary.

The people who lived in the house now had opened it up to the curious. Cage reckoned they had no choice. If the doors had not been open the crowds would have taken them off their hinges and carted them away. As it was, those who were not lined up at the front door to see the rooms were busy plucking blades of grass and blossoms from the garden bed, and there were even children scraping paint chips off the walls to take home as holy relics. The house paint was a pale brown, which mixed queasily with the black curtains and valances.

His own thoughts were as darkly shrouded as Lincoln's house. After many years away he had come back to the raw political boomtown—grown now into an almost unrecognizable city—that had been his home as a young man. But there was no sense of nostalgia, no warm ache of times past and lives flown. He had done his best to keep his mind trained forward, to stay ahead of the hypo, but today he sensed a collapsing darkness, a black thing pawing at his mind. He wondered: Is this what it had been like for Abraham Lincoln? Was this the sort of anguish he experienced every time his smile faded and he disappeared into that melancholic stillness of his?

By a freakish good fortune in timing he had managed to get a room at the Chenery House; otherwise he would have had to pay for the privilege of sleeping on the floor in some crowded boardinghouse, or bivouacking in a tent on the outskirts of town. He was glad he had the room to return to now, someplace to go to purge himself of this bile of despair. He made his way against the crowds surging toward the Lincoln house and walked back to the center of town, wiping away the sweat that poured down onto his face from the tight brim of his hat. Once in his room he took off his coat and collar and threw himself on the bed. When he woke, it was hours later, almost dusk. It took him another half hour to shake off the stupefaction of emerging from such a fierce nap.

He went down into the crowded lobby to read the papers, disturbingly avid for every detail of the assassination and how it had unfolded. He noticed that even the opposition papers were still publishing "Breaking Through the Ice," the poem he had written in one sitting in a fury the night of Lincoln's murder. He had had no thought of trying to rekindle his career with it. Writing the poem had been as raw an act of grief as letting out a wail. But he had shown it to a friend at the *Chicago Tribune* and it had come out the next day on the front page, and was immediately reprinted in papers across the country, then issued as broadsides and handbills and read aloud on courthouse steps and even, he was told, set to music. He did not think it his best work, but it was unguarded and almost untouched by the vanity and yearning for literary immortality that had driven him in the old days. That his name was now famous for one spontaneous poem, and not for the product of years of passionate, concentrated labor, was an irony easily absorbed when so much shattering change was in the air.

Seward would survive being knifed in his bed, he learned from the pages of *The Illinois State Journal.* Harrold's trial was under way, and the captors of Booth were quarreling among themselves about the division of the reward. The papers were declaring that as many as three hundred people had been part of the conspiracy, but he rather doubted that. And then there was, as always, the war itself to read about. Richmond had fallen a month ago, and according to the latest dispatch from New Orleans Kirby Smith had surrendered, but who could be sure it would not all flare up again, or degenerate into something that was no longer a defined war but a series of dirty reprisals and counter-reprisals that would last for generations and destroy the Union after all?

He had missed his lunch. It was a good sign that he was hungry. The shock and sadness of Lincoln's death were still acute but the conviction that existence itself was a cruel and static thing had evaporated in the afternoon's sleep.

There was a long wait for a table in the hotel's dining room, and every other eating place and tavern in town was full as well. He went instead to the new Masonic Lodge, whose doors had been thrown open to the public and tables set up to create a temporary dining hall. It was an efficient operation and the line moved quickly. He did not mind, on this evening, sharing a table with strangers. Grief, like danger, excites the herding impulse.

He sat with a family from Alton. The father was a widowed manager of a lard-oil factory who had brought his three daughters and his late wife's blind mother to Springfield for the funeral. The man had seen Cage struggling to balance his cup and plate of stew with one hand and had rushed to his aid and ushered him to the table his family had claimed in the corner of the lodge. They wanted to know if he was a resident of Springfield and, if so, if he had known the president. Cage told them he had not lived in the city for almost twenty years, which was true, and that though he had seen Mr. Lincoln back then walking through the streets from time to time he had never known him or even been introduced to him, which was blatantly false. He excused himself of the lie readily enough. He told himself he did not want to aggrandize himself in this somber moment by impressing listeners with his intimate stories of long ago. That was true, but the starker truth was that it would hurt to tell those stories, to remember too acutely.

The youngest of the girls, ten or eleven years old, kept glancing at his empty sleeve. He was an old man to her and she could not have imagined that he might have lost his arm actually fighting in the war. Her father wanted to talk about Old Bob, the president's suddenly famous horse, whom the family had admired that afternoon as the animal posed for photographers outside the Lincoln home. They had also been among the first in line that morning at the statehouse. The blind mother-in-law said that although she could not see the president she had felt his spirit as she moved past the coffin. She experienced this as an unexpected flood of gladness and peace.

The father was a nervous, plan-ahead sort of man. He wanted to know Cage's thoughts about the funeral tomorrow. Where was the best place to form up so that they wouldn't be at the trailing edge of the procession? Would there be such a crush of people that the cemetery would not hold them all? Was it true that Mrs. Lincoln was still back in Washington, too grief-stricken to even attend her own husband's funeral?

He offered what insights he could, but was already thinking he might miss the funeral himself, leave town on the first train to Chicago. He had seen enough history firsthand. He did not need to be crowding in to see more. And there was a kind of sting in knowing he would not be at the front of the procession, not walking beside the hearse as a pallbearer. Old Bob now had more of a claim to Lincoln than he did.

After dinner, out on the streets at night, he felt foolishly alone. He was homesick for San Francisco, which he had not seen now in almost four years: the sea lions barking on the wharves, the moist, seeping fog; sights and sensations that had been unimaginable to him as a young man living on the Illinois prairie. Now Springfield itself was almost as foreign as California had once been. The streets were brightly lit with gas lamps and planked over—no more muddy hog holes to swallow up unwary pedestrians. All the buildings on the square were of brick. Most of the wooden buildings were gone, including the Palatine, the lodging house he had once owned. Chicken Row had burned down in a fire. In its place were stalwart new structures housing jewelry stores and haberdashers. There was a new governor's mansion, new halls and bank buildings, a new market house. The people promenading along the sidewalks tonight on their Abraham Lincoln memorial tour, buying slices of pie and card photographs of the Lincolns' dog from opportunistic vendors, were not just strangers to him but proof of his own ghostly irrelevance.

He walked south to Aristocracy Hill, where Ninian Edwards's grand house still stood, looking much the same as it had when he and the other ambitious young men of Springfield had congregated there for hops and balls and windy political talk, arrogant enough to believe that any room that held them was the staging ground of their futures. Those futures were now revealed—certainly Abraham Lincoln's was. He was venerably dead now, sealed already within a tomb of myth. Would anyone ever really believe he had once been young—young and confused and desperate for success?

As for Cage Weatherby, his future appeared to him on this bleak night to be just a listless pageant of increasing obscurity and age.

After another hour of wandering in the warm May darkness he walked back through the square on the way to his hotel and stopped on the corner of Washington and Fifth, remembering. Of course: this was where Speed's store had been. But it was not here anymore. It had been demolished or burned down and then swallowed up by another modern brick row.

While he was standing there he saw a doorway shingle: *Lincoln and Herndon.* This must be where the new law office was. New to Cage, anyway. When he had left Springfield in the damnable summer of 1846 the office had been on the other corner of the square. This building, like all the others, was a funereal display tonight, everything draped in black. But there was a light burning in one of the back windows overlooking the alley. It was late now, eleven o'clock. The streets were finally starting to empty, though there were plenty of people who apparently had no rooms to sleep in and were passing the night before the funeral just walking back and forth.

He tried the street-level door. It was unlocked. His lonesome, grieving mood gave him leave to enter. The stairway creaked and he trod heavily in the darkness to make it creak louder, worried that he would take someone by surprise and be greeted with a bowie knife in the ribs. At the top of the stairs a glass-paned door was wide open. Inside were two long tables formed into the shape of a T. Billy Herndon sat alone at one wing of the top table, staring down with more absorption than was warranted at a piece of pie. It was like a painting by some Flemish master—the clever pool of lamplight, the ruddy-faced subject, the untouched pie on its white china plate, the thick green folds of the baize that covered the working tables.

"Billy," he said from the doorway, "it's Cage."

Herndon looked up with no hurry and no apparent surprise, though the two men hadn't seen each other in twenty years. He stood up without a word and with tears in his eyes. He held out his hand. Cage crossed the room to shake it. The office was bigger but essentially the same as the old one had been—a messy, overflowing room with random stacks of books and papers and pleadings, floors that looked like they had never been scrubbed. Not the sort of place to inspire confidence in a man trying to win a lawsuit or escape a murder charge, but an initial impression of shabbiness was a vital part of the way that Abraham Lincoln had worked his spell.

"You want this pie?" Herndon said. "I hate the idea of it."

"All right."

Billy handed him a fork. Although he had eaten dinner, Cage was still hungry. Partly this was due to the hollowing effects of sorrow, but the memory of true starvation, of that Sierra winter, accounted for something more, a kind of fretful ravening that was now a permanent part of his consciousness.

"My wife made it," Billy said. "She's a good hand with a crust, but today of all days I do not want to eat a piece of pie."

He poured bourbon into a glass and then leavened it with a splash of water from a pitcher. He said he had another glass somewhere in the office. Cage told him not to bother.

"I don't remember you as a temperance man."

"I wasn't particularly, back then. I'm more inclined to it now, for some reason."

"Well, God bless you, sir, and God bless our murdered friend."

He took a deep sip of his bourbon and sat back, looking warmly at Cage.

"I read your poem, of course. Along with the whole country. By God it's a masterwork. It will be remembered."

"Maybe. It doesn't matter."

"Of course it matters and you know it. 'Those were the arms that swung the axe, that broke the ice and set the waters free.' Very fine. Very fine indeed. You see, I've memorized it already."

He didn't have the line quite right, though Cage didn't bother to correct him. The poem came from something Lincoln had told him many years ago, how as a young man he had been employed to break up the ice on the Sangamon to open a channel for a steamship trying to make its way past New Salem. Setting the waters free was too obvious a metaphor for emancipation, but that had not bothered Cage when he composed the poem and it did not bother him now. At a time of national and personal distress, subtlety was a fussy virtue.

"You saw him?" Herndon asked.

"This morning."

"How do you think he looked?"

"I wish I hadn't seen it."

Cage took another bite of his pie and pushed the plate aside across the table.

"He was coming back here to practice law with me," Herndon said. "He said we'd take up again as if nothing had ever happened. Though I doubt that when it came to it she would have let him. Do you know the name for her in Washington? The hellcat."

"Don't call her that. Not now."

"Have you heard how she treated Springfield? We bought the old Mather place for her, spent fifty-three thousand dollars. Hundreds of workmen working night and day to build a marble tomb. You can go see it now, I'll take you there. By God, the name Abraham Lincoln is already carved into it! But she turns her back on us, just the way she always did. Not good enough for her husband, not 'quiet' enough. Threatens to bury him in Chicago if we don't start all over again out at the new cemetery. She has no friends here, Cage."

He finished his drink in one quick, practiced swallow and poured another. Billy Herndon was no longer the fervent young clerk of Joshua Speed's store, ten years younger than Lincoln and Cage but always ready with passionate opinions about the abomination of slavery or the treachery of Jackson. He was emotional and high-tempered and had been nursing the hurt of Mary Lincoln's dislike of him for years. But he had worshipped her husband, of course. He now wore his own version of the president's beard, though in his case the unshaven upper lip contrasted too strongly with the robust whiskers below, so that the top of his face looked strikingly naked. The beard had some gray in it, but his hair was still dark and combed into a disorderly clump on top of his head.

Billy gestured with his glass, not subtly, to Cage's empty sleeve.

"Did you ever talk to him, after that?"

"No."

"Were you there when Baker was killed?"

"Not far away, but I couldn't see anything, or hear anything either."

"This horrible war. We could never have imagined such a thing back then, could we? How did you get here all the way from California in time?"

"I'm at Chicago now."

"Are you so? I didn't know that."

He had been in bed with Ellie when he heard the news. The illicit nature of their union—"union": there was the word again, inescapable forevermore—had long worn off and they had been lying there feeling, in their settled comfort with each other, satisfyingly chaste. A stout one-armed man and a still slender and still unattainable gray-haired woman, neither asking too much more of life than what was there before them. The news came by telegraph only an hour or so after Booth had struck. When they heard the excitement below Ellie's house on Clark Street he guessed what had happened—more than guessed. Though he had never consciously prophesied Lincoln's murder, he felt a calm confirmation flood through him. The moment he had been waiting for without knowing it had come to pass. They both dressed quickly and followed the crowds to the newspaper office. An hour or so later the door opened and someone stepped out with a piece of paper in his hand. Although Cage and Ellie were too far back to hear, an almost visible wave of shock traveled through the people massed in front of them and hit them with its full force. They clung to each other as they tried to absorb the news that he was truly dead, then walked back through the streets as the sobbing and wailing and cries of vengeance went on all around them. They stayed up all night, Cage writing his poem. Ellie's weeping maid brought in coffee and they drank it in amazed silence as they sat at the window looking down on the crowded streets, where people were racing back and forth, asking one another for news as if some urgent detail could countermand the finality of what they had already heard.

"The news was just too large," Herndon was saying now, as if he had somehow been sharing Cage's own recollection. "Too large to enter my brain."

"What will you do now, Billy?"

"Well, keep practicing law without him, I suppose. But that won't be any fun at all."

Herndon settled back into his hard wooden chair in a slouch. He looked out of his office window as if there were a view to be contemplated, but there was nothing to see but smudged glass and a range of tar-covered roofs that only deepened the blackness of this black night.

"All the lawyers in town got together a few days ago," he told Cage. "They asked me to put forth the resolutions: his noble character, kind heart, iron integrity, on and on. But it started to feel somehow not complete, not the full portrait. So I added one little phrase about how he wasn't maybe quite as broad-minded as some other men. Well, there was hell to pay for that, I can tell you! Logan himself jumping up to protest as if I'd blackened his memory forever."

"It's natural. People grieving."

"Well, ain't I grieving too, Cage? Wasn't he my friend as well? The thing is I don't care what Logan says. I don't care what the hellcat herself says. By God, if we let it happen they'll just steal him away from us, make him the most broad-minded man who ever walked the earth and it'll be like the real Lincoln never even existed."

He lifted a big volume of Kent's *Commentaries* with a secret ceremonial flourish, as if he were removing the lid from a tomb. Beneath it was a small sheaf of loose pages covered with his undisciplined handwriting.

"I've been up here scribbling for the last two nights. I believe I might write a book. What do you think about that?"

"There'll be many books about him. Why not one from you?"

"You misunderstand me. I'm not talking about just a book, I'm talking about something essential. The verifiable truth about him, not sentimental blather. And not just what I know firsthand but what I can find out from people like you—people who really knew him."

"Mary?"

"Mary too. But I doubt she'd even answer a letter from me. And what do you think the odds are of her telling the truth about anything? You know her—she's going to think she can hold history by the throat. That's why I need your help. Set down a few recollections, Cage. Send them to me. Do you promise?"

Cage said he was too tired to promise anything; he would think about it. But by the time he had stood and shaken Billy Herndon's hand and walked back down the stairway to the street he had decided he would not burden himself with presenting the true story of Abraham Lincoln to the world. To hell with history and to hell with everything just now that was not his quiet room at the Chenery House. As he walked outside every step registered his increasing girth and gravity. A single piece of pie seemed to have made a telling difference. His collar was too tight and he could feel the strain in his shirt and coat. The sense of constriction excited the phantom pains in his missing arm. He had once thought he had trained himself to recognize those pains as illusory and therefore disregard them, as a sleeper upon awakening can talk himself out of the reality of a nightmare. But he was as much in as out of a nightmare tonight, and the pains were real, a burning restlessness as the severed nerves probed and throbbed, trying to capture the shape of a thing that was gone and could never be again.

He did not need to write down his memories, for Herndon or anyone else. They would come unbidden throughout the remainder of his life, a life whose course had been formed, as the course of the country had been formed, by the spirit and will of one man.

But for all the memories, Lincoln was distant from him tonight, distant in power and fame, conclusively distant in death. Cage saw, walking through the empty square, that the lights were on in the statehouse where his friend lay, where the guards were still keeping him company and the mourners still filing through on the eve of his interment. The light leaking through the windows, though, looked forlorn and weak—a lonely hearth fire on a vast dark prairie. And above the statehouse, almost invisible against the night sky, flew the black pennon of death.

1832

TWO

◆ ◆ ◆

THE DAY BEFORE HE MET Abraham Lincoln was the most harrowing day of Cage Weatherby's life.

He was part of a thirty-man scouting party that rode out at daybreak onto the prairie from the battalion's camp on a swelling ridge known as Kellogg's Grove. They were looking for Black Hawk's war trail. They halted about a mile from the ridge and Major Dement sent a half dozen men to scout a tree line in the distance. No one spoke as the scouts rode out and disappeared into the trees. They were not expecting a fight. Weeks of marching and counter-marching all across Illinois to no apparent purpose had almost drained the possibility of real action from their minds. But everyone was aware of the terrible rout that had befallen Major Stillman and his men several months ago, and though their militia training had been haphazard, their survival instincts were sharp enough. It seemed wrong to be standing still on an open prairie with no cover anywhere close by. Cage's horse, New Fred, was nervous and disapproving. He and Cage were still getting used to each other and the relationship was not going well. Old Fred, the horse he had ridden since he enlisted in May, had foundered two weeks earlier outside Dixon's Ferry.

Cage watched Major Dement raise himself up and down in his stirrups, flexing the muscles in his legs, impatient for the return of his scouts. Then they heard gunfire from the grove on the far side of the prairie—urgent, uncoordinated discharges. Bob Zanger, on his horse next to Cage, looked up and said, "What in hell . . . ," but in that instant it was already clear what was happening. The six men Dement had sent ahead were galloping back to them out of the trees, pursued by what looked like hundreds of mounted Indians. Cage saw two of the Illinois men shot out of the saddle almost at the same moment, one of them protesting with a hideous cry of pain, blood showering out from his rib cage, the other slipping off his horse without complaint, his life simply, magically over in an instant.

"Charge, goddammit!" Dement shouted. "Now!" He spurred his horse forward and Cage and the rest of the men followed, riding to the support of the fleeing scouts. But none of the men were trained or equipped for a cavalry charge, and though they had practiced dismounting and fighting on foot, with every fourth man holding the reins of the horses so that the rest could aim steadily and fire in concentration, they had not drilled often enough for the lesson to take hold in the chaos of real warfare. All they could do was rein to a ragged stop and discharge their weapons at the advancing Indians. The volley threw up an obscuring fog of gunpowder smoke and there was a moment of unexpected silence in which they thought they might have turned the Indians' advance. But then rifle balls began to punch through the smoke and they heard the enemy's high-pitched yelling and saw them erupt into view. The hooves of their horses broke up the ground beneath them, sending up a cycling churn of dirt clods that advanced along with the mounted Indians like the spray of a breaking wave. The faces of the British Band were painted for war, their arms tattooed and their heads shaven except for waving scalplock crests. They were thin and hungry and many of them were wearing ragged white man's clothes. Cage was startled by the hatred in their eyes, hatred from which he absurdly thought he should be excepted or excused.

Dement called out for the men to retreat in the face of this renewed charge and head back across the prairie to the safety of Kellogg's Grove. Half of them already had. The rest galloped frantically toward the distant swell of land, some of the men taking the ramrods out of their muskets and beating the flanks of their horses to speed them on.

Cage heard—above all the screaming and shooting and hoof pounding—the sound of a bone cracking. It was Bob Zanger's horse, shot in one of its front legs. The animal collapsed and cartwheeled on the ground, but Bob was back on his feet in an instant, barely missing a stride, sprinting and panting, an expression on his face that was no expression at all—just a blank mask of survival.

Cage knew he ought to turn around and try to save his comrade, but the thought was too late the moment it was formed. Over his shoulder, he saw two of the Indians dismount at a run and grab Bob's arms and wrestle him to the ground. He saw them swinging their tomahawks as Bob cried out, "Don't! Don't!"

Cage faced furiously forward so he wouldn't have to see what happened next. Then he had the feeling somebody was looking at him. He turned to his right where a moment before Bob Zanger had been, and there was an Indian riding right alongside him, staring at him as if he were measuring him for a shirt. Cage would never forget what the Indian looked like. His face was sharpened by hunger and his eyes were shining. He wore a calico shirt whose collar had been cut away to show off his eagle claw necklace. He had smallpox scars on his grimacing face and a feather tied into the strip of hair that rose from his otherwise shaven head like the bristles on an angry dog.

The Indian swiped at him with a war club. Cage awkwardly parried the blow with his heavy antique musket. By that time his assailant's underfed horse was panting and stumbling and falling behind, and there was fire now from the ridge at Kellogg's Grove, where the rest of the battalion was covering their retreat from the Indians.

They made it to the top of the ridge. The Indians had stopped their pursuit but there was still heavy fire that seemed to come from everywhere at once and Dement screamed for the men to ground-picket their mounts and get into the goddam house. Ground-picket meant to dismount, drop the reins, and trust in the horse's judgment. As New Fred galloped off into the trees, Cage sprinted for the door of the rotting three-room cabin that some settler had long ago abandoned and that now served the men of Dement's battalion as a fort. There were over a hundred men crowded into that log house, fighting for space to punch out shooting holes in the chinking with their knives, breathing air that was immediately rank and grainy with gunpowder. They could see Black Hawk's warriors as they dismounted and filed into a ravine at the edge of the grove.

They were forted up all the rest of that day and through the night. Cage was sure the Indians would fire the cabin. He jostled his way to a shooting place near the door so that he would have a chance to escape the inferno and die in the open air. But instead of attacking the cabin, the Indians turned their attention to the horses that were still tied to the picket ropes fifty yards away. All night Cage and the rest of the besieged men listened to the hysterical, guttural pleading of the horses trying to get free. They heard the balls slapping into their flesh and their broken legs scrabbling on the ground. In general, the animals had been poorly cared for during the campaign, but now the sound of their suffering filled the men with an intolerable burden of sympathy. Some wept aloud and others got down on their knees on the dirt floor of the cabin and prayed for God to deliver them from the fate of their horses.

But before dawn the firing stopped and the Indians slipped away in the remaining darkness, perhaps too low on gunpowder to press the siege any further. Dement threw open the door and the men staggered cautiously outside. They stared at the horses the Indians had shot, some of them still miserably alive, the others lying there unmoving with the dead weight of their bodies still attached to the picket line. The horses that had been ground-picketed and able to run away came nervously back, New Fred among them.

Somebody yelled that there were horsemen coming and there was a moment of renewed panic as some of the men raced back toward the cabin. But it turned out the riders approaching were white men, a spy company from Fort Dixon that had ridden all night to their rescue. The men of Dement's battalion cheered their arrival as the newcomers rode up the ridge with the rising sun behind them and stared down with horror at the dead and dying horses.

The leader of the spy company dismounted and conferred with Major Dement, and then the major looked around and saw Cage holding the reins of New Fred.

"You," he said, forgetting Cage's name, or more likely unaware of it to begin with. "You've still got a horse. Ride out there onto the prairie with Captain Early's men and show them where they're likely to find our boys."

Cage led his still-saddled horse over to the group of three mounted men that Captain Early had detached to find and gather up the dead. One of the men nodded at him as he approached and leaned down from the saddle to shake his hand.

"I'm Abraham Lincoln."

He was young—or so Cage would remember him. He did not seem young at the time. No one did in that summer of 1832, during the hard and mostly meandering campaign of the Black Hawk War. Lincoln would have been his own age—twenty-two or twenty-three. He had ridden all night. He was gaunt and unshaven and hard-used, his feet caked in dry mud, the buttons gone from the placket of his shirt and his narrow sunburned wrists protruding from its tattered sleeves. He was a head taller than the five men who were with him, too tall for the little mare he was riding, too tall for even his own clothes, since the frayed bottoms of his jean pants were a good five inches from the tops of his brogans.

He was not as freakishly remarkable in his appearance as it would later become fashionable to recall. Lincoln was exquisitely self-conscious, thought he was ugly, and later reckoned he had no choice but to promote himself as such. But it was his height and strength that marked him in Cage's mind that day, his height and strength and something else—the fact that he introduced himself to Cage when none of the other men he was with bothered to do so, and the plaintive note of human comradeship in his eyes when Cage returned the handshake.

Lincoln must have recognized something in his face that Cage himself did not realize was there. The horror he had lived through during the last day and night must have still been visible.

"I expect some of these boys we're looking for are friends of yours," Lincoln said as Cage mounted his horse for an unwelcome return to yesterday's battlefield. Cage nodded in reply, grateful for the implied note of sympathy.

"Well, we'll do our best for the poor devils," Lincoln said.

While the rest of the spy company were starting breakfast fires and contemplating the work of gathering the dead horses together and burning them, Cage led the party out of Kellogg's Grove and down to the open Illinois prairie. They trailed three mules bearing packsaddles heaped with blankets and old tent canvases. New Fred had no interest in revisiting the site of yesterday's terror, and he let Cage know by contesting every forward step. After fifty yards New Fred gave up actively resisting, though the muscles in his neck were still taut and his head warily upright. As he fought his horse forward, Cage was aware that he had to goad his own unwilling self as well. The open land was ominous in a way it had not seemed yesterday when they had ridden out to scout. Riding back across the landscape this morning, the sun illuminating it with such clarity as it crested the ridgeline of Kellogg's Grove behind them, Cage remembered how impossible it had been to see after that first hectic volley, the whole field and Black Hawk's mounted warriors immediately obscured behind a gray shroud of gunpowder smoke.

"I don't see anybody yet," one of the men said to Lincoln. "We sure this is where they ended up?"

"Ask him, John," Lincoln said, indicating Cage.

"All right, I'll ask him," the man said. His name was John Stuart. He was round-faced and somehow clean-shaven, mild-looking in comparison to Lincoln, his voice crisper and stronger. Was he the leader of this group? Was there any leader?

"I don't know where exactly they would be," Cage told him. "I only saw one man fall. Bob Zanger. That happened about a couple hundred yards over there to the south. At least that's where I think it was."

"It could be the Indians dragged them into those trees," the third man said, pointing to a tree-lined ravine ahead. He was Jim Reed, someone Cage would grow to know very well over the years, almost as well as he would know Lincoln. Reed was older, in his thirties, rash where Lincoln and Stuart were intuitively cautious. "We should probe beyond the tree line and see if we can find signs of their camp."

"You can wander into the trees if you like, Jim," Stuart said. "But I'm more comfortable out here where I can see if somebody wants to split my head with a tomahawk."

Lincoln reined his horse to a stop as if he hadn't been listening to this conversation and was lost in his private thoughts. They all stopped with him. He took off his fraying straw hat and wiped his forehead with what might once have been a silk neckerchief but was now a colorless rag full of holes. It was only an hour past daybreak, though it was already hot enough for sweat to be running into his eyes. His black hair was thick but shorn close to his head, no doubt by some messmate with no claim to the barbering arts. He put his hat back on and balanced his musket across his knees as he tied the neckerchief back in place with a square knot.

Then he nosed his horse ahead and they all moved forward again. Cage decided he must be the leader after all, if not by formal designation then by practical effect. The still-rising sun cast a glowing light on the field before them. The grass barely stirred. New Fred jerked his head up and down, arguing with his rider's control of the reins. The muscles in the horse's neck were still taut and his mane was sodden with sweat. They were getting closer. Cage could feel it as well, the memory of their horrible, humiliating flight across this ground infesting him like a poison. And Black Hawk's warriors might still be hiding in the trees as Reed said, or they might be concealed in some slight draw or dip in the land ahead. His hands were trembling; he worked to keep his breathing steady.

"I see something," Stuart said, though almost in a whisper. He was pointing to the west at what seemed to be a tiny red disk, blazing with the brightness of a mirror in the light of the sun. When they got to where Bob Zanger was lying, they saw that the red disk was a half-dollar-sized hole in his severed head where the Indians had taken his scalp. The better portion of his body lay about twenty feet away, and the grass there had a coppery sheen of blood. They had taken away Bob's clothes and chopped off his arms and opened him up and pulled out all the soft parts and strewn them across the prairie.

Cage stared without comprehension at this heap of glistening human rubbish throbbing with green-headed flies. The world around him shone and shimmered with unreal precision. What was left of his working mind told him to dismount before he fainted and fell to the ground.

He watched Lincoln walk around Bob's dismembered and disemboweled body, staring at all the pieces as if wondering where they were all supposed to go.

"That's a hell of a mess," Reed said. "Maybe we should just bury him where he lies."

"No," Lincoln said. "I expect we better not. Him and his fellows ought to be gathered up and buried together. That's the proper way to do it."

He turned to Cage. "You know him?"

Cage responded with a vacuous nod and got down on his hands and knees and vomited. There was nothing much in his stomach to purge but it seemed there would be no end to his retching anyway.

"You don't have to help us with this part," Lincoln said as Cage cast up a final string of bile and spittle. Stuart had untied a moldy piece of canvas from one of the mules and spread it out on the ground. Lincoln reached down and gently picked up Bob Zanger's head with his big hands, holding its staring face away from him as he carried it over and set it down on the canvas. Stuart and Reed each took hold of a foot and dragged the torso and its mass of trailing guts over to join the other oddments of the body.

Bob had been a schoolteacher from Danville who tired of the classroom and sold his collected works of Cicero for a Kentucky rifle. Like most of the other young men who had enlisted in the volunteer army, he had been eager to join in the frolic, to earn the gratitude and good faith of their fellow citizens, which would be the capital they would use to advance themselves in Illinois.

"Got your needle and thread?" Lincoln asked Reed. "We need to sew him up in there pretty good so none of his pieces come tumbling out on us."

As Reed sewed what was left of Bob Zanger into his stiff canvas shroud, Lincoln squatted down next to Cage in the grass. With his long legs bent that way, he looked like a giant insect about to spring into the sky.

"Not the first time we had this job," Lincoln said. He had a creaky voice but there was a gentle tone to it. "That's why we might seem practical-minded about it. We haven't seen any real fighting like you have, but we sure have learned to do this kind of work."

Cage nodded in a distant way. He wanted to appear more grateful to this angular stranger, who had more than once gone out of his way to express his sympathy. But the idea that his schoolteacher friend was dead and butchered while he himself was more vibrantly alive than ever had not just seized his thoughts but seized them up. The experiences of this day were too vast, his mind too small an instrument to capture and make sense of them.

After they hoisted the shroud with its shifting, bulging contents onto the back of one of the mules and tied it down, they set off reconnoitering again, and after a few minutes spotted four more bodies lying in the grass, all of them with the same bright bloody circle on their heads where the British Band had taken their scalps.

" 'That host on the morrow lay withered and strown,'" Lincoln said in an awe-filled murmur. Cage had not expected to hear a gangly backwoodsman reciting Byron, but it was only a small detail to be added to the ledger of this searingly unreal day. Cage knew these dead men also, though not as well as he had known Bob Zanger, and the cauterizing shock of seeing that first defiled body made the horror of encountering the others less acute. He made a point of taking a hand in the work and pretended to himself that he was as accustomed to it as Lincoln and the other men of the spy company were.

They worked hurriedly, eager for the gruesome job to be over and still anxious about being alone and exposed so close to the concealing timber and to still-uncontrolled trails along which Black Hawk's warriors might be gathering for another attack. It was a relief finally to have the bodies in their blood-soaked blankets tied across the backs of the mules, and to be mounted and riding away again toward the safety of Kellogg's Grove.

The dead volunteers were buried later that afternoon. The men of Dement's battalion and of the spy company that had ridden all night to relieve them stood over the graves as Dement praised the sacrifice of the fallen, committed their souls to God's keeping, and stepped aside as the ceremonial volleys were fired. After the funeral, Cage was light-headed, so lacking in sleep and so weak with hunger that he felt the air trembling with the eerie atmospheric foretaste of a tornado.

He opened his wallet and gnawed on a piece of hardtack as the men of his mess began to build their cooking fires. He walked away from them to be alone for a while and sat with his back against a hickory trunk and looked down from the height of the broad ridgeline to the open grassland and distant groves and wooded ravines, a landscape that in the fading light of a summer afternoon would have lifted his heart a day or two previous. Now he saw it almost as an enemy in itself, a staging ground and hiding place for the Indians who had nearly succeeded in killing him.

From an oilskin pouch he took out his notebook and pencil and resolved to write, though he was so tired he could barely hold his head up or hold a thought in it. He had bought the notebook at a stationer's in Beardstown just before he took the militia oath. He had filled all the pages once and now he was halfway through again, holding the book horizontally and writing against the grain of his previous entries. It had been a rainy campaign and the pouch had not always been effective in keeping the notebook dry, so its cover was half-disintegrated and its pages swollen and stiff.

The grand and naive words he had written on the first leaf stared back at him now: "Sketches of the War Against Black Hawk and the British Band." He had envisioned—two months ago, two lifetimes ago—that these would be poetical sketches, but there had been time only for prose notations and weary fragments of imagery, written out dutifully at the end of each draining day, days taken up with pointless marching and counter-marching, with desultory training and drilling, with wrestling matches and horse races and card games with the army's Potawatomi allies. But this fraying notebook would still be the cornerstone of his career. Other men had joined the militia because they knew they would not be taken seriously in any future Illinois enterprise if they had stayed out of the war. As a literary man, or someone trying to be one, Cage felt the same. He had joined this fight purposefully, with an eye for the advantage it would give him, for the ballast it would set in his character. There were miscreants and idlers in the militia, but they were outnumbered by men with a goal in mind, a standard to live up to. Cage had come to Illinois more or less by accident, but had sensed early on that it was a place where things were brewing, a place with more than its share of serious people with hungry dreams. Bob Zanger had been one of them. He had talked to Cage of reading the law and being admitted to the bar, of marrying and fathering children and gaining some lucrative public office like state auditor, perhaps one day representing Illinois in the United States Congress. He had encouraged Cage in his own dream of poetic achievement. The world needed literary men, the former schoolteacher assured him, in proportion to its doctors and politicians and pork packers and mechanics. And a poet in war, if he survived, would have even more at account, even more to draw on. Bob had been right, though Cage had not truly understood how right until he had seen Bob's butchered body. Now at last there was something to write about, something horrible and vivid. But when he tried to set down his memories of the last few days, his mind kept slipping off the path, wandering into a thicket of dreams.

The face of the warrior who had been riding beside him, trying to kill him, flashed into his mind again and startled him back into something like normal consciousness. He could smell burning meat and hair from the still-smoldering pyre fifty yards from camp where the dead horses had been dragged and burned earlier in the afternoon. It was almost dark now. The men were at their fires, bacon frying in their skillets, dough coiled around their ramrods to bake in the flames. All over the camp men were pounding their parched coffee beans with their hatchets, creating a rhythmic sound like the percussive calling of a flock of birds.

Another sound: a sudden burst of laughter, like that of an audience at a play. It shook Cage out of his half-dreaming state and woke the camp out of its evening stillness. He turned to the sound of the laughter and saw a growing circle of volunteers around a campfire twenty yards deeper into the grove. Other men were streaming in that direction.

Cage put up his things and followed them. The source of the laughter turned out to be his new friend Lincoln, who was sitting on a rock and tossing chips of wood into the fire. He was talking about a visit he and some of the men in the company had made to the whorehouses of Galena, and how those Magdalene establishments reminded him of a story. It turned out to be a story of such byzantine length and brazen filthiness—about a widow woman who kept a trained eel in a rainwater barrel—that by the end of it Cage and the other listeners were almost as breathless from shock as they were from laughter.

No one was laughing as hard as Stuart, who no doubt had heard the story many times but who was bent over and wheezing just the same.

Lincoln looked up and happened to catch sight of Cage. He gave him a wink as if the two of them had not just met but were old comrades; then he gazed down into his cup and picked a bug out of his soup. The laughter around him had only just then started to die down.

"You know," Lincoln said, as if to himself, "this little animalcule here reminds me of another story."

It should not have been a particularly funny story: an old farmer, his fussy educated son, a piece of cheese full of wrigglers. But the look on Lincoln's face as he impersonated the unconcerned farmer pondering an imaginary cheese teeming with worms, or the haughty and embarrassed son pleading with him not to eat it, had the men around the fire wiping tears of hilarity out of their eyes even before he had finished.

"Let 'em wriggle. I can stand it if they can!"

Lincoln himself was so amused that he could scarcely get these concluding words out before doubling over in a laughing cramp. It was as if he had never heard the story himself, as if he were encountering it for the first time even though he was the one telling it.

"Let 'em wriggle. I can stand it if they can," he repeated, in a softer key. It was fully dark now, a soft July night, dead friends buried nearby, dead horses settling down to bone and ash, a growing suspicion in Cage's mind that the conflict they were engaged in was a sordid and pathetic thing.

The conversation around the fire switched from storytelling to political talk: the problems besetting Illinois that would have to be taken up again once this war was over, the urgent need for internal improvements—canals, navigable rivers, and railroads. He did not know then that both Lincoln and Stuart were already public men, both impatient for the war to be over so they could get back to the canvass, but both needing the war, since service in it would be the foundation of their political capital.

Cage himself was a private man by nature; he had become more private today, driven inward by all he had seen and felt and feared. But as the other men drifted away from the fire when the storytelling ended, he stayed. His interest in Lincoln only grew as the raucous attention receded.

Stuart was speaking now—the perfidy of the Democrats, the disaster that would come to pass if Jackson vetoed the bank charter. Captain Early, the leader of the spy company, was apparently a Democrat, because he took exception to everything Stuart said, saying the National Bank was and always would be a pestilence against the common man. Lincoln listened, nodded his head in agreement with Stuart, patiently absorbing Early's angry rebuttals. But he had somehow removed himself. A moment earlier he had been the consummate outward man, now he had sunk so deep into his own private musings that it seemed he might never come out again.

He shifted his weight, leaned back on a bony elbow and stared into the fire. For a moment he looked, with his long narrow head and with his looming brows casting dark shadows over his sunken cheeks, like a skeletal old man. The others were laughing at something Jim Reed had just said, but Lincoln remained silent. The absence of his good humor was so acute it seemed as if he had removed himself not just from the conversation but from the earth. In an instant he had gone from being the soul of this society to its self-banished exile.

Stuart and Early and the others argued above his brooding silence— ignoring it, no doubt used to it. But Cage had only just met Abraham Lincoln, and he did not seem like a man you could pretend was no longer there.

1836

◆ ◆ ◆

THREE

◆◆◆

SOMETHING CALLED THE ALAMO had fallen. David Crockett, the frontier wit and former Tennessee congressman, had improbably been inside the Texas fort and killed by the Mexican army along with the rest of the insurgents. There was a great stir in Springfield about the news, men gathered in the muddy streets gossiping and throwing out opinions as hogs grunted and foraged indifferently alongside them. It was winter still, but the sun was bright, melting yesterday's icicles that clung to eaves and business signs. The bell announcing a stage arrival rang out from the Globe Tavern around the corner.

Jim Reed was holding forth on the courthouse lawn in a state of righteous agitation, leaning against the whipping post and reading aloud from the pages of the *Sangamo Journal.* He announced that a Jonathan Lindley from Illinois was among the dead, though neither Cage nor the half dozen other men on the lawn recognized the name.

" 'The countenance of Crockett was unchanged,' " he read, shaking his head impatiently at the newspaper writer's maudlin prose. " 'He had in death that freshness of hue, which his exercise of pursuing the beasts of the forests and the prairie had imparted to him.' "

Reed turned to Cage with a pained grin. "Yes, of course," he said, laughing bitterly, "we all well remember the freshness of hue that death imparts."

Clean-shaven, wearing good clothes, his hair barbered close to his oversized ears, Reed nevertheless still had more than a trace of the feral intensity Cage remembered from that day at Kellogg's Grove. He liked Reed well enough and was friendly with him in a cautious way. A fearless, impulsive, go-ahead sort of man like Reed was a beacon in war,

33

but in the four years since Black Hawk's defeat he had not adjusted well to the torpor of peace, and had thrown himself into one ill-considered business after another out of sheer restlessness.

"Santa Anna didn't even bury the bodies," he announced when he returned to the newspaper. "They just burned them like dogs."

The men on the courthouse lawn seethed in outrage. Reed proposed forming a company of old Black Hawk War comrades to march south and represent Illinois in avenging the martyrs of the Alamo and in securing the liberation of Texas from the Mexican tyrant. If the enterprise went well, he said, they could all be wealthy and important men in a boundless new empire.

"I'll put my name to that list," Ashbel Merritt said. "I'll go to Texas right now without another thought." Ash was a doctor, though he took such a public and pugnacious role in Whig political battles that it was sometimes hard to associate him with the art of healing. He was slight, and had thinning blond hair, pale skin, and silken side-whiskers: bland-looking, except for the animating ferocity in his eyes.

Billy Herndon's father, Archie, always eager to be whipped up, also spoke well of the idea. But before the talk of riding to the rescue of Texas went any further one of the men pointed to a figure walking out of the land office. "Lincoln's in town!"

The group in front of the whipping post adjourned without comment and reconstituted itself in front of Abraham Lincoln.

"Yes, I just heard the news myself," he told them. "Crockett dead. That's a hard one to believe, especially since he's always promoted the opinion that he was sort of immortal." He was shaking hands as he spoke—"Hello Jim, hello Ash, hello Archie"—and when he shook hands with Cage he gripped hard and leaned in a bit. Cage stood at five feet and ten inches. Lincoln was even taller than he remembered, and was smiling down upon him just now with what felt like a lordly benevolence.

"Well, it's been a while," Lincoln said. "But I remember you and I hope you remember me."

"Of course I do," he answered. If Lincoln hadn't been a memorable personality in the first place, Cage would still have been aware of him and curious about him, since he was a rising member of the state's General Assembly now and was always being written about in the newspapers. But they hadn't seen each other for almost four years, since that day at Kellogg's Grove. Lincoln didn't live in Springfield, but in New Salem, which was twenty miles away, and most of his legislative activity took place in Vandalia, which at that time was still the Illinois capital.

"I'm glad I finally ran across you," Lincoln said, "because I read your—"

"Let's all go over to Speed's store," Reed interrupted, literally herding the men down the street. "When there are great questions to be settled we ought to be standing around a stove and not quacking on the street like ducks."

Cage joined the group as they walked down to Joshua Speed's store. More people followed and drifted in, until the open space at the back of the store was filled and the onlookers crowded against the shelves of hardware and medicine and the mattresses that were lined up vertically against the wall. Arguments rippled back and forth about the Texas adventure. Some of the men thought it ought to be none of their business because it had happened in a foreign country and the Americans in the Alamo had known—or should have known—exactly what they were getting into. Others decreed that any place where American blood had been spilled by a tyrant ought to by God be considered henceforth American soil.

"Mexico is unstable and corrupt," Reed said. "As a matter of principle, Texas should be salvaged from it."

He spoke in a tone of sonorous finality that suggested his should be the last word on the subject, but opinions kept blasting forth anyway. Joshua Speed, who owned the store and who was long used to his hospitality being taken for granted, mostly contented himself with opening the door of the stove and stirring the fire with a poker. He had dark wavy hair, a straight nose, a lean face. He had grown up in comfortable circumstances in Kentucky and, perhaps as a result, was in possession of one of the town's calmer spirits.

Cage stood at the back of the group, listening and not offering much in the way of opinions, though the memory of those dead men strewn on the prairie prejudiced him against enrolling in another war, this one not against a fraying Indian confederacy but the nation of Mexico and its professional army. The air was soon oppressed with cigar smoke, none of it emitted by Lincoln, who stood off to the side with one elbow resting on a windowsill and his opposite arm hanging by his side. In civil society, or as civil a society as this raucous, opinionated crowd represented, he appeared more singular than he had the day Cage had met him after the panic at Kellogg's Grove. He had gained some weight since that hungry summer, but he did not seem capable of gaining much, and his proper suit of dark jeans only accentuated his height. But he was still powerful-looking, his skin burnished and his frame taut from the surveying work he did to help piece together a living while he served in the legislature.

He was listening mostly, nodding his head reflectively every now and then in the manner of an actor waiting backstage for his cue, until there was a lull in the conversation and everyone automatically looked in his direction. "What do you think, Lincoln?" Speed finally asked him.

"Well, I think I ought to detach myself from these learned specula-tions pretty soon so I can get back to New Salem before dark. But if you're pressing me for an opinion on this Alamo business I'd say it's a terrible tragedy for those fellas and their families but they were Mexican citizens, or at least were supposed to be according to the colonization laws as I understand them. We could all head down there and get our-selves into the business of overthrowing a foreign government, as Jim and some of the rest of you think we ought to do, but I believe I'll stay here in Illinois unless Santa Anna takes a notion to invade the United States."

Lincoln's remarks didn't end the squabbling about what honorable men must do as a result of the events in Texas, but they had a mysteri-ous clarifying effect, shifting the course of the argument away from the need for instant and aggrieved action to leisurely philosophizing about national interests. By and by the talk swerved to the inevitable topic: the presidential election six months away, the Democrats and their god-dam convention ploy, Van Buren's high-handed scheme to give the vote to free Negroes.

"Van Buren lubs de niggers," one of the men said. "He lubs to see dey kinky heads at de ballot box."

This bit of minstrel mockery was contagious, the men doing their best to top one another in servile diction and darkie jokes. Cage laughed along—the jokes were funny, especially Lincoln's—though the sheer weight of ridicule directed toward their fellow human beings troubled him. He was a Massachusetts man, or at least had been a Massachusetts boy, a state where the word "abolition" could be breathed aloud. Not so in the supposedly free state of Illinois, where the papers were full of advertisements for the return of runaway slaves and household indenture was impossible to distinguish from outright Southern captivity. But he had wandered the world and scrabbled hard for purchase somewhere, and this was where he now was, among these ambitious young men of his own age. It was in their society that his fortune and reputation had to be secured, where his dreams could advance, and so there were opinions he knew he ought best keep to himself.

When the gathering finally broke up and the men were filing out of the store, Cage felt a hand on his elbow.

"Can't you spare an old friend a minute's conversation?" Lincoln asked. They fell into step beside the plank fence surrounding the courthouse, picking their way carefully through the muddy slough that was Springfield's main street.

"I was greatly agitated by your book," Lincoln said. "I should have written you a letter about it. I'm convinced there won't be a finer thing ever written about the war."

"Thank you," Cage said. "My own opinion is that I brought it out too hastily. Some of the poems I can't bear to look at anymore. I should have had the patience to look for a proper publisher rather than just print it on my own."

"No, it benefits from that very impatience. It has the feel of a book that was forged in the fire and brought out blazing hot. I've read it six times. I could recite it to you, if there's any part you've forgotten. How far did the war take you before it turned you loose?"

"I was at Bad Axe."

"Were you so? All the way to Bad Axe? You were in the way of some real fighting then."

He said this with a glum undertone that suggested envy, though Cage by now wished he had seen none of it, that he had not been part of the force trailing Black Hawk and the starving remnants of his people through the Trembling Lands. He wished that his own musket had not added to the fusillades that shot Indians out of the trees in the wooded islands between the Mississippi channels. He had watched them tumble branch from branch like squirrels. He had seen women and children gunned down in the muddy sloughs as they tried to escape across the river. By the time his fellow volunteers were carving strips of flesh from dead warriors to cure and use as souvenir razor strops he was thoroughly estranged in his mind from the war. In his *Sketches,* he had written about such things only obliquely, in lines infused with a shame and anger that he worried might seem unaccountable to a casual reader. But to write the literal truth of the obscenities he had witnessed would have meant disgracing poetry itself.

"Our little spy company got mustered out up there on the Bark River," Lincoln said. "We got close to finding Black Hawk's trail a time or two, but those were lean days and they didn't have anything to feed us so they told us just to forget about Black Hawk and to go on home. How we got home was a wonderment in itself. Another man and me got our horses stolen, so we had to walk back through those miserable bogs taking turns on John Stuart's horse all the way to Peoria. I was a wretched creature when I got home to New Salem."

"Not so wretched now, it seems," Cage said.

"Oh, I do my best to throw my weight around when the assembly's in session. I have a few weeks every year to accustom myself to being a big man and then it's back to scratching for my living as a postmaster and surveyor. What do you think about Reed? Would you ride off with him to Texas?"

"I'm content here."

"Content? I don't know anybody who's content. Why would you be an exception?"

"Because you and your colleagues have promised to bring the capital to Springfield."

"Ah," Lincoln replied, "you're a speculator, like everybody else."

True enough. The scheme for moving the seat of government from Vandalia was much in the air. A boom was coming to Springfield, and Cage had scraped to get in on it, eager to set himself up as a man of business so that he could have the resources to become a man of letters.

"I'm a speculator of a very low order. I have a city lot or two."

"Which is it? A city lot—or two?"

"One in possession, my eye on another."

Lincoln bent one of his long legs and shoved his foot gently at a hog that was blocking his way. The hog squealed in annoyance, then trotted off on its spindly legs to root a few yards away. The hog had not taken the insult personally, but Lincoln stopped and contemplated the beast with a sad cast to his face, as if he had regretted discommoding it.

"What's the worst thing you've ever done?" he said to Cage, his eyes still on the hog.

"Shot a starving Indian out of a tree. You?"

"We were trying to get some pigs onto a flatboat. They didn't like what they saw and wouldn't agree to the proposition, so some of the boys sewed their eyelids together. I wouldn't take part in it myself, but I didn't stop it either. I reckon if the Creator exists, those poor pigs are in my accounting book."

Cage noted the "if," was quietly heartened by it. He had heard Lincoln was an infidel, and he liked the thought of having someone to talk to whose mind, like his own, actively wrestled with the idea that there was either no God at all or perhaps a very indifferent one.

"I might have a better investment for you than a city lot," Lincoln abruptly said. They were standing in front of a brand-new two-story brick row that had replaced the log buildings that had been torn down after Cage moved to Springfield. Hoffman's Row was the latest encouraging sign that the town was destined to grow into something more thriving than the prairie settlements that surrounded it. "You might want to go over there to the land office and buy along the river over by Huron. Don't buy in Huron itself—the price is already too high—but just find you something nearby that you can get at the government rate. Then you can sell it for four times that."

"How do you know?"

"Because I'm the one who surveyed Huron with my own eyes and between there and Beardstown is where the canal's going to be dug. I just entered forty-seven acres myself at a dollar and twenty-five apiece. Between us, a lot of these internal improvements might not amount to anything. To get the capital moved to Springfield we had to trade a few votes here and there and say yes to some things we might better have said no to. But I think the Beardstown canal is a good prospect."

Cage thanked him and said he would consider it, wondering at the same time if Lincoln was any different than all the other speculators wandering around Illinois, urging everyone to buy now before it was too late and the canals and railroads were already built and the rivers already opened up to navigation and the capital moved here or moved there.

But he *was* different, different in ways Cage couldn't disregard. Most of the men who were going around promoting themselves and their schemes were smoother than Lincoln, not as raw, not as striking in appearance, not as obviously self-invented. During the war, when everyone had been clothed in rags and shriven by scant rations, he had not seemed so remarkable. Now that he was more or less respectably dressed, something in his appearance betrayed him. He looked like a man who did not quite fit in, whom nature had made too tall and loose-jointed, with an unpleasant squeaky voice and some taint of deep, lingering poverty. He seemed to Cage like a man who desperately wanted to be better than the world would ever possibly let him be. But in Lincoln's case that hunger did not seem underlaid with anger, as with other men it might, but with a strange seeping kindness.

"I once met Byron's gondolier," Cage declared without thinking.

"What!"

"I remember you quoting Byron at Kellogg's Grove. I once met the man who paddled him through the canals of Venice."

"But where? How can that be? By jings, you haven't been to—Venice?"

When Cage nodded, he thought he saw tears forming in Lincoln's eyes—but tears of what? Astonishment? Jealousy? Possibility?

"What are you doing now?" Lincoln asked.

"I've already thrown away half the day. I have to go back to work."

"Throw it all away, and tomorrow with it. Do you have a horse?"

When Cage nodded, Lincoln pointed to one of the upper windows of Hoffman's Row.

"I've got to go meet John Stuart. You remember him—he was with us that day. It won't take a minute. I'm going to borrow some law books from him and go back to New Salem. Come with me and we'll talk about Byron on the way. And Burns too. You must like Burns!"

"New Salem is twenty miles from here."

"Yes, you couldn't get back by dark, of course. You'd spend the night with me. We can talk about politics if you want but I'd much rather hear about Byron's gondolier."

Cage had been at his writing desk, forcing his hexameters onto a long poem that did not seem to want them, when the news about the Alamo arrived. Since all the ensuing gossip was so distracting, since his concentration was thoroughly broken, he knew the rest of the day would be idle. Why not put the time to use by riding to New Salem with Abraham Lincoln?

He went home and saddled the six-year-old mare he had acquired from the estate of a circuit-riding Methodist preacher who had lodged for a month while laid up with gout in the rooming house that Cage owned, and then abruptly died before paying his bill. The preacher had never really liked or trusted the horse and had named her Potiphar's Wife, after the Egyptian queen who had tried to seduce Joseph. Cage had no problem with her and just called her Mrs. P.

Lincoln was waiting for him in front of the stable on Jefferson Street, mounted on a sizable bay gelding with a star in his forehead. He had lengthened the stirrups as far as they would go, but his long legs were still considerably bent, and in his city clothes he looked less comfortable on horseback than he had when Cage had met him in the field four years earlier. He was holding two big law books in his left hand and cradled them as preciously as if they were infants. Though he had commodious-looking saddlebags, he held on tight to the books all the long way to New Salem.

They rode west on Jefferson and in only a few minutes had left the town behind them and followed a branch that turned into a brook that led them into a picturesque grove of ancient trees on the fringe of the heaving prairie. They veered onto the road following the Sangamon, catching sight of the river every now and then through the wintry trees lining its steep banks. The air was still and the afternoon was warming, but it was cold enough for them to button the collars of their coats around their necks and for Lincoln to note the vapor belching from their horses' nostrils and to remark that the eruption of steam from locomotives might soon be as common a sight on these prairies as horses' breath if he and his colleagues in the statehouse managed to find a way to pay for all the internal improvements.

But he did not really want to talk about internal improvements, not this afternoon. He pressed Cage for details about Byron's gondolier, and how he had met him, and how he had managed it to travel as far away as Europe, and how having once reached that interesting land he had decided to remove himself to the forsaken wilderness of Illinois.

"'"Tis but the same rehearsal of the past,'" Cage said by way of answering him. Lincoln recognized the line immediately and grinned in delight.

"A child of *Childe Harold!*"

"I took it too far, I suppose, but isn't that what you're supposed to do if you're under the sway of Byron?"

He told Lincoln how his father, a prosperous manufacturer of pencils, had sent him off for a year in Europe so he could get a leaping start on French and Italian and write some travel sketches in the style of Washington Irving to sell to the newspapers. Cage's father had believed his son to be a literary genius ever since he had written, at twelve years of age, an elegy in rhymed couplets on the death of his mother. It had been a precocious child's strategy of holding death apart, of examining it in verse in a futile attempt to disperse its impact. Grief had soon crashed through his bulwark anyway and flooded his bewildered soul, but poetry had remained, and over time it became an instrument for probing experience, rather than a means of holding it at bay. He eagerly took advantage of his father's generosity because he felt the need to get Europe into his bones, to invent some new kind of American poetry that he believed had to be birthed in the Old World before being liberated in the new. Such was his thinking. He had only been eighteen. But on his tour he struggled with the suspicion that his talent might not be as deep nor his nature as tempestuous as Byron's. Standing beneath the Arch of Titus in the summer rain as he stared at the Colosseum, entering the Grand Canal of Venice in a felucca, traveling by diligence along the perilous gorge of the Strettura: everything that made his heart swell with wonder also made it shrink with homesickness in equal measure. He was too young, too alone.

On his way back to Paris from Rome he had stopped off in Marseille at the offices of Dodge and Oxnard, where a letter of credit was supposed to be waiting for him that would finance the rest of his tour. It was not a letter of credit he found, however, but a cryptic and frightening note from his father begging his son's forgiveness for some unstated crime. The letter had been forwarded by his Paris banker. The banker supplied a letter of his own, informing Cage of his father's presumed suicide, the body having been found washed ashore in a sheltered cove on the Massachusetts seacoast, the pockets of its coat and waistcoat filled with rocks and then painstakingly sewn shut. The banker expressed his condolences at Cage's loss, and regretted the absence of the expected letter of credit, as the financial affairs of Mr. Weatherby had for some time been irregular and his pencil factory, house, dependencies, livestock, land, and other assets would necessarily be portioned out among his creditors. Recognizing Cage's predicament and finding his own heart welling with sympathy for one so bereft in a foreign land, the banker had taken it upon himself to authorize funds out of his own pocket sufficient to bring Cage home.

Cage's mother had been dead for six years. His two sisters had not survived past infancy. Now his loneliness was total. He walked along the Marseille port, through the crowded lanes of Le Panier, feeling as if the people he saw in their throbbing masses had actively conspired to exclude him from all human activity and understanding. He could speak passable French by then, but in his shock and isolation the language was suddenly alien to him. Even his native tongue felt distant and useless.

He had given much thought as a young man about what he would do with his life, but never what he would do for a living. His father had been very well off, if not exactly rich, and Cage was no more accustomed to fretting about his future material welfare than he was to worrying about whether he would have breakfast.

But when he returned home it was to a new world. The house in

Lowell where he had grown up was occupied by a new family, its shutters painted a garish new color. His father's friends might have helped set him up, but most of them, he now understood, were his creditors, and he was too ashamed to apply to them. He found a job in a hat maker's shop and saved enough money to repay the surprised banker who had financed his passage back to the States, and then he drifted west, romantically unmoored, vaguely intending to work his way to Spanish California and the Sandwich Islands and live and write in obscurity so that his greatness as a poet could be discovered after his death. His funds ran out in Gallipolis, Ohio, where he took a job in a shipping warehouse, staying for a year until he was offered work as a deckhand on a steamboat that was leaving from Cincinnati with the intention of unloading its cargo in Springfield and proving the navigability of the Sangamon River.

"Do you mean to say you were on the *Talisman*?" Lincoln asked. "Why, there I was out in front of you, clearing your way with an axe!"

He told Cage how he had been one of the New Salem youths dispatched to cut through the snags and drifts and overhanging tree limbs, and to dismantle the mill dam that the vessel had not been able to float over when, having finally given up on reaching Springfield, it had retreated back to the expansive waters of the Illinois.

"I probably saw you," Cage said. "But I didn't notice much. The river was so narrow and there was so much timber on the banks it was like trying to sail through a canebrake. It took all our attention to make sure the pilot's house didn't get scraped off."

"Yes, it turns out that the Sangamon is a fine navigable river for an Indian canoe," Lincoln said.

Cage asked Lincoln about his own history and Lincoln quoted poetry in response just as he had, saying that he guessed Thomas Gray had it about right when he wrote that the annals of the poor were short and simple.

His own annals: restless father, moving his family from one hard-luck situation to the next, from Kentucky to Indiana to Illinois. Mother dead of the milk-sick, sister dead giving birth. A kind stepmother, a few months in a blab school here and there, but mostly whatever he knew besides planting and rail-splitting and farmwork he had taught himself. His father had given him no encouragement when it came to reading or anything else and it wouldn't much bother him if he never saw the man again. He said he'd been all the way to New Orleans twice on a flatboat. He'd seen a slave auction there and was troubled at heart about it still. He'd run for the General Assembly once before and lost. He had a store in New Salem for a time but it had failed, miserably so.

"That's how I acquired my national debt. All the money I make from postmaster work and surveying and serving in the legislature goes to paying it off."

"Probably not all of it if you're buying land along that canal."

"Well, you've got to rise to an opportunity every now and then, even if it's discommodious to do so."

They arrived in New Salem before dark. Cage had last seen the place from the deck of the *Talisman* while they had been trying to get the broad side-wheeler over the mill dam. That had been during a cold winter and the branches overhanging the river were sheathed in ice, which sometimes fell loose and crashed on the deck, once almost breaking the captain's wife's foot. The town had not impressed him then and it did not now—just another river village of maybe thirty houses, most of them made of logs, strung along a main street above the banks of the narrow Sangamon. The trees on its outskirts were strangely naked, the bark stripped off by the village women to make dye. The failure of the *Talisman* to open up the river had hurt Springfield, but it had probably doomed places like New Salem, especially if they ended up being bypassed by the railroads and canals that Lincoln and his colleagues in the statehouse in Vandalia had promised to bring to Illinois.

They left their horses at the public stable. The stableman greeted Lincoln like a favored nephew and in a sly, sarcastic tone of voice demanded to know whether he had been corrupted yet by the toad-eating man grannies he had been keeping company with in the legislature.

They walked out onto the street, where Lincoln waylaid a young boy and asked him to run off to the Carman house, where he lodged and boarded, and inform Mrs. Carman he was bringing a guest for dinner. The boy took off in a sprint as if it was the most urgent errand ever conceived. It was late afternoon. Women were walking home from the shops and men were drifting into the groceries, but it seemed there wasn't a citizen of New Salem who didn't make a point of stopping what they were in the midst of doing to speak to Abe Lincoln. The men lectured him about the Little Bull Law and warned him by God sir to hold the line against Van Buren and his preposterous idea of Negro suffrage. The women fussed over him and offered to feed him themselves if Mrs. Carman couldn't seem to put any meat on his bones. They told him to please comb his hair every now and then and to make sure the next time he had a suit made to have somebody measure his arms.

Lincoln introduced Cage, and the New Salemites greeted him cordially enough, but he felt unseen beside his towering, interesting new friend. Someone named Mrs. Abell came running up to Lincoln and grabbed him by his arm and told him she'd just had a letter from her sister.

"She remembers you!"

"Well, I remember her."

"You know what I mean. She *asked* about you!"

She turned her head briefly to Cage, curious about who he was but not curious enough to allow Lincoln to say more than "This is my friend from—" before whipping her head around again and staring up into Lincoln's face.

"I'm going to Kentucky soon. Do you want me to bring her back?"

"Bring her back?"

"Don't pretend to be stupid, Abe," Mrs. Abell said. She had a sharp, impatient expression. "Do you want me to bring her here or not?"

"Well, I guess you better."

"It's a long way to come for nothing. You understand that?"

Lincoln nodded in a dazed sort of way.

"I'll write her, then. I'll write her and tell her that you'll be writing her." She looked at him sternly again. "Which means you *will* write her."

Lincoln agreed that he would. Mrs. Abell smiled, took the liberty of brushing some dust off his sleeve, nodded politely to Cage as if she had actually been patient enough to meet him, and walked off.

"I think I just agreed to marry that woman's sister," Lincoln said.

"You did? Did you mean to?"

"Well, I suppose so. To tell you the truth the case puzzles me a little."

"Always reading!" Mr. Carman pronounced at the dinner table for Cage's benefit. "He reads thoroughly and never forgets it, don't you, Abe?"

"Well, it's hard to scratch something into my mind, which is about as hard to penetrate as a piece of steel. But once it's scratched in it's generally there to stay."

"A piece of steel!" Mr. Carman repeated approvingly. He was a shoemaker, a reasonably young man still, in his thirties, but nobly bald, and he spoke with such enthusiasm and concentration it was as if the hairs had been sprung out of his head by the force of the thoughts within it.

"'Here's freedom to him that wad read!'" Mr. Carman said, quoting Burns as he raised his glass of homemade Madeira for a toast.

"'Here's freedom to him that wad write,'" Lincoln replied, in an impressive Scottish brogue that suddenly had nothing of Kentucky in it. But he was returning the toast with a glass full of water, and Cage caught the disappointment in Carman's eye.

"He needs the temperance vote, you see," the host said to Cage.

"Leave Abe alone, Caleb," Mrs. Carman said as she bustled nervously as a hummingbird around the table, setting down a plate of biscuits, spooning catchup sauce onto everyone's food. "The poor man can drink what he likes."

"Well, I'm not above putting on a show for anybody who's got a vote to cast," Lincoln admitted. "But the truth is it ain't politics that keeps me from drinking. I allowed myself to get flat drunk a time or two when I was younger and didn't care for the famous effects. When it came time to stand up, I felt like a slug trying to jump over a fence."

Dinner was catfish soup, mutton cakes, and cold slaugh. There were three young children, all of them with their eyes on Lincoln, waiting for what he might say next to make them laugh. From time to time they cast disapproving looks at Cage. They did not like strangers at their table.

Mr. Carman asked Cage what he did in Springfield. Cage said he owned a lodging house.

"A lodging house!" Carman saluted again with his glass. "I honor you for operating such a thing—cooking, cleaning, washing bedclothes, making repairs, tossing out lodgers who can't pay their bills. I don't mean Lincoln here, of course, who's always scrupulously prompt. No doubt they attack you with their fists when that happens—maybe with knives."

"I've never been attacked with anything. As for everything you mentioned, I have an excellent woman who manages the place."

"Leaving you as a man of leisure, then. Well done."

"Hardly leisure," Lincoln said. "He's a slave to poetry."

They demanded a recital, then and there. Cage turned to Lincoln for help, but his friend's voice was loudest. So he put down his napkin and pushed back his chair and stood, fortifying himself with a swallow of their host's overly sweet wine, which Mr. Carman had earlier bragged required twelve pounds of dissolved sugar candy to make.

Cage had worked toilsomely long for the past two months on a short lyric inspired by the meeting place of the Ohio and the Kanawha, near where he had worked in the shipping warehouse. He had watched cotton and peach brandy heading upriver from Memphis, and machinery and iron farming tools coming down from Pittsburgh, and thought he sensed in those differing goods a metaphor that could stand for the reckoning that must someday come between the hard righteous North and the evanescent South, with its perishable crops planted and harvested by slaves.

The thing was not finished really; its meter wanted slackening, and some of its rhymes were too direct and others too elusive. But he thought it good enough to satisfy a command performance at a host's table:

"There flows the broad Ohio,
As if by thought itself impelled,
As if 'twere more than moving water—
But History undreamed, nor yet beheld.

It knows its course, though in the way
the flower knows the light, or the child

In womb its mother's cryptic voice—
A summoning stir, all mute, all wild."

There were eight stanzas, building well enough, resolving well enough in lines about unseen snags and the darkening tunnel of over-hanging ice-heavy tree limbs that he had experienced himself on the journey of the *Talisman*. The children looked blank when it was over but the three adults applauded—did more than applaud. They leapt to their feet and Mr. Carman patted him on the back and congratulated Lincoln on his excellent choice of a new friend.

The Carmans lived in a teeteringly high log house of two floors, with two low-ceilinged rooms above. The children shared one of the rooms and Lincoln lodged in the other. It was a cramped space barely big enough for a narrow bed and Lincoln's surveying tools and saddlebags. There were books carefully displayed on a plank nailed to the wall—the lawbooks he had just borrowed from Stuart, along with Shakespeare, Burns, Gray, *The Revised Laws of Indiana,* volumes on grammar, on mathematics, and a collected Byron worn to tatters. Squeezed into one corner of the room were a desk and a wobbly chair, the desk covered with papers and notebooks and loose pages with his scribblings, which Lincoln gathered up and put into a drawer, explaining that they con-tained thoughts too raw for anyone to be allowed to see.

In their nightshirts, they crowded together on the bed beneath two fraying quilts. Besides being narrow, the bed was far too short for Lin-coln, whose feet and legs overhung it almost to the knees. In the room across the hall the children were noisy and it took them a half hour and several admonitions from their mother to finally settle down and go to sleep. In the meantime Cage and Lincoln shared a candle and read quietly, each from a different book, Lincoln quickly lost in Blackstone's *Commentaries,* Cage fitfully turning the pages of an essay by Dr. John-son on Addison in one of the anthologies on Lincoln's shelf.

When the children's room was finally silent, Lincoln closed Black-stone and stared up at the ceiling with the book resting on his chest.

" 'History undreamed,' " he quoted back to Cage from the poem his guest had recited at dinner. "What did you mean by that? Is history a dream, in your figuring of things?"

"It can be, in my little poetic world."

"So who would be the dreamer? God?"

"Now you've left poetry behind for philosophy. And anyway, it wasn't meant to be literal, just to sound true."

Lincoln smiled, closed his law book and stared at its black cover. "It might be I'll make a poor lawyer, because sometimes I like the sound of truth as much as the substance of it."

He reached across Cage and set the book on the makeshift shelf, then resumed his position on his back, staring up the ceiling, the knob of his shoulder bone pressing against his bedmate's. It felt good to Cage to feel the warmth of another human body against his own—when had that last been the case? For a short half hour in a Beardstown brothel, he reckoned, with a fleshy young woman with broken teeth who had been surprisingly kind to him and provided not only the release he was craving but a reprieve from engulfing loneliness.

Of course it was vastly different to lie in bed with a woman. With a man that sort of release was not to be contemplated. But reprieve from loneliness was still a possibility. Cage had friends, but not one like Abraham Lincoln was beginning to seem: an intimate, a confidant, a man with whom one could lie in bed while the candle flickered and discuss the dreams of God.

"Tell me about this woman in Kentucky you seem to have bound yourself to marry," he asked Lincoln after a while.

"Her name is Mary Owens. She's very pleasant, very quick-witted, fair-sized but not Falstaffian. A handsome woman—a keener intellect than mine, properly educated. I don't know what she sees in me but we spent some time together and to the best of my recollection we fell in love."

"To the best of your recollection?"

"Well, it was a few years ago. And something happened between-times that sort of distracted me from her. Distracted me from pretty much everything there is."

Cage watched Lincoln scrape a thin flake of bark off the log wall with meditative absorption. Cage started to ask what had happened but decided to leave Lincoln to his solitude. It was a few minutes before he spoke again.

There had been another girl, he said, named Ann. Her family lived in New Salem. Lincoln said her brother had been one of the people he had introduced Cage to when they had been walking up the street toward the Carmans' house. She was young, slight as a bird, blue-eyed. She had been engaged to another man but he had wandered off to New York and since he had not seemed much concerned about coming back, Lincoln had told Ann maybe she should marry him instead. She said she would. The fact that he had her love was a constant startlement, like waking up out of a dream of such engulfing happiness you knew it could not possibly be true—and then discovering that it was.

But then last summer Ann had died.

"They said it was brain fever. I don't know if that's what it was or not, but it came on fast and it came on strong and it took her away. I saw her right before she died. She didn't know me. She screamed when she saw me walk into her sickroom, like I wasn't Abe Lincoln at all but some stranger who had come to do her harm.

"After she died I sort of ran off the track. I was in a low stretch, low enough that the people around here thought I was going to kill myself."

"Were you?"

"Maybe, if I could have roused myself enough to do it. I would have liked to be dead. It would have been a mighty improvement. But I didn't have the energy to lift a razor to my throat, and there wouldn't have been much point, since my heart was buried with that girl anyway. That's what the hypo feels like to me—like you're down deep in a grave and you can hear everybody talking and going about their business way above you, and there's no way you can dig yourself out to join them."

"Well," Cage observed, "you're well above ground now, it seems to me. And you're on the way to becoming the DeWitt Clinton of Illinois, if all these canals and things go through."

Lincoln laughed. He sat up and turned around and drew his long legs up so that he was sitting at the opposite end of the bed, looking down at Cage. In the darkness, in the candlelight, his lowering, observing presence was almost fearsome—as if it was a golem and not a rising Illinois politician perched at Cage's feet.

"And you're already on your way to being the Lord Byron of Illinois." Lincoln smiled, but he grew solemn again. "I need to make a mark somehow. I don't think I can stand it if I don't. Do you think that's a peculiar thing to feel? Don't you feel it too?"

"Yes, I do. It's an intolerable thought, to be forgotten as if you'd never lived."

"I wish I had the gift of poetry like you do. That would settle the matter."

"The matter is hardly settled. Not that many people have read my book, and I've just had a manuscript sent back unread from Hilliard and Gray."

"But your success is inevitable, and you know it. You have a great gift, and all I have is my national debt and a ridiculous talent for ingratiating myself. Why do I think Mrs. Abell's sister would even want to marry me?"

"Do you even want to marry her?"

"Well, I've got to marry somebody, Cage! And so do you. Aren't you tired of being alone?"

"I suppose so."

Lincoln ruffled his hair as if he had lice and then stood up and walked over to the desk and blew out the candle. He sat down in the chair. One of its legs was a bit shorter than the others and he lurched rhythmically back and forth, seeming to think it was a rocking chair.

"They say Davy Crockett came from nothing. A bear hunter from West Tennessee, and there he was in the Congress of the United States. And a Whig into the bargain, just like me."

"Crockett is dead," Cage reminded him.

"Well, that's a bothersome sort of thing, I admit. But maybe being dead won't bother you so much if you can just get people to remember your name."

FOUR

◆ ◆ ◆

A FTER AN EARLY BREAKFAST at the Carmans' table and a warm handshake from Lincoln, Cage rode home to Springfield. It was not long after daybreak and the sun shone luminously on the icy dew covering the prairie. There were swans overhead, and prairie chickens unseen in the stirring grass—he could hear the booming and moaning notes of their courtship songs. It was cold yet but steadily warming, and he encountered no traffic except for a few of Illinois's omnipresent hogs, released from their owners' pens at the close of the winter to graze on the woodland mast at the edge of the prairie.

The road between New Salem and Springfield was not much more than a trace, but it was still reasonably smooth and defined, and it seemed to Cage that Mrs. P plodded along with satisfaction, her mood uplifted as was his by the birdsong breaking through the stillness, and by the silent suspirating rhythms of a prairie morning.

His mind was fastened on the new friendship he had forged with Abraham Lincoln. Cage's life up until now had been a mostly solitary one. He had not sought out this solitude, though in his youthful confusion he had formed the idea somewhere that to commit oneself to the written arts required forsaking common varieties of human fellowship.

It was his fault, he knew. He held himself apart, perhaps held himself too high. He was twenty-seven, no longer such a young man, already two years older than Keats had been when he died. If Cage were to die now he would leave only his privately printed *Sketches of the Black Hawk War* and a scattering of poems published in the *Sangamo Journal* and a few other Illinois newspapers. There were also prose fragments and extensive notes, their context now largely forgotten, written during his travels in Europe. Whatever dreams he had once had to make a book of those travels had been cauterized by the shock of his father's suicide. There were as yet only the beginnings of a body of work. His book had impressed the few people who had bought and read it, but he shared Lincoln's nervousness—his terror almost—that he might live out his life without making any case that it had been a life worthy of remembering.

He had been successful so far, in a minor way, as a man of business. After the war, the pay that was due the volunteers had been held up for months until the federal paymasters arrived to give cash for their claims. Cage had managed to resist the temptation to sell out beforehand to speculators, as so many of the volunteers had. So he was paid in full for his service, and by living thriftily was able to invest in some land near Jacksonville, paying as little as $1.25 an acre near the center of one of the many Illinois towns that had been laid out but did not yet exist. Thanks to all the talk of the internal improvements that were on the way, the town took root, the bet paid off, and he was able to sell the land for five times what he had paid for it, enough to buy the Palatine, a failing boardinghouse of six rooms just off the square on Adams Street, betting that as more and more of the state's business became centered in Springfield he would have a reliable clientele of legislators and influence peddlers.

He lived at his own establishment but took most of his meals in taverns, feeling conspicuous in the company of his lodgers and not inclined to play the gregarious host. He left the running of the place to Mrs. Hopper, the formidable cook and housekeeper he had had the good fortune to engage after her husband, a lawyer on the circuit, had drowned near Metamora while crossing a ford of the Mackinaw River in high water.

The income from the house was steady, his tastes were far from extravagant, and he lacked the drive for financial aggrandizement. He was not caught up in the frenzy of speculation that went on all around him. It was enough to be in funds, to seize opportunities as they came along but not to spend his days plotting and searching them out. Cage preferred to suffer at his desk in his room, a bust of Shakespeare gloating at him as he worked himself deeper and deeper into thickets of verbiage from which there was, as often as not, no release. After his work he would take long walks through Springfield, stopping inevitably in its one bookshop, going to the theater at night if there was a company in town, or to a lecture on colonization, or on Napoleon, or on the natural history of volcanoes.

As often as not he went out on his own, unless in the company of Joshua Speed or Ashbel Merritt or one of the other restless single young men of Springfield. He was on the outside ring of their buzzing circle, good for recruiting at a game of town ball, a listener and not an arguer, thoughtful, steady, helping to soothe tempers when somebody drunkenly challenged somebody else to a duel. Though his life's work was poetry, not politics, he kept finding himself among political men, drawn to their circle by his own kindred yearning to live a life of consequence. Their talk was feverish and recondite, their personal aspirations and the salvation of the nation urgently entwined. There were set times for elections, but it seemed to Cage that everything was always happening at once, one all-consuming never-ending canvass. It was hard to know the difference between the legal and political professions since so many of the office seekers were lawyers and were often suing each other and running against each other at the same time. Everything and everyone was enmeshed, jostling elbow-to-elbow and nose-to-nose in a scrummaging for advancement that never paused.

One way to gain advantage, of course, was to marry, and as Springfield began to be the coming place there were more young women with lighted candles in their windows, more cotillions, more sisters and cousins coming to visit from Kentucky or Ohio or Virginia in hopes of meeting a rising man on the western frontier. In that enterprise too Cage stood outside the circle. His mother's early death and his father's fatal disgrace had prevented him from learning the hidden rules of social navigation. He did not know how to court a woman. He did not know any women to court. On his nighttime meanderings he would often stop and stare up at the lighted candles, the signal that the lady was at home and willing to receive company, and wish he had the courage to walk up to the front door and present himself.

This morning he had a hopeful sense that his isolation, his hesitation, were just the artifacts of a stalled existence. Perhaps a vibrant, consequential friend such as Lincoln promised to be would change all that.

What he had needed most in life, Cage now realized, what had been missing up until now, was just someone to talk to.

But it would be a while before their conversation could resume. Lincoln was not often in Springfield during that spring and summer. He was busy with his surveying work, with his solitary law studies, and above all with the need to get himself reelected to the legislature. The 1836 campaign in Illinois was a traveling entertainment that moved from town to town and grove to grove, its cast of characters giving their speeches at every stop, debating their opponents, insulting their honor, sometimes leaping at them and wrestling them down into the dirt. The show came to Springfield in July, just a few weeks before the election.

The event was planned as a sort of debate, with a revolving cast of Whig and Democratic candidates denouncing each other in turn. It promised excitement and was the sort of thing that even a politically wary man like Cage would not think of missing. He arrived at the courthouse at nine in the morning, an hour before the speeches were to begin, and even so he barely made it into the building before it filled up and the doors were shut. The rest of the crowd would have to stand on the courthouse lawn listening to the debates through open windows.

Even with the windows open, it was stuffy and hot inside as the mid-morning July sun bore down upon the city. All the seats were taken, and Cage stood in the back in a tight press of onlookers, among them Joshua Speed, who was already wiping sweat from his neck with a silk handkerchief. He greeted Cage with his usual openhearted, self-assured delight.

"Look at Edwards," Speed whispered. "Somebody should tell him he's never going to be reelected if he can't get that scowl off his face."

Ninian Wirt Edwards, who had the same name as his father, the former Illinois governor, spoke first for the Whigs. It could be argued that he was Springfield's leading citizen—he would certainly argue it himself—but from what Cage could gather people only liked him for his money and for the parties he and his wife put on at their house. The house stood in a part of Springfield known—proudly to Edwards, cheekily to most everyone else—as Aristocracy Hill.

Edwards was tall and elegant, but unfortunately his sour superiority was on full display and quickly turned the day against him. He started out at the rostrum attacking his Democratic opponent, who was none other than Jacob Early, the captain of the spy company that had ridden to the rescue of the men at Kellogg's Grove. As far as Cage knew, Lincoln and Early were still on good terms, even though they were opposite each other politically.

Edwards, however, appeared to quiver with outrage at Early's very existence. He promised his fellow citizens that once they understood the full extent of his opponent's greed and mendacity they could not but be appalled and would determine to drive the reptile from his shell. But Edwards had no sense of rhythm or timing, no understanding that you had to gather the audience slowly along with you if you were going to call an opponent a reptile. As it was, the way he blurted it out without preamble created a chorus of gasps and boos and only a few thin cheers. It had taken no more than a minute or two for Ninian Edwards to rally most of the listeners to the defense of the man he meant to pillory.

Cage noticed Lincoln in the crowded room as Edwards's screed continued. He was standing behind the other Whig candidates, his long neck protruding from his collar like a cork in a bottle, his dark hair fuller than when Cage had seen him last and combed forward in the manner of the times but without much devotion to the effort, so that it ended up in a haphazard tangle. The rest of the Whigs were doing their best to huzzah Edwards on, but Lincoln was clearly having trouble pretending that his speech was anything but a disaster.

When Early stood up to reply, he had the sentiment of the room behind him. He looked much the same as he had in the war, though his face looked blank as a baby's without its stubble, and the hair he had worn close-shorn on the campaign against Black Hawk was now swept up into a pomaded crest. What right, he demanded, did a toad such as Edwards have to call another man a reptile? No, upon reflection a toad ranked too high on the chain of being to bear comparison to Ninian Wirt Edwards. And so did a slug, and so did a worm. Ninian "Wart" Edwards stood alone among all creation, a veritable carbuncle of a man, a pustule, nothing but a fur-collared human abscess.

Early searched for a lower epithet, but before he could come up with one Edwards had leapt up on a table, frothing with invective as the crowd surged forward, eager to see some sort of fight. Edwards was on the verge of challenging Early to a duel, which was illegal and would have disqualified him from office, when Lincoln reached up to grab him gently by his wrists and slowly pry him off the tabletop and back onto the floor. Edwards's face was red and swollen with anger, though still handsome in its princely way, and it was interesting to see him slowly and silently deferring to Lincoln. In his dress and deportment Lincoln was clearly Edwards's social inferior, but none of that mattered, and everyone could see it: his self-possessed bearing placed him in his own category.

Lincoln was next to speak, and as he took the rostrum the room was still agitated. The Whig and Democrat partisans crowded together in the courthouse sweatbox were jeering at and jostling each other.

Lincoln's reedy, twangy voice was a poor instrument, or at least it seemed to be when he first opened his mouth and said "My friends," and one of the Democrats on the other side of the room shot back that he'd just as soon have a rattlesnake for a friend as a goddam Whig who looked like a goddam ape.

"A rattlesnake and an ape!" Lincoln said. "That makes two more creatures we can include alongside our familiar toads and reptiles and slugs. If we were electing animals to put in a menagerie, instead of men to send to the statehouse, well, I expect we'd be pretty well set up."

Lincoln said he would set aside the question for now of whether a man or an ape could better represent the people of Illinois, but he was pretty sure a Whig toad would be a far sight better at getting a canal dug and roads built than a human Democrat.

The room, and not just the Whig side, blossomed with laughter. Lincoln's voice, once it had warmed up a little, was not really so bad. Though it was thin and high it carried somehow, threading out to the back of the room where Cage and Speed could hear it plainly. Judging from the laughter from outside the windows, it was discernible out in the square as well. And there was a warmth and calmness to Lincoln's public demeanor that helped to puncture the wild histrionics of a moment before, and to bind the people in the room into a shared sense of what was reasonable and what was funny.

Lincoln's opening words were improvised, occasioned by the stir Edwards had created, but he shifted so seamlessly into his speech it was hard to tell where his spontaneous thoughts left off and his prepared remarks began. He offered the standard Whig bill of fare—banks, tariffs, internal improvements—but the familiar ideas sounded newer and bigger as he presented them.

"We may well ask ourselves this question," he said. "What is government? Is it just a reluctant gathering up of individuals who would rather be left alone? Or could it have something more of harmony to it? Could it be that it doesn't have to be a collection of grumbling voices but a rousing chorus of people who see the need to act together and to accomplish things that would be impossible to do otherwise?"

There was enough partisan sting in his speech to keep it free of airy philosophizing, but there was gravity too, the sense that the man speaking was not just a political operative but a thoughtful steward of the people's business. The audience was stirred, the audience was moved to reflection—a condition the Democrats could not allow to persist.

"This young man will have to be taken down," George Forquer said when he stood up to follow Lincoln, "and I am truly sorry that the task devolves upon me."

Forquer was the register of the U.S. Land Office in Springfield, a lush patronage job that had not so coincidentally come his way after he had decided to renounce the Whigs and become a Democrat a few years before. Cage knew him casually—anyone who had bought land in Springfield did—but he had never seen him speak in public. Forquer stood there in silence for a long moment, his head down, as if summoning the will to discharge his painful duty.

He reminded the audience that he himself was not a candidate. He had just come here to speak his mind about matters of deep importance for the future of our beloved Illinois and our beloved country. He would appreciate the indulgence of his friends' attention, though he knew he had done little to deserve their notice, except perhaps to discharge his duties as register as honestly and diligently as he could. He had no ambition for higher office but he admired men who were willing to put themselves before the electorate, if they did so honorably and were untainted by base ambition. Alas, he could not attribute these qualities to Mr. Lincoln, for whom ambition was everything, for whom lies were but common discourse, for whom personal advancement superseded public duty.

"Now it's true," Forquer said, pointing directly at Lincoln, who was standing not ten feet away, "that a man can't do much about the way he looks. But when I study Mr. Lincoln there, with his comical phiz, with his long arms and his clothes that don't quite fit, I see a man who wants you to think he just wandered up the road from New Salem. I see an actor playing at honesty as he connives and schemes to enrich his friends and to impoverish his state with 'internal improvements' that he and his mendacious comrades in whiggery have no idea how to pay for."

Cage could see that Lincoln was struggling to master himself during this attack, to remain patient and expressionless. He carried the act a little too far, his face such a mask of polite attentiveness that it might have seemed to a disinterested observer that he was agreeing with everything his denouncer said. There was a case to be made, of course, that Forquer was right. As would become painfully obvious in only a few years, the Whigs, Lincoln included, had no real idea how to pay for all those canals and railroads without taxing the citizens into penury.

"Mr. Forquer has struck at me, and he has struck hard," Lincoln declared when it was time for him to speak again. "He has given me a mighty wound. He says I have contrived to look this way on purpose."

He stood there in silence, with his bird's-nest hair and his arms sticking out of the sleeves of his coat, giving the absurdity of this proposition time to sink in. "I submit to you that only the Creator could have come up with such an apparatus as myself."

The audience laughed and then, laughter not being enough, applauded. For the second time that day, Lincoln had discharged a blustery accusation and won the crowd over to his side.

"Now, Mr. Forquer commenced his speech by saying I would have to be taken down, and that he was the one to do so. Whether he has ably performed that task is something for you to decide, as it is for you to decide which of us is more practiced in the tricks and trades of politicians.

"I noticed as I was riding into town yesterday that Mr. Forquer now lives in a very large, very handsome new house, and on top of this very large and very handsome new house is the first lightning rod I believe I've seen in Springfield. I congratulate Mr. Forquer for having the foresight to install this device, which will no doubt protect his very large and very handsome new house from the storms that rage from time to time in our beautiful Illinois skies.

"But the more acquaintance I have with Mr. Forquer, the more I wonder if his fears are strictly atmospherical, or if they arise from some other worrisome source. Because as you know, he was able to pay for that house and for that useful ornament on top of it by virtue of his appointment to his present office, which was bestowed upon him by President Jackson himself in gratitude—or shall we say in recompense—for his eagerness to jump over the broom and attach himself to the Democrats. My fellow citizens, I may be young as Mr. Forquer says, I may be ill-made, I may even have been 'taken down' as he promised to do, but I doubt that I will ever come down so low as to change my politics, my party, and indeed my principles, for the chance of an office worth three thousand dollars a year, and then have to erect a lightning rod over my house to protect a guilty conscience from an offended God!"

The room erupted. There were jeers and halfhearted cries of "unfair" from the Democrats, but the applause grew louder and drowned them out. Lincoln stepped back with a studiously blank expression, as if he was not aware that he had just delivered a killing blow.

"Come on, let's go up and congratulate him," Speed said. The two of them tried to make their way forward, but they were caught in a surging crush of people who were on the same errand. Lincoln himself was overwhelmed, doing his best to shake all the hands that were stretched out to him. He was smiling and nodding, but still working hard not to let the triumph show on his face.

"A very able speech," Speed told Lincoln when they finally reached him. "Very able. You nailed him in a box and you buried him deep."

"Well, I expect George'll dig himself out soon enough."

He saw Cage and eagerly shot out his hand. Cage was heartened by the beaming smile on Lincoln's face.

"There you are. It's about time we saw each other again. No doubt you've forgotten all about me. I ran across a poem I want to show you. If you and Speed can come over to—"

Before he could convey the rest of the sentence he was seized by John Stuart, who proclaimed he had delivered a perfect skinning—and then Lincoln was gone, vanished into a congratulatory crush of Whig political operatives.

"To the young man who needed to be taken down, but was not," Joshua Speed said that evening, holding aloft a glass of beer. "You know what will have to be taken down, don't you? Forquer's damned lightning rod. Can anybody look at it now and not break into laughter?"

They had come to the Globe for dinner after listening to the remainder of the day's oratory—most of it the usual forgettable gasconading. The tavern was crowded, the taproom a hive of opinionated men putting forth their blustery assessments of Lincoln's rhetorical victory over Forquer. Speed set down his glass and began cutting up his fricasseed chicken with elegant strokes of his tableware—his cultivated Kentucky upbringing never far from the surface.

"What do you think about our friend?" he asked Cage. "He liked plunging the knife in, didn't he?"

"He was doing his best not to let us see how much."

"Are you talking about Lincoln?" Stephen Douglas had just appeared at Speed's side and was standing there with one fat, short leg propped up on the bench next to him. He reached onto the table, helped himself to a pickle, and temporarily removed the gigantic cigar that was in his mouth in order to eat it. "It's well known old Abe has a cruel streak. We saw it today, didn't we? I think he'd just as soon smother a baby bird as smell a flower."

"Be careful that you don't accidentally describe yourself," Speed said.

"No sir, my blood runs hot. Any baby bird that died at my hands would have to call me a name first."

Cage knew Douglas casually. It was impossible to live in Illinois and not know him, since he took such delight in electioneering and appearing at chopping bees and husking frolics, studiously turned out in homespun to appeal to his rustic electorate. Through political guile if not through legal brilliance he had gotten himself appointed the state's attorney, and now he was running for the assembly from Morgan County. His opponent was John J. Hardin, whom people called the handsomest man in Illinois when they were not calling John Stuart the handsomest man in Illinois.

Stephen Douglas was not the handsomest man in Illinois. He was squat as a toad, with beady eyes and a bulbous nose. But he was such a lively and agreeable toad it was no task at all to overlook his appearance. And the titanic self-regard that would have been reprehensible in other men somehow made Douglas even more agreeable.

"But even we Democrats," he said, "have to admit that Forquer misjudged his enemy, and for that he was reduced to a quivering pudding. But enough of that. Tell me what I can do for you gentlemen once I get to the statehouse. How can I help you prosper? How can I turn your journey through life into a beautiful never-ending song?"

He bantered with them a few moments more and then shook their hands and slapped their backs and continued working his way through the tavern, laughing and promoting himself, reaching up on his tiptoes to throw taller men into affectionate headlocks and breathe into their faces.

Cage observed this display with the same fascination he might have watched an arcane mating ritual or some other puzzling manifestation of natural history. Then there was a sudden bustle of interest near the door. Cage and Speed looked up to see Lincoln entering, along with John Stuart, Ninian Edwards, and most of the rest of the Whig partisans. Stephen Douglas greeted Lincoln with a theatrical bow, then as if the mock praise was not deep enough, went to his knees and greeted him as the savior of the merchants, farmers, mechanics, and pork packers of Illinois. In the same ironic spirit Lincoln leaned down and bade his Democrat foe to rise, and the laughter among all the political men rippled back to where Cage and Speed were eating their meal.

"It's amusing to watch, isn't it?" Speed said. "Do you think you could ever be a public man like that?"

"Not for an instant."

"The interesting thing about Lincoln," Speed said, "is that he's both the most public man and the most private man I've ever known. He has to hover rather precisely between the poles of his personality. Any deviation might pull him apart."

"You make him sound fragile."

"Oh, we're all fragile, I suppose," Speed said indifferently, his mind now set on a different object. "How is your house? Is it fully occupied?"

"Yes, at the moment. Why? Are you looking for a place to live?"

"A friend might be."

"Who?"

"A friend."

Speed's grin was delighted and conniving. His blue eyes shone through the smoky tavern atmosphere. He held the pose until Cage finally understood his meaning.

"Do you mean to say—a woman?"

"Well, I can't keep her with me, can I? I live above my store. And I don't want to set her up in a dark alley someplace. She's not a common whore, for God's sake. A room in a lodging house, with perhaps a discreet entrance, is what's needed. You could count on me paying her bill, of course."

"There's no vacancy. And if there were, and Mrs. Hopper discovered the arrangement, which she would, she'd quit in outrage. And there I'd be with no one to keep the house."

"Then you'd be free to hire somebody else who wouldn't be so starchy about it! But I can tell by the way you're looking at me you're starchy yourself. A New England puritan, bound by your iron code of whatever."

"Not at all. If you want to keep a woman that's your business."

"She could be your woman too."

"What?"

"Cage, she's not a *wife*. Why can't she be shared?"

Speed reached across the table, slapped Cage affectionately on the arm, and went back to the enthusiastic cutting-up of his fricassee. His breezy attitude, his jocular charge of an "iron code," left Cage a bit unsettled. He did not think himself a servant of propriety, a pious enforcer of conventional morality—but perhaps that was what he unknowingly was.

1837

FIVE

◆◆◆

WHEN THE NEWS REACHED SPRINGFIELD that it had been finally chosen as the site of the new capital, there was jubilation in the streets that amounted almost to rioting. Cage gave up trying to write and went down to the square, where a bonfire had been built in front of the courthouse. The old whipping post had caught fire and the drunken men pouring out of the groceries stood there and watched it burn, happy to say goodbye to this symbol of the rude frontier settlement that Springfield had been but would be no more.

It was a bitterly cold February night, snow on the ground, boys with hand sleds grabbing onto horse-drawn sleighs and sluicing wildly and dangerously down the street, the members of the Springfield Singing Society proudly lending their voices in celebration. Cage joined Mrs. Hopper and some of the residents of the Palatine in front of the bonfire. He felt the ferocious heat of it on his face, the slicing cold of the prairie wind at his back.

"The Creighton farm is going up for sale," she told him. "Mrs. Creighton buried her husband last week and is going back to Ohio to live with her sister."

"And you want me to buy it?"

"I want you to buy it and I want to be the agent for the sale. It's only a mile up the Pekin Road and will lie within the center of town within five years. You need to make an offer immediately, before somebody else does. The town is already overrun with speculators and now that we're the capital you can be sure there'll be twice as many tomorrow morning. For heaven's sake, Mr. Weatherby, your lethargy is maddening."

Mrs. Hopper turned to scowl at him fondly, the brim of her tied-down bonnet rippling in the night wind. She was in her forties, strong-featured, restless, always chafing at people—like Cage—who were slow to seize opportunities that were so plain and urgent to her. She was born to run things and Cage felt fortunate to have her in charge of his house. In addition to her housekeeping and managerial skills, she was a great cook, famous in Springfield for her voluminous yeast rolls, which she served to the boarders at every meal and then sold to the populace at large on Saturday evenings.

He told her he would think about making an offer on the Creighton farm, but he had no real intention of doing so. Mrs. Hopper was a practical woman, but in an excitable moment like this he sensed that it would be too easy to make a mistake, too easy to be convinced nothing could ever go wrong. He had little enough money and he did not like to part with it except in a nimbus of deliberate calm.

He would be glad for his caution. There was a financial panic on the way that would last for years and sweep the ground away from men who had invested too wildly in the future. But on this February night, as the bonfire illuminated the old courthouse that would soon be torn down and replaced with a grand statehouse, as the wolves' howls from the still-unbroken prairie infiltrated with a weird harmony the anthems of the Springfield Singing Society, he could not help but feel that the world had shifted westward, and that he was a little closer to its center.

A few months later, in April, he went alone to a performance of *Fazio* put on by a well-known company that was touring central Illinois, another sign that the sun of civilization had begun to shine on Springfield. The play took place not in a proper theater but in the commodious upper room of a store, with board benches set up in what passed for the pit, the air smoky with burning whale oil. There was a wooden column partly obscuring Cage's view and the actors' speeches rang harshly in a space built with no particular concern for the projection of the human voice.

The play was a Florentine tragedy rendered in stiff Shakespearean language, played out against a painted backdrop that had been crated and uncrated one too many times on its journeys across the western hinterlands. None of this mattered to Cage. Even an indifferent play was an intoxicating opportunity to him, a chance to slip away for a few hours from the oppressive demands of his own imagination to bask in someone else's attempt to present another world. He watched the young actress playing the central part of a wife who mistakenly believes her husband has wronged her. She was overly trained in the teapot school of acting, striking expressive poses and attitudes as the mood of the story demanded. It was the last night of the play, the last performance of a long western tour. Though the actress moved fluidly, though she was agitatingly beautiful and spoke her lines with confidence, Cage could sense her boredom and homesickness, her longing to return to the East.

When the play was over he applauded with the rest of the audience as she took her bows and disappeared behind the heavy drop curtain with its painted Tuscan landscape. Then he remained in his seat, held in place by a provocative thought. To the actress and the rest of her company, Illinois was the last stop on the tour, the last place on earth. Why should that be so? he asked himself. Because it was a place that had not yet been made, a place that canals and railroads had yet to penetrate, where log houses were still more common than brick buildings. Other men—men like Lincoln—might create the internal improvements and banking systems and government edifices that would one day turn Illinois into a place of wealth and sophistication. But who would create its literature? Who would make it into a capital not just of commerce but of culture? In that moment, he was aware in a way he had never been of the real subject of his poetry: the hopeful towns and cities of the West and all that they were displacing, the men and women whose dreams of advancement and achievement were no less acute than those of their eastern countrymen whose lives took place in a world that was already established, already known. His work would be all about raw beginnings. He would be the poet of the unfinished, the still-to-come, of those who reached out for greatness from unlikely places.

He left the theater and walked along the darkened streets jotting thoughts and random phrases in the tiny notebook he always carried in the pocket of his waistcoat. It was eleven o'clock when he got home. In the parlor, facing each other as usual from twin wing chairs, sat Theophilous Emry and Roger Victor. Emry was a retired riverboat captain in his sixties. Victor was ten years younger and owned a struggling hat shop on Adams Street. Both men were widowers and lived at Cage's establishment; both of them were bored and boring and eager to entrap any passerby with endless questions about where he had been and what he planned to do for the rest of the day and what were his plans for the evening. Since they strategically stationed themselves in the parlor facing the front door they were impossible to avoid.

Emry looked up from his French grammar when Cage entered. For the last few months he and Victor had been occupying themselves by puzzling out together a translation of one of Balzac's stories.

"Vous avez un lettre, Monsieur Weatherby," he said in a barking accent.

Emry stood up and took a letter down from the mantelpiece and handed it to Cage. "Mrs. Hopper has gone to bed but she was concerned that we give it to you."

"It's from that awkward-looking fellow," Victor said. "The young politico. He came looking for you and when we told him you weren't here he sat down at that chair and wrote it out."

"You mean Mr. Lincoln?"

"Yes, Mr. Lincoln indeed. And before he left he gave us a very remarkable story about a monkey who could shit bananas."

He read the letter as soon as he reached his room. It was a brief note with a poem pinned to it. "Dear Cage," the note read, "I am now at last an attorney and counselor at law—sworn in Vandalia last month. And today I am moved to Springfield!—in league with Stuart in his law practice. J. Speed knowing that I have no money is letting me live in the upper room of his store and giving me half his bed. We are there now. Assuming you return home and receive this at a reasonable hour, come over and talk! And read this poem on your way if you don't already know it. I have copied it out for you—tell me what you think of it."

The poem was scrawled out in Lincoln's hand and he had failed to supply either the title or the name of the author. Cage read it hurriedly. It wasn't bad, though its iambic regularity was boring and its central idea—that everybody dies—was hardly novel. Each stanza featured one more example of things moldering or being erased or turning to dust. It built to nothing except a reaffirmation of what it had been declaring all along.

But he could see Lincoln in it. Its fatalism, its melancholic gloom, struck Cage as being as authentic to the new Springfield resident's divided personality as the raucous poetry of Burns or jokes about banana-shitting monkeys.

He could see the lamplight shining in the windows from the upper floor of Speed's store, though by now it was almost midnight. The door was open. He made his way past the stocked shelves and counters to the stairway that led up to Speed's living quarters.

It was a spacious room that took up the entire second floor of the building. Speed's big double bed was against one wall. Lincoln lay in it fully dressed and with his boots on. Speed, John Stuart, and Ashbel Merritt were all talking at once, standing or sitting or stretched out on the floor.

When he saw Cage, Lincoln sprang up off the bed and clomped over to him with his hand out.

"Everybody's drunk except for me," he said. "Somebody get Cage a glass. Temperance is a terrible vice and I don't want him to fall into ruin on account of my example."

Speed wiped out a glass with his untucked shirttail, filled it with what he proudly proclaimed was Kentucky bourbon, and handed it to Cage.

"Nobody could find you," Speed said.

"I was at a play."

"The Italian one?" Lincoln wanted to know. "Is it any good? I'd like to see it but first I've got to win a case for Stuart here so I can get paid."

"It's not bad," Cage said, unwilling to betray the restless mood the play had put him into. "So you've moved to Springfield?"

"I'm in the lion's den! It feels strange to have planted myself here at last. It feels exciting. And I haven't even been here a day and we're already trying to figure out how we can get the doctor here elected to probate justice of the peace."

Cage turned to Merritt and raised his glass in salute. "I'm sure you'd make an exemplary probate justice of the peace, Ash. Whatever that is."

"It's a very important and lucrative position," Lincoln said, "and no one would serve the public better in it than our friend. Unfortunately we have an obstacle in his opponent."

"James Adams," Ash Merritt said to Cage. "Do you know him?"

"Only to see him on the street."

"He's a liar, a forger, a thief, a fool, a traitor to his country, and a whining, wheedling windbag."

Ash had only a sip of bourbon left in his glass but he gulped it down to punctuate his angry verdict.

"But he's also the incumbent," Lincoln said. "So he's had a chance to do some favors and sew up a sack of votes. But we think we can find a few votes of our own and maybe put a hole in Mr. Adams's sack.

"John," he said, turning to Stuart, "how many members in the Mechanics' Institute here in Springfield?"

"I'd say fifty, fifty-five active."

"Who do I talk to?"

"Ezra Heath's the president, but Ezra's pretty far into the drink these days. Maybe Tom Tucker."

"What about the Methodists? What do they need?"

"I've already talked to Reverend Wiley. They could use a new roof after that hailstorm last month, but we can't count on the whole congregation. Methodists tend to be independent-minded."

On they went, Lincoln and Stuart and Merritt, factoring out who controlled the votes for the masons laying the foundation for the new state capitol building, for the draymen and teamsters and the stable owners, the Presbyterians and the temperance societies, for the stagecoach drivers and boardinghouse owners and innkeepers and militiamen and the vendors who supplied tents and chairs for camp meetings. Who had influence, and who was willing to use it for the good of the cause and who needed a couple of cured hams or a new suit of clothes or a new window frame for his house. Speed offered an opinion from time to time but mostly he just joined Cage in listening in amazement. Cage knew that Lincoln was the floor leader of the Whigs in the statehouse, but he had never seen him in action. Lincoln knew the names not just of the operatives called big little men who were counted on to deliver blocks of votes, but of seemingly each individual voter and that voter's needs and desires. He knew the men who would stand firm when they told you they were with you and the men you had to visit time and time again, shoring them up, reminding them what the stakes were.

"It's too damned tight," Ash said, when they had finally finished their imaginary plebiscite. "If you don't find me some more votes I'm going to be wasting my time running against him."

"Well, there is such a thing as campaigning, Ash," Lincoln said. "The problem there, though, is your gloomy and combative temperament."

"He's just not likeable," Stuart agreed.

"I know it," Ash said. "I try to be agreeable, but the problem is I value common sense so much I'm offended by anybody who hasn't already made up their mind to vote for me."

Lincoln nodded appreciatively at Merritt's self-diagnosis and confirmed that it presented a problem. "But we'll triumph over your deficient personality somehow, Ash. Don't forget we have the power of the press at our disposal. A lot of people already agree that Adams is a bloodsucking tick, and we'll make sure that everybody who reads the *Sangamo Journal* has the benefit of that opinion."

He turned to Cage with a lightning-fast change of topic.

"What did you think of that poem I left off for you? Isn't it the best poem in the world?"

"Did you write it?"

"What!" Lincoln looked around the room in astonishment. He stood up on Speed's bed, his head bent against the ceiling. Then he proceeded to recite the poem from memory.

"'O why should the spirit of mortal be proud!'" he declaimed. "'Like a fast flitting meteor, a fast flying cloud . . .'"

He made his way through the whole thing—kings and herdsmen and saints all alike doomed to the grave, human emotions and thoughts fleeting and meaningless—as he bounced up and down on the mattress, the poem making him exuberant with its solemnity.

"He thinks I *wrote* that!" he said to Speed when he was finally finished. Then he turned to Cage.

"How could somebody as ordinary as me write something as profound as that?"

"Who wrote it, then?"

"I have no idea. I've known the poem for years. It struck me to my heart the first time I read it, but there was no name given in the anthology where I found it. Some anonymous soul—'hidden and lost in the depths of the grave.' When you think about it, what could be more fitting?"

"We'll all be anonymous souls someday," Stuart mumbled to himself. "We may think we won't but we will."

"Stuart has the thing exactly," Lincoln said. He collapsed back onto the bed with all the finesse of a stork that had been shot out of the sky. "When an elegant summation is wanted, look no further than Stuart."

Stuart smiled and saluted Lincoln with the smudged glass Speed had given him. He was only a few years older than his new junior law partner but in his bearing and his dress and his overall polish he seemed a decade or more removed. His status was more apparent now than it had been that day at Kellogg's Grove, when they had all been winnowed down and made equal by hardship. He was a cousin of Ninian Edwards's wife, yet another member of the famous Todd family of Kentucky who had been steadily infiltrating Illinois and assuming positions of influence. Yes, he was indeed glaringly handsome, with his serious black eyebrows and thin authoritative mouth. He carried himself with the ease of someone who had known from birth that somewhere in the future a place was being held ready for him. But Cage knew that beneath the surface he was boiling with ambition and frustration like all the rest of them. He had just been beaten in a run for U.S. Congress by Big Red May and was furiously plotting the next chapter in his political career, no doubt planning to load Lincoln up with all the distracting legal work in the meantime.

They talked and connived for another hour, until Speed declared he had to go to bed or he wouldn't be able to get up in time to open his store. Ash Merritt was drunk enough by then to hesitate at the top of the stairway and ponder the steep descent like a boatman trying to chart a course through a treacherous rapids. Stuart grabbed him by the arm before he could take a first fatal step and led him down the stairs, calling good night as he went and warning Lincoln to show up at the office on time for his first day of work.

Cage was about to leave as well, but Lincoln declared that he was too excited by the idea of living in Springfield to ever close his eyes again.

"Let's leave Speed to sleep his storekeeper's sleep while we ramble through the capital city."

Cage was just agitated enough—from the play he had seen earlier and the course it had set him on, from the excitement of Lincoln's unexpected appearance in Springfield and his contagious enthusiasm—to agree.

They strode forth into a pleasantly chilly April night—the lamps on the streets out, dogs barking after them. They walked around and around the square, then across Town Branch toward Aristocracy Hill, past Ninian Edwards's grand house, out along a vacant road where the starlight shone upon open farm fields.

"Why do I love that poem so much?" Lincoln asked himself more than he did Cage. "The more melancholy a sentiment is, the more despairing it is, the more beautiful I find it. Is that normal?"

"You have a greater capacity for laughter than any man I know."

"Yes, but I'm not really a man you know. We've spent one night together and had a few memorable conversations."

"We've gathered up the dead together."

"I haven't forgotten. That's a sacred bond, I reckon. You know what we should do? Start a poetry society. You and me and Speed and Ash and of course Ned Baker—you know him?"

"Not well."

"We'll fix that. He's one of those men it's important to know well. He's a couple years younger than we are—twenty-five, maybe twenty-six. But he's riding a fast horse. If he hadn't had the bad luck to be born in England, I'd predict he'd be president someday. His poetry is excellent, what I've read of it. A little pompous, but so is Ned. Of course when it comes to poetry, it's unfair to place any of us in the same room with you, so if you think it'd be beneath you—"

"No, a poetry society sounds like a fine idea."

They came to the end of a rail fence; beyond it was a stretch of unbroken ground, and then closed-in forest. The treetops swayed in a soft spring breeze, stirring like some sort of beast of the night that could not be still. Cage remembered the feeling of being watched from the trees by Black Hawk's warriors. Lincoln must have too, because without speaking about it they both turned around and walked back toward town.

Lincoln gripped the back of Cage's neck in his big hand and shook it playfully back and forth. Under the force of his friend's grip, Cage's neck felt pliant as a stalk.

"I've been observing you all night," Lincoln declared. "Close observation of humankind is the first business of a sharp-witted lawyer like myself. So what's stewing up there inside your head? I sense turmoil of an animalistic nature. Women maybe."

"I'm thinking of the work I need to do. Hoping it's the work I'm meant to do."

"I wonder if I'll be any good at the law. I confess my arm trembled a bit when I raised it in front of the supreme court clerk the other day and took the oath."

Cage started to reassure him but decided not to, didn't think he needed to. So they walked on through the night in silence until Lincoln spoke again.

"Has Speed told you about this girl he's set up?"

"Yes, and it sounds like he's wasted no time in telling you as well."

"He's proud of her some."

"Proud of having her is more like it. Did he offer to share her with you?"

"As long as I pay her. I wouldn't mind a turn with her. She's bound to be reasonably good-looking, knowing Speed's taste. But I don't have the money to spend and I'm not as carefree as our friend. Besides, there's that other thing."

"Other thing?"

"I told you about her, don't you remember? Miss Owens."

"So you're marrying her?"

"Only if you advise it."

"How can I possibly give you advice one way or the other? I've never met her."

"But you will," Lincoln said. "There's going to be a picnic, to which you are going to be invited for the purpose of laying eyes on her. And your judgment will weigh mightily."

SIX

◆◆◆

S O Y O U ' R E M R . S P E E D ' S F R I E N D who has no room to rent
to me?" she said when she opened the door. She swept back in welcome and he walked into the room, eager to be out of sight of passersby,
though it was night and the house on Jackson Street where she lived
was far away from the center of town. She lived in an upper room with
a separate entrance, reached by an outside stairway. From the house
below, he could smell greasy meat and onions cooking and hear an old
woman complaining about something or other in a spiritless monotone
to someone who was not bothering to reply. A dog had joined Cage as
he approached the house and had escorted him up the stairs. When she
closed the door the dog was sitting on the stoop with a look of satisfaction, as if conscious of having served some important function.

He had been in a state of anxiety in the days and hours leading up
to this encounter, but now that the door was closed and he was in the
room alone with her he felt unexpectedly comfortable and unhurried.
She asked for his hat and set it on the pier table between the windows,
whose shutters were discreetly closed. The room was orderly and well-
kept, with one corner given over to a great deal of sewing and pattern
work. Elsewhere there were pictures on the wall, a writing desk, several
cane-backed chairs, and a bed with a better bedstead than his own. No
doubt Speed had seen to it that she had these things—probably supplied them from his own store—but Cage had the sense that the quiet
presiding taste was her own.

"I could call you Mr. Weatherby," she said, "or I could call you—it's
Cage, I believe, isn't it?"

"Yes, Cage—for Micajah."

"Ellie for Ellen."

She smiled, and her warmth and ease startled him a little. She was four or five years younger than he was. She wore a blue muslin dress, tight at the waist and at her slender throat. He was not sure at the start of that first meeting that he cared so much for her face—it was rather blunt and broad, he thought—but very quickly its plainness began to represent for him a confounding new benchmark of beauty. She wore her hair in the style of the times, parted in the center so that it framed her face, the tip of her left ear showing through the loose plaits like the tender shoot of a plant.

"I know all about you from Joshua," she said as she settled into a chair and gestured for him to do the same. "He said he was surprised when you told him you wanted to see me."

"He doesn't really know me."

Her eyes brightened a little. They were brown.

"He doesn't really know me either. But I pretend that he does. There's no harm in that. What should you and I pretend about?"

He searched for a witty answer but he was too flummoxed by her teasing wit and by her bold availability. He was ashamed to be so bashful. There was no need to impress her, but he wanted to. She was nothing like the whores in that Beardstown brothel, nothing like the respectable ladies of Springfield, though in her simultaneous sexual frankness and social acuity there was the embodiment—perhaps the mimicry—of both.

When she realized he was not going to be able to find anything to say, she unclasped the bracelet at her wrist and leaned forward to set it on the writing desk next to his chair. It was a gesture both casual and electrifying, a silent overture to the drama of her undressing. Her outstretched arm was only inches from his head. He smelled the perfume on her wrists, and then felt her fingertips idly grazing across his sidewhiskers, and then her hand on his cheek. She was looking at him with what he knew was only mild interest, though he felt caught in a gaze of such intensity that he looked away, at the bracelet she had set down on the writing desk. Two strands of gold links, with a bezel depicting a Roman temple in tiny mosaic tile.

"Do you like it? Joshua said it was the Temple of Minerva."

"He's wrong. It's the Temple of Hercules."

"How do you know that?"

"Because I've seen it. I've sketched it."

She sat back, lifting her leg so that the toe of her boot just barely touched his knee. "In Rome?"

He nodded. Perhaps it was just his wishful thinking, but he thought there was more curiosity in her eyes than before.

"What would a man who's been to Rome like to see me remove next?"

He nodded toward her earrings. She took them off with a slight tilt of her head to either side, tightening the muscles in her neck, and once again reached out to lay them down next to the bracelet, this time not returning to her chair but sliding onto his lap. She seemed to weigh almost nothing as he stood with her in his arms and carried her over to the bed.

He had been stirred up ever since witnessing that beautiful teapot actress in *Fazio,* and had needed some way to resolve his bewildered longing. Ellie supplied the physical resolution in short order—she was clearly accomplished at that, unembarrassed by it—but as he lay with her in her bed afterwards the longing remained. She was now the source of it. Her candid sexual nature, her air of contentment and independence, was unexpectedly wounding. The ease with which she bestowed herself ran counter to his own nature. It undercut the sense of romantic destiny that he was disposed to feel. But the obvious fact that they did not belong together, did not fit together, felt irrelevant. Something about her confused him, excited him, threatened the settled rhythms of his life.

She was from Maryland, she said. Her father was a millworker who had been robbed and murdered at night on the National Road. Her mother married a widower who already had eight children of his own, and she was infatuated enough with her new husband to agree to his suggestion to send Ellie and two of her sisters off to Louisville, where they could board with distant relatives and be out of the way. She found employment in a millinery workroom and at sixteen married her fore-man, a dreamer and tinkering-minded man who staked everything on moving himself and Ellie to Illinois, where he believed he could find investors for an invention he called the prairie car, a great Noah's Ark-like conveyance that would roll over the landscape powered by steam, assisted when the winds were favorable by a towering mast and a great canvas sail. He had solicited interest in Springfield, where she had met Joshua Speed at a gathering of potential investors. But whatever enthusiasm her husband had been able to generate evaporated when it became clear he had never taken the trouble to secure a patent.

As some men do when they are unhappy and disappointed he began to beat his wife, and she was obliged to burn him with a hot iron, and afterwards to hold a knife under his throat and order him out of the state. The ensuing arrangement with Speed did not trouble her. She liked him, understood that young men needed sporting relationships until they found someone of their station to marry (and often needed them afterwards). When it came to religion she was an infidel, a deist at best, and saw nothing at all unnatural in a frank exchange of sexual favors for material support.

She revealed everything about herself. She lay beside him, unhurried, indifferent to her own nakedness. There seemed to be nothing closed off about her, nothing he couldn't touch or reach, and yet there remained an intoxicating boundary. Her very openness to him felt like a kind of rejection.

"Why does Speed share you?" Cage asked, when he had sensed that their time was over and had begun to put on his clothes.

"Why shouldn't he? He's a generous man. He likes his friends and wants them to share in his pleasures."

"Has he sent a lot of his friends around?"

"Very few. Only people he trusts and thinks I might like. I like you well enough. I hope you'll come back, but of course you know you must pay me."

"I know that," he said. Awkwardly, he emptied coins out of his purse onto his palm as she watched.

"You may pay me in guineas if you like. I'd rather have real English money than a paper shinplaster from some bank that may already have gone out of business."

He counted out what Speed had told him to pay, and then, flustered, added half again as much to it. He stood there holding the money in his hand, not quite sure what to do with it.

"Don't be embarrassed," she said. She got off the bed and onto her feet, still blazingly naked, and he set the money into her open palm. Cage was aware again of the cooking smells from the rooms below, and the man who had been silent before as the old woman lectured him was now venomously defending himself, yelling at the top of his lungs that she should go straight to hell and see if she liked the men there any better.

"You can see why Joshua wanted a better situation for me," she said as she pulled on her robe. "He doesn't like coming here. But there are so many people flooding into Springfield right now there's hardly any-place else to live. And I suppose that even if you did have a room that my character wouldn't be the sort that would—"

"Your character is not at issue," he blurted out gallantly.

"Oh, of course it is. But I have plans to improve it."

She kissed him, an unrequired gesture of genial affection that he had to remind himself had nothing to do with love. She opened the door. The dog that had walked up the stairs with him was still sitting there, wagging his tail in excitement.

"The dog will see you out," she said.

"You have a particular air of satisfaction," Joshua Speed told Cage a few days later, "that can only be supposed to be the result of a particularly satisfying experience."

It was midmorning on a hot June Sunday. Cage and Speed were mem-bers of an expedition of a dozen people that had set out from Spring-field on horseback, leaving the roads behind to ride across country to a picnicking spot ten miles away on a shady bluff above the Sangamon. They had fallen back to retrieve Speed's hat, which had blown off in a gust of wind. Though they had not quite caught up to the main party, Cage was worried that their voices would carry, and he gave Speed a cautioning look to that effect.

"If you're referring to your friend—"

"Yes, for God's sake I'm referring to my friend. You don't have to whisper. They can't hear you, you know. They're all upwind from us. Did you like her?"

"Of course I liked her."

"You can see why I wanted to get her into a decent house somewhere. I don't like the people she's boarding with—a lazy, worthless clerk of some sort and his horrid old mother. They're nosy, too. Her only friend there is that dog, and nobody even knows who he belongs to."

Speed was riding a very fine gray stallion that was impatient at trailing so far behind from the main party. The stallion pranced about and shook his head as Cage plodded along on Mrs. P, who was older and more patient and had no nervous energy to discharge. Speed was an elegant rider—he kept his mount in check with almost invisible adjustments of the reins, and his posture in the saddle and his overall conformance seemed to mirror the high physical standards of his horse.

"You should get her to mend your clothes," he said. "On top of everything else, the woman can sew."

"What exactly are your plans for her?"

"Why should I have plans? I enjoy her company, I enjoy knowing my friends enjoy her company. I'm a happy man. Besides, Ellie's not the kind of woman who's going to let somebody else plot out her life. As soon as I tried, our delightful little arrangement would be over."

Cage was well aware that he had no right to be irritated by Speed's breezy contentment. If anything, he should credit him for generosity. But the idea that Ellie could be so indifferently shared cut across his sense of what was right, or at least what ought to be right. Perhaps there was no great offense in keeping a woman if the terms offered an advantage to both parties, but this business of sharing gave the whole thing the taint of indenture. Cage didn't want to be a part of it, though he wanted very much to share in it and see her again.

"Shall we catch up with our friends?" Speed suggested.

They trotted forward in pursuit of the main party. It was still early in the summer and the carpets of sunflowers had not yet emerged, but the grass was tall and in its boundless reach seemed more infinite than the sky above. Cage experienced a vestigial spasm of something that it took him a moment to identify—the fear of being caught on horseback on open ground. The Black Hawk War kept surfacing that way in odd moments. Up ahead, twenty yards or so in advance of everyone else, Abraham Lincoln rode with Ash Merritt and Simeon Francis, the editor of the Whig newspaper the *Sangamo Journal*. The three of them were locked in an intense political discussion.

The outing had been arranged by Mrs. Abell and her husband, Bennett, as a strategy, it seemed, of introducing some of Lincoln's Springfield friends to her sister Mary Owens. This was the young woman who had come from Kentucky with the intent of marrying him, or at least of taking his measure prior to making a commitment. Whether they were engaged or not Cage didn't know. Nobody did, and Lincoln and Miss Owens seemed particularly uncertain of that fact themselves.

If they had been happily betrothed, surely they would have been riding together. But Lincoln was twenty yards in advance of Miss Owens, listing perilously in his saddle and gesticulating with his long arms as he plotted some political maneuver with the editor and the doctor riding alongside him.

When they caught up with the rest of the caravan Speed fell into conversation with Bennett Abell while Cage reined up next to Mary Owens. He had met her only that morning, but she had been so friendly and curious he had warmed to her immediately.

"Here's Mr. Weatherby at last," she said. "Did you find Speed's hat?"

"We did."

"He should go to a different hat maker. A man's hat should never blow off like that. It should fit properly, even in a high wind."

"My sister has all sorts of opinions," Mrs. Abell said to Cage. "About men's hats and everything else."

Mary Owens smiled patiently but kept her eyes ahead on Lincoln and his friends. She was a big, well-proportioned woman, not beautiful but alert and intelligent, with a conniving sense of humor. Cage had known her for a mere few hours, but his clear impression was that Lincoln ought to marry her at once.

"What do you suppose they're talking about up there?" Mrs. Abell was asking.

"I can tell you exactly what they're talking about," Miss Owens said. "They're conspiring about what to say in the next Sampson's Ghost letter. Do you know about Sampson's Ghost, Mr. Weatherby? I'm assuming you're a Whig and read the Whig paper."

"I do read the *Journal,* though I'm not what you'd call a fire-breathing Whig. I'm not a fire-breathing anything. Sometimes I even read the *Register* to stretch out my mind a little."

"I suppose a poet needs a stretchy mind. Tell me this. Do you always sign your name to your work?"

"Of course."

"What do you think of people who write things and have them printed in the newspaper under a made-up name? Do poets do that?"

"Sometimes. But I think mostly politicians do that. They do it quite a lot."

"No doubt because if they signed their names they'd end up having to fight a duel."

She said this flatly. She was referring to the letters Lincoln and some of his Whig friends had been writing for the *Journal* and signing as Sampson's Ghost. This was the invention they had come up with to darken the name of James Adams, Ash Merritt's opponent for probate justice of the peace. Sampson's Ghost was a character like Hamlet's father. He had risen from the dead to claim that Adams had cheated him out of his property. But that was only half of it. In the corporeal world, Lincoln, just out of the gate as a lawyer, was energetically suing James Adams on behalf of a widow and her son who were claiming he had fraudulently seized the title to the family's homestead.

When he had read the first letter, Cage had wondered whether it was a good thing for a lawyer to create a fictional stand-in to slander the character of the man he was soon to face in court. If there were any boundaries left between law and politics and character assassination, Lincoln had been very busy lately trying to erase them.

Cage had merely followed all this in the papers. He hadn't spoken to Lincoln about Sampson's Ghost. A man's business and his manner of conducting that business were his own affair. And he had seen enough of politicians to know that they had different standards of conduct, brazen and underhanded ways of doing things that were so pervasive and so widely acknowledged to exist that to criticize them was pointless.

Mary Owens, however, was apparently not so philosophical. She had been introduced to Lincoln's Springfield circle only this morning, and so far the encounter had been a mixed affair. She clearly liked Speed, who was always even-tempered and never took anything too seriously. Cage thought she liked him as well, but she definitely did not like the way that Ash Merritt and Sim Francis had commandeered her supposed suitor and ridden off with him to plot political strategy. And she didn't like the fact that Lincoln had let them do so.

"What do you think of Dr. Merritt?" she asked Cage. "Is he going to win his election?"

"Do you care?"

"Not a bit. But Mr. Lincoln does, so I suppose I should try to pretend for his sake. Though he's doing a fair job of ignoring me."

"Don't you think you're being too sensitive?" her sister said.

"I'm sure I'm not, Betsy, but thank you for alerting me to the possibility."

The track they were following narrowed as it led them into a dense screen of sycamore and cottonwoods bordering a branch of the Sangamon. The warmth of the sun vanished in an instant beneath the overspreading branches and the latticework of leaves and pea vines, and suddenly there was a crypt-like coolness to the air. There was a ford ahead, though the bank leading down to it was rather steep and muddy and the water was higher than usual after a wet spring. Lincoln and Merritt and Francis had already crossed and their horses were picking their way up the slippery opposite bank, their legs covered with mud and the stirrups of the riders dripping water.

Mr. Carman, who was with the party, was now solicitously escorting his wife across the branch behind the leading riders.

"You'd better stay close to me, Betsy," Bennett Abell said, riding up to his wife's side.

"Well, who's going to see my sister across? What in the world is Abe doing? He's just riding on with those men as if there were nobody back here at all."

"I'll be glad to ride with Miss Owens," Cage volunteered. Under her bonnet Miss Owens's face might have been sunburned from their summertime ride across the prairie, or it might have been flushed red with anger.

"Thank you, Mr. Weatherby," she said distractedly as she kept her eyes trained ahead to the crest of the far bank, where Lincoln and his companions were disappearing again into the trees.

The crossing was not particularly hazardous, and Mary Owens was quite capable of accomplishing it without Cage riding by her side. But the stony bed of the ford was slick, and the water was high enough that the horses would have rather not ventured into it in the first place. They had to be urged through to the other side. Mrs. P was so eager to be out of the water that she scrambled up the bank with heedless energy, then slid backward for a moment when she couldn't find purchase on the steep trail. The mare Miss Owens was riding was more sure-footed but at one point during the crossing she shied and skittered so violently she might have unseated a less skilled rider.

"I don't blame her," Miss Owens told Cage when they were onto firm ground again. "She saw a snake. I think it was a cottonmouth. Do you have those in Illinois?"

"Yes, of course, though we have lots of other water snakes as well."

"Well, I didn't get a good look at it. I was too busy trying to stay in the saddle. But my horse is definitely of the opinion it was a cottonmouth."

Her skirts were wet and her clothes and face had been spattered with mud kicked up by the horse's exertions. Nevertheless, she had enjoyed the challenge of crossing the branch and would have been grinning if she had been in a better mood.

"You were very gallant to a helpless abandoned lady."

"He gets preoccupied. Don't be too hard on him."

"Oh, you can be assured that I'll be too hard on him."

They crossed another stretch of prairie and when they approached the shady bluff above the main course of the Sangamon that was their destination, Cage asked Miss Owens if she would mind him taking leave of her and riding ahead.

"So you can warn Mr. Lincoln that there's a storm coming? No, I think it's best that you stay right here."

To make things worse, Lincoln and his confederates were already ransacking through the picnic supplies. When the rest of the party rode up, he was eating a doughnut and had his back turned to them. He was in the middle of telling a story to Merritt and Francis, who were so intent on hearing it they also did not notice that they had just been joined by the women.

"He comes out of the tavern and there in the street is a dog licking its balls. The dog is performing this service for himself in such an industrious and satisfying way that Stephen Douglas turns to his friend and says, 'I wish I could do that'"—

"Lincoln," Cage said.

But Lincoln was already laughing so giddily as he approached his conclusion that the world was shut out to him.

"And his friend thinks about it for a spell and turns back to Douglas and says, 'I wouldn't try it. He might bite you.'"

It was only the sudden horrified look on his listeners' faces that caused him to turn around and see Mary Owens glowering down at him from her horse. He choked for an instant on his own laughter and then did his best to rescue the unrescuable situation. He walked up to Mary with the half-eaten doughnut in his mouth and offered his hand to help her dismount.

She might have been justified in swatting it away, but as it was she just ignored it and slipped off her horse and picked pieces of dried mud off her dress as Lincoln stood there chewing, his big Adam's apple nervously heaving up and down.

"Well, Mary," he cautiously said, "I'm glad to see you got across that branch all right."

"Are you? You didn't even bother to look back to see whether or not I'd broken my neck."

"Why, because I knew you could take care of yourself."

He laughed, but it was no joke to her. She was doing her defiant best not to break into angry tears, and she walked away to join her sister so Lincoln wouldn't be there to see it in case the dam of emotion broke.

The party loitered on the riverbank for several hours, eating cold chicken and cornbread. They were in the middle of an old Kickapoo sugar camp and there were gashes on the trees where the Indians had collected sap. Miss Owens never left her sister's side, so it was impossible for Lincoln to break her off and try to make a suitable apology. They all rode back to town in the heat of the afternoon, crossing that same troublesome branch, this time Miss Owens issuing a curt "No thank you!" when Lincoln did his awkward best in asking to safeguard her.

"Well, Cage, what do you think she wants?" Lincoln asked as the two of them drifted behind the main party together. "She won't stand still for me to say I'm sorry and she won't allow me to do what she says I didn't do in the first place."

"She'll cool down and then the two of you can have a civil conversation about it."

"A civil conversation about everything that's wrong with me? You can be sure I'll look forward to that. What do you think is wrong with me, so I can get a head start on her?"

"Where that woman's happiness is concerned it seems to me that everything on God's footstool is wrong with you. For one thing, you don't pay any attention to her."

"I do when we're alone."

"Well, for God's sake, do it when you're in company, instead of riding off to hatch one of your many plots. And that's another matter: she doesn't like Sampson's Ghost, she doesn't like character assassination in the newspaper, and she doesn't like you being the anonymous author of either."

Lincoln looked over at Cage, raising his eyebrows in surprise to such a degree that the movement lifted the brim of his new straw hat.

"You say that with enough heat," he told Cage, "that it might be your philosophy as well."

"It is my philosophy. Put your name to what you write, or don't write it at all. In any case, I like Miss Owens. She's intelligent and thoughtful and good-looking into the bargain. I think you ought to marry her."

"I think I ought to myself."

"Then adjust your character immediately, or you won't stand a chance."

SEVEN

✦ ✦ ✦

ELLIE LEANED AGAINST THE WINDOW FRAME in the sunlight as she read the pages Cage had brought her. Her hair was undone, spilling down upon the bodice of the linen petticoat she had just put back on. The strings of the bodice were untied, its border of fraying Moravian stitchery running gracefully beneath her bare shoulders and across the tops of her breasts. She read in silence, and he watched the suddenly enticing fabric heave slightly with her breathing.

She finished reading, neatly folded the two sheets on which he had copied out the poem, and reached out to hand them back to him without saying anything.

"Keep it. It's for you."

"Thank you."

She set the papers down on her writing desk and stood looking at him from across the room.

"It's about me, it seems."

"More you than anybody else. Do you like it or not?"

"As much as I like any poem. Probably better."

"Well," Cage said. "I suppose I won't try that again."

She sat on the bed and gestured for him to join her, but to reinforce his self-respect he remained sitting in his chair and smiled casually at her as if his feelings had not been crushed.

"You've put me on the spot," she said. "I don't know how to react to something like this when the author is sitting there in front of me as I read it. I'm not a critic of poetry, though I'm sure it's very good. And I'm not sentimental, you must know that. It seems to me that if you want to say something to me you ought to say it outright and not in verse."

She turned and stretched herself down toward the foot of the bed, facing him.

"It would be silly for you to be in love with me."

"I agree. You've misread the poem if you think it's a declaration of love."

"Well, poems are so easy to misread. And I told you I'm not a critic."

She had reached out to entwine her hand with his—playfully, fondly—and this time he gave in and joined her on the bed, lying with her as they looked up at the cracked ceiling. It was mid-afternoon on a stultifying summer's day, the heat suppressing everything but the noise of the wagon teams rumbling down the streets carrying blocks of stone from the quarry to the town square, where the old courthouse had been torn down and the new statehouse was slowly rising in its place. There was, for once, no screaming from the old woman and her son who were Ellie's landlords. Perhaps they had finally succeeded in killing each other.

"Whether it pleased you or not," Cage said, "I was moved to write it."

"Don't think I wasn't pleased. But what's the point? You don't plan on marrying me, and if you did, I wouldn't let you."

"And why not, just out of curiosity?"

"Because then I would be your wife, and you would want to show me around to all the people on Aristocracy Hill, and the people on Aristocracy Hill would not like me very much."

"I have nothing to do with Aristocracy Hill. I don't care about those people."

"You don't want to advance yourself?"

"I do, but on my own terms, in my own way."

"Well," she said, smiling at him, "then we're more alike than I thought. Which means you should definitely never try to get me to marry you."

"You have my sacred pledge that I will never marry you. I want a wife who would pretend to like my poetry."

She laughed gently, turned her head from him to look across the room at her overflowing sewing basket and heaps of fabric.

"Would you ever want to be in business with me?" she said after a deliberating moment.

"In business? You mean . . ."

"No, I don't mean *this* business. I mean a proper shop. A millinery shop."

Cage sat up in bed and drew up his knees, staring down at her where she still languidly lay. But the teasing look and tone she had been using in their discussion of marriage was gone. In fact, he thought he had heard a tremble in her voice when she introduced the topic of business.

"This would be a terrible time to open a shop," he told her. It was true. Eighteen thirty-seven was turning out to be a very bad year indeed. Property wasn't selling because nobody had any money, farmers who had not already lost everything were in a deepening welter of debt, banks everywhere had suspended specie payments and were facing liquidation.

"The bubble has burst," Cage stated.

"Bubbles burst and then rise again, don't they? And Springfield is the capital now. It won't go completely bankrupt."

"You should read the papers. We're not the capital in reality quite yet. We've only just begun building the statehouse and the legislature is still meeting in Vandalia. And you can be sure there'll be an attempt to repeal the law so that the capital isn't ours after all."

"I'm sure your friend will keep that from happening."

"Who? Lincoln?"

"Joshua says he's lonely and should come around to see me. I've heard he's irresistibly ugly. Is that true?"

"Of course not, though you'll have to make up your own mind about his appearance, just as you make up your own mind about everything else. By the way, you might want to have him 'come around' soon, since it looks like he'll be getting married. Shall I arrange it?"

"Don't be like that. I don't like the jealous tone in your voice."

"It's an impatient tone because everyone is always trying to push me into business when all I want is to be left alone to write, even though you find my poetry worthless."

"Of course I never said it was worthless." She slid off the bed and began to dress. "I just prefer that you would write it about somebody other than me. And I wasn't pushing you into business, I was doing you the favor of presenting you an opportunity."

"Shouldn't you present this opportunity to Speed first?"

"He likes our arrangement as it is."

"So do I."

"Dear Cage, I know this much about you: you like nothing as it is. You want more."

He knew he should not say it, but he did: "More of you."

"Oh, but I have to protect you." Her smile was warm now, her eyes deceptively bright. "You already have more of me than is good for you."

When he left Ellie's presence he was irritated with himself. He should have known that she was not the kind of person who would be moved by an unexpected poetic offering. Whatever he'd meant to say—and what was that, exactly?—he ought to have said in plain bold language. The poem had been an impulsive gesture, the product of several sleepless nights during which he had been tortured by a need to claim her full attention. He realized now what a juvenile stroke it had been, a blundering broadside of metaphor designed to impress rather than to truly communicate. She had seen through him at once, which only made her more damnably appealing to him.

It was election day. He waited in line in the summer heat to approach the voting window in front of the courthouse. Half of the men in line with him were staggering under the effects of the free beer given out by the buckets by Whig and Democrat operatives, and drunken scuffles—exacerbated by men deriding opposition candidates at the tops of their voices—were breaking out all around him. He stared at the tickets he had clipped from the pages of the *Sangamo Journal*. Lincoln's name was not on the list of candidates. He was not up for reelection this year, but he might as well have been, since he had been so busy campaigning out in the open and behind the scenes for his fellow Whigs. Cage had barely seen him since the disastrous outing with Mary Owens, but he was visible enough in the papers. Depending on whether it was a Whig paper or a Democratic one, Lincoln and his colleagues were either spending long days and nights in a desperate attempt to keep the state bank solvent in the face of an economic collapse, or working to bankrupt Illinois on behalf of rapacious speculators.

Two men were clawing at each other a few feet away from the line

Cage was standing in. They expressed their political convictions in outraged grunts as they rolled into a mudhole. They were so equally matched and held each other so tightly that neither could get a hand free to slap his opponent or shift his center of gravity, so they just ended up in an exhausted stasis as if they had decided to take a nap together in the mud. The men in the voting line watched the wrestlers eagerly at first and then as the contest stalled regarded them with no greater interest than they watched the carriage traffic on the street.

Cage too turned his attention away, looking down at the ticket he had clipped out of the paper. Ash Merritt, running for probate justice of the peace, was one of the names on the list. He happened to turn the ticket over. Printed on the back was a fragment from a letter to the editor. Cage's spirits sank. It was yet another Sampson's Ghost letter, written by but not signed by Lincoln, once again attacking the character of Ash's opponent. The letter was witty but exuberantly mean-spirited. Maybe James Adams really was a land-swindler, really was the defrauder of innocent widows, as Lincoln kept claiming in these anonymous letters, but Cage couldn't recall reading anything that amounted to real evidence.

This gleeful, freewheeling character assassination disturbed him, disturbed him even more as he sweated in the heat waiting for his turn to cast his vote. When he was in Lincoln's presence, Cage couldn't keep himself from being beguiled, convinced he was a man of noble purpose, his powerful ambition harnessed to the common good. But from a distance, in the pages even of the Whig newspapers that were so friendly to Lincoln, he saw only another grasping politico.

As it turned out, Cage must not have been the only one who thought Lincoln had overreached, because all the Whigs running for county office were elected except for Ash Merritt, who was overwhelmingly defeated by the supposedly villainous James Adams.

Lincoln was rebuked. He was chastened. And a few days after the election he was at Cage's door, looking drained of blood, his hair lank with sweat and his face alarmingly gaunt. He was one of those men who could go for a decade without gaining an ounce but might lose fifteen pounds in the course of a single stressful week. Even his knock had been mournful, and when Cage opened the door Lincoln seemed almost to fall into the room. Without saying a word he undid his tie as if it was strangling him and then sprawled backwards onto the bed.

"Do you want a glass of water?" Cage asked.

"I don't want anything." He lifted his head and glanced around the room, staring at the books on the shelves.

"I'm finished, Cage."

"I doubt that's true."

"You may doubt it all you want, but if I can't get even the simon-pure Whigs to vote for my candidate what kind of future do you suppose I have?"

He suddenly fixed Cage with a concentrated look.

"Did *you* vote for Ash?"

"Yes, but I was tempted not to, after that last Sampson's Ghost letter."

"Well, there you have it. There's your proof that I don't have a friend left in the world."

"You have a friend still, but I don't care for anonymous letters and I won't pretend that I do."

"That sounds like the righteous thinking of a man who won't come into the fight."

"Is it a fight or is it a game?"

"Well, I reckon it's both. Anyway, it doesn't matter. Fight or game, I'm out of it now. I might as well leave Springfield. Anyone can see I don't belong here. Everybody flourishing around in carriages, and I'm in debt and despised and unfit for marriage."

"Who says you're unfit for marriage?"

"Who do you think? Mary Owens."

"Did she tell you that?"

"In her elegant Kentucky way. I made a kind of proposal in a letter, leaving the matter of marriage for her to decide."

"That sounds like no proposal at all."

"Well, it seemed like the right course to me, but I don't know anything about women and so it wasn't. She said her training had been different from mine. I lacked—let me see if I can remember it exactly—'those little links which make up the great chain of a woman's happiness.'"

"I'm sorry, Lincoln. Were you much in love with her?"

"In a partial sort of way, I guess I was. I wasn't in love with her the way I was in love with Ann, but she was quick-minded and agreeable and I could have done a lot worse, and no doubt will do worse if any woman will ever consent to have me."

He continued lying there flat on his back, his eyes open and staring upward at nothing, his legs hanging over the end of the bed. He breathed heavily. Cage watched him from the desk, where he had been sitting, where he had been busy putting together a short collection—which he thought of as a kind of overture to his great Western symphony—to send off to Little and Brown, the new publishing firm in Boston.

"You just have the blues," Cage told the dispirited, angular shape on the bed. "There's a Shakespeare play in town. Let's go see it."

Lincoln was silent for a full two minutes before he turned his head to the side and asked, "What play?"

"*Much Ado About Nothing.* A very decent company from Philadelphia is putting it on. Come with me. It'll do you good."

Getting Lincoln to the theater was not easy. Cage first had to get him to eat something, which in his martyr's depression he was loath to do. But Cage called down for Mrs. Hopper to bring them up a plate of cold beef and hard-boiled eggs, and Lincoln set upon them with the indifference of a grazing cow.

Walking through town, Lincoln was sure the citizens of Springfield would avoid him, or perhaps actually jeer at him for his role in Ashbel Merritt's loss to Adams, but people greeted him as if the embarrassment had never happened and he was still a favored son of Sangamon County. He sat next to Cage in the crowded theater, his knees drawn up practically to his cadaverous chin in the tight space between the rows of seats, and as the banter between Benedick and Beatrice began in earnest Cage could sense Lincoln mentally uncoiling, light once again entering his sunken-eyed face.

When the actress playing Beatrice struck a pose and proclaimed, "I had rather hear my dog bark at a crow than a man swear he loves me!" Lincoln's abrupt laugh shot through the audience, and people in the rows ahead turned to look at him and smile, taking pleasure in his pleasure, grateful for his infectious enthusiasm. The man who thought he had not a friend left in the world settled easily back in his seat, smiling at Cage, his hypo lifting as he discovered that his humiliation in politics and in love were things that perhaps could be borne after all.

"You've restored me, Cage," he said as they left the theater. "You and Shakespeare. It's remarkable how something as simple as a well-wrought phrase can make you want to live again. How can I thank you, except to—wait a minute, will you?"

He had spotted two of his Whig house colleagues walking out of the theater onto the street. He rushed up to them and, within moments, as deftly as a sheepdog cutting lambs from a flock, had parted them from their wives and begun talking to them about the election.

"We shouldn't let ourselves think for an instant that because Adams beat Ash we're weak," Cage heard Lincoln say to them. "We won every other race on the ballot and the Democrats can't pretend we didn't. They're going to come at us hard next year and we've got to be ready if we don't want Douglas to take over the Third District and the rest of Illinois along with it."

Cage listened to the strategizing, intrigued in the way outsiders can be intrigued by an intense discussion of a foreign craft. Lincoln had placed a big hard-knuckled hand on the shoulder of each man, not gripping them like someone claiming dominance, just touching them in a confident, comradely way. He was fully recovered now, bursting with ideas about how to keep the Whigs in line and the Democrats off guard.

"Look at Van Buren's subtreasury, his obsession with hard money. Look closely at that and we have our theme for 1838: the ruin of Illinois, just waiting to happen. Paper depreciated, banks shut down, the government itself suddenly the supreme steward of what's left of the people's money."

The two wives pretended not to notice that their husbands had been captured and started a side discussion about the merits of the play. Meanwhile Cage stood off by himself, listening to Lincoln lay out plans for driving a wedge on the subtreasury issue between reasonable-minded Democrats and their hardened Loco Foco allies. The strategy was simple in outline: keep the Whigs together while splitting the

Democrats. But Cage had brushed up against enough politics to know that it was dauntingly complex in practice. Once again, he marveled at the way Lincoln seemed to know not just every public man in Illinois but every common voter as well, and to know what that voter wanted or needed, what favors he expected, and what developments he feared.

"You're a patient man," he told Cage when the impromptu political strategy session had finally broken up and the two legislators were returned to their wives. "First I imposed my pitiable self upon you, then I proceeded to ignore you. Let me buy you a drink. What sort of drink do you want? Or I have a better idea. Don't you have a collected Shakespeare in your room? Let's go there right now and read *Much Ado* aloud. There are parts I'd like to hear again right away, particularly that speech of—"

"No, I'm too tired."

"Lend me the book, then. I'll read it myself and return it tomorrow. And I promise in the future I'll be a better friend to you. I'll make sure there'll be less ado about me and my woes."

EIGHT

◆ ◆ ◆

I, TOO, AM A WAVE on a stormy sea," Ned Baker declaimed, as he struck the cork ball with his hand, slamming it into the backside of one of the new brick buildings on the square. "I, too, am a wanderer driven like thee!"

The newly formed Springfield Poetical Society had no fixed location in which to meet, but they often convened behind the square where the back walls of the buildings, not quite flush with one another, created a kind of court in which to play fives. The challenge the members of the society had set for themselves was to recite their new poems while making the ball strike the wall in rhythm with their stresses.

Ned Baker—Edward Dickinson Baker—was the man Lincoln seemed to believe was a figure of destiny, and who he had decided must be one of the first recruits to the poetical society. Ned was big and square with sweeping hair and soaring eyebrows and hypnotically pale blue eyes. He was only twenty-five but gave the impression of someone who had impatiently vaulted past youth to assume the air of a supremely confident middle-aged man. And he moved with surprising speed and finesse. He was a better player at fives than any of them, better even than Lincoln, who had an advantage with his long arms and big cave-man hands.

Ned was a lawyer and had recently defeated Candlebox Calhoun in a special election for state representative. He had also been a Campbellite preacher. Even as he raced around the court to hit the ball in rhythm, he recited his poem with the urgency of a man reaching out from the pulpit to souls in danger of damnation.

He had come to the last stanza—"For the land I seek is a waveless

shore / And they who reach it shall wander no more." He said the closing word with savage finality as he struck the ball one last time, letting it
bounce and dribble to a stop as his powerful voice seemed to reverber-
ate in the empty makeshift ball court.

"'For the land I seek is a waveless shore,'" Lincoln repeated with
reverence. "By God I'll be the first to shake the hand of a man who can
write a line like that."

It was growing dark and they decided to continue their meeting at
the county clerk's office, which was vacant at night and just down the
hallway in Hoffman's Row from Lincoln and Stuart's own office. The
room had a commodious black walnut chair that Ned commandeered
before the lamps were lit. He was a man blessed with the assumption
that he should always be expected to preside. It was hard not to confirm
him in that expectation. If someone had asked Cage in October of 1837
which man in the room that night would soar the highest, might even
one day lead the entire nation, he would have thought of Ned Baker
in an instant. Lincoln himself held that opinion. Ned's election had
made him a new member of the Long Nine, the legislative delegation
from Sangamon County that included Lincoln and whose nine members were all six feet or more in height. John Stuart had once stood the
nine men against the wall of the house chamber in Vandalia, measured
each with a yardstick, added the sums together and announced that
if stacked head to toe the Long Nine would reach fifty-four feet eight
inches into the air.

"'A waveless shore,'" Lincoln said as he took his own seat on a hard
chair in the county clerk's office. "'A waveless shore.' I don't know that
there could be a better metaphor for infinity. I assume that's what it
represents."

"You're correct," Ned replied. "I had in mind a sort of spreading
watery flatness. Also very foggy. Before we left England, my father used
to take me to the Kent marshes."

Cage thought Lincoln's excitement about Ned's passable poem was
a little excessive. Baker wrote poetry as well as he did everything else,
with casual if not consummate excellence, but the idea of a wave as a
restlessly roving spirit, searching for a "distant shore" where it would

find peace and oblivion, strained under the weight of its own obvious-ness. Still, Ned's cadence was strong and consistent—not always the case with the other members of the society who thought of themselves as poets. And Cage was in favor of anything that helped keep Lincoln in a lively mood instead of the demoralized paralysis he had displayed that night after the August election, when he had suffered his simulta-neous rejection from Mary Owens and from the voters for Ash Merritt's candidacy.

Simeon Francis was the next to read his composition. Sim was older than the other members of the society, already into his forties. He had the face of a lean man, a sharp nose and a thin-lipped, downward-sloping mouth, but his body was so discordantly broad and fleshy it overlapped his armchair. His poem was an ode to the power of the printed word and a vibrant press, a predictable bit of self-congratulation from the editor of the *Sangamo Journal.* After him came Ash Merritt, his spirit more or less recovered from losing his election to James Adams. For his contribution, he reverted to his doctor's expertise and read a few awkwardly constructed comic lines about bodily eructations:

> *"Now hear the belching of the wind*
> *The body's noble trumpet!"*

Billy Herndon jumped up after Ash had finished, and from the fiery look in his eyes it was apparent he was determined to change the tone. Billy was the youngest of them, only nineteen. His father was Archie Herndon, a choleric Democratic member of the state legislature. Archie had sent his son off to college in Jacksonville where, freed from the stric-tures of his father's tyrannical thought, Billy had drunk himself wild and become a heathen abolitionist. Illinois College wouldn't have him back, and neither would Archie, so now he clerked in Speed's store and lived in the increasingly crowded upstairs room with Speed and Lincoln.

"I've been trying to write a poem about the evils of Negro bondage," he said. "But the theme is too important—there's no greater theme, in my opinion, except for maybe the existence of the Deity—and I can't make my language rise to it. So with your indulgence I'll just read 'The Slave's Lament' by Robert Burns."

Everyone knew that Joshua Speed's family owned plenty of slaves in Kentucky and they turned to see how he would react, especially since Speed had recently given Billy a job and a place to live. But Speed just smiled indulgently, even tapped his knuckle on the county clerk's desk in time with the poem's refrain: "And alas! I am weary, weary O."

Billy was not yet a lawyer nor even a student of law, and his rhetorical skills had not been honed. His voice was thin and had no drama in it, so that the endless refrains of "I am weary, weary O" became tedious and even comical. Nevertheless, the group could see the last one coming and joined in rowdily, as if for a drunken chorus—not the effect Billy Herndon had wanted.

"I don't see that Negro slavery is a fit subject for laughter," he told them.

"We weren't laughing at slavery," Lincoln reassured Billy, putting his hand on the younger man's shoulder. "Much less were we laughing at you. We were just caught up in Burns's musicalness and it got the better of us."

Billy reached into the battered haversack that had contained his copy of Burns and pulled out a sheaf of handbills and started passing them out. "We can sit around here and listen to poetry about Negro slavery, or we can do something about it."

Speed took the paper, a notice for an upcoming lecture by an abolitionist preacher named Porter, wadded it up—not angrily—and tossed it into the wooden wastepaper basket. Lincoln studied the paper for a moment and neatly folded it over and over again until he was able to file it away into his waistcoat pocket, where it could be judiciously forgotten.

"I'll go hear Reverend Porter," Cage said. "In my opinion slavery is an injustice without parallel and I'll listen to anyone who wants to speak out against it."

"I will too," Ned Baker said. "What about you, Lincoln? Are you coming?"

"I'm entombed in legal matters. Stuart is out on the circuit and I have to manage our caseload here in Springfield."

"What Lincoln means to say," Speed translated, "is that if he's spotted at an abolitionist rally he might as well drink hemlock."

"When it comes to political suicide," Ned said, "caution can sometimes kill you just as dead as poison. I'm not an abolitionist radical, but why not hear the man out?"

"I'll do better than that," Lincoln said. "I'll read every word of Reverend Porter's lecture when it's published."

Ned Baker, nobler and more reckless than Lincoln, laughed out loud, half in exasperation, half in admiration at his friend's rhetorical evasiveness. The great issue of slavery was still avoidable in those days, if you danced nimbly enough, if you didn't let your principles entrap you.

"I think of slavery as a regrettable infirmity," Speed said. "Like a fever. A strong body politic will eventually throw it off, but if you subject it to the deadly remedy—like abolition—you're likely to kill the patient. Anyway, if we don't get back to being a poetical society we'll turn into a debating society and all hope for harmony will be lost."

"There should be no harmony!" Billy said. "Harmony is an evil in this case! Haven't you read what's been happening in Alton? A man like Lovejoy speaks out against slavery and mobs tear apart his printing presses, not once but three times!"

"The harassment of Lovejoy is a great wrong," Lincoln said.

"Yes, it is, Mr. Lincoln, and slavery is a far greater wrong."

They went on talking about Lovejoy, the famous preacher and abolitionist editor, and even Speed agreed it was an admirable thing for him to risk his life for his beliefs, extreme and unproductive though they were. Abolition was no kind of answer, he said, a remark that led the conversation inevitably to the topic of colonization, which Lincoln and most of the others favored as the most humane and ingenious solution.

"It's no sort of solution at all," Cage said. "It's a wild dream to think we can send all the Negroes back to Africa."

"Henry Clay doesn't think so," Lincoln said.

"Henry Clay!" Billy Herndon sputtered. "Is Henry Clay God? Is every sentence he utters sacred text?"

"Oh, I guess pretty much." The statement was so guileless and absurd and Lincoln's grin so lazily conniving that there was no high ground left for Billy to stand on. Lincoln had a way of turning the mood of a room this way or that as it suited him. And now that he had managed not to ensnare himself in the abolition question, he announced that after staying up almost all night writing various pleadings and petitions and praecipes he had managed to scratch out a poem of his own.

It was a short, bad poem, written in a tone of humorous chivalry in defense of fallen women. He had not had time to commit it to memory, so he stood in front of the group and held up the expired legal document on whose back the poem had been written. He struck theatrical poses as he read it and, infected by the laughter of his audience, began to chortle as he came to the final stanza.

"Whatever spiteful fools may say—
Each jealous, ranting yelper—
No woman ever played the whore
Unless she had a man to help her."

There was applause and appreciative hooting, and Ned Baker declared the poem should be put to music and sung in taverns, the drunker the singers the better.

"Well, Cage," Lincoln said, "what sayest thou? Is it the work of a natural poetical critter or just a four-o'clock-in-the-morning lawyer?"

"I can only point out the obvious. A man who would use the word 'yelper' is a man who is very desperate for a rhyme."

They laughed at Cage's lighthearted riposte, but Lincoln's poem had had a cold effect on him. His mind was too preoccupied with Ellie these days not to be struck by the jarring word "whore." Lincoln's poem meant nothing, of course. It was thoughtless doggerel. But the simple fact that he had written it, had probably labored over it, chuckling to himself late at night as he crossed out lines and counted out its stresses, was vaguely disappointing.

Cage kept his disquiet to himself, and Lincoln—a brilliant reader of other men's thoughts—didn't seem to notice it.

"But we've yet to hear from the master," he declared.

Cage stood and read some lines he had written in the last few weeks, lines that had yet to find their place in a finished piece of work with a discernible theme. It was a notion he had been working on since that spring morning a year and a half ago when he had ridden home alone after spending the night with Lincoln in New Salem. The birdsong breaking through the stillness had made him think of musical notes, and to wonder if music itself was not a human invention but a code buried in the suspirating rhythms of the world. It was a complex thought that kept flying out of his grasp, and he knew, even as he read his lines aloud, that he had not yet caught it. There was appreciative nodding and grunting on the part of his friends as he finished, but the poem sounded abstruse to him. Worse, it sounded useless. Cage looked over at young Billy Herndon. He could tell that Billy had barely listened to his poem. He was still fuming over the issue of slavery and the persecution of Reverend Lovejoy, and how Lincoln with his mocking trifle and Cage with his hazy ponderings had helped turn the conversation away from the great moral question looming over them all.

NINE

◆ ◆ ◆

IT WAS A BRIGHT OCTOBER MORNING but the sky rippled
with darkness as unending flocks of passenger pigeons flew above
Springfield on their southern migration, depositing a light snowfall of
bird waste that spattered the hats of the crowd gathered in front of the
First Presbyterian Church.

There were in fact two crowds, a smaller one with the intent of entering through the front doors to hear Reverend Josiah Porter speak about
abolition, and a larger one resolved to prevent them from doing so.
Jacob Early was there, standing with the latter group, his arms reso-
lutely crossed.

"Well, hello there, Jacob," Ned Baker called out as he approached
with Cage and Billy Herndon. He offered his hand with such hearty
goodwill that Early—compromised by his own essentially friendly
nature—had no choice but to uncross his arms to shake it.

"What are you doing standing out here in front of the church?" Baker
asked him.

"You know damn well what we're doing, Ned," Early said. "We have
a peaceable community here, and we don't care to have some abolitionist who calls himself a preacher come along and stir everything all up."

"You're planning to keep a preacher from walking into a church?"
Cage asked.

"Do I know you?"

"Second battle of Kellogg's Grove."

Early peered at Cage. Early had been a captain at Kellogg's Grove
and Cage only a militia private beneath his notice. But Cage remembered him vividly, as he remembered every other deeply incised detail

of that day. He had last seen him during the courthouse debate when Early and Ninian Edwards had been bombarding each other with lowly insults. Face to face now, he was struck by how young Early looked, how young he must have been at the time he had commanded Lincoln and Stuart and Reed in his spy company. He still had traces of that native authority, though his waistcoat strained against the weight he had put on since. The angry men at the church door shuffled behind him as if it were a settled thing that he was in command.

Early finally nodded at Cage but—still acknowledging the gap in their long-ago rank—declined to say anything to him.

"I don't see your friend Lincoln here," he said instead to Baker. "He's got the sense to stay away, and you aren't likely to be growing any turnips here either."

"I don't care a thing in the world about a turnip. I just like to hear a learned man speak from time to time."

"Open a sack and let all the niggers loose at the same time?" a man standing next to Early said. "That doesn't sound like the teaching of any kind of learned man to me." He shifted his attention to Cage. "And just so you know, I'll knock you or anybody else in the head if you intend to help get that preacher in here."

Cage had seen this man holding forth in the taverns and hotels and coffeehouses of Springfield. He was a wealthy landholder and failed Democratic candidate for the assembly named Nimmo Rhodes. He was of normal height but so powerfully thick in the chest that the sleeves of his coat were pinched and creased under his arms. He had a marvelously round face that was incongruent with the menace in his eyes.

"You might as well try to knock me in the head now," Cage told him, "because that's exactly what I intend."

"Let's not get excitable, Nimmo," Early told Rhodes, gently pulling him back by the arm. "This isn't a mob."

But it was a mob, or turned into one almost as soon as the Reverend Josiah Porter was spotted walking down the street on his way to the church, gripping his Bible so hard that his knuckles were white. He was a fierce-looking man to begin with, and he was surrounded by five or six acolytes who were clearly acting as bodyguards. About fifty people, including Cage and Baker, had come to hear him speak, but there were twice that number blocking the doors to the church.

The confrontation that took place came on swiftly and was hauntingly silent. The crowd guarding the doors tensed up and closed ranks, Reverend Porter's men stepped forward and shoved into them without saying a word, and suddenly the two groups closed into a grunting, heaving, trampling mass. No one spoke, no one struck anyone else with fists or deadly implements, but it was violent all the same, a press of men with their feet planted grinding into one another in such a tight mass that in an instant Cage was afraid for his life. He might have fallen, or someone (Nimmo Rhodes being a likely suspect) might have kicked his feet out from under him; in either case he went down onto the street. He tried to stand but was packed in so tight by the shoving men still on their feet that there was no room to bend his knees. Looking up through the thicket of flailing arms, he could see the sky only in flickering glimpses. He gasped for breath but there was no air, only a growing cloud of street dust. He had almost passed out by the time he fought his way back to the surface. He gulped air and watched as one of the combatants—pro- or anti-abolitionist, it was impossible to know—lost his footing and fell, his head cracking into Cage's cheekbone on the way down.

"That's enough! That's enough!" Ned Baker was shouting. The confrontation had been going on for some time now, but Baker was the first person who seemed to have actually spoken any words since it began, and as his voice rose out of the confused silence it had an arresting force. "We're neighbors! We don't have any reason to be fighting each other."

He reached out and grabbed an ashen-faced Reverend Porter by the shoulder. "All this man wants to do is—"

"—free all the niggers!" someone in the mob shouted. Men were still shoving and surging against each other, but the struggle was more like a loosening knot now. Behind the colliding front lines, there were pockets of calm.

"No," Baker said. "He wants to walk into a church of God! Is Springfield the sort of town that won't let a man do that? Are we the kind of people who will *kill* a man to keep him from doing that?"

He turned to Early.

"Is that who we are, Jacob?"

"Nobody wants to kill anybody," Early had to admit. "But we don't want to listen to his kind of talk."

"Then *don't!*" Baker yelled, almost laughing at the obviousness of the solution. "Just don't listen!"

Early thought about that while he put out an arm to settle down Rhodes and the other still-agitated men who were standing immediately next to him. Then he turned around and took a step back so he was facing the crowd that was blockading the church.

"Gentlemen, we hold strong views and we've expressed them strongly. No one can be in doubt about where we stand on the question of abolition, which at its heart is not a principle at all but a devious tactic to disrupt comity and civil behavior. You've seen the abolitionists at their work already this morning. They would like nothing better than to keep us all agitated and off our guard. But we're the opposite of agitated, we are calm in our convictions. And having made those convictions known, we're now at liberty to go home to our hearths and our families and enjoy this beautiful God-given day."

Cage, his eye swelling shut, noticed Early exchanging a satisfied nod with Ned Baker and then walking away, Nimmo Rhodes and the rest of the crowd hesitating at first and then following him down the street, roughly jostling the members of Reverend Porter's audience as they went.

When Reverend Porter finally began his lecture the church was only half full. Cage sat with Ned and Billy Herndon in the front, staring at the preacher through his one open eye, feeling the satisfying and righteous pain in his injured sinus. There was no blood but he was sure the left side of his face was grotesquely swollen and discolored. He could not wait to present the wound he had suffered in the abolition war to Lincoln, who had probably watched the confrontation on the street from the safety of his law office window. It was partly Lincoln's slipperiness on the matter that had made Cage determine to attend the lecture in the first place. Cage was naturally wary of men who were sure of themselves, whose beliefs and prejudices and ambitions were purposefully visible to all the world. That was why Lincoln's hidden motives and even more hidden self intrigued him more than Ned Baker's open passion. But there were some issues, a very few, that would find you out no matter how cleverly you disguised yourself. And so he had to be here, where history was brewing.

If Porter was still shaken by the melee outside the church, his voice did not betray it. His own church was in Sugar Creek, but the call of God and the demands of justice had sent him all around Illinois to speak out against slavery. He spoke with a benevolent South Carolina accent but his tone was chastising and firm. He had prepared for the ministry in Cincinnati, he said, where he had tried but failed to keep the great question of human bondage separate from his theological studies. Slavery was God's challenge to the human conscience. It was the crisis of our time, it would not go away, it could not be resolved by impractical expediencies like colonization. The only thing that would resolve it, that would restore God's blessing upon this morally blighted country, was the immediate liberation of all the men, women, and children of the imprisoned Negro race.

He urged his audience to disregard the confrontation that had taken place outside the church this morning. It was nothing. It was the reflexive spasm of ignorance and prejudice. The harassments he himself had suffered in preaching God's truth about slavery did not compare to what Reverend Lovejoy had endured in Alton. Bandits had tried to tar and feather him, they had repeatedly destroyed his printing presses, yet not only did the *Alton Observer* continue to appear on the streets but Lovejoy himself had called for a statewide antislavery meeting for that next week.

During the two hours the reverend spoke, Cage's eye swelled tighter, and by the end of the talk he was light-headed and his cheek was throbbing with pain. Baker and Herndon congratulated him on his noble wound. He went home, ignoring Mrs. Hopper's horrified look as he walked through the parlor and up the stairs. At his desk, he set down his memories of the eventful morning, conflating the righteous creative energy he felt with the vivid pain in his cheek.

· · ·

One night a little more than a week later the usual Whig crowd was once again gathered at the back of Speed's store when Billy Herndon burst through the door and ran past the merchandise and appeared in front of them with tears streaming down his face.

"They shot him dead!"

He was crying so hard that it took him a moment to calm himself and deliver the rest of the news about who exactly had been shot. Elijah Lovejoy, the abolitionist editor and minister whom Reverend Porter had praised in his lecture the week before, had been killed by a mob in Alton.

"They shot him dead. He was trying to keep them from destroying his new printing press and they killed him. Five times he was shot."

The men in the store reacted with grim silence. Their Whiggish views on slavery and its extension into other states and territories were various—a few of them were theoretically in favor of abolition, some believed in the dream of colonization, some like Speed came from families that still held slaves and therefore could not denounce the institution without hypocrisy, others like Lincoln stood cautiously to the side, observing, waiting, testing the ground for a place to take a firm stand. But they were united in their horror at the outbreak of mob rule. They were ambitious but conscionable men, and a society without order was a threat to their dreams.

"We would not have allowed such a thing to happen in Springfield," Speed said.

"It almost happened last week," Cage said. He knew his observation was supported by the appearance of his face. When he had looked in the mirror that afternoon the grotesque swelling was finally gone but there was still a many-hued bruise below his eye. "And it might happen yet."

"Anarchy is bad for business," Ash Merritt said. "The citizens of Alton will find that out soon enough. No one will leave their homes to go to the shops."

They took turns making economic and political and ethical pronouncements. To anybody who read the papers, it was plain that what had happened to Lovejoy in Alton and what could have happened to

Reverend Porter in Springfield was not unique. The national economy was in crisis, the populace was on edge, lawlessness was everywhere, self-appointed avengers springing up in the streets of every American city. A pickpocket had been lynched in Vandalia only a few months ago, all across the country there had been riots and inchoate attacks, and recently a free black man in St. Louis, suspected of murder, had been chained to a tree and set alight without any thought of formally charging him with a crime.

"They say he sang a hymn while he was on fire," Ned Baker solemnly remarked.

"It would be very difficult for a man to sing a song while he was burning to death," Ash observed with his doctor's knowledge. "The mind in such a case is too distracted."

"You're talking about irrelevancies!" Billy Herndon shouted. His eyes were dry now, but they were still red with emotion. "Mobs exist because slavery exists and there are men who are trying to stop it. The thing to do, the only thing to do, is to root out slavery in the first place."

"There's no grub hoe that big, Billy," Speed said. "I wish there was."

Speed sounded sincere. Probably he was, momentarily setting aside the fact that his own fortune had grown root and branch from his family's slaves. There was nothing unique in his situation. Springfield was full of enlightened men in whom sincerity and hypocrisy were woven tight.

"Well, somebody here should do something," Billy said. "Somebody here should at least *say* something."

Lincoln had been silent during much of this conversation, his face set in its familiar aspect of tortured thoughtfulness. Now when he looked up he noticed that the men in the room had all turned their eyes toward him and were waiting for him to speak.

"Well, I reckon Billy's right," he considered, running his hand thoughtlessly through his hair until it ended up looking like a clump of crow feathers. "Something has to be said."

1838

TEN

◆ ◆ ◆

L ET REVERENCE FOR THE LAWS be breathed by every American mother," Lincoln orated from beneath a molting buffalo robe in his law office, "to the lisping babe, that prattles on her lap—let it be taught in—"

"Stop right there," Cage said. "You should choose one. The babe should either lisp or prattle."

"Why can't the babe do both?"

"Because lisping and prattling will collide in the mind of the listener and create a distraction. Also, it's too ornate. Is this a speech or is it a sonnet? By the way, there's a terrible smell in here."

Lincoln said he hadn't noticed but that he would join in the search for the source of the offensive odor. He stood up from the narrow bench on which he was lying, clutching the buffalo robe around his shoulders, and then lay lengthwise on the floor so that he could see beneath a couch against the opposite wall. He retrieved a plate on which lay a half-eaten piece of cheese whose surface had grown a fungal blush as green and shiny as a velvet waistcoat. He opened a window, letting in a freezing January wind, and tossed the cheese out onto the street.

"If the defenestration of the cheese has had the desired effect," Lincoln said, "I will continue."

Cage sat in the office's hard client chair, bundled up in the under-heated room with his fur hat and gloves on, a scarf around his throat, and resumed listening to Lincoln practice his speech. He was to deliver it later that week to the Young Men's Lyceum, and he was nervous about it. A high-minded speech about the undesirability of mob rule, if it succeeded, would help restore the public's trust in his judgment after the unpleasant reaction to his Sampson's Ghost letter-writing campaign.

Stuart and Lincoln's law office was on the second floor of Hoffman's Row, just above the courtroom. In fact, it must have originally been envisioned as a storage room for court documents, since a hinged door in the floor connected it directly to the courtroom below. The room was spacious enough but so crowded with books and piles of legal papers that it might have been half its size. Since Stuart was so often gone—out on the circuit or campaigning for Congress or both at the same time—the office had been left to conform itself to the character of the firm's junior partner. It was a shambling but intriguing mess, in which nothing ever seemed close to hand, but at the same time never quite out of reach of its long-armed occupant.

"New reapers will arise," Lincoln read, dramatically casting off the buffalo robe. It fell to the floor in a mighty moth-eaten heap, and Cage would not have been surprised to see a host of burrowing animals scurry out from under it. "And they, too, will seek a field. It is to deny, what the history of the world tells us is true, to suppose that men of ambition and talents will not continue to spring up amongst us. And, when they do, they will as naturally seek the gratification of their ruling passion, as others have done so before them."

Cage was a little startled by where Lincoln's thoughts led him next, because it seemed these "men of ambition" were not to be trusted at all. He declared that public men who would find themselves satisfied with a traditional public office—even the governorship or the presidency—"belong not to the family of the lion, or the tribe of the eagle."

Lincoln struck a teapot pose, his arm flung high in the low-ceilinged room. "What! Think you these places would satisfy an Alexander, a Caesar, or a Napoleon—Never! Towering genius disdains a beaten path."

Cage was so infatuated with his friend's eccentric and fervent performance that he didn't think to interrupt him again. He sat in his chair and listened to the whole thing all the way to the end. The speech seemed to be a call to arms against the "mobocratic spirit," against the Napoleons and Caesars who would destroy the country's political institutions and its common history, but there was a degree of infatuation with the family of the lion and the tribe of the eagle that Lincoln couldn't quite mask. Was he warning the people against the rampaging leader he feared was resident in his own ambition, hidden within his own heart?

"I don't know what to make of it," Cage told him honestly when he had finished and had struck his last lunging pose. "Read me the part about reason again."

"Cold, calculating, unimpassioned reason must—"

"You make the cure sound more forbidding than the disease. I want to live in a warm-blooded country, not the Republic of Logic."

"You just complained that it was too ornate! I'm being forceful and direct here. And honest, by the way. Do you want me to imply that reason should be warm and soggy?"

"I thought this speech was going to be about slavery."

"Why did you think that?"

"Why would I not think that? It's the great issue of the day. It's what's driving the mobs in the first place."

"You can give a speech about slavery, if you want," Lincoln said. "Your future doesn't hang on your reelection, but since mine does, this speech is about the perpetuation of our political institutions, which are under threat—not from slavery but from disorder."

He said this crossly as he sat down on his bench, shivering, his breath frosty. Cage kicked the buffalo robe across the floor to him—a gruff peace offering—and Lincoln bent down and wrapped himself once more in the hideous garment.

"There are some nice phrases," Cage admitted. "Something about artillery?"

"The silent artillery of time."

"Yes, that was it. Very effective."

"Thank you."

Lincoln sat there musing for a long moment, troubled by Cage's criticism, or by something deeper.

"When I was a boy in Kentucky," he finally said, "this place we called Knob Creek, we were right on the edge of the turnpike. I remember seeing slaves being marched down the road to Nashville. My father's been a hard man all his life but you would have thought he was tender-hearted as a deacon, the way he looked at those coffles of poor Negroes when they were walking past, all manacled together. I guess he'd been treated poorly enough himself—the land titles were all shingled up in those days and he'd already lost his claim to two farms by then—that he didn't see those men as nigger slaves but just poor unfortunate souls like himself.

"And those two times I went down to New Orleans on a flatboat I saw the slave markets there. Right in the middle of town, there'd be those Negroes in their pens and people standing there auctioning them off. No difference than if they were selling cattle. Signs hanging out in front like it was a dry goods store—'So & So and Co., Slaves for Sale.' It seemed so normal it turned your mind in on itself, till you thought there was something wrong with you for thinking it was strange. It's odd what us humans can make room for in our minds."

"That's a speech I'd like to hear," Cage said.

"Well, you're going to hear this one instead, I'm afraid. Listen, Cage, if slavery isn't wrong, nothing's wrong. But outright abolition's impossible—it would tear the country apart. The Constitution itself protects it. And if I start preaching abolition the only thing that's going to get abolished is me. So take me as I am if you still want to be my friend—I'm not going to get any better than what you see right now."

He gave the speech that Saturday night, taking a few of Cage's suggestions but ignoring most. The babe lisped and prattled both, Lincoln struck his poses and warned against Caesar and Napoleon and safely called for the crumbling temple of liberty to be rebuilt, "hewn from the solid quarry of sober reason."

The crowd that had gathered at the Baptist church to hear him was not nearly as critical as Cage had been. Speed and Baker and Herndon and Merritt and all the usual Whig crowd were there, and since the Young Men's Lyceum was a nonpartisan group there were Democrats as well. Even Jacob Early was in attendance. He had been maintaining since the Reverend Porter incident that he had never been the leader of a mob, only of a civil-minded protest against radical and incendiary ideas.

There was little to disagree with in Lincoln's remarks—who didn't want a peaceful society uninfected by mob savagery?—but despite his reservations Cage found himself stirred just as strongly as the rest of the audience. Beneath the staginess, there was authentic passion, and beneath the passion there was something stronger, a steadily ensnaring grip of logic. When Lincoln reached his concluding rhetorical burst—"The gates of hell shall not prevail against it!"—his listeners responded with boisterous applause that he had engineered with great craft throughout his speech, and finally made as inevitable as a reflex. It was done. Abraham Lincoln had banished the memory of Sampson's Ghost. He was no longer an anonymous character assassin but a lone voice crying out for honor and decency in a time of chaos.

Cage got to his feet with the rest and put his hands together, applauding for the tame sentiments that had been written and delivered with such conviction. Joshua Speed stood across the church aisle, huzzahing. When he caught Cage's eye he smiled and jerked his head slightly backwards, indicating something or someone behind him. And two rows back, there she was. The club was called the Young Men's Lyceum but it had always graciously opened its doors to women who might want to hear a lecture about the properties of water or the moral question of capital punishment. Still, it was a shock to see Ellie there, standing contentedly by herself, politely applauding with her gloved hands. She wore an austere woolen dress of pale green, and over her shoulders a carriage shawl of a teasingly different shade. He had never seen her outside of her rooms, and the fact that she was so suddenly and blatantly visible to him and to all the world filled him with anxious longing.

She saw him, didn't smile but tilted her head in complicit acknowledgment, slipped out of the pew and toward the back of the church as the rest of the audience was surging forward to congratulate the speaker. In her hurried pace as she retreated, in the firm set of her shoulders, he recognized that she was sending him a signal not to follow her, that they had no business meeting each other in public. Of course he wanted to disregard this. Why should he care about his reputation? He wasn't running for office. But he knew that his eagerness was a dangerous thing—it was the enemy of her respect for him.

So he went home, waited a week, working late into the night, driven by a sudden mood of despairing solitude. He was twenty-eight years old and he held in his hand a letter that had come that afternoon from Little and Brown: "Though we see much promise in these skillful verses, we feel that your exclusive focus on Western settings and themes may not coincide with the interests of our reading audience, whom we perceive as being mostly of the city-dwelling type. Therefore we regret that we cannot make you an offer of publication. If you find that your work begins to extend beyond the geographical boundaries you appear to have set for it, we would be very happy to consider further submissions."

The small-minded, dismissive response infuriated him. But the verdict that came with it—no publication—scared him. Was he staking his time and his talent on a literary enterprise that the rest of the world would find to be of no interest? Was his project of a real western literature just the defensive reaction of a man trapped in the provinces, far from where things could actually be expected to happen?

He could have thrown the letter away or burned it in the fireplace, where the coals were glowing, waiting to receive it. But instead he folded it and slipped it between the pages of his notebook, where it might serve as a goad should his confidence ever begin to recover. "Towering genius disdains a beaten path," Lincoln had said in his speech. "It thirsts and burns for distinction." He had meant it in the form of a warning against the dictatorial usurpers of democracy, but wasn't just such a raging drive necessary to accomplish anything lasting? He certainly could not imagine Lincoln—or Baker, or Stuart, or even young Billy Herndon—without it.

But his own engine was going nowhere, thirsting and burning though he was. It was off the track, the gears frenetically spinning. He felt this acutely after witnessing Lincoln's triumph at the Young Men's Lyceum, after seeing him applauded and huzzahed for a speech that took no chances, that was full of sentiments that everyone—civil-minded Whigs and Democrats alike—could agree with. It would not be until many years later, when his friend proved willing to prosecute a relentless war against disorder and disunion, that Cage realized that the speech had not been empty after all, that Lincoln really did believe the things in it. He hated slavery, yes, but he feared chaos more. And perhaps he feared his own "towering genius," the ruthless racing thing inside him.

It was nearly midnight but she would be awake. He had visited her at this hour before and found her at her dressmaker's dummy, contentedly sewing by candlelight, happy to interrupt her work. He stood up and assessed himself in the looking glass. A neutral face, small and sharp-featured, though his brown eyes were earnest and searching. His hair was awry and he brushed it downward and forward, so that it curled at the brow and at the edges of his side-whiskers in the style of Byron and Bonaparte and others who disdained the beaten path.

He walked with care through the hallway, avoiding the familiar warped floorboards that would creak and disturb his lodgers. Most would be asleep, including Mrs. Hopper, who had a righteous bed-time and was not to be disturbed after nine thirty. Theophilous Emry, however, was usually awake well into the early hours of the morning, playing his fiddle so softly—and so well—that the other residents never complained. Cage could hear "Brightly Speed the Hours" as he passed Emry's closed door.

The night was clear, the stars scattered like ice droplets in the frigid vault of the sky. It was very cold but there was no wind to drive the temperature down farther. Springfield felt exquisitely static and empty, a perfect little snow cave of a town, protected from the tumultuous world around it.

"The beaten path," he whispered in this silence, stealing the phrase from Lincoln, testing it out for a title or first line of a poem. Path. Wrath. Math. Hath. Bath. Faith, if he wanted the effect of a glancing rhyme, though he rather doubted he did. Of the rhyming words that sprang to mind, "wrath" was the only one that suggested a hard surface upon which his forming ideas could be beaten into shape. "And winding on, through something-and-something, leads to the very seat of wrath." Or to the very heart of wrath. Or to a strange flowering grove of wrath.

A cold poem for a cold night. But toying with the idea revived his spirits a little, made him feel that the editor at Little and Brown had read hastily, and with a provincial defensiveness of his own. Perhaps, even at twenty-eight, there was a future still looming for Cage. He had only to look to his friend Abraham Lincoln for an example of how to revive your fortunes when they were at a low ebb.

He came to the isolated house. The bottom floor where the disagreeable old woman and her son lived was dark, but upstairs there was weak candlelight visible through the curtains. She was awake, no doubt calmly sewing. She would be unsurprised when he climbed the outside stairway and knocked softly on her door. She would smile, just enough to give him heart, to allow him to believe he meant something to her, or could. She might be playing out a charade of affection, but she might just as well be playing out a charade of indifference, afraid for practical reasons—or for hidden emotional ones—to reveal the normal human longings that had to be there, and that for some reason Cage thought he must uncover.

He saw the nameless, ownerless dog curled up by her door—someone had covered him with a cast-off blanket. Cage was striding toward the stairway when Ellie's door unexpectedly opened and the dog leapt to his feet, throwing off the blanket. The figure that emerged was almost too tall for the doorframe, an unmistakably familiar figure, tall and thin with narrow shoulders and untamed black hair. He would have seen Cage if he had not immediately bent down to pet the dog, who—like everyone else—danced around his feet in adoration.

Cage drew back, out of sight in the night shadow of a neighbor's barn. Lincoln made his loose-jointed way down the stairs and took off toward the center of town, striding through the cold with a self-satisfied gait, his condensed breath streaming behind. It required an effort from Cage not to scramble out after him, to demand what he had been doing with her, what right he had to be here. But of course he knew what Lincoln had been doing, and he knew that he had every right. To accost him, to berate him for no coherent purpose would only mean piling on more humiliation than Cage already felt.

But he couldn't check himself from climbing the stairs, once Lincoln was out of sight, and rapping angrily on Ellie's door. The dog rose to greet him, but seeing that he would be ignored he burrowed down into his blanket as Ellie opened the door.

"I saw you standing down there," she said. She held the door open for him to come inside. She was wearing a dark blue dressing gown, her hair was undone and hanging loose in a way that tormented him with its casualness, its hints of an intimacy he could witness but not share.

As they stood looking at each other, she brushed her hair with a brush whose silver backing depicted a goddess in a chariot.

"You look very angry," she said. "But you know, don't you, that you have no right to be?"

"It must give you some sort of satisfaction to pretend that normal human emotions are a violation of nature. Do you think I'm perverse for wanting you?"

"You're not perverse. But you're making yourself very miserable trying to imagine me as something other than I am."

"Did you charge him the same as you charge me? Or were you so stirred up by his speech that you—"

"Oh, stop it. I went to hear his speech because everybody's always talking about him and I was curious about what he had to say. I'm not stirred up, I'm not infatuated. In fact it's very late and I'm very tired and I think it would be better if you went home."

"He wrote a poem about a whore. He read it to our poetry society."

She looked away from him, made a show of surrendering to disappointment as she resumed pulling the brush through her hair.

"I don't care if he wrote a poem about a whore. I don't care if you're trying to shock me with that word. That's not the way I think of myself, and I don't think it's the way you think of me either. I'm something different. And you and I together are something different than people would expect, maybe than either one of us would expect."

"What do you mean?"

"He was here for an hour, Cage, and then he was gone. I doubt very much he'll even come back. He doesn't think of me the way you do. Only you think of me the way you do."

"But you don't think of me at all."

"I'm thinking of you right now," she said. "I'm thinking of how welcoming I'd be if you went home now and came back when you weren't feeling angry at me and sorry for yourself. I would be so pleased to see you in that condition."

ELEVEN

◆◆◆

THE TWO YOUNG MEN Billy Herndon brought to Cage's room looked familiar. As he was pulling out the chair from behind his desk to make sure that everyone had a place to sit, he realized why. They had been part of the Reverend Porter's entourage that day when the scuffle had broken out in front of the First Presbyterian Church.

Their names were Benbrook and Westridge, both attorneys from Alton. Benbrook was disheveled-looking, his coat smudged with cigar ash, his hair cut short as if he were emerging from an illness. Westridge was tall and trim and wore his clothes well. He sat with his thin legs elegantly crossed and one arm hooked casually over the chairback. But otherwise there was nothing casual about either of them. They were direct and fervent.

"Mr. Benbrook and Mr. Westridge were both close associates of Reverend Lovejoy," Billy said. "Of course they're grieving his death terribly."

"His murder was an outrage," Cage said.

"It was a shock but not a surprise," Benbrook said. "We were well-armored, you could say, because we had been preparing ourselves for it, or for something like it, for quite some time."

"But nothing can really prepare you for such savagery," Westridge said. "Well, you yourself saw a little taste of it here in Springfield when Reverend Porter tried to make his way into the church."

"As you say," Cage said, "only a little taste. But how can I help you?"

"They've come to see you about a woman," Billy said.

"A Negro woman," Benbrook said. "Her name is Cordelia, or at least that's the name she goes by now."

"As you know," Westridge said, unhooking his arm from the chair-back and leaning forward to fix Cage in his earnest gaze, "Illinois is a free state, though the word 'free' is really only a rhetorical construction. Section Three, Article Eleven of our state constitution, for instance, blurs any real distinction between indentured servitude and slavery, making them in essence—"

"Don't bore him with articles, Gideon," Benbrook said.

"And of course a runaway slave has no right to reside here at all," Westridge went on, ignoring his friend. "If such a person were to set foot in Illinois and be apprehended and turned over to the sheriff, she would be sent straight back into bondage."

"So this Cordelia is a runaway slave?"

"We have not said that," Benbrook said. "And will not say it. Let's just say instead that Cordelia is a young woman of elusive origins who can read and write and is extremely skillful in the domestic realm. She's someone who needs employment, and who we can guarantee will return value to her employer. Even more than a job, she needs the appearance of having a job, of being part of the warp and woof, so to speak."

"A woman with that sort of situation," Westridge said, "employed by a reputable citizen, is less likely to be asked to show a certificate of freedom."

"And what would it take to obtain a certificate of freedom?"

"A thousand dollars," Benbrook said.

"That's a lot of money."

"It is," Westridge said. "If it were only the case of this one woman, we could raise it, but there are many others with the same plight, and we feel the best we can do for them is to find them a job where over time they could save enough money to buy the certificates for themselves."

"Why do you come to me?"

"You were willing to hear Reverend Porter speak, for one thing," Westridge said, "and Mr. Herndon has implied your ideas aren't so far out of line with ours. Also, we've read your poetry about the Black Hawk War. Your sympathy for those poor wretched Indians is evident on every page. It wasn't a great stretch to think that feeling might extend to Negroes as well."

"There might be a grain of risk," Benbrook explained. "Probably not physical risk, but if this girl was indeed a runaway slave—a fact we have not communicated to you, by the way—you could for instance be fined for employing her."

"I understand," Cage said. The grain of risk, the hint of conspiracy, was welcome. Anything was welcome that could distract his jealous mind from recalling last night's covert sighting of Lincoln leaving Ellie's room.

"I don't have anything for her here at the Palatine," he told the two abolitionists. "I have a strong-willed housekeeper and can't impose a new staff member on her. But I might be able to turn up something helpful if you can give me a little time."

"Why do you keep asking me about what I thought of Lincoln's speech?" Ellie was carefully cutting a strip of pale green fabric with her long shears. "Is it because you like to hear me talk about him? Because you like to be jealous? I don't like jealousy. I have no tolerance for it."

"I'm interested in your answer for its own sake."

"All right, here's my answer. I think that if I could vote, I would vote for Frances Wright, if a woman could run for something, and I wouldn't concern myself too much with what Abraham Lincoln or any other man had to say about anything."

"Even if you could vote, you wouldn't have the luxury of ignoring men. We would still tend to be in your way."

"You're in my way now," she said, brushing past him to look for something in her sewing basket. She smiled, busy, preoccupied, but happy enough to have him there. It was a professional visit—the only kind she gave any indication of allowing—but she was not in a hurry and certainly he wasn't either. He craved the illusion that they were companions, that the time they were together could be freely wasted and was not a commodity. It was an illusion he was trying hard to maintain, though he was still burdened by the sight of Lincoln at her door.

She sat down again to her sewing, making a show of ignoring him. It was four in the afternoon, still January, still cold, snow falling. He had not taken off his gloves, though his new John Bull hat hung on the bedpost.

"As for the speech itself, I thought that what he had to say was something that I already knew: people should behave themselves."

She was aware of him watching as she worked, the needle in her hands darting in and out of the cloth with frenetic precision.

"If I could," she said, "I'd walk up to all the women of this town and rip off their mutton sleeves. It would be a great favor to them. Your Mr. Lincoln could build his railroad in the time it takes for word to arrive from Philadelphia that the styles have changed."

"He's not my Mr. Lincoln."

"Good. He's not mine either." She stared up at him from her chair. He was still standing. He hoped his tortured thoughts didn't show in his face, but of course they did. In another moment or two she would put down her sewing and stand up and walk over to him, turning her back so that he could slowly undress her, aware that he craved the illusion of slow-moving normalcy.

"Are you going to confront him?" she asked. "Challenge him to some kind of fight?"

"Why would I do that? It would be petty of me."

"So you won't even speak to him about it?"

"No, I wouldn't think of speaking to him about a private transaction."

"Men are interesting."

"We're placed in the position of being interesting by women like you. You mentioned some sort of millinery idea. Tell me about it. Aren't there enough shops in town already?"

"No," she replied without expression. He saw she was making an effort not to appear too interested in the question. "We have clothing stores, and dry goods stores, and women who sew in their homes, but not a shop like I have in mind. Not just a place where ladies buy their accessories but where they can have a dress run up by somebody who knows what's in fashion and, more important, what's not. A place that will give them somewhere to go. Women like to get out, you know. Since there's no longer any doubt we're the capital, somebody is bound to open a shop like that. Women will need clothes. There'll be parties and cotillions all through the regular sessions of the legislature. And there'll be special sessions because nothing will get done in the regular sessions, and so there'll be more parties and cotillions for those."

He asked her where she would put such a place. She told him the rents in the center of town, where the new statehouse was going up, were already too extravagant, but that didn't matter anyway, because people were accustomed now to searching out intriguing shops off the main square. Jefferson Street, perhaps, or as far east as Seventh.

"If a person were far-sighted enough," she said, "he might even buy Chicken Row, tear down those ugly stinking stalls, and build something nice out of brick."

"I'm not that far-sighted, and I'm not that rich. What would you need in the way of help?"

"A girl at two dollars a week, to start with. A good needlewoman."

"I might have someone."

"Do you? Someone who can do a vertical stitch?"

"I don't know what that is."

"Then I don't know why you would want to recommend her."

"She would have to be part of the enterprise."

"Why?"

"Because she's a runaway slave and I want to help her."

"That's ridiculous."

"You don't care about slavery?"

"No, I don't. And if we were in business together I would never allow you to make a decision based entirely on sentiment."

"Then we won't be in business together."

"Have you even met her?"

"No."

She slumped in her chair, making a show of her disapproval. But the sense of opportunity he had awakened in her was still keen.

"What about the rent?" he asked her.

"Are you serious about this? Why would you want to set me up in a shop? Is it so you can possess me?"

"It was your idea in the first place."

"Because I've had enough of men possessing me. You must accept that, because if you can't there's no way I would go into business with you."

Her face was flushed with sudden emotion and she dabbed with her handkerchief at the corners of her eyes before the fat tears that had formed there could fall. Nothing he had ever said or done had unsettled her before. She reacted to the possibility of him setting her up in business as another woman might to an offer of marriage. He made a determination to stay where he was and not move toward her. She did not need or want comfort, and would swat him away just now if she sensed he was trying to edge too close to her vulnerable core.

He spoke to her in a flat voice. "If you could find a suitable location, and could make a plan for your shop that would make sense for me, and agree to hire this Negro woman, something between us might be gotten up. In that case I assume you'd want to break your arrangement with Speed."

"So that I can start a new arrangement with you? So that I can't be shared?"

"It has nothing to do with that."

"I don't consider myself to be Joshua Speed's chattel, and if we open a shop together I won't consider myself to be yours. So nobody will be 'sharing' me. I'll share myself, of my free will, and with whomever I want.

"And at the moment," she said, slowly unbuttoning her dress, "that happens to be you."

Lincoln's new poem was about suicide, an unexpected topic for someone who had just given a triumphant speech. He introduced it to the members of the poetical society with a grin by saying he had been wandering in a dark forest on the Flat Branch of the Sangamon, deep in thought about specie payments and the subtreasury and the state bank, when he came across a skeleton, still gripping this suicide note in the bones of its hand.

They all laughed, of course, thinking they were in for another dose of Lincoln's ribald verses. But the poem really was about suicide, starkly so, with lines about self-imposed dagger thrusts ripping up organs and sending out showers of blood. Lincoln succeeded alarmingly in putting himself in the mind of this miserably solitary creature who had killed himself, who thought of the hell he was destined for as a place where the screams of the damned and the searing flames would help him to "forget."

Forget what? Was something unendurable in his own spirit driving the theme of this poem, or was it just an exercise, a brief abstract glimpse into what he imagined a man with a tormented mind would feel? He read the poem without giving much of a clue, without a touch of oratorical flight. There was nothing original in the language—"lonely hooting owl," for God's sake—but there was a frightening conviction at the poem's core that made it seem, just then, in that room, that an unrevealing man had suddenly laid himself bare.

The group was caught a little off guard by the raw sentiments in the poem and it took them a moment, once he had finished it, to proclaim it the finest product so far of the Springfield Poetical Society. It should be published in the *Sangamo Journal* without delay.

"Maybe," Lincoln said, "but people might get the wrong idea. If they think I'm planning to stab myself they might decide it would be the waste of a vote."

"That's easily solved," Speed said. "Don't put your name to it. After all, *you* didn't write it. You told us that yourself. It was written by the poor fellow whose bones you found."

"Yes," Lincoln said, "and the skeleton belonged to Stephen Douglas, who killed himself at the prospect of John T. Stuart beating him for Congress. Except of course if I'd found Douglas's little skeleton in the first place I would have thought it was that of a squirrel."

It was Cage's turn next. His "beaten path" musings had led to the first draft of a poem, written one night in a strange feverish rush. He had not had a chance to reflect on its meaning, or even to determine if there were any meaning to it at all. He knew that it was in a somber key, that it was vaguely apocalyptic, that it was some sort of declaration to himself that he had his own course to run.

> *"The beaten path, the traveled way,*
> *The turnpike leading on*
> *Through forests dark, 'neath burning skies,*

The trail imprinted on the earth,
Though Earth itself be gone."

Years later, in the snowbound silence of a Sierra winter, when he was no longer Micajah Weatherby but just some ravening thing conscious only of the need to keep itself in existence, this poem would come back to him. It would seem almost like a predictive dream, something he had created in an earlier life to alert his future self that there was a way ahead, a way over the mountains and out of the starving winter camp. His poetic ambitions would by then have come to nothing, his very imagination something his being no longer had the strength to fuel. But he would keep saying the lines to himself as he fought through the waist-high snow—the lines that declared against all evidence that there was some kind of road ahead.

But he was not that person yet. That ordeal was still to come. He was in the county clerk's office in Springfield, Illinois, on a Wednesday night in March, surrounded by young men like himself, each of them eager to applaud the extraordinary accomplishments of his friends but each believing in secret that it was he that would be judged most remarkable when the history of their circle was written.

Cage was not immune to this illusion. He was not immune to the applause that followed his recitation. Lincoln stood up and said the next bones that would be found in the forest would be his own, the skeleton of a man who had killed himself from envy. Cage laughed and waved off the compliment, but he thought he could indeed see a jealous pall in his friend's face, a variant of the jealousy he himself had felt that night when he saw Lincoln scratching the ears of the dog who was the self-appointed guardian of Ellie's door.

They had not spoken of it—what was there to speak of? Cage was in no position to question another man's private recreation. He had never told Lincoln he regarded Ellie as "his," he had never exactly expressed that to himself. And he had no business in feeling possessive about a woman whose allure in the first place had something to do with the fact that she would not be owned even as she allowed herself in effect to be bought and sold.

The meeting broke up earlier than usual, but Lincoln asked Cage afterwards to head down the hall with him to his office.

"Did I succeed in striking a true tone with that poem?" he wanted to know. "Or was it just an exercise in gloom?"

"I thought it was good. A little too theatrical in places. Are there as many exclamation points in the written poem as there seemed to be when you read it aloud?"

"Probably more. There are points that need emphasis, after all."

"Let the meter carry the emphasis. Try to limit the exclamation points. But it's stronger and more daring than anything you've written before. I agree you should publish it."

"I always trust your judgment. I never know how much attention to pay to the praise of the others. I don't want just encouragement. I want to matter as a poet. I don't have your talent, of course, but I think I could matter. Have you heard anything from Little and Brown?"

"They don't want it."

"I'm astonished. How could anybody not want to publish work of such obvious merit?"

"They regard it as provincial. Irrelevant."

"They're fools! Did you hear? I've just used up one of my limited supply of exclamation points to emphasize that fact. Don't be discouraged, Cage. None of us should be discouraged. There's a long road ahead and we'll get to where we're meant to be by and by."

His tone was so warm and his friendship so gratifying that Cage was able to forget, at least for a moment, his unreasonable jealousy toward him. But it was just as well when Lincoln announced he had to get back to work—he would be up all night, he said, amending a complainant's bill about the death of half a dozen sheep due to foot rot. The longer Cage stayed in his presence, the less sure he could be that he would not lose his resolve and bring up the subject of Ellie.

He was on his way home from Hoffman's Row when Jim Reed spotted him and took him by the arm. "Come over to the Globe with me and I'll buy you a drink. I've got something I want to talk over with you."

When they entered the hotel they saw Jacob Early in the sitting room, contentedly reading a thick book by the fireplace. He greeted Reed—

his old spying company partisan—with hearty goodwill. Toward Cage he was more reserved.

"I believe we were on opposing sides when that damned abolitionist came to speak."

"We were," Cage said.

"But you were at Kellogg's Grove, so I'm happy to extend my hand in comradeship."

"I'm happy to accept it, Captain."

The three men chatted for a moment about nothing of consequence, and then Cage and Reed left Early reading by the fire as they sat down at a table on the other side of the room.

"What does the capital of Illinois have?" Reed asked after he had ordered a gin sling. "It has saddlers, watchmakers, blacksmiths, tinsmiths, doctors, booksellers, mechanics, and of course more lawyers than anything else. It's got brickyards, it's got mills, it's got a foundry, but do you know what Springfield doesn't have?"

"What doesn't it have and what do you want me to throw away my money to get for it?"

Reed laughed with hearty complicity, making Cage even more cautious when it came to considering going into business with him. He had a long face, a long straight nose, protruding ears, piercing eyes: overall the feral intensity of a born salesman.

"A tallow chandler is what we don't have! Think of the freight charges we have to pay to bring candles from Philadelphia when we should be making them right here, in the capital of Illinois. And soap! If we had a soap boiler and—"

"I'm asking you if you are the author of that damned resolution!"

Cage and Reed turned to the sound of the outraged voice that was suddenly echoing in the sparsely populated room. Cage had never met Henry Truett, the man who was standing there shouting at Jacob Early, but he knew who he was. He was the son-in-law of Big Red May, the Democrat who had been elected to Congress in 1836. Big Red had gotten Truett appointed as the land office register in Galena, a very cozy position that came with a nice salary and boundless ancillary ways in which to speculate and fill one's own purse. But the appointment had spurred infighting and intrigue among the local Democrats—pitting Big Red against the rising power of Stephen Douglas—and according to the papers the Little Giant and his faction had issued some kind of resolution calling for Truett to be removed from office.

Just now Truett looked like a man who should not merely be removed from office but put into a cage. His face was flushed with rage and the glow from the fireplace had turned it monstrously livid, a shiny waxen mask from which two unreasoning eyes stared down at Jacob Early.

Early was calm. He remained in his chair as he inserted a silk bookmark into his volume and set it down on a nearby table.

"Who told you that I wrote the resolution?"

"I'm not going to tell you that."

"Well, if you won't tell me where your information came from, I won't tell you whether I wrote it or not."

"You are a damned scoundrel and a damned hypocrite! I know you wrote it, but you're a coward and won't admit it."

Early remained seated and struggled to remain calm. Despite the insult from Truett, he appeared to want nothing more than to be left alone to sit by the fire and read his book.

"If you want a formal confrontation with me, Mr. Truett," he said after some deliberation, "will you do me the kindness of putting your complaint in writing as a gentleman should?"

He then picked up his book again and dismissed Truett with a wave of his hand. Inflamed, Truett leaned forward. From across the room Cage saw the handle of a pistol in Truett's overcoat pocket. Early must have seen it at the same moment, because he dropped his book and stood up and lifted his chair to shield himself from the armed madman confronting him. Truett clumsily pulled the pistol from his pocket. It was already on full cock. The two men began circling each other around the fireplace, Early with the upraised chair, Truett waving the gun around looking for a clear shot.

Cage's instinct was to remain where he was, but Reed had a bolder temperament and he sprang out of his chair and started to stride across the room to take the pistol out of Truett's hand. "Now listen here," Reed was saying, but before he could finish his sentence Truett had found his shot. He pulled the trigger and the sound of the explosion filled every atom of atmosphere suspended in the quiet tavern. Early collapsed to the floor with a surprised shriek, his legs buckling under him as the rest of his body fell as straight as a plumb bob. The heavy wooden chair he had been holding came crashing down at the same instant, one of its arms splintering as it hit the Turkey carpet. The gunpowder smoke that instantly filled the room hurled Cage back to that crowded and besieged cabin at Kellogg's Grove. Truett, looking almost as surprised as the man he had shot, bent down and laid his pistol rather formally on the floor. He looked around as if he expected somebody to tell him what to do next, and when nobody did he ran out through the back door of the hotel.

"By God I think that man has shot me!" Early said when Cage reached him. He was lying on his back with his arms spread, blood already soaking the fibers of the carpet beneath him.

"Yes, you've been shot," Cage said. "But we'll get you to Dr. Merritt immediately and all will be well."

Cage and Reed and three other men lifted Early with great care and walked out of the hotel and down the street to Ash Merritt's house, only half a block away.

"Well, I don't think he ought to have done that," Early observed as they bore him along. There had been a sleet storm the day before and they were careful not to slip on the still-icy ground. Early's lips were pale and drawn back in pain, but his sense of bravado demanded that he entertain his bearers with a commentary. "Such a thing is uncalled-for and it makes me mad."

Ash was waiting at the door. He had heard the shot and was expecting someone. "Hello there, Dr. Merritt," Early said as Cage and the others carried him through the parlor and set him on the narrow surgical bed in the doctor's office. "I'm a Democrat who has been shot by a Democrat, so I guess I shouldn't complain if now I have a Whig for a doctor."

"Well, it's a topsy-turvy business all around, Jacob," Ash said. "But I'll do my best for you."

Early said he desired to shake hands with the men who had carried him out of the tavern. He gripped Cage's hand tight and asked him to go back over to the Globe and see if the carpet was ruined.

"If it is," he said, "tell them that if I'm alive I'll replace it, and that if I'm dead I'm sorry."

When Cage and Reed got back to the tavern, a crowd had already gathered to analyze the shooting scene, though the chair had been righted, the bartender was in the act of blotting up the blood on the carpet, and the pistol that Truett had dropped had been picked up and safely stored behind the bar.

The air was still full of the grainy smell of gunpowder and the slick scent of blood, and the shock of what had happened still ruled the room and the thoughts of the people in it.

"I thought there was something wrong about Truett the minute he walked in," Reed said, picking up the gin sling that was still sitting on the table. "And then I saw that pistol butt in his pocket."

"You saw that too?"

"Damn right I did. He came in here to murder Early, no doubt about it."

Jim Reed drank with a steady hand. In the moment Cage was impressed. He envied Reed's commanding coolness, the satisfaction he seemed to take in being in control of his nerves and his mood at a time of such distress.

"Did you see where the bullet went in and where it came out? I'm no anatomist but you can be sure Early's got a hole in his liver. He'll be lucky if he lives till morning."

He set down his glass and lit a cigar and released a cloud of smoke, adding to the deadly brew of smells already circulating in the room.

"Well, Truett's dead, too, for that matter," Reed continued. "As soon as they find him. That was as clear a case of outright murder as I've ever seen."

Cage wasn't feeling well. He was light-headed and his hands were shaking and he had to master the need to vomit. Witnessing a man being shot did not have the same steadying effect on him as it had on Reed. It made him revisit the horrors of the Black Hawk War—the face of that Indian who had tried to kill him on their retreat from the prairie,

Bob Zanger's butchered body, the emaciated warrior he had shot out of a tree at Bad Axe. These memories resided in his mind like a sepsis. Most of the time the infection was barely detectable, but now it swelled malignantly, the sense that human life was without value or purpose, that it was lived in tedium and ended in pain and stink.

Reed wanted to resume the conversation they had been having when Truett walked into the room. If they didn't open a tallow and soap business in Springfield someone else would. If Cage would be his partner, provide some working capital, Reed would—

Cage stood up and excused himself. He said they would talk later when they were not so distracted by the evening's excitement. On the way out of the hotel he encountered Lincoln hurrying along the street.

"Is it true? Henry Truett shot Early?"

"It's true."

"Just shot him? In cold blood?"

"Just walked right in and shot him."

"How bad off is he?"

"Pretty bad, I think. We carried him over to Ash's."

"Well, I'd hate to see it end like that for Jacob. He was a fine captain in the war. And Truett is a worthless little shit. Stuart and I had to collect a debt from him for one of our clients. He's got a big money pile from being land register but the son of a bitch won't pay his bills. Are you all right, Cage? You don't look well."

"I just watched a man be shot, and that's not a thing I like to see. I'm going home."

He took a step and his feet skidded out from under him on the icy street. He was not hurt but he sat there for a moment, haunted by the memory of the appalling swiftness with which Early had fallen to the hotel floor after being shot. It could all be over that fast. He had seen it too many times now not to believe it.

"Well, Cage," Lincoln said, "do you want to sit in the street all night or do you want to go home?"

TWELVE

◆ ◆ ◆

J ACOB EARLY'S FUNERAL was an angry, austere affair, presided over by a Methodist minister who begged the Creator to bring down his terrible justice upon the cold-blooded murderer who had robbed Springfield of a war hero and leading citizen—a man who, as a minister himself, had brought many souls to God.

Cage sat in the back next to Lincoln and John Stuart and Jim Reed, Early's former comrades-in-arms. Cage had barely known Early, but he felt like a comrade-in-arms himself, since he had seen the man shot and helped pick him up off the floor, and then shaken his hand before Ash Merritt had done his futile best to save his life.

It was the second funeral he had been to that week. Roger Victor, one of his annoying parlor sitters at the Palatine, had been buried two days before. He had been sitting at the communal table, speaking in French to Theophilous Emry, when an alarmed look appeared on his face and his head dropped onto the table with the force of a dead weight. In one thrombotic moment he was gone. Or at least that was how Mrs. Hopper described it. Cage had not been there when it happened. He had been lying in Ellie's bed, going over her figures for the rent and overhead costs of her dressmaking business while the old woman and her son who lived below continued their never-ending argument. He came back to the Palatine to find Victor's body lying on the floor of the parlor where Mrs. Hopper and the other residents of the house had moved it from the less seemly locale of the crumb-strewn dining room. They had covered Victor's contorted face with a silk pillowcase, and were doing their best to comfort one another as they waited for the undertaker. They had the same numb look as Cage himself must have had after witnessing Jacob Early's murder.

"A silly political dispute," Speed said to Cage as they walked away together from the town cemetery where Early had just been laid to rest. "And a man lies dead. It could happen to Lincoln, you know. He's always writing the same sort of anonymous letters and resolutions that got Early killed."

Lincoln wasn't there to heed the warning, not that he would have heeded it in the first place. He and Stuart had left the cemetery as soon as the last prayers were said, racing back to their office to catch up on their legal work and to plot out the final months of the 1838 campaign.

"A young enough man, too," Speed went on. "How old was Early? Thirty-one? Thirty-two? Life can be so goddam short, so goddam pointless."

Cage shrugged in acknowledgment of his friend's cynical wisdom. Stephen Douglas rode past them in one of the carriages that were leaving the cemetery. He touched the brim of his hat when he saw them and shook his head mournfully as if to declare what a dreadful business it had all been, then settled back in his seat as the coach bore him away to plot his own strategy.

"I want to live a meaningful life," Speed blurted out. "I want to depart the earth surrounded by a loving wife and grieving children. Not shot dead on a saloon floor."

"Stay out of politics."

"I'm serious. I'm going to put my mind to business, drink only modestly, look for a proper wife. I haven't been living deliberately enough. Carefully enough."

"I want to talk to you about Ellie," Cage said.

"She told me. You want to set her up in business. It's a fine idea. She has talent and energy and will no doubt succeed."

"Her living situation can be improved. There's a room available now at the Palatine."

"I thought you said your manager wouldn't approve of her visitors."

"She won't need those visitors anymore. She'll be in a different line of work."

"Is that so? Do you intend to live with her?"

"I intend for her to have a place in my lodging house, that's all. She'll be charged for room and board like everybody else and can come and go as she pleases. If that means that every now and then she finds herself in my rooms that's her affair."

"This coming and going into rooms—how would it apply to the man who introduced you to her in the first place?"

"You just said you were looking for a proper wife."

"That doesn't mean I plan to suspend my existence until I find her. Cage, do you imagine that you're in love with her? You have to know that she has too much of an investment in herself to love anyone else. She has an indifferent heart."

"I don't care."

"Well, then you are in love, or in something dangerously like it."

A week later a widow from Jacksonville named Mrs. Bicknell arrived at the Palatine. While the draymen carried her furniture and possessions into Roger Victor's now-vacant room, Cage introduced her to Mrs. Hopper not only as a new resident but as the proprietress of a soon-to-be-opened dressmaking and millinery shop in which he had retained an interest. Mrs. Hopper surely had suspicions, but Ellie had too much invested in her new circumstances to give the game away. And for that matter it wasn't a game. She wasn't acting. She was exactly the firm-minded businesswoman she wanted the world to perceive her as being. Her married name was indeed Mrs. Bicknell, and though she was not officially a widow her husband was gone from her life and there was a reasonable chance, given his drinking and helplessness and violent manner, that he had died or would soon die from one unheralded cause or another.

A month or so after she moved into the Palatine, Ellie met Cage at the property they had rented for her store; it was east of the square, the site of a small watchmaker's shop that had gone out of business a year earlier. Carpenters were already at work, putting in shelves to hold fabric and building cabinets for pins and hair combs and jewelry that would be offered for sale at Bicknell & Co., Women's Fashions and Accessories.

"You are the 'Co.,'" she told Cage. "Unless you would like your name spelled out on the sign."

"No, I'm content to be a silent partner."

Cordelia, the Negro woman that Benbrook and Westridge had urged him to employ, was already at work, seated on a stool in the back of the store, sewing amid the chaos of construction. When she saw Cage she stood and greeted him by lowering her eyes, waiting to be spoken to.

"It's all right, Cordelia," he said. "Please don't interrupt your work on my account."

She sat down again quickly, as if his casual request had been a command. She had a concentrated servility of manner, but her wide-set eyes were ferociously alert. Cage guessed she was twenty-three or twenty-four. She was slightly built, her skin a deep brown, a raised scar on one cheek. On the advice of her sponsors, he and Ellie had been careful not to ask her too many questions about her background, though she had arrived ready with a fabricated story that she had been a housekeeper for a family in the free state of Indiana. The family was in the yarn business, but it had foundered with the economy, and she had come west because she heard there might be work in Springfield. At first she told the story like someone under interrogation. In the following weeks she had grown more relaxed, but still attacked her work with the intensity and vigilance of someone determined to be invisible.

"So she's suitable?" Cage asked Ellie after they had finished inspecting the shop-to-be and were standing in front of it, on a street a few blocks removed from the main shopping district. But there were new signs of industry here as well. Ellie's shop wasn't the only business being built or revivified.

"She can sew, she knows clothes. She obviously knows how to stay in the background and not cause any trouble to anybody. Good needlewomen with good eyesight and good sense are rare anywhere. So yes, fortunately for you, she's suitable. If she wasn't, you would have heard from me about it."

"I have no doubt."

"I'll need a sign, by the way. Do you know a good sign painter?"

"I'll ask around. How are you settling in at the Palatine?"

"Very comfortably."

"I'm alone in my rooms at night. My hinges are well oiled and the carpet in the hallway is thick."

She smiled up at him, having read his thoughts long before he spoke them.

"We could still be discovered by Mrs. Hopper."

"I don't mind."

"You're getting too careless. We have a business to build." She tilted her head to the shop behind her. "We can meet here instead. One or two nights a week."

"Three or four."

She laughed—affectionate, grateful, happy. All the things he wanted her to be.

THIRTEEN

❖ ❖ ❖

EIGHT O'CLOCK ON AN AUGUST EVENING, the astral lamps just now lighted, a mighty bowl of Mrs. Edwards's famous chicken salad weighing down the mahogany sideboard next to pyramids of beaten biscuits and airy macaroons. Young women with bare arms and bare shoulders, holding glasses of champagne, smiling up at men basking in the power conferred on them by the Whig victories in the election two weeks before.

Newly elected United States congressman John T. Stuart stood in front of a massive bureau in Ninian Edwards's parlor. The bureau was crowned with a mirror that gave the people in line waiting to congratulate him a view of the back of his sculpted head. Since meeting Ellie, since setting her up in her shop, Cage had begun to notice what people were wearing, what fit and what didn't, what was produced by a talented tailor or dressmaker and what was thoughtlessly bought ready-made. Stuart's frock coat, he recognized, was expertly cut, with no outdated padding in the shoulders. His dark checkered waistcoat was tight against his trim torso, the ends of his wool trousers hovered at some precise perfect point above the top of his booted feet.

Lincoln, holding forth on the other side of the room, was as negligently dressed as ever. There was no way, apparently, to make his sleeves come out right. His funereal-looking coat gaped at the shoulders and the big soft knot of his cravat swallowed up his skinny throat. None of it mattered. He was as much a man of the hour as Stuart was, reelected to the state legislature for a third term, winning more votes than anyone else from Sangamon County. The Whigs had done all right generally, though Ninian Edwards's uncle Cyrus had lost the governor's race and Stuart himself had had to ride out a confusing and contested election, finally being declared the winner over Douglas by only three dozen votes.

But it was a full-throated Whig victory celebration that Ninian Edwards was throwing nonetheless. John Stuart had no qualms about treating his treacherously thin victory as a shattering mandate, and he was proudly showing his purple swollen thumb to everyone who came up to shake his hand. The injured thumb was even sweeter to him than his election. It still had Stephen Douglas's tooth marks in it. The two candidates had been debating in the market house a few days before the vote when the Little Giant's haughty, wheedling invective had succeeded too well, and Stuart had suddenly lost his lawyerly composure, launched himself at his diminutive opponent and wrestled with him all through the building and out onto the lawn, Douglas hitting and gouging at Stuart like a hysterical monkey in the claws of a leopard. He had finally escaped by the expedient of biting down hard on Stuart's thumb.

"I know all about you." Elizabeth Edwards had suddenly appeared at Cage's side. Ninian Edwards's wife was not nearly as starchy as her husband, but Cage could see at once she was formidable in her own way, her smile as assessing as it was welcoming. "I've read your marvelous book. Lincoln told me he was bringing you, and I was glad to hear it—but he's left you becalmed in the middle of the room. I don't think he has any manners, do you?"

"Lincoln's thoughtful enough, Mrs. Edwards, he just—"

"Oh, it's not his fault. He's risen from nothing at all, all by himself, and there are naturally things he still doesn't know the first thing about. We have to be patient and teach him how to behave."

She put her arm through his and guided him to the sideboard and ordered him to fill a plate and eat. The chicken salad, she said, was an old Todd family recipe, made with butter instead of oil. Everybody knew that Mrs. Edwards was a Todd, one of the members of the famous Lexington family who kept emigrating in stages from Kentucky to Illinois, seeding the whole state with influential characters. Stuart himself was a Todd cousin, so was John Hardin, the Whig leader from Morgan County, and so was—distantly—Stephen Logan, a prominent Springfield attorney and political operative. Mrs. Edwards introduced Cage to her married younger sister, Frances, and informed him that still more Todd sisters were on the way.

"There are dozens and dozens and dozens of us," Mrs. Edwards said. "But it's Mary's turn to come out here next. Do you think she can find a respectable husband in Springfield, Mr. Weatherby? She has very strong opinions, and she's a perfect take when it comes to political matters. So he'd have to be someone who could stand up for himself."

That was the first time Cage heard the name Mary Todd, and he would remember later that as she talked about finding her sister a husband Mrs. Edwards's eyes were roving around the room, settling for a moment perhaps to consider Joshua Speed, just then in earnest conversation with Ned Baker, who could possibly be another candidate. He would not remember her gauging Lincoln for the assignment. The Todds were as notoriously refined as Lincoln was rustic, and everybody knew he had already failed to make a match with another well-bred Kentucky lady who had also been named Mary. The union of Abraham Lincoln and Mary Todd was as unlikely in theory that night as it would later prove to be in reality.

As for Cage himself, he was under no scrutiny as a marital partner either. He was in Ninian Edwards's home not as a member of the triumphant Springfield junto but as a civilian observer, and in this crowd men without political aspirations were something to be puzzled over. In any case, though he recognized that any man his age ought to be actively looking for a wife, he was preoccupied with his privately scandalous and exquisitely unfathomable arrangement with Ellie. They met as she proposed at her shop, the number of times per week depending on her volume of work and level of exhaustion. At the Palatine they kept up a charade of neighborly friendliness when they dined together or sat with others in the parlor. At night, he struggled to fall asleep without torturing himself by listening for footsteps on the stairs or the almost inaudible whisper of her door opening to receive a visitor. He didn't think it would happen now that she had an enterprise and an income of her own—or at least happen often. She was no longer in the keeping of Joshua Speed but if she chose to see him or anyone else she would certainly do so. There had, he thought, been only that one time with Lincoln. But Lincoln was a man people tended to develop a deepening fascination with, struck by his powerful alternating moods of animation and melancholy.

He was supremely animated tonight. There he was, with his hand on John Hardin's shoulder, looking down on him, pausing before he delivered the sidesplitting conclusion of some story that Cage and Mrs. Edwards, across the noisy parlor, couldn't hear.

John Hardin: distractingly handsome and commanding, dark-eyed, dark-haired, intimidated by no one. He was the Whig representative from Morgan County and lived in Jacksonville, not Springfield, so when he walked into a room there was a "Hardin's-in-town" ripple among the guests, heads turning, hands offered in greeting. He stood with Ned Baker, listening to Lincoln's story. Ned was equally imposing but not quite as splendid-looking. Hardin had precise features and immaculate grooming. Ned's face was large and florid, and he was balding in a spectacularly inelegant way, with wayward strands of hair flopping this way and that. It was odd that neither of these two remarkable-looking individuals drew the eye as compellingly as the man they were listening to, the awkward and arguably homely Abraham Lincoln.

"Do you think he would really want to kill himself?" Elizabeth Edwards asked Cage. She had apparently been studying Lincoln as intently as he had. There was no need to ask why this thought had come into her head. Sim Francis had recently published "The Suicide's Soliloquy" in the *Journal*. It was the same curious reverie Lincoln had read aloud to the poetry group that night last March when Jacob Early was shot. The poem was published anonymously but everyone knew Lincoln was the author, just as everyone had known he was the author of the Sampson's Ghost letters that had derailed Ash Merritt's campaign.

"I think it was just a literary exercise," Cage told Mrs. Edwards.

"Well, you're a literary man, so I suppose you would know. But to write well, don't you have to write with conviction? Don't you have to mean what you say? I think you and the rest of his friends should keep a close eye on him."

She excused herself to go off and lecture one of the liveried servants who was standing over a half-empty punch bowl. He was a young black man—a free man in a free state, in theory—but her sharp tone as she instructed him to for heaven's sake fill the punch bowl indicated that Mrs. Edwards had no interest in such distinctions.

Cage drifted over toward Lincoln, who was standing now in a group with Ash Merritt at its center. Ash was holding forth about Jacob Early's fatal gunshot wound, looking up periodically to make sure no ladies were in earshot. He and another doctor standing next to him had performed the autopsy, which they said revealed that the ball had nipped the ureter at its upper part.

"I suspected as much while I was treating him," Ash told the group. "The flow of matter was very great, and it had a urinous smell."

"A hard way to go," the second doctor said.

"Yes, to die in great pain is one thing, but to die needing to piss will test your faith in a just God."

They talked in great detail about the angle of the bullet that had entered Early's body, how it had passed through the upper part of the sigmoid flexure of the colon, narrowly missed the spine as it exited just to the left of the fourth lumbar vertebra, and had caused—so often the case with injuries of the kidney, Ash observed—a retraction of the testes.

Lincoln was silent, listening to this grisly postmortem discussion with determined concentration. Cage remembered him saying in the Carmans' house that he had to work hard to learn something but once it was learned it was etched into his mind as if into a piece of steel. Cage could almost hear the sound of engraving as the doctors' words entered Lincoln's mind. He thought it curious at the time. But at that moment he didn't yet know that Lincoln had been hired to represent Henry Truett for the murder of Jacob Early.

FOURTEEN

ABRAHAM LINCOLN BEGAN his cross-examination as if he had
never met the man in the witness chair, a preposterous conceit
that Cage found unsettling and insulting, as perhaps Lincoln meant it to
be for some strategic legal reason. Since he was peering at Cage as if he
was a stranger, Cage returned the favor, assessing Henry Truett's lawyer
as if he was encountering him for the first time.

Lincoln had risen steadily from his chair and was standing with his
hands locked behind him and his head inclined toward Cage in an
anonymously friendly way. He was so tall that if he had put on his top
hat it might have almost touched the trapdoor in the ceiling of the courtroom, the door that conveniently opened in the floor of Lincoln and
Stuart's office overhead.

Cage had been questioned that morning by Stephen Douglas, acting
as the state's attorney in the murder of Jacob Early. Douglas had kept his
flamboyance in check, saving it no doubt for his summation, as he led
Cage through the events of that March night with numbing specificity.
Cage certainly didn't mind his thoroughness. It was odd to be on the
side of the Little Giant, the political enemy of all his friends, but on this
occasion Douglas—in prosecuting Truett—was the friend of justice.

Cage was the first prosecution witness—Reed and the others who
had been in the Globe and witnessed the shooting were to be called
later—and it seemed to Cage that if there was such a thing as a sure outcome to a murder trial they would all provide it.

Truett, sitting next to Douglas, looked meek and miserable. He had
lost considerable weight and his skin had a jailhouse pallor, and from
the way he stared fatalistically out the window it appeared he could

allow himself no real cause for hope. Behind him the benches were full. The trial was a public excitement, every bit as much an occasion as a political debate.

"Now," Lincoln began, "you told Mr. Douglas you saw a pistol in Truett's pocket."

"I did."

"And that upon seeing the pistol himself, Early jumped to his feet."

"Yes."

"Did you and Early see the pistol at the same moment?"

"I don't know."

"Is it possible Early saw it at a different moment?"

"Yes."

"He might have noticed it later than you did."

"I suppose so, but I doubt it, because—"

Lincoln smiled and nodded as he cut Cage off.

"I'm just interested in the 'suppose so' right now. Is it accurate to say that Early might have noticed the pistol later than you did?"

"It's accurate to say that."

"In which case he might have jumped to his feet before he ever saw the pistol."

Cage was saved from answering this by Douglas's objection.

Lincoln said "hmmm" as if the judge, in sustaining the objection, had given him more to contemplate. He grabbed the lapel of his coat and walked a few steps to the left and then a few steps to the right, then turned to face Cage again.

"You told Mr. Douglas he raised a chair in his arms."

"Yes."

"He raised the chair after he jumped to his feet?"

"Of course."

"Just want to be sure. But I reckon it would be kind of hard to raise a chair and remain seated at the same time."

Lincoln gave Cage a sly smile as the people in the courtroom laughed. It was the first hint Lincoln gave that he and Cage might know each other and share the same sense of the absurd.

"Since as you say it might be possible that Early noticed the pistol later than you did, then is it possible that Early raised the chair before he saw the pistol?"

Cage saw where it was going, that Lincoln had already drawn him into a world where the things he saw with his own eyes and the principles of logic were ruthlessly beside the point. There was no answer to his question, of course, but yes.

"Can you show the court by standing and raising your hands the approximate angle at which Jacob Early held the chair?"

Cage stood, raised his hands at shoulder height, as he remembered Early doing.

"That is the attitude of the deceased, to the best of your memory, at the time he held the chair?"

"Yes."

"And that is the approximate height—again, to the best of your memory—at which he held the chair?"

"Yes."

"It was a wooden chair?"

"It was."

"Substantially made of oak or hickory or some similar substance?"

"Probably."

"A heavy chair?"

"I didn't lift it."

"But you saw Early lift it. Did it appear to be a heavy chair or a light chair?"

And so on it went, Lincoln slowly taking hold of the narrative, the self-evidently malicious and premeditated murder of Jacob Early by Henry Truett, and twisting Cage's testimony until it supported the idea that Truett had killed Early in self-defense.

Cage's testimony was over in an afternoon, but the trial lasted three days. He had resolved to put the whole unpleasant episode out of his mind and get back to work, confident that justice would inevitably be done and Truett would be found guilty, but he couldn't keep himself away from the crowded courtroom when it was time for the attorneys to address the jury. Like everything else in Springfield the final courtroom arguments represented a proxy political battle, in this case the first of many contests to come between Douglas and Lincoln.

"This man who lay dying on the floor of a tavern," Douglas began, "was he a petty knockabout, a shady denizen of the criminal ranks? Was he a gambler, a debtor, a man on the run from the law or from his own immoral confederates? No, I think he was not any of these things. I *know* he was not any of these things, and so do you, gentlemen."

Douglas sighed, he stared at the floor in a pose of despair over what had befallen the human race. Then, after a pause in which Cage could almost audibly hear him counting out the beats he thought would be required for the maximum dramatic effect, he raised his head and stared at each man of the jury in turn. They were all seated and he was standing, but he was so short he was already at eye level with them.

"He was one of you, one of us. A patriot in the war against Black Hawk, a Methodist preacher vouchsafed to deliver the Word, a man who stood against all forms of extremism and depravity. He was, in short, gentlemen, the very heart of our hopeful prairie community, this citadel of temperance and goodness, the moral bricks of which it could be said he laid with the hand of a master mason."

The longer he went on, the more extravagant his claims for Early's character became, and he spent an equal amount of verbal energy sketching the low, vindictive, and unscrupulous behavior of the accused. It went on and on, a great set piece of legal coloratura that the packed courtroom enjoyed more than subscribed to.

Lincoln's summation by contrast was short. It was direct. Where Douglas had tried to flatter the jury by painting them as the sole bulwark against a spreading evil, Lincoln provided them with a single idea to consider.

"Gentlemen," he said, "I don't know what happened that night in the Globe. There were men there who saw it, and who testified in this courtroom with honest intent, so that you could arrive at the truth and deliver a fair verdict. You heard them. You heard them say that Jacob Early raised a chair, that Henry Truett raised a pistol. What none of them could say with the confidence required to send a man to the gallows is who raised which weapon first. The idea that a heavy chair could be a weapon is no little matter. It is no defense lawyer's trick. It is a fact of our physical world. Henry Truett was angry at Jacob Early. We don't dispute that. He spoke intemperately. We don't dispute that either. And in speaking intemperately he provoked Jacob Early, and what we will never know—what we can never know—is whether Early had it in his mind to smash Truett over the head with a crushing blow that could have splintered his skull. But it's that very fact—the fact that we *can never know*—that must be the challenge to your consciences as you go off to the jury room to determine whether Henry Truett will live or die. *Can never know*—those are the words you must live with into your old age, those are the words that will haunt you if you make a decision today that will end a man's life, a decision that can never be undone."

Cage heard that the jury had found Truett innocent three hours later, when he was picking up a book of poetry he had ordered from a New England publisher. Suddenly people ran into the bookshop to talk about the startling verdict. The whole city was like an audience flooding out from an energizing time in the theater, desperate to talk about the surprise ending they had just witnessed.

But Cage had been in the room when Jacob Early was shot, and what he had witnessed was not theater. It was cold-blooded murder, and the man who had committed it had been set free because of an absurd, made-up counter-argument that Early had been the aggressor.

He left the bookstore and walked outside, dodging the carriages that now crowded the street, making a simple walk home a hazard for pedestrians. For all its new status as the state capital, Springfield still had boggy streets. And despite a new city ordinance against pigs, the creatures still ranged freely, doing their part to stir up the filth. The statehouse was still unfinished—the assembly would convene once again in Vandalia for its upcoming session in December—and construction debris and shouting workmen and drays loaded with building materials added to the chaos.

He understood that Lincoln had had a role to play and had played it well, but he was sick at heart with the miscarriage of justice he had just witnessed, and angry at the way Lincoln had maneuvered him to play a part in it. To try to settle his mind he unwrapped the book he had just bought: *Voices of the Night,* by a new Massachusetts poet—his age? younger?—he had read good things about. The author had the improbably perfect name of Longfellow. It was a slim volume, a first modest offering to the world. As he walked, he thumbed through the uncut pages, reading a line or two at random and then glancing up to make sure he didn't collide with a teamster's wagon or a rooting sow.

"I heard the trailing garments of the Night," was the first line of one of the poems. He didn't read on, didn't want to. There was no way the poem could sustain the mysterious pitch of that one perfect line. He read it again as he made his way down the street, and was about to read it again when one of the stray dogs that the town trustees had vowed to keep off the street raced silently up to him and buried its teeth in the flesh of his calf. The pain was unthinkable and inescapable. He yelled unashamedly and looked down at the dog in disbelief. He hit it on top of its flat head with Mr. Longfellow's thin poetry book, but the dog's jaws just clamped down tighter, producing new horrible harmonies of pain. He kicked at the animal with his untrapped leg but only succeeded in falling down onto the dirt street.

People swarmed to his aid without accomplishing anything as the dog kept growling and thrashing. Lying in the street, Cage was so preoccupied with the ever-escalating pain that he couldn't open his mouth to communicate with the people who were trying to help him.

Just when it began to seem to Cage that his situation was a hellish nightmare out of Dante, that this creature would gnaw on his leg throughout all time, a huge human foot intervened and kicked it splendidly hard in the ribs. Cage heard the dog yelp and at the same moment felt the release of its jaws. It raced off whimpering in pain and outrage down Adams Street until it disappeared into some secret lair.

"Think you can walk?" a familiar creaky voice said from above as Cage lay there panting in pain.

Cage nodded and let Lincoln help him up. He was in his tall hat and was carrying a law book and a bag of raisins. He bent down to inspect Cage's bloody leg.

"I can see the tooth marks through your trousers. Looks like you got punched with an awl. We better get our friend Dr. Merritt to clean it out and put a dressing on it."

"I was carrying a book with me."

"I picked it up. Got it right here. Is it any good?"

Cage took the dusty book from Lincoln's hand and drew in his breath. The pain was still outlandish. "I can't concentrate on a literary discussion right now."

"Understandable."

With Lincoln at his side, he hobbled the few blocks to Ash Merritt's house. Lincoln couldn't keep himself from chattering away about the dog problem, which was far worse than the pig problem had ever been back in the old days. The market house was full of ownerless dogs fighting over meat scraps, biting little children, barking at horses, and causing wrecks on every corner. He was a town trustee now and was thinking of proposing a dog eradication committee, fully armed and with the authority to shoot every suspect canine on sight.

"I hope that dog that bit you didn't have the rabies."

"I don't want to think about that."

"They say that the rabies makes a man hard as a railroad spike and he can't stop himself from ejaculating. It's like your pecker has the hiccoughs. Rabies is a bad way to die but if you're shooting off like a geyser all the time I reckon there's a silver lining in there somewhere."

They reached Ash Merritt's house and the doctor ushered them into his office and without asking Cage's permission cut off his good wool trousers at the knee. The wound that was revealed—a dozen or so perfect punctures—commanded Cage's fascinated attention but was of no particular interest to Ash, whose mind as usual was fixed on politics and the upcoming legislative session. He rattled on about the new Democratic governor as he almost incidentally washed out the dog bite on Cage's leg with cold water and Castile soap.

"He may call himself a Democrat but as far as I'm concerned he's Loco Foco all the way," Ash groused. "He's anti-bank, he's hard money, he wants to gather up all the gold and silver in treasury vaults and leave the people with nothing but worthless shinplasters."

"We can beat back a subtreasury scheme for Illinois," Lincoln said, glancing at some legal papers he had taken out of his hat. "Carlin can attack the banks all he wants, but he's still going to need a way to fund internal improvements."

He took one of Ash's scalpels and, without asking Cage, began to cut the pages of his new poetry book. He sat there reading with his usual unearthly absorption while the doctor applied ointment and a lint bandage.

"Do I pay you in specie or in shinplasters?" Cage asked Ash when he had finished binding the wound.

"You're a friend, so you pay me not at all."

"That's a dangerous course," Lincoln said, looking up from Mr. Longfellow. "Friends should pay for services as well as enemies. It's nature's plan and it's a good one."

Cage pressed a silver dollar on Ash. Then he left and walked awkwardly home with Lincoln still insistently at his side.

"You should take to your bed immediately," he said.

Cage waved the idea off but in fact that was what he planned to do. Ash's ointment and dressing had a slight analgesic effect, but he was still in pain and still bearing a quiet but murderous rage toward the creature that had come out of nowhere to assault him.

"I think I may have broken that dog's ribs when I kicked him," Lincoln told Cage. "I heard a bone crack."

"Good."

"I hate to think of an animal in pain. Even one that bites."

Cage made himself walk on without speaking, but the pain of the dog bite was still severe, and the outrage that had been building in him since his turn on the witness stand finally broke through as they approached the Palatine. He turned to Lincoln and, to his own astonishment, knocked the sack of raisins out of his hand.

"You talked a jury into letting a murderer go free, and you used me to help you. No doubt you'd take that dog as a client and do the same for him. Before you were through you'd have everybody convinced I was the one who attacked *him!*"

Lincoln looked down at the raisins scattered on the dirt street. He gave a nervous sort of laugh, as if Cage's anger might turn out to be a performance. But Cage's anger was real, and as he limped away he had the satisfaction of seeing that fact register on Lincoln's face.

He slept not at all that night, kept awake by the pain in his leg and by a turbulent, confused anger, directed both toward the dog that had assailed him and toward the friend who had so blithely used him in court. At four thirty in the morning he heard Mrs. Hopper and her assistant, an orphan girl named Betsy who had fled to Illinois after her Mormon parents had been killed by a Missouri mob, walking out to the kitchen at the back of the house to start breakfast. He heard them setting the table in the dining room and smelled coffee and cornbread and fried ham. He heard the dinner bell softly ring and then the voices of the boarders as they walked into the dining room and greeted each other good morning and began to chat about the news of the day. He could not make out all of their conversation but he heard the words "Lincoln" and "Truett" and "Could you believe it?"

He heard Ellie's soft voice among the others. She was already a favorite among the residents of the Palatine. If they thought there was anything unusual about her circumstances they seemed perfectly willing to keep their speculations to themselves. Cage had thought at first she might hold herself apart from them, but instead she had quickly become an eager participant in the family-like conditions of the house, sharing in the parlor gossip, volunteering to mend clothes, treating Mrs. Hopper and Betsy with a professional consideration that was gratefully reciprocated. Toward Cage she was courteous and fondly teasing at times, but because so much depended on her new station there was a business-like correctness between them that could be broken only during their after-hours meetings at Ellie's dressmaking shop.

While the others were at breakfast he got up and washed and dressed and went down the back stairs to the privy, then up to his room again. His morning routine now was not to take breakfast but to go directly to his desk, with the purpose of composing poetry but more and more turning his attention at this productive time of day to his accounts. He was holding on to four town lots, thinking the ripest time to sell them would be when the statehouse was finished and the assembly was at last settled in Springfield, and he had two farm properties to manage, in addition to the Palatine and Ellie's shop. All of these matters—rent income, repairs, tenancy arrangements, town taxes, salaries, procurements—were increasingly complicated and vexing, with money always never quite where it needed to be. The work of accountancy had something in common with writing poetry, in the way the elements had to be shifted and weighted and prodded to achieve what was often an impossible effect. And it worried Cage sometimes that his own creative ambitions were neither as heroic nor as necessary as he thought, that whatever impulses he had to make a mark on the earth might be better realized by adding figures to a ledger.

He heard Ellie bidding a cheerful goodbye to Mrs. Hopper and then the front door opening and closing. He looked down at her through the window as she walked to her shop in the gusty October morning, people on the street smiling at her, nodding to her. She walked with her back straight, her gloved hands folded in front of her, her slender arms cocked outward on either side of her body with unthinking perfection, like the handles of a jar. Every day he discovered something new to arouse him. This morning it was the simple symmetry of the way she held her arms.

He watched her disappear around the corner. He was turning back to his work when he saw Lincoln striding down the street in an agitated fashion from the direction of his law office. No doubt he had slept there, since there was stubble on his hollow cheeks and his clothes—the same clothes he had been wearing yesterday—were so spectacularly wrinkled that Cage could see their condition from his second-floor window. Lincoln, he saw, was making straight for the front door of the Palatine. He heard his distracted "good morning" to Mrs. Hopper and the residents reading the newspaper in the parlor, then the sound of his hurried, loose-jointed tread on the stairs. Cage limped to the door and opened it as Lincoln was walking down the hallway with his arm upraised to knock—or perhaps to pound. He looked bad, his great Adam's apple bobbing nervously on his neck, his eyes sunken and fierce, his hair when he took his hat off greasy and uncombed and straying all over his head.

"Are you aware what you accused me of yesterday?" he demanded.

"For God's sake, Lincoln, don't berate me in the hallway. Come inside."

Lincoln walked into the room and kept walking, pacing toward the opposite wall and back again to where Cage had just shut the door.

"If another man had said that I was without honor, I would have challenged him on the spot."

"I didn't say you were without—"

"Then what did you say? What did you mean? I've been up all night trying to puzzle it out and that's the only conclusion I've been able to come to. Tell me this, Cage. Should I have tried any less to get Truett off? If so, how much less? Half as much? What is the proper level of effort to defend a man who is on trial for his life? Would you excuse me—would *God* excuse me—from fighting on behalf of an accused man because one of the key witnesses happens to be my friend?"

"The man he killed was your captain in the war!"

"Yes, he was, and if I had the power to bring him back to life I would, Democrat though he was."

Lincoln leaned back against the wall and then slid dramatically down to the floor, running his big hands through his already agitated hair. "Everything you seem to be accusing me of is beside the point. Surely you understand that it's not my duty as a lawyer to judge the morality of my client. That's the judge's duty, and the jury's, and God's. I'm there to represent the poor devil with all the vigor and—"

"I think you need some breakfast," Cage said.

"I can't live if my friends think I have no honor."

"Stay here." He went down to the kitchen, took several big pieces of leftover cornbread off the breakfast table that Mrs. Hopper was clearing, and brought them back to Lincoln, who was still sitting disconsolately on the floor. He accepted the cornbread and joylessly ingested the first piece in two bites. Cage handed him the second piece as if he were feeding an ape in a cage.

Lincoln was then so silent for so long that Cage went back to his desk and his accounts, letting him sulk on the floor for as long as he needed. Ten minutes passed before he spoke again.

"You rebuke me for having no principles, but I do have them, Cage. There are things I stand for. Without the law, for instance, without the full and dispassionate application of the law, there would be anarchy."

"Anarchy—and no way for you to make your living."

"If I didn't believe in what I do, I'd go back to rail-splitting. I'd go back to being a flatboatman."

"Let's not talk about it anymore. Your apology is accepted."

"I'm not apologizing! I'm challenging you to a duel!"

Cage laughed at the absurdity of that idea, and Lincoln despite his misery could not quite keep from laughing in response.

"I'm unsettled," he said after a moment. "You unsettled me with your accusations that I'm a man without a soul."

"You unsettled me by seeming to be one."

"Will you, as my friend, take my word that I am not? I want always to do the right thing. A man like Truett goes free, and you may call that injustice, but there's a larger pattern of justice into which that verdict fits. There has to be that pattern. Without it our society falls apart."

"That's ingenious. You do good by doing bad, so there's nothing left to argue about."

Lincoln shrugged his narrow shoulders, acknowledging Cage's superior logic without somehow allowing it. He did stand for something, but as Cage would look back on that morning from a great distance in time he understood that Lincoln was still struggling, had not yet found out what that something was. That was true with Cage himself, of course, and with all of the young men of Springfield, but none of their internal struggles would prove as consequential as Lincoln's, none would demand so much sacrifice from a nation that he would not allow to be broken apart.

The question crossed Cage's mind that morning: was there really a future for Abraham Lincoln? He could descend so swiftly and completely into brooding melancholy, he was such a fatalist when it came to God and salvation and the truth of the Bible, he let himself revisit so frequently the theme of self-annihilation, that for all his great promise he seemed like a man who might not live.

He needed friends who would believe in him, to keep him from destroying himself with sorrow and self-doubt. Cage knew he had no real choice but to accept that role. But he also suspected that friends would not be enough. Lincoln, he thought, really needed a wife.

1839

FIFTEEN

◆◆◆

I SAW HER," ELLIE SAID. "She came in yesterday."
"Saw who?"

"Miss Todd from Kentucky. Mrs. Edwards's sister. Everybody's been talking about her coming, and now here she is."

They were in the little office at the back of Ellie's store after closing hours. They had left the door to the office open, but all the store's shades were drawn and the lamps out, with only a single candle whose light was invisible to passersby. Ellie saw to these precautions each time he visited. Discretion mattered more to her than it did to him. He had watched caution seep into her character. Her new respectability as the proprietress of Springfield's best millinery shop—patronized by all the ladies of the coterie on Aristocracy Hill—was not to be risked.

The shop had been open for a little over a year now and Ellie had managed the business with efficiency. She had briskly met her projections, repaying Cage for the expenses he had forwarded and counting out his monthly share of the profits after they had gone over the books together and had satisfied their pent-up urges in the cramped back room. She had always been cooler and more pragmatic than he when it came to sexual matters, but the act of explaining her monthly expenses and profits to him greatly loosened her up. It almost seemed that letting him into her books was the same to her as letting him into her heart. She was thrilled by her success, so happy to be his partner that their common enterprise might, in her mind, be confused with the goal of marriage.

She was sitting back on a settee, a glass of wine in her hand, wearing only her chemise and the silk stockings she had not taken off during their lovemaking. Her feet were in Cage's lap, and she wiggled her toes to remind him that it was time to resume massaging them. Through the open office door both sides of the narrow shop seemed upholstered in sumptuous bolts of fabric—printed or regally plain—and open copies of *The Lady's Book* and books of fashion plates lined the accessory counters.

"She ordered two pelerines from me, one of lace and one of cotton lawn. She knows clothes and knows what she wants."

"Is she here for a long time?"

"I hope so. I can use her business. Why don't you marry her? That's why she's here, of course, to find a husband."

"I've never seen her."

"You will. She'll be at the big cotillion they're having at the new hotel, to which I'm sure you're invited, unless you've broken with all your political friends. She's pretty enough, and frank, and very spirited. By which I mean bossy. She must be used to ordering slaves around back in Lexington."

"There's no place in my life for another bossy woman," Cage said. "Let her make somebody else miserable."

"Vous parlez français!" Mary Todd exclaimed to Cage the next week when he was introduced to her at the great cotillion the Whigs had gotten up at the American House. He had not meant to speak French to her, but she and her sister had been rapidly gossiping in that language in a corner of the ballroom when Elizabeth Edwards had hooked his arm and drawn him in for an introduction. He had become reasonably conversant in French during his European sojourn, and had just been idly translating Lamartine's *"Le Lac"* for his own amusement, and so it was almost instinctive on his part to offer a schoolbook *"Très hereux de faire votre connaissance."* Or perhaps it was more calculated than that—perhaps he meant to impress her.

But she chattered on in French faster than he could follow, and seeing the look of growing incomprehension on his face she abandoned the pursuit and subtly shifted to English with no more of a break in the conversation than if they had been speaking in their native tongue all along.

She was young—hardly more than twenty—and lively and sharp. She leaned forward when she talked, her diamond-hard blue eyes drilling into him. The candlelight in the room created enticing hollows in her bare throat and shoulders. She had a firm, proud chin and her face was interestingly wide. She was asking what he thought of General Harrison. Wasn't it a shame that the presidential nomination had gone to him instead of Henry Clay, who deserved it so? There could not be a greater man than Clay in the whole country.

Stephen Douglas, who certainly considered himself a greater man than Clay, suddenly appeared at the edge of Cage's sight, bowing toward Miss Todd as a quadrille was starting up. She accepted the Little Giant with a brief curtsy, flashed a backward smile at Cage, and disappeared. There seemed to be a sudden hole in the atmosphere where she had just been standing, so definitive had her presence been. He could not see the dance floor from where he was standing. Everyone in Springfield appeared to have shown up at the cotillion, if only to escape the wet and dreary December weather that had been oppressing the city all week. And of course the party was an excuse to see the new hotel, which had been built with far more alacrity than the new statehouse, which still stood unfinished after two years of construction. From the look of the toolsheds and piles of building stone littering the square, Cage wondered if it would be another two years yet.

The American House was a huge edifice that was already a political hive, Whigs and Democrats and hardened Loco Focos buzzing about in its meeting rooms, plotting their way forward into the 1840 presidential contest, which everyone had chosen to believe would be an apocalyptic one, the election of Harrison or Van Buren offering a chance to save the country or cast it into its final ruin. But politics was, astonishingly, something of a side issue tonight. Both Lincoln's and Douglas's names had appeared among the cotillion managers on the invitation Cage had received, which also featured an illustration of the national eagle with a banner in its beak pointedly reading "E Pluribus Unum." The idea of a greater good to which all partisans were ultimately pledged was of course nothing more than a warm illusion, but it was almost Christmas and people were in the mood to sustain it.

Cage wedged his way through the Turkish splendor of the American House toward the dance floor. The hotel was stuffed with opulent furniture and appurtenances, with beckoning landscape paintings and brilliant wallpaper whose patterns seemed to pulse in time with the music. He stood finally on the edge of the thick carpeting and watched the dancing. The quadrille ended fluidly and a high-spirited Scotch reel began. Cage watched Miss Todd weave among the dancers in her green dress, briefly connecting with Stephen Douglas, detaching, connecting again. Though her movements fit the same pattern as those of the other dancers, she seemed to be creating a living garment of her own. The tempo increased and the dance accelerated, the participants laughing, the audience gathered around them clapping in time. When Miss Todd swung past where he was standing, Cage noticed the sweat on her forehead, the delighted expression on her face.

He saw Lincoln on the far side of the room, wearing his cotillion-manager ribbon. He was talking to James Shields, the Irish-born state auditor. They were grinning, Lincoln gripping the smaller man's shoulders with both hands as he told a story. At its conclusion Shields threw his head back and laughed. He gave Lincoln an appreciative pat on his lapel and walked off shaking his head and smiling. He had a limp, the result of a fall to a ship's deck when he was a young merchant seaman. The limp was not pronounced but maybe enough to make him self-conscious on the dance floor. Cage did not really know Shields but was aware that he was not well-liked. He had a temper, though it was not on display tonight. And he had a very high opinion of himself. But who in this particular room did not?

As Shields walked away, Lincoln turned his attention toward the dance floor, watching the dancers as if their activity was as exotic as that of circus acrobats. Perhaps Mrs. Abell or one of the other married women who fussed over Abraham Lincoln had taught him some basic dance steps, but the blurry, whirling activity in the center of the room clearly outran his expertise.

"Is that Mr. Lincoln?" Mary Todd had suddenly appeared at Cage's side again. The music had stopped and she was fanning herself and gasping delightedly for breath.

"It is."

"Well, I don't think he's nearly as ungainly as his reputation says he is. You must be a friend of Mr. Lincoln. What's he like?"

"Hard to sum up."

"Well, he is rather monstrously tall. And Mr. Douglas is short enough to be stepped on. Are all Whigs and Democrats in Sangamon so ridiculously mismatched?"

"I'll introduce you to him," Cage said.

"Thank you, but my brother-in-law is jealous of introductions. I'd better let him do it."

Then she was gone again, gathered up by her friend Julia Jayne and some of the other young women who were repairing en masse to the ladies' lounge.

The next time he spotted her she was on the other side of the room, standing next to her brother-in-law, Ninian Edwards, as he presented her to Abraham Lincoln. Cage would remember the sight for the rest of his life—Mary's hand possessively on Lincoln's forearm as she gazed up at him, smiling, chattering, almost shaking with laughter at something he said in reply. And Lincoln bending down toward her, his expression both bashful and confident. She was probably not a beautiful woman. But she had so much liveliness and candor in her character that beauty was something people just naturally assumed she possessed as well.

That she was a little woman with very big needs was not yet obvious, though Cage understood from his first conversation with her that she had a restless will that any man who sought to marry her would have to accept and accommodate himself to. The American House that night was full of potential suitors—Stephen Douglas among them—and Cage would not have guessed that Abraham Lincoln would have ever found his way into the first rank. He looked oddly meek in her presence, towering over her like a tame camelopard.

"She knows Henry Clay!" Lincoln told Cage in wonderment toward four in the morning, when the party had at last begun to unravel and even Miss Todd was showing signs of fatigue. "She lived only a few miles from him in Lexington and used to visit him as a girl. She mentioned it as if it was a thing of no great importance. Why, I'd say it was a thing of great importance. It's like living down the road from George Washington!"

He said this as they were standing outside the American House with Speed and Billy Herndon watching Mary Todd disappear into a carriage with Mr. and Mrs. Edwards. The Edwardses were exhausted but their charge was still calling goodbye to everyone and waving from the carriage window as it drove off through the rain.

It was determined that with dawn so close at hand it would make no sense to go to bed, so the four of them, along with Ash Merritt and Ned Baker, walked through the rain to Speed's store, where they spent the rest of the night drinking Speed's Kentucky bourbon in the upper room. Since it was near Christmas and the cotillion had been such a marked success, Lincoln allowed Speed for once to pour a drop or two into his water cup, and he raised it in a toast, declaring that to live on the Illinois prairies at the close of the year of 1839 was like living in Eden before the Fall. Or would be if the state bank was solvent enough to pay out its notes in specie. Or if the money for the internal improvements system, all of those new railroads and canals that he and the rest of the Whigs had so feverishly sponsored, had not been squandered due to theft and mismanagement.

Speaking of the Garden of Eden, Lincoln said, reminded him of a man named Cain who owned a mill in Adams County. His pecker was of such a remarkably long and slantindicular character that it was said that he could fuck a farmer's wife two counties over while lying flat on his back reading the *Quincy Whig*.

There was another story after that, of course, a long one about a hunter who skinned a bear in an ingenious manner that left its pizzle intact and still functional. One night, during the Deep Snow of 1830, he and his wife were lying under the bearskin shivering . . .

Cage fell asleep long before the end of the story. He was shaken awake by Lincoln just as the sun was coming up. Speed and Herndon were snoring on the double bed, lying foot to chin. Baker was passed out on the floor and Ash Merritt had apparently slipped away at some point to go home.

"Let's play ball," Lincoln whispered to Cage.

The rain had stopped and an icy early-morning sunlight presided over the city. They walked to the makeshift playing court behind the square. The city was waking up and they could smell bread from the bakeries. From the kitchens of homes and taverns and lodging houses came the aromas of coffee and hoecakes and frying meat. Cage enjoyed the sensation of being ravenous, of knowing that soon—but not yet—he would have his breakfast. They took off the good wool coats they had worn to the cotillion and unbuttoned their waistcoats and played ball in their shirtsleeves, building up a fine sweat in the cold air as they listened to the rhythmic *thunk* of the ball and the hammering and clinking of the stonemasons who were already at work trying to finish the long-overdue statehouse.

They played silently, losing themselves in the intensity of the game. Cage was quicker than Lincoln and had a better eye for where the ball was going to be, but his opponent's arms were still hazardously long, and dodging them was like trying to dodge the blades of a spinning windmill. When they had finally decreed an end to the contest—Cage up by a game—they were both heaving for breath. Lincoln said that despite the fact he had not slept all night he must go home and get cleaned up and be in his office by eight thirty. There were a number of cases that needed attention immediately, and Stuart's continued absence in Washington City added exponentially to Lincoln's workload. A "damned hawk-billed yankee" kept writing him about the eighty dollars that he said his client was owed; and Mr. Wright, who lived up in South Fork, was anxious about some deeds that Stuart had assured him were in the office somewhere but that Lincoln had never seen.

"A two-man law office runs better when there are two men running it," he said.

"You may have forgotten that I'm also a damned hawk-billed yankee."

"I meant no offense to Massachusetts men, or for that matter to the avian race. Should I pursue Miss Todd?"

"Do you like her?"

"I don't know. I like the idea of her. She scares me a little."

"I wouldn't marry a woman I was scared of."

"I don't mean that. I could wrestle her down in a fair fight. But she's formidable, don't you think? She speaks French as natural as a dog barks. And did you see her dancing? I could never keep up with that. I shouldn't even try it."

"Then why?"

"Because she unsettles me in a way that I like. She's too good-looking for me, she's too proper for me—she's a Todd, for God's sake!—and she's too smart for me. Therefore, to one way of thinking, she's perfect for me."

He bounced the ball on the ground a half dozen times, catching it in his hand with an increasingly agitated swipe as he pondered the issue.

"Be careful you don't set something in motion you won't be able to stop," Cage said.

"I'm a long way from that. I'm just starting to get my thoughts in order. And of course she would have to like me back, and as we know I'm rough and peculiar and not fit for a woman's company. The whole affair would likely be me and Miss Owens all over again."

He turned his head, squinting against the low winter sun as he looked at Cage.

"What about you?"

"What do you mean?"

"Well, she's come to Springfield to get married. She won't leave until she does. Why don't you marry her yourself and put an end to my deliberations in the matter?"

Cage had thought about it, just for a moment when he had first been introduced to her by Mrs. Edwards, caught up in Mary's beaming smile, her intoxicating enthusiasm for all the commotion going on around her, the way her eyes searched the crowded hall as she talked to him. But he knew almost instinctively that their natures could never be compatible, that her appetite for excitement—for victories and defeats and all-enveloping contests, for friends and enemies and ceaseless campaigns waged with her whole heart—was something that would seek to obliterate the quiet reflection he knew he needed for his work.

"No," he told Lincoln, as if the thought of marrying Mary Todd had not occurred to him. "Stephen Douglas might be in your way, and who knows who else, but not me."

Lincoln accepted this answer with a thoughtful grunt, but as they were walking back in the direction of Speed's store he turned to Cage and asked, "Who *will* you marry, then?"

"I'm not sure that I have to marry anyone."

"So it's enough—what you have with her?"

"What I have with whom? Are you talking about Ellie?"

"Of course I am. You moved her into the Palatine, you went into business with her. Do you think your friends are completely unobservant? You know, of course, your attachment to her being what it seems, that we would never think to . . ."

Unable to find the words to complete his thought, he left it unfinished. Cage felt his habitual burden of jealousy lightened a bit.

"I know"

"As soon as it became clear . . ."

"Yes."

"Let me ask you this," Lincoln said, "are you happy with her?"

"I don't know. I would like to be, if she would allow it."

Lincoln smiled, his sunken, fatigued eyes lightening. His face was unshaven and his hair was plastered with sweat. "I don't know if I would be happy with Miss Todd, or even should be. They say happiness can slow a man down, and I don't have time for that."

SIXTEEN

THE SLEIGHING PARTY SET OUT in late afternoon beneath a flawless blue sky, the sun still blindingly bright on the new snow covering the road to Mount Auburn. The members of the high-spirited coterie that had sprung into existence with Mary Todd's arrival in Springfield had sorted themselves into four sleighs, two of them belonging to Ninian Edwards and his wife, one to Joshua Speed, and the other—a two-seater bobsleigh—leased from the town livery. Just after dark they pulled up to a tavern outside of Mount Auburn. The proprietor, knowing it would be a full moon and that there would be sleighing parties heading out in every direction, had the big public room ready, a great fire going, the japan candlesticks out, the floor cleared for an impromptu frolic. He serenaded the party with his fiddle as they pulled up, and kept the music going past midnight while one son worked the bellows at the hearth and the other passed out crullers and quinomie cakes. Everyone was drinking toddies and the ladies were throwing back their heads and proclaiming, "Whig husbands or none!" It was a "William Henry Harrison for President" crowd. No Democrats had been invited, especially Stephen Douglas, whose manners at present were deemed wonderfully inexcusable. He had recently attacked Sim Francis for something the editor had allowed to be published in the *Sangamo Journal.* His weapon had been a cane borrowed from Candlebox Calhoun—leading to many jokes about Douglas's own "diminutive cane," its lack of "sufficient length," etc.

The dancing was loose and ragged, no one afraid to hold back for fear of making a fool of himself, as had been the case at the cotillion before the turn of the year. Lincoln was in the middle of it, clomping when he should be gliding, looming above everyone else, helplessly off-beat, turning what started out as a contra dance into a series of form-less collisions. He was not drunk like everyone else, but neither was he the preoccupied observer he could become on such occasions. It was one of those rare nights when individual worries and ambitions became somehow irrelevant, forgotten in the flood of music and friendship, light and warmth. If Lincoln had decided after all to begin a campaign for the affections of Mary Todd, Cage saw no evidence of it tonight. The dozen or so people in the party had squeezed into the sleighs hap-hazardly on the way out, with no special maneuvering to sit with any-one in particular, and the dancing was too chaotic and energetic for any valsing that might have separated the partygoers into couples. But Mary Todd was very much aware of Abraham Lincoln, laughing at his awkward footing, constantly turning her head and glancing upward as if to make sure he was still in the room.

At one in the morning Ned Baker walked among the men holding out his hat, and they put in four and sixpence apiece to pay the exhausted tavernkeeper and his sons, then they all trooped out into the snow again for the ride back to Springfield. It happened that Cage and Mary found themselves in the backseat of the bobsleigh, with Lincoln and Sim Fran-cis crowded together on the narrow seat in front with Mercy Levering, who was visiting Springfield from Baltimore and whom Mary had adopted as one of her great coterie friends. Francis handed the reins to Lincoln, pleading blind drunkenness.

"Also," he said in a slurry, sarcastic voice, "I shouldn't drive because I must at all times remain vigilant. I live in terror that Stephen Douglas may jump out of a tree and attack me with a cane again."

They all laughed because Sim was such a big man that people called him the White Bear, and because the only damage that Douglas had done to him with Candlebox Calhoun's cane was to squash an apple he had been carrying in his coat pocket.

Lincoln was an inexpert driver, but a sober one, and the two horses that had been leased along with the sleigh from the livery knew the way back home to their warm stalls in Springfield and were quite willing to head in that direction without a guiding hand. The little sleigh caravan took off, the moonlight illuminating the mounded snow at the sides of the road and the great surging fields of whiteness beyond with such intensity that any lamplight or candlelight would have been a corruption. The moon was brilliant enough that Cage could see its light actually sparkling on the snow, he could read every line in his palm when he held his hand up to his face in wonder. Even the horizon was visible, and the wolves calling to one another from the heart of the night expressed themselves with a symphonic complexity. The sound of the sleigh bells teased around at the edges of this great natural orchestration, sometimes eerily harmonizing with the voices of the wolves.

The sleigh glided along on the new-laid snow covering the road, moving as silently as the scraps of cloud overhead. The mood of the expedition was still high, but no one was speaking anymore. They were listening to the wolves and the bells and studying the eerily bright landscape and the glowing clock dial of the moon. Mary and Cage sat with a buffalo robe up to their chins, both of them staring at Lincoln from behind as he held the reins. He was wearing his usual tall hat and a heavy wool scarf whose bright blue color was as detectable in the moonlight as it might have been in daytime. The scarf covered his face to the bridge of his nose. Sim and Mercy were slumped down in the seat beneath their blankets. She was a slight girl and bundled up next to the White Bear she appeared even slighter. Lincoln sat upright as he drove, the profile of his towering body vividly clear against the sky. He and Sim Francis were speaking about the *Old Soldier,* the pro-Harrison newspaper that Francis was publishing out of his office along with the *Journal,* but they were speaking in low tones and the sound of the sleigh bells obscured most of what they said.

"He looks like Father Jupiter," Mary whispered to Cage.

"A little," he admitted.

"Or like the Ancient of Days. Is it blasphemous to say that?"

"I don't know what God would think. I doubt that Lincoln would appreciate hearing himself described that way."

"Do you think he heard us?"

Lincoln was still listening to something Francis was saying so Cage shook his head, guessing he had not.

She leaned closer to him, so close that their cheeks touched, and he could feel her cold flushed skin against his own. Her whisper was barely audible.

"I don't know if he's handsome. Well, I'm sure he's not. But it's interesting for a youngish man like him to look like Father Jupiter. What do you think?"

"Yes, I suppose it's always more interesting when people stand apart a little from the expected."

"*You* stand apart." The intimate declaration, combined with her breath tickling his side-whiskers, startled him. Her whisper was so low now he wasn't entirely sure if he had heard her correctly. But he needed to reply and so he did.

"I don't know that I do."

"Oh, I'm quite certain of it. I've read your poems. I read the one last week in the *Journal*."

She was referring to a piece of Cage's that Sim Francis had published just before Douglas had caned him. It was called "The Indifferent Beast." Cage had begun writing it shortly after he had been bitten by that dog on the square. Something about looking down at the top of the dog's head as it gnawed on his leg had produced a meditation in six stanzas on the frightening implacability of nature, each living thing locked in its own mind, following its own unshared directives. The poem had flirted rather boldly with the theme of an uncaring universe, of a God implicitly absent. But as far as he knew he had not been charged with infidelity by the citizens of Springfield. Very few of them, he supposed, had even noticed the poem at all.

"You must read the paper thoroughly," he said to Mary.

"Oh, every word, of course. I don't want to miss anything. You have a gift. I can understand why you don't want to spend all your energy on politics, like the rest of us do. When will you publish another book so the world can properly take notice?"

"As soon as a publisher decides not to turn me down."

"Turn you down? That's nonsense. I'll write to my father in Lexington. I'm sure he knows publishers in Boston and Philadelphia who would be pleased to bring it out."

She said this so casually he hardly knew whether to credit it, but she clearly came from a different world, a world in which certain obstacles that ruled most people's lives simply didn't exist, in which frosty, unapproachable publishers were family friends.

"That would be generous of you," Cage told her.

"Generosity has nothing to do with it. I'd do it for my own pleasure."

She smiled in a conspiring way and bumped her foot against his beneath the buffalo robe. It was a casual, unreadable gesture—perhaps flirtatious, perhaps not—but it summoned his attention in a way she must have meant for it to. She was not interested in Cage as a future husband. That was clear enough, despite her seductive, confiding conversation. She was a natural-born denizen of the political world, and she would not want a husband who could not place her in the middle of the constant excitement that that world kept manufacturing for itself. But the touch of her boot suggested that it was natural in her to lay a claim where she could, just for the purpose of doing so.

"Lincoln!" she called out, breaking without warning the web of intimacy she had just spun for Cage. "Stop the sleigh!"

"For what purpose, Miss Todd?"

"For the purpose of a snowball fight, of course."

Lincoln reined the horses to a stop and the sleighs behind followed suit, and in a moment the whole party was climbing up the snowbanks on the side of the road and into the virgin whiteness beyond, stumbling about as they sank to their knees and packed the snow tight in their gloved hands. Mary Todd declared that the fight should be the women against the men, so the two sexes formed battle lines several dozen yards apart and launched snowballs until their arms were exhausted and their extremities numb. After everyone else had raced back to the sleighs and bundled themselves under blankets and quilts, Miss Todd declared that she would continue the contest even unto frostbite if only there were a man willing to stand against her.

"Mr. Lincoln!" she demanded as he was heading back with the others to the sleigh, "where is your courage?"

"Miss Todd, where is your sense?"

She already had a snowball in her hand and when he turned away from her to climb into the sleigh she hit him with a perfectly aimed throw on the exposed stalk of his neck.

There followed a general commotion in which Lincoln and Speed and Ned Baker chased the wild Kentucky belle through the snow and wrestled her back to the waiting sleighs. Cage hung back, feeling that he had had enough for one night of being a participant in one of Mary Todd's tableaux-vivants. He stood next to Ninian Edwards, who watched his sister-in-law laughing and writhing as the three men carried her back like a rug. He was a priggish man and though he had given himself over to the evening's dancing and toddy-drinking and snowball-fighting, his priggishness had returned. Or at least it had seemed to, judging by the look of stony assessment on his face as the men set Mary down in the double sleigh, in the front seat this time. It was Lincoln, not Speed or Baker, whom Ninian had his eye on now. Of all the men in the coterie, it could certainly be argued, he was the least likely fit for the latest Miss Todd from Kentucky: too tall, too poor, too coarse. But Ninian must have known that his sister-in-law was the sort of woman not to allow herself to be entrapped by anything expected.

For the final drive into Springfield Cage ended up in the backseat of the sleigh again, but this time he was joined by Mercy Levering and Sim Francis, both of whom promptly fell asleep, lost to drink and exhaustion and the narcotic schussing sound of their conveyance as it sped through the snow. Mary was in front now, next to Lincoln, her face turned toward his as he watched the road ahead and nodded and smiled as she spoke to him in confiding tones. Suddenly ignored in the backseat, Cage strained to hear what she was saying: how beautiful Lexington was, with its wide streets and great houses and venerable shade trees, but how it was the scene for her of a "desolate childhood." Her mother dead in childbirth when Mary was six, her father remarrying a horrid selfish woman who kept populating the house with an endless succession of her own children, treating Mary and her full siblings as if they were of no more concern to her than the slaves. She was better treated at her boarding school than in her own house!

Cage wondered what Lincoln made of all this, whether someone with his own penniless and forlorn upbringing could regard the emotional distress of a young aristocratic lady as something remarkable. But he seemed to be listening to her as patiently and sympathetically as if he had never heard of any such trouble visiting anyone, and when Springfield came into view—the soon-to-be-finished capitol building glowing alabaster in the moonlight like something from *The Arabian Nights*—Lincoln and Miss Todd had veered from her past troubles and were competing to see who could do the best impression of Stephen Douglas's stentorian pomposity or James Shields's Irish accent. She was as good a mimic as he was, precise and lacerating. The two of them, Cage thought as the horses picked up their pace at the promise of home, could be dangerous together.

1840

SEVENTEEN

✦✦✦

I F T H E R E W A S A R O M A N C E to be pursued between Lincoln and Mary Todd, there was much other business to distract from it. Eighteen forty was a crowded year. Not only was Lincoln running for a fourth term in the legislature, but he was an elector for Harrison, meaning that he was away from Springfield for weeks and months at a time campaigning for the Whig presidential candidate in the southern part of the state—known for some eccentric reason as Egypt. When not among the Egyptians Lincoln was riding the Eighth Judicial Circuit, arguing cases in more than a dozen counties in central Illinois. During that spring Cage received occasional letters from Lincoln. Was it true that Ned Baker had gotten into a street fight over the new city charter, and that his opponent had fallen back on that fiendish Democratic trick of sticking his thumb deep into Baker's eye? Had Cage seen any farmers in Sangamon flying Tippecanoe flags on their plows? You would not believe the bedbugs to be encountered in Egypt—a plague out of Exodus. He felt he was holding his own in his debates, even though the Democrats were putting forth their crack nags against him. Only deep into the letters would he inquire about the coterie and specifically about Mary Todd. He had heard that she had arrived home late one night at the Edwards house on a drayman's wagon. True? Had Cage been to any more hops or cotillions? Please describe them in detail, with emphasis on Miss Todd's activities vis-à-vis potential pursuers. Should he write her? Would that mean he was in the race? Should he be? Was she the sort of woman who could make him happy? Was she too headstrong, too full of opinions, too rich for him? Was she beautiful, or at least very handsome? Was it unfair and unrealistic of him to aspire to marry a woman with enticing physical features when he himself would be such a painfully opposite counterpart?

In his correspondence, Lincoln wondered about Mary Todd's disposition. She seemed to expect a steady supply of distraction. How could he possibly match his moods to hers, when he was so subject to self-doubt and emotional lethargy? How could he possibly pay for the things she would need—clothes, conveyances, excitements? No, Lincoln almost always concluded in these letters, as Cage followed the turnings of his correspondent's mind, he should remove himself from the field of action in the case of Miss Todd. He should tend to the business of his reelection and that of old Tippecanoe, and chart his future from there.

Cage answered the letters, of course, but he steered clear of outright advice. He could make an abstract case for a marriage between Abraham Lincoln and Mary Todd. They were alike in that the heat of politics warmed their souls and gave their lives purpose, and it was possible that their individual ambitions could be better satisfied if they were united. But he was reluctant to make this case in writing, for fear Lincoln would somehow seize upon his opinion as the decisive factor. If there was a misalliance brewing, as he rather suspected there was, Cage didn't want to be responsible for it.

In March a letter came from Gray and Bowen, the Boston publisher. "A mutual friend whose judgment we value has written to us about your poetical work. We are in the business of getting up some titles in that line and would like to know if at present or in the near future you might have a manuscript and if you might favor us by sending it our way. We are looking for a voice or two from the Western regions and if your poems strike us as favorably as they did our informant we will hope that an agreement for their publication by our firm can be reached."

Mary waved away Cage's thanks when he saw her the next day on the street as she was walking with Julia Jayne to a performance of the Tippecanoe Singing Club. They were both wearing Harrison banners, which conformed gracefully—and provocatively—with the swell of their bosoms.

"It wasn't a favor at all," she insisted. "It was simple duty. The world must know of your genius. My father read your poems and was very happy to send them on with his recommendation."

"I'll write and thank him."

She took him by the arm and pulled him close as if for a confiding word, though Julia still stood next to her and did not show any reluctance about listening in. "If you're going to write anybody, write your friend. Tell him some of us in Springfield are getting tired of just reading all about the campaign in the newspapers. It would be very nice to hear from somebody who's out on the canvass, on the front lines so to speak."

He did as she asked, but Lincoln wrote back from some flea-ridden boardinghouse on the far side of the circuit that he would hold off writing Mary Todd, at least for now. "The truth is I would very much like to trade opinions with an active-minded woman of that sort, but I think there could be a hazard in doing so from a distance. What if I were to write something to her in passing that she would seize on and not let go? What if I accidentally proposed marriage? I don't know if her accepting me would be a good thing or a bad thing. I tell you, Cage, I am capable of every sort of miscalculation out here on the circuit, where the snoring lawyers are three abed and the food is usually a greasy wonder. 'Beware all siren songs' is my watchword just now."

Cage was glad to see that Lincoln knew his own mind, at least a little— that he was aware that he was helpless where women were concerned. Reading the letter made Cage remember that night in New Salem, when his new friend had lain in bed sobbing over the girl he had loved and who had died. Maybe the loss had been so hard for him that he was afraid to put himself in the way of that sort of tragedy again. Or maybe his skittishness around Mary Owens and now Mary Todd had less to do with old grief than with the fear that he was more intrigued than in love, and that in marrying he would foreclose forever the possibility of finding again what he had found with that poor girl in New Salem.

What wisdom could Cage offer, when he himself was hostage to a similar dilemma, in love with a woman who, though not dead, was so contentedly indifferent to him that she was as ungraspable as a ghost? At least now he had the possibility of publication to distract him.

Throughout that spring of 1840, while the minds of Springfield's citizens were trained on the contest between Harrison and Van Buren, he worked on the manuscript he would send to Gray and Bowen. It would not be the same book that he sent without success to Little and Brown. It would be not an overture but the full symphony, each poem its own singular expression but also lending substance to the overall theme, the chronicle of a developing civilization. In the intensifying political season the meetings of the poetical society had been suspended. He was glad of it. He needed to work in solitude, to force himself forward without entertaining the opinions of others. He would not allow himself to be in a hurry. He wrote to the publisher to tell them it might be a year, even two, before the manuscript was completed to his satisfaction. He wanted to compose without comment, without even understanding. He still saw his friends, went out to the theater, still accepted invitations to the parties that were put on all throughout the legislative season. The people he saw there did not know the intensity of his private reflections, did not see him by his lamp late at night, alone, confused, ruled by the need to pursue phantom thoughts and scratch them into existence with his pen.

"Respecting as I do your high concerns and your distaste for all slippery occupations," Lincoln wrote in May from Egypt, "never have I thought to ask you for money. But the race between Van Buren and Harrison is I think about as much a crusade as a political contest can be. Will you give forty dollars to help bring out the Whigs in Springfield in June? Ash is the treasurer of the event. You can hand the money to him. It will be the biggest Harrison rally of the campaign and his election will help the country recover itself from stagnancy."

Cage complied without reluctance, knowing that in the political world donor and friend could not be thought as separate things for long. When Lincoln finally returned to Springfield Cage didn't see him until the rally itself, when he stood on a wagon in front of the nearly finished capitol building to address the crowd. Afterwards the *Journal* wrote that there were fifteen thousand people there, though the *Journal* was a Whig paper and bound only to its own partisan truth. But there certainly seemed to be fifteen thousand people helping themselves to the free barbecue that Cage's contribution had helped pay for. They were seated at tables in the square that must have each been 150 feet long, and they ate with the single-minded rapacity of people who never expected to be fed again. The Whigs were running a "Log Cabin and Hard Cider" campaign, and there were log cabin replicas and barrels of cider that were not replicas at all, and that men in their Harrison coonskins had been getting drunk on since the night before.

Women did not have the vote, of course, but that did not stop them from turning out onto the square, waving their banners and calling out "Two dollars and roast beef!" along with everyone else.

Just before Lincoln was introduced, Cage heard his own name called and turned to see Mary Todd pushing toward him through the crowd accompanied by two unsmiling middle-aged men who seemed to regard themselves as chaperones. Mary introduced them as Uncle John and Uncle David. Apparently the entire world was now peopled with nothing but Todd relatives.

"Uncle David," she said to Cage triumphantly, "fought with General Harrison at Tippecanoe."

Cage touched the brim of his hat and bowed slightly to Uncle David, saluting his place in history. Uncle David acknowledged this tribute with a grunt. Neither he nor Uncle John, who was merely a doctor, looked particularly happy at the behavior of their brazen niece, who had evidently been wending her way through the crowd without regard to their chaperoning authority, her face sunburned and flushed with excitement. A political rally was better than a hop, better than a cotillion, better than a moonlight sleigh ride.

She was wearing her Harrison banner, which no doubt further aggravated her uncles, who looked like the sort of traditionalists who disapproved of the new fashion of women allowing themselves to get excited about elections. One of them opened his mouth, probably meaning to give her a lecture on this point, but she moved away from him toward Cage, dismissing his concerns with a wave of her hand and telling them that they all needed to be quiet because Lincoln was about to speak.

They were thirty or forty yards away from the speakers' wagon, and the diminutive Miss Todd found her view blocked by a forest of men in tall hats. "Tell that man to take off his hat so the ladies behind him can see," she ordered Cage. Her voice was loud enough for the man in front of them to hear it himself. He complied, but satisfied himself with a grudging look backwards. Lincoln was speaking now. His voice was even reedier than usual from overuse, but on this clear June day it carried well enough: Van Buren and his fussy aristocratic ways, how if he were to partake of a single swallow of Harrison's hard cider he would ruffle up like the cuffs of his shirt. Cage was amused at the idea of Lincoln, the scrupulous non-drinker, presenting the consumption of alcohol as a test of character. But he knew enough politicians by now to understand that they were more likely to be invigorated by hypocrisy than to be shamed by it.

There were a few stony-faced Democrats scattered through the crowd but it was mostly a fervent Whig audience, and after several more jokes mocking Van Buren's pretensions Lincoln had them all laughing and waving their Tippecanoe banners and spontaneously bursting out into campaign songs, Mary singing lustily along with everyone else—"Van, Van is a used up man"—as her uncles rolled their eyes in helpless disapproval.

"Do you suppose he's afraid of me?" Mary said into Cage's ear as the singing was dying down.

"Lincoln? Afraid of you? Why would you think that?"

"Because he hasn't written me. It doesn't matter, I don't care in the least, but the thought did cross my mind."

She turned her attention to Lincoln again, who had stood there waiting patiently for the hilarity to die down before resuming his speech. He was enjoying himself a great deal, and the enjoyment was contagious. As soon as he opened his mouth, the audience laughed again, this time not over something he had said, but from anticipation of what he would come out with next. From where Cage was standing he looked almost normal, taller than most men, scrawnier than most, but reasonably well turned out in a good broadcloth coat with a velvet collar and sleeves that some decent tailor had finally cut to the right length. He had inevitably lost weight on his legal and campaigning travels and as a result his eyes looked darker and more penetrating, his jawline sharp as a plow. But his ready smile and obvious comfort in standing in front of thousands of people undercut anything stern or forbidding in his appearance.

He himself, he told the audience, was a former flatboatman and rail-splitter who wouldn't know a ruffled shirt from a rattlesnake. He carried no gold-plated cane, but he did have a blue streak around his leg where you could still see the mark where the buckskin breeches he had worn as a boy had almost cut off the circulation, due to the fact that his family could not replace them as he grew. In fact, he was glad he was through growing and had a good pair of trousers because the endless war the Democrats were waging against the Bank of the United States probably meant that he and the rest of the good people of Illinois would soon have nothing but the clothes they were wearing. Meanwhile all the free Negroes that Mr. Van Buren said ought to have the vote—yes, he said it, right there at that convention in New York!—would be wearing kid gloves and gold watch chains.

The crowd booed and bellowed at the preposterous idea of Negroes voting. At Cage's side, Mary Todd was calling out "No! No!" with the others and grinning in delight at the apocalyptic abolitionist scenario Lincoln had so deftly presented.

"Why do you have that odd little smile on your face?" she said to Cage.

"I don't know what you mean."

"A scowl, I think. What are you scowling about?"

"Well, if I'm scowling it's because he's painting Van Buren as an abolitionist, which Van Buren certainly is not. And maybe I'm scowling because Lincoln is happy to say anything if it will win an election."

"What would you like him to say? That Negroes *should* be able to vote? He'd have to leave Illinois. I suppose you can say such a thing in a poem if you like but you can't say it in front of people you're asking to vote for you."

She turned away from him to listen for a while to Lincoln, who was talking now about how Democratic policies had driven men from their farms, families into hopeless debt, while Van Buren and his speculating friends were ever more prosperous. Then she abruptly turned back to Cage and leaned close and spoke into his ear so that no one could overhear.

"Are you an abolitionist, Cage? Are you that extreme?"

She was smiling at him, a fond smile but a challenging one. He saw that she liked pinning people to the wall.

"I suppose I am." He gestured toward Lincoln, whose long arms were now theatrically spread. "Unlike our friend."

"Oh, yes," she mused. "He's the farthest thing from an abolitionist. As am I, of course. But I like the idea that you are one."

She turned her eyes back toward Lincoln, thoughts of abolition and abolitionists evaporating as she returned to the theme of her own situation.

"I suppose I'll have to get him to write to me myself."

EIGHTEEN

❖❖❖

THE DAY AFTER THE GREAT Whig barbecue and speechify-
ing spectacle, Lincoln stopped Cage on the street.

"I'm going to Florville's to get a haircut. So are you. Your hair's so
shaggy you could be mistaken for a poet instead of a respectable man of
business."

It was mid-afternoon on an airless June day. The log cabin replicas
and tables and floats and banners had not yet been taken down, and
as he stared out at these forlorn artifacts a few minutes later from the
window of Florville's barbershop Cage felt a mild twinge of despair,
as if history had come and gone, and would come and go again, and
the world would still be tediously the same. The barbershop smells of
cologne water and lavender soap and pomatum only added to the sense
of time itself being trapped and pickled in a specimen jar.

William Florville was the best barber in town and until recently had
been the only one. His shop was usually crowded but on this lazy afternoon Lincoln and Cage were the only two customers.

"Didn't I tell you your money would be well spent?" Lincoln had
gone first and was sitting in the barbering chair, his head poking out
from the cloth tied around his neck. "Ned Baker thinks there were even
more people there than the *Journal* said."

"So in your calculations the more of my money was spent the better
spent it was?"

"Exactly."

Billy Florville laughed as he scooped Lincoln's black hair into a top
knot and started snipping away. He was a black man, a Creole from Haiti
who had fled the troubles there as a boy, ending up somehow in Spring-

field working as a servant for a local merchant, who had helped set him up in his barbering business. A free man, not enslaved, not indentured, he was a savvy entrepreneur who also owned a laundry and was calmly and methodically making himself wealthy. Somehow he had created his own world, a world that was parallel to the one that the other black people of Springfield inhabited.

"Cage here is upset with me, as usual," Lincoln explained to Florville. "He thinks I was too eager to embrace the prejudices of the electorate in my speech. I put a fling on Van Buren, you see, for saying he wanted free Negroes to vote."

"I heard your speech, Mr. Lincoln," Florville said in his Caribbean-inflected accent. "And in my thinking, Negroes would sooner get suffrage if Harrison got elected than if Van Buren did."

"That's my thinking too, Billy. Our minds run on the same track."

If Florville objected to this illusion, he did not say so out loud. He was a cautious man of business who strived for a neutral complacency and kept his thoughts hidden deep. Meanwhile Lincoln smiled at Cage as if he had just proved to him that emancipating slaves and then giving them the vote was his first order of business as a public man, even though there was scant evidence that his principles ran very far in that direction. But there was no point in pressing Lincoln into an argument. He might not be the first person you would turn to in the cause of ending slavery, but at least he had a tender conscience and an awareness that human suffering was generally a bad thing.

"What did she think of the speech?" Lincoln asked Cage.

"Who?"

"Miss Todd, of course. I saw you standing with her out in the audience."

"I would say Miss Todd received your remarks in a generous and uncritical spirit."

"I never did write her."

"She told me that."

The sound of Florville's scissors occupied the room as Lincoln fell into a pondering silence.

"I guess I'd better go see her. Will you come with me? I'm afraid of what I'll say if I'm alone with her. I might push the case too far."

"The case?"

"Will you go with me?"

"If you want to see Miss Todd," Florville said, "you'd better go soon. Her brother-in-law Mr. Edwards was in the chair this morning and said she was going away for the rest of the summer."

"What? When is she leaving?"

"Very shortly. Maybe tomorrow."

"Well, then we have to go see her right away. Sorry, Cage. I'm afraid you don't have time for a haircut after all."

Yes, Mary confirmed as she sat in the parlor of the Edwards home with Lincoln and Cage, she was on her way to Columbia, Missouri, to spend a few months with her uncle David and his family. She didn't mind going in the least. The cotillion season in Springfield was winding down, it was getting hot, and she was getting bored because so many interesting people were out of town on the eternal canvass.

"You and Mr. Douglas, for instance," she said to Lincoln. "You've been going at it like ancient gladiators all over Illinois, I hear."

"We meet in the arena from time to time, though he's so short it's often hard to spot him."

She smiled thinly, uncharacteristic for someone with such a robust sense of fun. Cage thought Mary had a naturally shrewd understanding of human behavior but that she was too accustomed to being at the center of attention herself to put that understanding to much use. And just now she seemed as confused as Lincoln was by his intentions in calling on her. She sat upright on a black horsehair couch, her two gentlemen callers facing her formally from across the room, aware of their reflections in the glass-fronted bookcase behind her. A young Negro woman came in to serve them lemonade. Mary paid her no notice except for a perfunctory nod that might have been a gesture of thanks, or of dismissal. She had obviously grown up being waited on by slaves. Since Mary's sister and her husband lived in the free state of Illinois, this girl in their home was not technically a slave, but thanks to various creative laws she was employed on a "contract" that probably paid her nothing but her board and the clothes she was wearing.

Mary took a sip from her glass and fingered the little pocket watch she wore on a chain around her neck. She was wearing a light silk day dress the same pale color as her lemonade. Her legs were crossed beneath her skirts and one delicate foot bobbed up and down in expectation. She waited for Lincoln to make some momentous announcement.

But no momentous announcement came. The conversation slid into campaign banalities, then into poetry, with Mary reciting a Shakespeare sonnet and Lincoln reciting Burns and Cage wondering what he was doing here in the first place. When Mary turned to him for a verse, he started out with the opening lines of "Tintern Abbey"—"Five years have past; five summers, with the length / Of five long winters!"—but had not gotten very deep into the poem when tears started pouring out of her eyes.

"I'm sorry," she said. "But there's something about the way Words-worth makes things sound, just in those few words—'Five years have past.' It's as if you can hear time itself rushing by. You can hear your youth disappearing. It's so silly of me to cry."

"Wordsworth would like it that you do," Cage said.

"Do you think so, as a poet yourself?"

"Here's a poem that will make you cry worse," Lincoln said. He tapped the crown of his beaver hat on his knee in rhythm as he recited another of the grave and fatalistic poems of which his memory seemed to hold an inexhaustible supply. It started out with something about tumbling out of the womb into a dark and silent grave, then marched on after several more dispiriting stanzas to conclude that "All our laughter is but pain."

"Well," Mary said. "I was feeling wistful a moment ago, but now I think I should go kill myself."

The look of momentary confusion on Lincoln's face caused her to break out laughing.

"I'm sorry," she said. "But why do you like such *sad* poems?"

Lincoln finally caught her teasing mood and laughed back. "I reckon I'm just peculiarly fond of black despair, Miss Todd."

"Oh, shall we please drop the pretensions of miss and mister? The both of you are friends, and so the both of you should call me Mary. No, one of you could call me Molly instead. That was what my brothers and sisters called me back home in Lexington—the real brothers and sisters, I mean, not the half ones that came along after my horrid stepmother entered the scene."

"Why should just one of us call you that?" Cage asked.

"Because that's my rule. You should continue to call me Mary, Cage, because you strike me as a man who is better off using a name with an 'r' in it. That means Lincoln has to call me Molly."

Lincoln agreed that he would, and Mary—or Molly—nodded her head as if some great issue had been decided. She took pleasure in keeping him unbalanced and confused about how to react to her. She wouldn't have gone to all this manipulative effort—drawing Lincoln in, pushing him out, teasing him, taunting him, making him feel the force of her capricious will—if she weren't taking his measure as a potential husband. And Lincoln must like it, Cage thought, bantering with a woman who was so sophisticated and confounding.

They stayed for another half hour, Lincoln finally standing and explaining that he had to leave and file a demurrer for a client, attend to some other legal business, and then head north to Tazewell County to campaign for Harrison.

"Then I won't expect to see you again until the fall," Mary said. "When I'm back from Missouri. Do you think the Whigs can carry Illinois?"

"I think we can, but it'll be a hard fight, Miss—"

"Molly, remember?"

"It'll be a hard fight, Molly."

"Good. I like a hard fight. Goodbye, Lincoln."

He stood still for a moment, searching for something to say, a parting comment to save him from the impression he had just been dismissed. But nothing came and he just smiled awkwardly and turned to go. Cage nodded goodbye to Mary and started to go with him, until she reached out and touched his arm.

"But you don't have to file any demurrers, do you? Can't you stay for a little while? Let's read some more Wordsworth together. I'm sure my sister and Mrs. Edwards have a copy of *Lyrical Ballads* somewhere in the library."

Cage glanced at Lincoln, who was now even more confused, and gave him an apologetic smile.

"Let's watch him from the window," Mary said after Lincoln had left the house. They stood beside the curtains and watched as he ambled up Second Street toward his office in the center of town.

"He's too tall and his hat is too tall," she said. "Does he have any idea of the vertical effect he makes?"

"He's not the sort of man who gives much thought to his clothes."

She kept staring out the window, watching the vertical figure recede, down the barely perceptible slope of Aristocracy Hill.

"I thought we were supposed to be reading Wordsworth," Cage said.

She turned her head, gave him a sly look, and then at last backed away from the window. She stood in the sunlit center of the room in her pale yellow dress, clasping her hands in front of her waist, her elbows bent to show off her slender arms to best effect. It was a fetching pose, a portrait of thoughtful female gravity. Her face was perfect, in its way: a little round, a little soft, a mouth that was straight but not stern, eyes that were clear and frank. But there was no serenity in that face—there never had been, probably. She was a woman who could strike a pose of physical stillness but could not conceal the fact that her spirit was always plotting, wanting, needing more. Just like the men she had surrounded herself with—Lincoln, Douglas, Ned Baker, Ash Merritt, Cage himself—she had a governing appetite, a need to identify opportunities and then to seize them before they were gone.

"Does he like me?"

"He's uncertain around you."

"For heaven's sake, what does that mean?"

"He grew up very plain, Mary."

"Of course he did. That's obvious. I like that he grew up plain. It's one of the admirable things about him. It's no doubt part of what makes his mind so fascinating. I know that he more or less schooled himself in a log cabin and I was very rigorously educated in Madame Mentelle's academy, but why should that make a difference to me? Do you think I'm such a terrible snob that I would not be interested in a man who had faced obstacles? My advantages and his disadvantages might be a perfect fit."

"They might."

"But does he like me?"

"I think he does."

"You're no help at all."

She sat down in her chair and stared at him in exasperation. "Did he visit me today for any particular reason?"

"He heard that you were leaving, and I think it scared him, that you would get away without him . . . saying anything. And I think he brought me along because it scared him that he might . . . say something."

"So what do you advise?"

"Advise? I don't know what to advise. I don't know what you want."

She held her pose in the chair for a moment, then stood up and walked to the window again, moving about like a character in a play. Maybe she *was* a character in a play, very much alert to her own unfolding performance.

"I've been at Springfield for—what? Six months? I've had a chance to look around at some of the gentlemen in this town. Their attention has been very flattering. As yet there's no principal lion. As yet. But that won't be the case forever and if I'm going to marry somebody—which I am—I would very much like that somebody to be an interesting person, a person with an evident future ahead of him."

"Do you want me to tell Lincoln he has a chance to be your principal lion?"

"Of course not. Do you think I'd be so obvious and grasping as to have you carry a message like that to him? But I'm off to Missouri and I'd like somebody to know how I feel about him. I'd like *you* to know it. It's comforting to share a secret with someone you trust."

Her confiding tone, her open and innocent expression—it could have been stagecraft. But Mary Todd was the sort of person in whom artifice and authenticity were always richly entwined. Cage understood why Lincoln had wanted him in the room today. Lincoln was captivated by her energy and intelligence, but aware that her surface emotions were manifestations of deeper currents swirling and boiling below. They were a match that way, and he must have sensed it just as she did, though whether those currents would merge or collide was the great question.

"And what about you?" she asked Cage in a different tone of voice, cordial and businesslike. Her posture had straightened; her vulnerable and confiding mood had passed. "What will you do in the long summer ahead?"

"Devote myself to my book, and to my business affairs."

"Anything else? Or anyone else? A principal lioness?"

He smiled and told her no, but he must have inadvertently given something away, because he caught a calculating flash in her eyes. Did she know about him and Ellie? It was unlikely but possible. She was, after all, a young woman of unabashed curiosity.

"Mr. Edwards's young relation Matilda is coming for a visit in the fall," she said. "I should be home then as well. I'll make sure you receive a suitable introduction. She's eighteen, I think. I'm twenty-two, so compared to her I'm ancient. And unlike me she's very beautiful."

Cage made the necessary rebuttal about her looks. At that moment—in that summer of 1840, before all the bitterness and horror and heartbreak that would later rule her life and stamp her character—he did think she was beautiful. Or at the least she was beautifully presented. Every detail of her appearance—her dress, her hair, the tiny watch hanging from her throat—seemed in perfect conformity with every other part. She was looking at him, half smiling now, her blue eyes shining with candor.

"You're a gentleman for saying such kind words. But don't be too much of a gentleman. Because if you decide you want to marry Cousin Matilda, you'll have to fight everybody else off."

NINETEEN

✦✦✦

T HE MAN RUNNING AGAINST LINCOLN for his reelection to the assembly was Jesse Thomas. He was a Democrat who had begun political life as a Whig and was of course for that reason regarded by the Whigs as a turncoat. He was now a judge, and had presided in court during the Henry Truett trial. To Cage's mind he had presided fairly enough, though there had been something odd about him as he sat behind the bench. He rarely spoke during the proceedings, but when he did his voice was as high as a girl's. He was not fat, but he had a swollen-looking body, along with bulging eyes and a strange placidity of manner that made you think of a frog sitting on a log, observing the world in front of him while taking no apparent interest in it. Every now and then his lips would rise into a quizzical half smile whose meaning, if there was one, remained provocatively hidden.

It was partly because of Thomas's unreadable frog-like facade that Cage was curious about how he would conduct himself in a debate with Lincoln that was to take place a few weeks before the election. His curiosity grew enough that he abandoned work one Monday morning to go to the courthouse to witness it. He got there nearly an hour early, knowing that the courtroom would be crowded with people eager for a contest between two such opposite personalities. Thomas was already there in the front of the packed courtroom, pacing back and forth and conferring with his Democratic friends who were huddled near the witness chair, now and then taking a seat at the judge's bench as if to remind himself and the onlookers that it was still his property. A half hour before the debate was to begin, Lincoln had still not arrived, and Judge Thomas was growing agitated. He reminded Cage of a boxer who had prepared himself too early for the fight and could not hold on to his nervous energy any longer. Finally Thomas stalked once more back to the bench, standing behind it as he called for silence with his gavel.

"When Mr. Lincoln arrives," he announced in his high-pitched squeak of a voice, "our conversation will begin in earnest, but I see no reason why I should not issue a few remarks as preamble. And let us begin those remarks by reacquainting ourselves with Abraham Lincoln's long record of calumny and insult in the pages of the so-called newspaper the *Sangamo Journal*. If you'll recall, only a few years ago he was disguising himself as a character named Sampson's Ghost, who—"

Cage was sitting on the aisle on a bench toward the rear of the courtroom. He sprang up and left the room and sprinted across the square to Speed's store, where he found Lincoln in the upstairs bedroom in front of the looking glass, getting dressed for the confrontation that was not scheduled to begin for another half hour. Speed and Billy Herndon were with him.

"You'd better get over there right now," Cage said. "Thomas has already started the debate by himself."

"Started the debate? How can he do that if I'm not there?"

"See for yourself."

Lincoln ran down the stairs and out onto the street, pulling his coat over his shoulders as he went. His neckwear was askew and one side of his shirt collar, not yet buttoned, flapped up and down as he dashed across the square. When he made his way into the crowded courtroom, he stood at the back with Cage and Speed and Billy. Thomas was still speaking. He had not yet noticed Lincoln, and was so wrapped up in his oratory that he failed to register the hum of excitement that Lincoln's presence had brought to the room. The judge now stood in front of the bench, his hands clasped in front of him, his bug-eyed face with its eerie half smile swiveling slowly as he swept his head from left to right, right to left. He was talking now about something that he said had happened two years ago, when Lincoln or one of the Whig junto had published anonymous anti-Douglas letters in the *Journal* and set in motion a rumor that Thomas was the author.

"To what purpose was this done?" he asked the audience rhetorically. "Well, I think it's obvious. The Whigs could not abide me switching parties and wanted to discredit me among my new Democratic friends. Well, no one was fooled by their device, and—"

He had seen Lincoln now, who called out amiably from the back of the room as he finished tying down his collar. "Please continue, Judge. I didn't know I was going to hear all about myself before the debate started. I feel like the man who sat up in the casket at his own funeral and wanted to know who this exceptional individual was that everybody was talking about."

In one easy verbal swipe he had won the audience over to his side. Though Jesse Thomas did his best to get back on track, he couldn't concentrate with Lincoln there grinning at him from the back of the room. He kept to his theme of Lincoln's underhanded political maneuvering, but nobody cared any longer, and after a few minutes he muttered some concluding remarks and sat down.

This left the floor clear for Lincoln, who walked down the center aisle and stood in his courtroom posture in front of the judge's bench, staring at the floor. He was smiling a thin smile and shaking his head in wonderment at Thomas's charges. Cage knew him well enough to know he was angry, but the impression Lincoln sought to convey was that of a man saddened and stupefied by the low depths to which his opponent had sunk.

He dispensed with the high oratorical style he had used in his speech to the Young Men's Lyceum, and he didn't speak with the exaggerated folksiness he displayed at large campaign gatherings like the rally on the courthouse lawn. The courtroom was an unimposing setting that would hold only a few hundred people, so he barely needed to lift his voice to be heard. He spoke as if to a group of intimate friends.

"Thank you, Judge Thomas," he said, glancing over at his adversary, who was sitting now at the defense table, "for that expansive introduction. It's not every man who can say he has been handed a complete inventory of his failings. I believe if I go down the list and correct everything that Judge Thomas says is wrong with me, I'll emerge about as pure as a newborn Democrat."

It was such a graceful and good-natured riposte that even Thomas allowed himself to laugh along with the courtroom audience.

"And I'm also fortunate," Lincoln went on, "in that I've discovered in Judge Thomas such an example of learning and eloquence. He is inflated with those qualities as few men are. In fact, he is a veritable balloon of humanity, growing ever bigger and more perfect, swelling with wisdom until it seems he might float away from us and take up residence in the ether."

As he spoke, he began to somehow transform his angular face into an impression of Thomas's bulging amphibian features. He moved his eyes from side to side in imitation of his opponent's blank all-seeingness, and he also managed a perfect parody of his inscrutable grin. He held the pose for a good thirty seconds, saying nothing, just letting the absurdity of Judge Thomas's appearance wash over the audience, who were already not just laughing, but gasping. Then he began to mimic the judge's high-pitched voice.

"And he speaks," Lincoln said with the timbre of a mouse, "with an Olympian majesty that befits such a superior being. Now, if anyone were ever to dare to put a pin into this singular man, who is filled with so much wonderful air, the result of course would be a catastrophe. But who would do such a thing? Not me! I like him just the way he is!"

He continued to hold his face and body in the froggish aspect of Jesse Thomas, letting the impersonation linger. Cage was laughing, but he was starting to feel uneasy, thinking maybe the jest was going too far. But it went farther still, as Thomas's smile disappeared and his face began to turn red with embarrassment. Lincoln couldn't, or wouldn't, stop himself. He pantomimed what would happen if his opponent were in fact stuck with a pin, all the air sputtering out, his voice growing even higher, his eyes spinning wildly in confusion.

The laughter in the courtroom was delirious, but there was another sound beneath it, one that for a moment Cage found hard to credit. He turned to Speed, who was looking at him, an expression on his face of both confusion and confirmation. Someone was not just weeping, but sobbing. Then they both directed their attention to where Judge Jesse Thomas stood in front of the jury box, covering his reddened face with his hand and weeping in loud, convulsive heaves, exactly like a child. Lincoln was so involved in his comical character assassination that he failed to notice that his audience's quaking laughter had begun to subside into embarrassed silence. It was not until the laughter had almost entirely disappeared that Lincoln became aware of the awful bleating emitted by his shattered opponent.

"And if the good judge would only . . . ," he said, before letting the thought dissolve and staring at Thomas with a mixture of pity and horror. Thomas met his eyes, stuffed his hat on his head, and ran down the center aisle of the courtroom, still covering his face, still wracked with sobs as he burst out the front door.

Lincoln opened his mouth to speak, but he didn't know what to say. An accusatory silence enveloped the courtroom, and a voice called out, "Cruel! Cruel, sir!" The Democrats in the room took up the cry, or variations of it, and the Whigs seemed to understand it would be unseemly to mount a too enthusiastic defense of Lincoln when he had just reduced a man to tears. Lincoln just kept standing there uncertainly, absorbing the jeers, until Cage and Speed and Billy went to his rescue and removed him from the scene of the offense.

They retired to a curtained booth in Cornelius's coffeehouse, where Lincoln sat without touching a drop of his tea, looking perplexed and stricken.

"I admit that I meant to give him a skinning," he said in a hollow voice. "He deserved it. He came clawing at me before the debate started, when I wasn't even in the room."

"You were well within your rights," Billy said. "The man did you a terrible wrong."

"But was I cruel?"

No one answered him. He fixed Cage with an almost frightened look.

"Was I cruel?"

"You went a little far."

"I wouldn't worry about it," Speed said. "Some men can't bear ridicule, can't control their emotions. Poor Thomas. He'll never be able to live that down: crying like a child who's been slapped by a bully in a schoolyard."

"Maybe I'm the one who'll never be able to live it down. Maybe I'm the bully who slapped him."

They tried to cheer him up, to talk of other things, but Lincoln couldn't get his mind off the thought that there was something in his character, and not his opponent's, that had turned the day sour.

"I enjoyed it too much. I knew I had him, I could feel the hook in his mouth. A man ought not to enjoy another man's misery so much. He ought not to enjoy his misery at all. I've got to find him. I've got to apologize!"

He stood up abruptly, pulled back the curtain and left the booth. The coffeehouse was crowded and oppressively smoky, and the patrons noticed Lincoln as he walked out. They tracked him in silence for a moment until he disappeared out the door, and then turned busily back to arguing and gossiping among themselves about his satirical ferocity.

"What else was he to do after being attacked like that by Thomas?" Billy said to his companions in the booth. "He was within his rights. That's for sure."

"Still, he took it too far," Cage said, "and he knows it."

"Now that he's out of our hearing," Speed said, "I'll tell you what I thought. It was savage. He was trying to kill him with ridicule and you could tell by the look in his eyes that he meant no mercy. I didn't know Lincoln had that sort of savagery in him."

"We all do," Billy said, picking up his hat. "We're all merciless creatures at heart and sometimes it shows in even the best of us."

He stood up and walked away, leaving Cage and Speed to silently consider the black rot at the base of the human character. Speed poured sugar in his coffee and then stared into the cup with the look of a man who had just performed a scientific experiment and was waiting to examine the results. When he looked up again his eyes were filmy.

"I'm thinking of moving back to Kentucky."

"Why would you move back to Kentucky?"

"My father's dead."

"Oh. I'm sorry."

Speed blinked in an exaggerated manner, trying to blame the tears on the irritating effects of the smoke hovering in the dark room. He generally carried himself with insouciance, but there were Byronic moods in his temperament as well. He was as susceptible as Lincoln to the hypo—

perhaps that was why they got along so well. Likewise his loyalties—to friends, to family, to place—were dramatically deep. His father's death, which he was only now bothering to disclose, must have hit him hard.

"It happened a few weeks ago. My mother is overwhelmed," he explained. "You can imagine how much there is to deal with on a hemp plantation like ours. We've hired a temporary manager. He's a good man and can keep us on course for a while, but not for the long term. I'll have to move back. There are just too many things—estate issues, bills, crops, and then of course the slaves. We have a responsibility to the slaves—some of them I've known my whole life."

"Well, of course you have to go where your responsibilities take you, though I can hardly imagine this place without you. When will you leave?"

"Not until the spring, probably. Don't tell anyone yet, particularly not Lincoln. He has enough on his mind right now without having to think about finding a new place to live."

"He'll regret the absence of a friend more than the inconvenience."

"I don't think he's quite himself. Well, it's not a matter of just me thinking that. We saw it confirmed today. He's overworked. Campaigning for Harrison all over the state, as well as campaigning for his own reelection, then running his legal practice. At least the assembly's not in session, or he'd be dealing with that on top of everything else. He's exceptional, but it's so easy to imagine him coming to harm. He has to learn to govern himself. He wants things too hard."

Cage nodded, thinking as he did so how Speed's observation applied not just to Lincoln but to himself as well. The manuscript pages covering his desk, his anxiety that Gray and Bowen would find his collection acceptable, his hope that it would be exceptional; the image of Ellie, now at work in her shop, overseeing Cordelia and the other girl that she (and he) now employed, and the anticipation he felt that this was to be one of their nights together. If Judge Thomas or anyone else threatened to take all that away from him, wouldn't he attack just as hard, even as cruelly, as Lincoln had? How would Speed react if someone threatened to take away his hemp plantation and his slaves?

"If I leave," Speed said, "that makes one less person around to talk sense to him. He has a great capacity for errors in judgment. For instance, I'm afraid he might end up marrying the Todd girl."

"He might."

"Please don't try to tell me it wouldn't be a disaster. I like her, of course, but she's not for him. She's mercurial and dramatic and demanding. She'd come at him like a tornado. You should marry her instead."

"No thank you. And she's not interested in me."

"No, I suppose not. You're going to make a name for yourself, but you won't be scaling the particular heights she has in mind. If you ask me, she wants to be the wife of a president. Living down the road from Henry Clay would give you ideas of that sort, if you were an ambitious woman like she is."

"She and Lincoln might make a formidable team that way."

"Or she and Douglas, if she could stand to marry a tiny little Democrat. I bet she'd do it, but I think our friend interests her more."

Speed seemed to ponder this thought privately for a moment, then leaned back in his chair until it was tilted on its back legs and regarded Cage from across the table.

"And how is our other friend? I hear she's made quite a success in the millinery line. Don't stare at me like that. Are you worried I want to reclaim her somehow? Nothing could be further from my thoughts. She's a delightful girl and I'm glad she's making well. Are you and she still—"

"Yes," Cage said.

"I wonder. Can something like that—what you have with her—be enough to fill out a life?"

"I don't know."

"I suppose I'll find somebody to marry in Kentucky," Speed said. "And that will be that."

He said this in a gravely musing tone. He had turned sideways and was looking through the opened curtain of the booth at the window on the other side of the room. The great statehouse now rose commandingly in the center of the square, most of the scaffolding taken away so that its grandeur was plainly visible. It was not ready for occupancy yet, and the ground around it was still raw and dug up and filled with construction detritus, but it stood out cleanly in the heat of this July afternoon—a great prairie temple consecrated to the principles of human striving and conniving.

"By the way," Speed said after a moment, "do you want to buy me out? I'll make you a fair price. You can keep it running as a store or use the property for something else, I don't care."

"My money's tied up. I'm buying land in the Military Tract."

"That's a sound investment. The Military Tract will pay off once this state gets going at full speed. Well, I'd hoped you'd buy the place so Lincoln would still have a place to live, but I suppose he can get a room at Butler's. He already takes his meals there. In any case, it probably won't be long before he comes to rest in the arms of Miss Todd."

Lincoln succeeded in making his apology to Thomas and shaking hands with him in the middle of the square in full view of the citizens of Springfield. He went out campaigning again and came home a few weeks later. Cage saw him only briefly at Speed's store. He looked exhausted and depleted, interested only in huddling with Baker to try to come up with some strategy or other to keep the Democrats from packing the polling places with Irish railroad and canal workers they had brought in from St. Louis. The great national contest for president was still several months off, but the state and local elections were immediate, and on the day of voting there was scuffling in the streets between the Whigs and the imported Democrats, who had been drinking their patrons' free whiskey and apparently had been told that the polls needed to be defended from members of the opposite party who might be so brazen as to cast a vote.

Lincoln won reelection but by too thin a margin to justify rejoicing, and his victory over Thomas only served to remind voters of his relentlessness in turning his opponent into a blubbering heap. Overall, the Whigs suffered badly, losing to the Democrats in both houses of the assembly. Before Cage could even console him, Lincoln was gone again, back to Egypt for more campaigning to deliver Illinois for Harrison in the November election, back on the judicial circuit to manage more cases for his and Stuart's over-stretched law firm.

There was another party at the Edwards house when Mary returned from Missouri in September, but Lincoln was out of town for that too.

"Good God," Ash Merritt whispered to Cage when he saw Mary enter the room. "Is that the same person?"

She was a small-statured woman and even a few pounds would have made a difference in her appearance, but she must have put on fifteen or twenty during the months she had been away, months no doubt of endless nighttime parties and buffets and afternoons of exquisite Southern idleness. The sufficiency of weight suited her, in a way; it certainly didn't seem to bother her and it made her even more of a presence. She moved through the room tearfully hugging Julia Jayne and Mercy Levering and all the other young ladies of Springfield she had so sorely missed. When she made her way to Cage she asked about him eagerly, about his writing, about his business, then grabbed him by the elbow and dragged him a few feet away from the vortex of the party, next to a little table bearing a stern-looking statuette of Dante.

"He's been writing me," she whispered. The added volume in her face enhanced her smile and seemed to take some of the acerbity out of her manner. "Did you tell him to?"

"Of course I didn't. If he's writing to you it's because he wants to."

"The poor man is having a rough time. On horseback all day, wearing the same hickory shirt from one stop to the next. He seems very tired, and his accommodations are wretched. But I think he revives himself somewhat when he has to debate or give a speech."

"Yes, that's a reliable remedy for Lincoln. Does he say when he's coming back?"

"Not until after the election in November. He says he wants to see me as soon as he gets home. What do you think that can mean?"

"I don't know. I'm unschooled in such matters."

"Such matters as what? Please be specific."

"I can't be specific. I don't know anything." He lowered his voice, though they were alone in their little corner and could probably not be overheard. "I don't know if he's making love to you or not."

But he was afraid that was what was happening. Weary horseback miles, bad food, crowded flea-infested beds in substandard rooming houses, dirty clothes, anger at the lies told by political opponents in debates, submerged concern about the falsehoods he was telling in return, chronic anxiety about whether he could deliver Illinois for Harrison; and along with all of that the stress of the many cases to be acquainted with and argued for or against on the legal circuit, leading inevitably to overwork, confusion, loneliness: it was enough to make any man start writing letters to a woman, particularly a woman like Mary, whose letters in return would be so sharp and witty and full of bracing political understanding. The kind of letters that could convince a man he had fallen in love.

TWENTY

✦✦✦

L INCOLN'S VOICE WAS STRAINED from months of speaking
and debating all around Illinois. His spirits were strained as well.
"The last thing I want to do right now," he confessed to Cage in a rasp
as he tried to make himself heard above the conversational noise in the
crowded space of the Presbyterian church, "is give another speech."

All those days and nights of bad food and long horseback miles and
dirty inns filled with snoring men showed in his appearance. He had
lost weight again, of course, which had the effect of exaggerating his
verticality, turning him into a lonely, shriveled human tree. He was
wearing a once-good suit that had been much abused in his travels and
had lost its drape and now hung on his thin body like a funereal sack.

The church had become a de facto public space ever since the assembly started meeting there until the final touches could be put on the
statehouse. The gathering on this November night was a Whig victory celebration. Harrison had just decisively won the presidency over
Van Buren. But for Lincoln the triumph was muted, since he had been
determined not just to elect a president but to make sure the Whigs carried Illinois, and in the end the Whigs did not carry Illinois.

"So is *she* here?" he asked. His neck looked as long as a snapping
turtle's as it swayed back and forth over the crowd.

"I haven't seen her."

"I think I may have gotten myself a little bit embriggled with her."

"Yes, that's my impression."

"It is? When did you talk to her? What did she say?"

But there was no time to answer him because Ned Baker had just
taken the pulpit and was asking the crowd to welcome that great Whig
stalwart and towering state legislative leader Abraham Lincoln.

The weariness and doubt that had been in Lincoln's demeanor an instant before vanished as he turned from Cage and headed to the front of the church, where he shook Ned Baker's hand and led the victorious Whig faithful in a hurrah for Harrison. He promptly began to paint a vivid picture of the national paradise that was to come under President Harrison's leadership, with good sound currency in good sound banks, with men rewarded fairly for their labor and the farmers and pork packers and manufacturers of Sangamon County and the rest of Illinois blessed with a system of internal improvements untainted by speculation and graft.

He had been speaking for ten minutes when the door of the church opened and Ninian Edwards and his wife entered, followed by Mary Todd arm in arm with the most beautiful young woman Cage had ever seen. This must be, he realized, the Edwards niece Mary had told him about last summer. Matilda. She was three or four inches taller than Mary, who—still carrying the extra weight she had accumulated during her time away—looked almost squat beside her. Cage had seen Matilda walk only a few steps, from the door to the side of the church, where the crowd was thinner and the view better, but her gracile gait was mesmerizing, the skirt of her dress ebbing and flowing in a way that revealed to the imagination the long and perfectly formed legs that were hidden under it. She was blond, judging by the glimpse of parted hair visible beneath the crown of her bonnet with its discreet flowery trim. Her brilliant blue eyes surveyed the church with interest and curiosity, unaware or choosing to be unaware that everyone was trying not to stare at her.

Lincoln was still speaking, finishing his remarks as fluently as if this beguiling distraction had not entered the room. But he had seen her too, and Cage knew Lincoln well enough to detect that even as he continued speaking—about Harrison and Tyler and the duty of all Whigs to stand solidly beside them for the good of the country—he was not in full command of his own attention. He roused the audience to cheers even as his own expression betrayed a sudden and bewildered yearning.

"Of course," Ellie said to Cage that night in the back of her shop. She was sitting in a chair in her chemise, her hair down, catching up on backed-up work orders as she sewed lace onto the collar of a client's pekin dress. "I know all about Miss Edwards. Everybody's been talking about her for weeks. They say somebody—a Mr. Strong, I think—believes she loves him and has asked her to marry him but she's not eager just yet to tie herself down. I suppose she wants to have a look at what's available in Springfield."

She looked up at him from her sewing.

"Did you see her?"

"I saw her. I didn't have a chance to talk to her."

"Well, you will. And anyway, I understand that it's not necessary to talk to her to fall in love with her. Is she as beautiful as everyone says?"

"Yes."

"So will you?"

"Will I what?"

"Fall in love with her?"

"Would you like me to?"

"Yes. I think you ought."

She spoke lightly, banteringly, but Cage could feel the steel of truth in her voice as well.

"And what would become of you if that should happen?" he asked.

"Nothing would become of me. We'd still be friends. We'd still be business associates. As long as the shop continues to make money."

"If it didn't, I would cut you off. Is that what you think?"

"If I didn't make money for you, you should very well cut me off."

"I'm not that inconstant."

"Constancy's a term of love, not a term of business. You should understand which is which."

She had him off-balance, as usual. She enjoyed seeing him uncertain about whether she was speaking with ruthless honesty or with teasing domesticity. He wanted to kiss her but that was over with for the evening. She liked to talk after they had been to bed but now that she had so much work to do she seemed to regard lovemaking itself as a session with a defined beginning and end.

"Anyway," she went on, "you'll finish your book and publish it, and the world will hail you as a genius, and I'll no longer be enough for you. You'll need a wife, a proper wife like Matilda Edwards."

"You and Mary Todd both seem to think I should marry her, but for different reasons. In your case, it's because you want to get rid of me. In hers, I'm pretty sure, it's so she can make sure she's off-limits to Lincoln."

"I don't want to get rid of you," Ellie said. "You make me sound much colder than I am. I like this—" With the hand that held her sewing needle she gestured around the room, a gesture that included her in her chemise, Cage in his shirtsleeves and unbuttoned waistcoat creaking back and forth in a rocking chair, two people who had fallen into an undefined, unsettled, unyielding dependency. "I want it to go on and on until we tire of it."

"Good," he replied. "So do I."

He saw Matilda again a few days later when Ninian and Elizabeth Edwards once again hosted a party, this one to mark the start of the legislative session. Edwards himself was in a sour and formal mood, still simmering over the fact that he had been dropped from the ticket in the last election, a casualty of the rest of the Whigs in Illinois believing that too much power was concentrated in Springfield. But he had swallowed his outrage and was now doing his part, standing with Mrs. Edwards to receive his guests as they came out of the early winter cold into the mansion.

Billy Herndon and his new wife Mary Ann were among them. One day last March he had announced that he was moving out of Speed's store and getting married to the daughter of the town marshal. Billy was younger than all of them and on the surface his unbendable political passions and his abiding anger at his father would have appeared to make him the least inclined to domestic happiness, but here he was, with his calm and affectionate new wife. He was studying law now too, talking to anyone who would listen about Blackstone and Chitty and all the other weighty tomes he was working his way through. The Herndons drifted over to the edge of the small cluster of dazzled young men—Cage among them—who had gathered around Matilda Edwards.

"Oh, I love it here!" she was saying. "It's so dull in Alton. Springfield seems like the center of the world."

"Springfield's having a hard time just now being the center of Illinois," Joshua Speed said. Poor Speed. He could not hide the radiant want that lit up his face, the tremor in his voice when he spoke to her.

"Oh? Why is that?"

"Well, there are all these internal improvement projects that are unfinished, debt is piling up, and the rest of the state thinks all the problems originate in the capital, which of course they do."

"Well, the rest of the state should understand that big things like railroads take time," she said. "I certainly do. I can wait."

"That's because you're young," Speed said.

"Oh, are you old, Mr. Speed? You don't look old to me."

She touched his arm and laughed when she said this, showing her gloriously even teeth. She was comfortable with being adored; it made her generous and eager to put other people at ease. Cage saw in Speed's expression that the feel of Matilda's hand on his broadcloth sleeve registered with the force of a burning iron. Bat Webb, an assembly member from White County, who really was old—close to forty—stared at Matilda with dumb admiration, as did Billy Herndon, despite the fact that his new wife was standing next to him. Cage didn't know if the hunger showed in his own eyes as vividly as it did in those of the others. Her physical perfection drew him in, of course, but it made him uncomfortable as well, because there was no escaping it, no way to stop gauging whether there might be a reciprocal interest on her part. For that reason it was exhausting to be in her presence. And she had the kind of beauty that seemed like it ought to be the outward manifestation of deep intelligence and wisdom, but so far she had said nothing beyond expected pleasantries.

She had asked him about himself and when he told her he was at work on a book of poetry there was a mild look of alarm in her eyes, as if she didn't know what to say next. It was easier to have a conversation with her if you just asked her questions about herself. How long would she stay in Springfield? Was she looking forward to the cotillion season? Did she have sisters and brothers back home in Alton?

While they were all quizzing Matilda, Cage swept his eyes from time to time to a corner of the big parlor, where Lincoln and Mary Todd stood by themselves, deep in conversation. Or at least Mary was deep in conversation. Lincoln stood with his hands hanging at his side, bending down from his great height to meet her eyes, to nod at whatever she was saying, but now and then his attention would pivot in a way he thought subtle to Matilda Edwards and the admirers surrounding her. After keeping him to herself as long as she could, stranding him on the other side of the room, Mary brought him over to introduce him to her dear friend Matilda.

"Oh, I'm glad to meet you!" Matilda said with a beaming smile. "I know all about you, of course. Everyone does. I read about you in the newspapers all the time."

"I hope you're doing all your reading about me in the Whig papers," Lincoln said. "They tend to be more charitable about my defects."

"Your defects are never mentioned, Mr. Lincoln, and I doubt that they even exist."

She regarded him with radiant eyes and a lingering smile that left Lincoln incoherent. After a moment Ninian Edwards came and captured his cousin and drew her away to another group of legislators who had demanded to meet her. With Matilda no longer there to hold them in thrall, Cage and the others dispersed, accepting drinks from the liveried and indentured Negro waiters or helping themselves from a platter of glistening oysters.

Mary had Lincoln to herself again, chattering away to him, rising up on tiptoe to whisper in his ear, laughing, evoking distracted laughter from him in return. Her face, with its healthy new bounty of flesh, seemed lit from within like the globe of a lamp.

The conversation in the room died off as a group of bell ringers that Ninian Edwards had hired for the occasion trailed in playing "Jim Along Josie." Mary broke into a delighted smile and clapped her hands in time to the lively song, and turned to Lincoln and bid him to do the same. He obeyed, but his clapping was mechanical and off the beat and he looked like a man who was struggling to wake from a perplexing dream.

Cage and Speed left the party together at eleven o'clock that night, slipping past the other departing guests standing outside the Edwards mansion waiting for their carriages to be brought up. The temperature had fallen but there was no wind and it was a fine night for walking.

"Have you ever seen a creature quite that exquisite before?" Speed asked.

"No, I don't think I have." But the truth was that, for Cage, Matilda's beauty was like a thing in itself, a completed thing like a painting. With Ellie, there seemed something always to be added, something yet to be understood. So when Speed abruptly announced his intention to marry her, Cage felt no competitive resentment, just a sense of comradely caution.

"You'd better waste no time in trying," he said. "Did you see the way she was surrounded tonight?"

"Of course I saw it. And she saw it too, of course. She knows exactly what a prize she is. It's driving me crazy already."

They had gone several hundred yards when they heard frantic footsteps from behind and turned to see Lincoln sprinting to catch up. When he reached them he planted his feet and came to an awkward accordion-like stop. It took him a few seconds to collect his breath as he bent over, his hands on his knees.

"I need to talk," he gasped.

They walked to Speed's store, where they watched Lincoln as he crouched in front of the stove stirring up the flames with a bellows. He did this for a disconcertingly long time without bothering to speak. He looked miserable, and the reflection of the flames—highlighting the despairing hollows of his eyes—made him look more miserable still. His urgent need to talk seemed to have evaporated and he had sunk into a solitude from which Cage—impatient and sleepy now—decided it was time to rouse him.

"For God's sake, Lincoln," he said, "what's the matter?"

Lincoln moved from his crouch into a nearby chair. He had taken his boots off and his feet, clad in ragged gray wool socks that needed washing, looked as disproportionately large as a rabbit's.

"The matter is that I don't think I want to marry her."

"Mary Todd?"

He nodded solemnly.

"Well, then don't marry her," Speed said. "People don't marry other people every day."

Lincoln was silent, wiggling his great feet by the fire.

"Wait a minute," Cage said. "Are you saying you've asked her?"

"I don't know. We were sending letters back and forth for a month or so. I may have gotten a little caught up in the spirit of it."

"So you're engaged?"

"I can't remember everything I wrote to her. It doesn't seem to me that we are, but she might have a different view. You know how it is when somebody writes you a letter. When you write it's like you've heard the tone they're using and you naturally try to match it."

"Did you tell her you loved her?" Cage asked.

"It's possible. I might have told her that."

"But you didn't specifically ask her to marry you?"

"No, now that I reflect about it, I'm pretty sure that I didn't."

"That's good," Speed said. "That's very good. You haven't quite put your foot into the bear trap yet."

"The thing is," Lincoln mused, "I want to marry that other girl."

"What other girl?"

"Miss Edwards. The one who was at the party tonight. I think that if I married her I'd be happier all around."

Speed shifted his eyes to Cage, but said nothing to betray that Lincoln had a rival around the fire. Since the rivalry for Miss Edwards was thick to begin with, maybe it wasn't even worth mentioning.

"I'm going to write Molly a letter," Lincoln declared.

"Who's Molly?" Speed asked.

"His pet name for Mary," Cage said.

"Good Lord, you have a pet name for her? You can't break it off too soon!"

"I'll write her tonight and tell her I love Matilda Edwards instead."

"Are you insane?" Cage said. "Don't do that."

"Well, I think I have to give her a reason, don't you? And I have to be honest. I won't lie to her."

"For one thing, you can't possibly be in love with Matilda Edwards. You hardly know her. And for another, you'll make an enemy of Mary if you tell her you're dropping her for somebody else, and Mary Todd is someone you don't want for your enemy."

"What do I tell her then?"

"I don't know," Cage said. "Tell her that you've greatly enjoyed your conversations with her, both in letters and in person, but you find you're so presently oversubscribed with your political and legal activities that regrettably you must fade away from such rich companionship, but trust that sometime in the future . . . and cetera and cetera."

"She'd have to be very stupid to believe a word of that," Lincoln said. "And she's very far from stupid. And like I said, I have to tell the truth, or at least some part of it. Maybe I don't have to mention Miss Edwards but I have to tell Molly that I don't love her. It has to be clean and it has to be fair. I'll write her tonight."

"No," Speed said, "don't write her. You have to tell her face to face."

"Why?"

"Because it would be the coward's way. And because once you put your words in writing she can read them again and again. In her poor broken heart, they'll be a living and eternal monument against you."

Lincoln chewed over this advice with a look of deepening anguish, finally turning to Cage.

"What do you think?"

"Speed's right. You have to do her the honor of telling her in person."

TWENTY-ONE

◆◆◆

THE NEXT AFTERNOON Speed showed up, frantic and unannounced, at Cage's door.

"You've got to take Lincoln off my hands!"

"What are you talking about?"

"He says he wants to kill himself, and my store is full of kitchen knives and axes and razors and all sorts of deadly implements."

"He says what?"

"Do you have guns here? Knives?"

"No guns. I have a bowie knife from the war. A letter opener. A razor. I can't think of anything else."

"Hide them away. Leave them with Mrs. Hopper or somebody. Come on. Billy Herndon is with him now, but the sooner we get him out of the store the better."

As they walked across the square Speed did his best to relate what had happened. "He went to the Edwards house this morning to break it off with her like we told him to do. Face to face, no ambiguity, a clean break. But she started crying, of course, and he didn't know what to do, so he dug himself in deeper. He said he took her on his knee and kissed her, and now she thinks they're in love again. It's a bad lick, Cage. He's in deeper than he was before."

"So he wants to *kill* himself?"

Speed answered with a fatalistic shrug as they entered the store and climbed to the upstairs room where he and Lincoln lived. When they opened the door they heard Lincoln give a startled yell and saw him back across the room to stand against the far wall, exactly the way a caged wild animal might have reacted to an expected intruder.

"Calm down, Mr. Lincoln," Billy Herndon said. "It's just your friends.

"I can't get him to talk to me," Billy said to Cage and Speed. "He just keeps saying he wants to die over and over."

"You know me, don't you?" Cage said softly to Lincoln.

"Of course I do. I haven't gone insane. I know everybody I'm supposed to know."

But his eyes were darting back and forth, his breathing was rapid, and there was a frightening animus in his expression. Some internal spring had broken and as a result the whole mechanism of his being appeared to be racing but going nowhere.

"I'm going to take you home with me," Cage told him.

"Why? I don't want to go home with you. I don't want to go home with anybody. I don't want to be anywhere. I just want to be dead and you gentlemen are in my way. Please leave me alone."

"You know we won't do that."

"If you were truly my friends you would."

For a moment, Cage thought Lincoln's derangement might be an elaborate jest. It didn't seem possible that a man of his intelligence and acuity could lose his bearings so utterly, and for such a character reversal to happen in the course of a single day. But as brilliant as Lincoln was at telling stories, he was no actor. He could not have faked the pain and despair that were in his eyes.

For all his agitation, he was strangely compliant, obedient as a child when Cage walked across the room and took his hand. He led him down the stairs, Lincoln walking behind and muttering that he would kill himself one way or another no matter where Cage took him. It was only a matter of time and opportunity and there was no reason to postpone the matter.

"All right," Cage said, "but if you're determined to do it there's no hurry and no reason why we can't discuss it."

Lincoln was immune to logic, but a commiserating tone seemed to have some sort of calming effect. Or perhaps this was due to the fact that they were now out on the street, in full view of his friends and constituents, and there was enough of the politico still residing in his tortured mind to not want to be shamed in front of them. For that reason Cage let go of his friend's hand and simply walked close to his side the few blocks to the Palatine and pretended to be in an intense conversation with him. Passersby nodded or tipped their hats to Lincoln and he had enough wits left to smile vacantly in return.

When they got to the house, Cage ushered Lincoln rapidly through the parlor, where Theophilous Emry still worked in an orphaned way on his French. "Is that Mr. Lincoln?" he called out in surprise, but Lincoln didn't answer and Cage pretended that neither had heard him. They managed to get to the stairway without encountering Mrs. Hopper, but on the landing they passed Ellie on her way out on an errand. She smiled and opened her mouth to say something but must have seen the grim look on Cage's face, so she just nodded a quick greeting and went down the stairs.

Cage opened the door to his room and ushered Lincoln inside, then ordered him to take off his coat and hat and sit down. Lincoln complied distractedly, handing his coat and hat to Cage as if to a servant, but he was too agitated to sit. He paced around the room, glancing at the pictures on the walls, grabbing books off the shelves and putting them back without looking at them. Before he had left with Speed, Cage had taken his bowie knife out of his desk drawer and his razor off the washstand and hidden them beneath his mattress. But the way Lincoln was so nervously inspecting everything made him worry that he would happen upon them.

"Do you think you could make an effort to sit down and tell me what happened?"

Lincoln sat down in a chair but then sprang up again. A sudden wave of lucidity passed over his face. "Nothing happened. Well, nothing that was supposed to. I'd written out and memorized what I was going to say to her. I thought it was best to get the brutal truth out as soon as possible, so I told her I'd made a mistake and that I didn't love her. You should have seen the look of shock on her face, the power of her suffering. It was like I'd hit her over the head with a skillet. And then she started crying, of course, and begging me to say it wasn't true."

"And that's what you said?"

"Yes, I told her I loved her after all. What else could I do? The poor woman was so miserable! When I recanted, when I told her what she wanted to hear, it was like watching a child wake up from a terrible nightmare. And now the nightmare is mine, and I have to end it."

"There are ways to end a nightmare without killing yourself."

"So it might seem to you. I have no interest in any other course, and if you and Speed think you can talk me out of it, or keep me from it, you've deluded yourselves."

"Hasn't the session started? Shouldn't you be there?"

"What does it matter? The whole internal improvements system is a disaster. The bond payments alone might bankrupt the state. And it's all my fault. It would be a favor to the voters if I were dead and unable to cause any more mischief. And if the Democrats want to destroy the state bank, let them! I'll be happily underground. Nobody will remember me, nobody will care about me, and that's the way it should be."

Cage tried to make him eat, to take coffee, or to set aside his temperance habits and have a glass of whiskey, but Lincoln would hear none of it. All he wanted to do was talk about how he had no choices left but to destroy himself or live the rest of his life with a woman he did not love.

"I think you must love her at least a little bit," Cage ventured at one point.

"No, I love Matilda Edwards."

"You've barely met Matilda Edwards."

"It doesn't matter. I can't have her in any case. If I have to live, I have to marry Molly. Honor demands it. To get rid of myself would be an act of kindness to her, and the poor bewildered creature deserves at least that much."

He talked on for hours, his eyes wild with fatal determination. He said the same things over and over again, sometimes varying the words a little but never straying from the themes that were torturing him—the futility of his life, the demands of honor, the hurt he had caused an innocent soul. Cage was growing hungry but he could not take Lincoln out in this condition or leave him alone in the room while he saw to his own dinner, so he steeled himself for a long, hungry night. At about midnight he managed to talk Lincoln into getting into the bed, making sure his restless guest occupied the side next to the wall so he couldn't slip away without Cage being aware of it. After they were in bed Lincoln talked with perfect but manic coherence for an hour more about how he wanted to die, unable to let go of the topic, unable to recognize that everything he was saying he had already said four or five dozen times before. At some point in the early hours of the morning he fell silent, but it was a loud silence, a brooding so intense it radiated outward like the heat from a stove. Lying next to him, Cage drifted off for a few minutes and woke to the sense of Lincoln next to him in the bed. He was sitting upright, staring into the center of the dark room, maybe even silently plotting the details of how he would depart from life.

Cage dared not speak to his ghostly bedmate for fear that doing so would stir up another endless soliloquy. This was the second time he had shared a sleepless night in bed with Abraham Lincoln, and that other night now came back to him with heartbreaking clarity: the two of them in Lincoln's cramped room in the Carmans' cabin in New Salem, talking until dawn about poetry, about love, about destiny and death and the imperative of being remembered beyond the grave. Sleep had been impossible because there was too much to be said, too much life to be desperately lived. How had it happened that that wondrous future life had suddenly become such a burden and a horror to him, something that needed to be swatted away like a crawling spider?

Cage remembered standing in a bank office in Marseille, reading the suicide letter that had been handed him by his father's banker. His father had been a quiet-mannered man, kind to everyone, much admired by his friends, a companionable and indulgent figure to his only surviving child. He was unlike Lincoln. He was not a captivating storyteller and his political philosophy, if he had one, was a personal secret. But he had been a man of rigid honor and, as with Lincoln, that honor had turned somehow to shame.

Lincoln finally lay down again and Cage fell into a vivid half-sleep, in which he saw a scene clearer than he could have encountered it in life. A man sitting on a rock, waiting patiently for the tide to come in, a man who had never before touched a needle and thread clumsily sewing shut coat pockets filled with round, sea-washed stones. A seal lifting its head out of the water twenty yards offshore, staring at the man, the man staring back, the tide coming in and the cold water filling his boots. Feeling resolve more than fear; in fact no fear at all, no regret, just a harrowing, relentless need whose satisfaction was now the towering goal of his life.

It was the material of a poem, arising from terrible real-life memory and from hallucinatory sleep, a poem that might help provide his unfinished collection with a binding resonance. He sat up in bed, meaning to go to his desk and write something down: the face of that seal, its neutral curiosity. But his desk was occupied. While he had been dreaming, Lincoln had apparently risen. He was searching through the drawers of Cage's desk.

"What are you doing?" Cage asked, afraid that Lincoln was looking for some novel instrument to kill himself with. "Stay out of there. There's nothing that will help you."

Lincoln turned to face him. "I was looking for a piece of paper so I can write you a note. I didn't want to tear a page out of your notebooks."

He rubbed the stubble on his face and stretched his arms. He looked weary and resigned, purged of the frightening energy that had kept him awake all night. His suicidal mood had broken in the night like a fever. "I didn't want to wake you but I thought I owed you a few lines of gratitude. Don't worry, I decided to go through with it."

"Go through with what?"

"With being alive. Being alive and being married to Molly. Like my father always told me, when you make a bad bargain you hug it the tighter."

"That sounds like the worst sort of advice."

"Well, Cage, you can have me dead, or you can have me hugging a bad bargain. Which is it? And where can we get some breakfast?"

"Will you come see me this afternoon?" was all that the note from Mary Todd said. There was a question mark at the end of the sentence, but he could guess from the authoritative brevity of her message that she was not really asking a question but issuing a summons. Her handwriting, with its cramped, thickly inked letters, gave off the same starchy sense of expectation.

It was a few days after Lincoln's catastrophic interview with Mary, the incident that had driven him to the edge of the precipice. He seemed to be functioning well enough now, but once a man had gone that crazy there was no guarantee that suicide would not remain a chronic entice-ment. Cage was not sure he wanted to see Mary right now, especially when he felt ordered to do so, but he was curious about the nature of the strange embrigglement between Mr. Lincoln and Miss Todd, and thought that the more he knew about it, the better the chance he had of keeping his friend's sanity secure.

"Have you heard?" she said when he presented himself yet again in the parlor of the Edwards home. "He's jumped out of a window."

"Is he dead?"

She blinked at him in surprise. Her face had been tense, her eyes red, perhaps from crying, but now there appeared a look of mordant amusement. "Of course not. Why would you think that? Is that even possible? I don't think there's a building in Springfield that's taller than Abraham Lincoln. No, he hasn't killed himself, just embarrassed him-self, I'm afraid."

She had heard the news from her brother-in-law. The papers would no doubt be full of it tomorrow. It had happened this morning at the Presbyterian church, where the assembly was still meeting before mov-ing to the new statehouse next week.

"The Democrats were conniving to require the state bank to redeem its notes in specie. Well, of course, that's just their way of killing the bank and sowing havoc and making people miserable, which is all that Demo-crats care about. They came up with a trick of adjourning sine die and when the Whigs tried to keep them from having a quorum the sergeant at arms rounded them all up—even from their *sickbeds,* some of them— and locked them—locked them!—in the church. So the Democrats had their quorum, but apparently Lincoln thought he could still defeat it so he and two Whigs jumped out the window. It didn't work, though. The quorum held—or at least the Speaker ruled that it held. Which is what you would expect, since he's a Democrat. Now everyone is laughing at Lincoln and saying there's something wrong with his mind."

She stared at Cage. "Is there?"

"He hasn't been his normal self."

"In what sense has he not been his normal self? For heaven's sake, his normal self is not normal in the first place."

"I think he's confused."

"About me? He told me he loved me. Does he not?"

"If he told you he did, of course he does."

She sat perfectly still on the horsehair sofa. She had not called for one of the servants to offer him anything to eat or drink. They could hear women's voices from upstairs, singing.

"That's my sister and Matilda. They like to sing together. I don't recognize the song, do you?"

Cage said he didn't. He could only make out bits of an unfamiliar melody, and none of the words. But Matilda's voice was clear and strong, a perfect match for her note-perfect beauty.

"You're right," she said. "He's very confused. I suppose he told you that he came to see me."

She saw that Cage was stalling for an answer and said, "Never mind. Maybe he didn't tell you. Women talk about these things openly with each other but I don't suppose men do. Or if they do they pretend they don't. I don't understand men at all. I doubt that I ever will. Are you finished with your book?"

"Not yet."

"Please do hurry. I don't understand why it's taking so long. Why does everything have to take so long? I can't stand how slow the pace of life is. If things happened faster, people would be happier."

"Maybe, but life might be over too soon."

"What do you care? All you do is sit at your desk. I notice you haven't yet offered your affections at Matilda's shrine."

"There are plenty of other men doing that. I don't like being in a crush."

"You shouldn't be so solitary. No, I take that back. You should be solitary. It's your nature, and it's interesting. So whether you court Matilda or not—whether you court anybody or not—I don't care."

But she did care. She wanted someone to take Matilda off her hands, and soon. Lincoln hadn't told Mary he was in love with Matilda—or that he thought he was in love with her—but she was shrewd enough to understand that the crisis between her and the man she had thought was her suitor had come upon the heels of Matilda's arrival in Springfield.

"Anyway," she continued, "that's not the reason I asked you to see me. We're getting up an expedition to Jacksonville over Christmas. Mr. and Mrs. Hardin have asked us to visit them in their home. It's said to be lovely and they are so gracious to invite us. Lincoln will be there, and Speed, and two or three others. Will you join the van as well? I'm praying for snow so we can have a sleigh ride there. I want you along for the pleasure of your company, of course, but also because Lincoln seems to be in a confused state and I'm worried about him. He needs his friends around him."

Mary was right. The papers were full of Lincoln's leap out of the window. In the *Sangamo Journal,* Sim Francis saw to it that the act was portrayed as a heroic last-minute effort to deny the Democrats a quorum and postpone a vote that would have the effect of destroying the state bank and ruining the economy. But since the vote had already occurred, that interpretation was only the Whig press trying to make the best of things.

"I was feeling peculiar," Lincoln admitted to Cage and Speed around the stove in the store that night. "You know how it is in that church. We were all packed together in the first place, and they had locked all the doors and the sergeant at arms had stationed guards in front of them. After the vote, I just couldn't breathe. I don't know why. I just had to get out of there, so I ran upstairs and opened a window."

"You could have broken a leg jumping out of a window like that," Speed said.

"It wasn't that far off the ground. I just sort of eased myself out. Maybe if I'd broken a leg people wouldn't be laughing at me so hard."

He laughed himself, not too bitterly, a hint of his old self-deprecating good humor. Cage and Speed exchanged a quick look, gauging each other's impressions of the state of their friend's mental health. Lincoln had moved back to Speed's the night after the suicide vigil in Cage's room, and seemed generally sound again, but there was always the possibility that the armature that supported his remarkable character was somehow permanently askew.

"I would have done the same thing," Cage told him now.

"What? Jumped out of a window?"

"I remember what it was like in that cabin at Kellogg's Grove before you and the rest of those men rode up. I felt like I was going to suffocate."

"Well, it's kind of you to say that, Cage. I'd like to think that being surrounded by Democrats is about the same as being surrounded by hostile Indians, but my common sense rebels."

He was sitting in a hard wooden chair, his legs stretched out, his coat off, his cravat untied, his chin resting in the spreading wings of his collar. He wore a velvet waistcoat that needed laundering, gravy having been spilled on it several meals past. He looked slowly from Cage to Speed and back again.

"Does it seem to you gentlemen that I'm losing my wits altogether?"

"Sometimes," Speed admitted.

"And now news comes to me by way of Miss Todd that we're all going to Jacksonville together."

"Would you rather we didn't?" Cage asked.

"No, it'll be a grand party, I'm sure. And it's always good to be out of town after you've made a fool of yourself. And I've made a fool of myself twice over this week."

He stood up and grabbed another oak log to feed the fire in the stove, tamping it into place with the poker. "Speaking of making a fool of yourself," he said, "I'm reminded of this old sucker we knew back in Indiana. A peculiar-looking fellow, with the biggest, shaggiest eyebrows you've ever seen. Well, one morning he goes out with his rifle hoping to shoot a squirrel for his breakfast. He spots a lively one on a tree branch not twenty yards from the house. He primes his rifle and takes aim and shoots, but he doesn't hit the squirrel and what's more the squirrel pays no attention at all to being shot at. So the old sucker loads and fires again, and the squirrel's still wriggling on the tree branch but staying in the same spot and still no more concerned about the sound of that rifle shot than a cloud passing over. The man loads and shoots thirteen more times and the squirrel's still there. He turns to his little son, who's been standing there watching all the time, and tells him, By jings, there's something wrong with my rifle. I been trying to hit that squirrel all morning and he's still standing there on that tree branch. So the son says, I don't see any squirrel at all, Pap.

"What do you mean you don't see any squirrel? the man says. Hell, he's right there, how can you miss seeing him? But the son still can't see the squirrel, and finally he turns to look at his old dad. And he looks at his face some more and breaks out laughing. I see your squirrel, Pap, he says finally. Why, he's right there and he ain't on a tree at all. Your squirrel ain't nothing but a louse in your eyebrow!"

When Lincoln began telling the story, the solemnity of his own mood bled into it, so that Cage was not expecting a funny tale at all but some sort of gloomy parable. As Lincoln continued to tell it, his inflection remained flat, and sometimes as he poked at the fire he affected to have forgotten his own narrative, and had to pause to recall it. He let the humor creep up on his two listeners and the story was explosively funny in the end, less for its merits than in the way the pleasure of telling it brought life back into Lincoln's face.

He was himself again for a moment or two, laughing along with Cage and Speed, but as the laughter fell off he withdrew once more into a black cloud of reflection. There was silence around the stove until he spoke again.

"I like her well enough, I reckon. There's no reason in the world not to marry her. She's the smartest woman I've ever met and a good-looking woman too, even with extra tonnage she's carrying around these days. I just panicked, that's all, the way I panicked being shut up in that church. But I couldn't break her heart when it came to it, so I guess that means I must love her or have some similar emotion about her after all."

"But you're still not formally engaged?" Cage asked.

"Well, nothing specific has been said in that regard, but I'd be surprised if she didn't think we were—so I guess we are."

He was seated in the chair again now, tilting back, staring up at the ceiling, his arms hanging at his sides.

"The two of you don't have to keep looking at me like I'm going to stab myself any minute. I'm clearheaded now. There's no reason Matilda Edwards should have any interest in me. There's no reason I should feel about another woman the same way I felt about my poor Ann back in New Salem. That's all over with. I know my future. I know what it has to be. I embrace it gladly and will complain about it no more."

TWENTY-TWO

◆◆◆

THE NEXT WEEK the doors of the new statehouse were officially opened. There were nightly receptions for the public, with free punch and cakes and a choir singing lively songs and Christmas ribbons hanging from the Corinthian columns. The building was still not finished, but the house and senate chambers and the governor's office were open and the legislature was now meeting at last in a public space consecrated for that purpose.

Cage walked alone through the edifice, listening as the voices of the singers and the chattering of the visitors echoed off the polished surfaces of Sugar Creek limestone. There were grand buildings like the American House in Springfield now, but this was different. This was like a great anchor thrown into the sea with the promise of holding the city in place.

"The thing is done at last!" Ned Baker said when he saw Cage. He was with Ash Merritt, the two of them pleasantly inebriated on multiple glasses of punch as they stood at the head of the stairway in the gleaming new legislative temple.

"What about Lincoln?" Baker asked Cage in a whisper. "What the hell is the matter with him?"

Cage told Baker and Merritt about the suicide vigil. He was under no obligation that he knew of to keep it a secret from Lincoln's friends, especially after he had made such an odd spectacle of himself by jumping out of the church window.

"He should drop that girl and have done with it," Ash said. "She's too smart and too cunning for him. She's got him completely confused."

"Maybe, but he might do well to marry her after all. That would settle the matter and settle his mind," Ned said. "And there are worse things than a smart and cunning wife."

But a crowded, echoing rotunda was not the place for an intimate conversation about Lincoln's marital prospects and mental health. As Baker turned to acknowledge the congratulations of one of his constituents, Cage excused himself and drifted off to have a glimpse of the house and senate chambers where so much solemn mischief would be enacted in the future. He noticed Stephen Douglas, whom the governor had just appointed secretary of state, grandly gesturing to a group of visitors, his stubby arms flung upward and outward as if to somehow fuse the building's magnificence with his own.

Among the men and women who had gathered to listen to Douglas's impromptu oration was Ellie. She saw that Cage had noticed her and discreetly stepped away, joining him where he stood at the staircase railing. The choir stood on risers behind them, singing "The Lakes of Pontchartrain."

"Do you like our new statehouse?" she asked in a tone she would have used with a near stranger. Unaccustomed to meeting each other in public, uncertain if they should, they stood a few feet apart.

"Yes," he answered. "It's suitably grand."

"It's permanent. That's the most exciting thing about it. A very good thing for men and women of business."

"Let's get out of here," he whispered. "I'll follow you to the shop."

"It's not our usual night."

"Why does that matter?"

"I suppose it doesn't. I'll see you in a while."

She left him and walked down the staircase. Ten minutes later he followed. The night was stark and clear. The choir could still be heard as its singing drifted out of the new statehouse and through the comfortable streets of Springfield and the still-hostile winter emptiness that lay beyond.

The door to her shop was unlocked and she waited for him in the back, all her clothes already removed, her body half-visible in the dim lamplight as if she were swimming toward him from the depths of a murky lake. Indeed, she fell on him like a selkie, her own desire fully and uncharacteristically exposed, with no coyness or coolness to mask it. It seemed to Cage that she meant to reveal something deeper than sexual hunger—a fondness that might have reached a point that bordered on love, a flash even of vulnerability. But there was no way for him to press his curiosity. When they had finished and were lying together quietly in the subdued light, he joked that she must have been stirred into a frenzy by the Little Giant's oratory.

"I was stirred by what a city we're becoming. By the sense that things are taking hold. There were so many things I never dared to think about that now seem almost possible."

"What sort of things?"

"Being really free." Her expression was guileless. "To do as I care to do, and to become rich and do even more that I care to do."

"That's the sum of your ambition?"

"Yes. I know you disapprove, Cage, but I don't care. You may have your lofty dream about living beyond the grave, but my dream is to do very well for myself before I'm ever buried."

"Don't you want anyone to remember you?"

"No, I'd be very happy to be forgotten about."

"Not if you had children."

"I don't have children, as you may have noticed, and don't plan to have any, as you may have also noticed."

She settled against him, tracing a finger through the whorl of his ear. Her voice grew a little tighter but she did not lift the spell of physical intimacy.

"If that's what you want for yourself," she said, "you know what a simple thing it is to have it. But you must have it with someone else."

"I don't want children," he said, assuming it was true though he had never seriously tested the idea with himself. But he could not fathom her indifference to any sort of legacy. An unremembered life, an unvisited grave, an empty posterity—those were the fates he worked against at his desk, deep into every night.

He changed the subject and told her about his upcoming Christmas trip to Jacksonville with Mary Todd and the coterie. He might have hoped for some trace of disappointment in her expression about being deprived of his company, about possibly losing it forever to Matilda Edwards or some other appropriate young lady. But he had to satisfy himself yet again with the fact that she was who she was and meant what she said.

"Is it true that Lincoln and the Todd girl are going to marry?"

"I don't know. It's not a settled issue."

"It's certainly the impression that people have. Everybody who comes to the shop talks about it."

He told her about how Lincoln had tried to break it off with Mary, but in the attempt had only succeeded in making the bond tighter.

"Well, that was a ridiculously clumsy thing. He knows nothing at all about women."

"Is that what you learned when he came to see you that night?"

It was exactly the sort of question he had managed to keep himself from asking her for over a year. She wriggled away in surprise, sat up on her elbows so that she could peer down disapprovingly at him.

"You still haven't put that out of your mind?"

"I have, but it keeps returning."

"I thought you didn't like me to talk about such things."

"I don't. Tell me what it was like. What you were like with him."

"I have no interest in tormenting you, even though you think I enjoy doing so. And by the way, in case you've wondered, which I suppose you've been doing obsessively, it really was only that one time. It hasn't happened again."

"Would you ever let it happen again?"

"No. There'd be no point."

She laughed a little, saying this. She wasn't unaware of how cold she could sound, how cold she could be.

"Besides, he would never think to come see me again. He really is your friend, Cage."

She slipped back down beside him. They were silent for a moment, staring past the open door of the back room at their barely detectable reflections in one of the glass sales counters, two bodies beneath a quilt, two heads with peering eyes.

"If you want me to tell you what he was like," she whispered, "I will.

He was just like you were that first time—not knowing quite how to behave or what to say. Except even worse. Both of you thinking that a night spent with a woman binds you to her forever in a solemn contract."

"I'm not that naive."

"He is. Almost. He'd been to whorehouses, I suppose, so he knew how the thing was done, though no idea what it was supposed to mean or not mean. If I'd said we have to be married now he would have put on his hat and walked me to the church. You should have seen the confusion on his face when he paid me—much worse than you, and you were bad enough."

"Stop talking about it."

"Even if he hadn't found out how you felt about me, I doubt that he would have ever come back. I don't think he could bear to think of himself as nobody special, just another sex-starved male creature who needed to—"

She noticed the look on his face and broke off, having no interest in provoking his jealousy further. "Anyway, maybe Mary Todd is what he needs. A firm woman who knows her mind might make him happy."

"I don't think so. He said he wanted to kill himself."

"Did you believe him?"

"Yes."

Cage felt her unclothed body shifting comfortably against his. "What a dreadful trap the whole idea of love is," she said.

Mary's wish for enough snow for a sleigh ride did not come true, so most of the party ended up taking the stage for the Christmas excursion to Jacksonville, with some of the men following behind on horseback along a road that was rutted and boggy, the horses' hooves melodiously breaking up the remaining splinters of melting ice. Cage rode Mrs. P, who was no longer in her prime but still delighted to be out in the open air in company with the horses ridden by Lincoln and Speed and John Hardin. It was to Hardin's house that they were all headed, to celebrate the season and the end of the legislative session. Cage had not seen Hardin since the party at the Edwards house to celebrate the Whig victory in the 1838 election. That had been almost two and a half years ago, and Hardin had not changed in the interim. He looked even more composed and self-assured than he had that night, and he seemed immune or at least inured to the sideways glances of the female members of the party. He was steadfastly, unflappably married. Like most politicians, he took a crucial interest in getting to know and subtly assessing the potential value to himself of the people he met. As they rode along he quizzed Cage with flattering intensity about the craft of poetry, about whom he ought to read, and whether or not the great music of the Renaissance could ever have been composed had it not been for the words that underlay it.

"Yes, music is music," he theorized, "but the shape and tempo of a piece has to start from somewhere. Words firm music up, they give it direction and purpose, that's what I think. Otherwise what do you have? Just notes."

Mary and Matilda and the rest of the group inside the stage were in high spirits, and one or the other of the ladies kept peering out of the windows and looking back at the trailing horsemen, insisting that they join in their Christmas songs, warning them that if they did not Saint Claas would leave them nothing in their stockings, or they might even be visited by the evil Bersnickle. Lincoln was doing his best to take part in the revelry, but he still looked like a man ensnared, and whenever Mary's insistent and energetic face appeared at the window Cage could see that Lincoln felt the bonds drawing tighter still.

Hardin was homesick and eager to see his wife. The session had been trying and tendentious and he had made the mistake of boarding in Springfield at an establishment that served second-rate food. How he looked forward to his own home, he said, his own dear Sarah, the food from the cooks in his own kitchen. For now the disappointments of the session, the coarse maneuvering of the Democrats to destroy the state bank, could be set aside. There would be a lively round of parties in Jacksonville for the next week or so, but also time for rest and reading and discussions with the fine gentlemen riding alongside him.

He rode a black gelding as handsome as himself. Watching him in the saddle, Cage was aware of his own posture and made adjustments, raising his head, squaring his shoulders, stiffening his back. He knew he could not match John Hardin's bearing and physical confidence, but he could not keep himself from trying. Lincoln of course made no effort in that direction. Even when he was in the best of moods, his own appearance was an afterthought, and he was not in the best of moods today. He rode in a stooped and sloppy manner, his mind removed from his body, which teetered obediently to the rhythms set by his horse.

They were in Hardin's grand house on State Street in Jacksonville by early afternoon, Sarah Hardin greeting them all—even those like Cage whom she had never met—with an overflowing warmth. She was glad enough to see her husband that there were tears in her eyes. She was a match for him physically—slender and dark-haired and arrestingly attractive—and her calm domestic spirit was a perfect fit to his vaulting ambition. She briskly sorted out all her guests into a multitude of comfortable rooms, and even had Christmas stockings for each of them, hung in a long festive row on the mantelpiece.

For several days there was an unending round of parties, during which Mary stuck tight to Lincoln's side. She touched his arm familiarly as she chatted with the Hardins' Jacksonville friends, smiling up at him as if to register their dual appreciation whenever a witticism was uttered or a poignant chord was struck at the pianoforte. If they were not officially engaged, she gave every impression that they soon would be. Lincoln was distracted but compliant. His body was as motionless as a plank for the most part, his arms dangling at his sides, a perfectly pleasant smile on his face. He listened and laughed and told stories, but he was a different Lincoln, a half-Lincoln, his attention divided between the audience in front of him and the swirling confusion in his head.

By Christmas Eve they were all exhausted from the festivities, and there was a quiet night around the fire with just the Hardins and their guests from Springfield. They sprawled comfortably in the parlor, singing Christmas songs in rounds orchestrated by John Hardin's delightfully vibrant sixteen-year-old sister, Martinette. Afterwards they ate three kinds of pie and the political men told stories about the battles of the last session. Matilda Edwards sat half-reclined on a settee, a cup of eggnog balanced in her hand, the lovely bones of her wrist set off against the ruffled cuff of her sleeve. The glow of the firelight revealed the perfect angles of her face to unbearable advantage. Her expression was one of intoxicating contentment, suggesting that she was aware of her outward beauty and that this awareness brought peace to her soul.

Her voice when she laughed or when she sang had a raspy, throaty quality that conveyed the possibility of sexual abandon. It was hard for the men not to stare at her, for the women not to notice they were doing so.

Somehow Speed managed to get Matilda off alone, the two of them seated on matching chairs in a far corner of the room, his head bent to hers. They talked for half an hour while Sarah Hardin played the pianoforte and Mary took over from Martinette and organized a new round of carol singing with the energy of a choir director. She kept Lincoln in his place during a rousing "Joy to the World" but his eyes, tormented with jealousy, kept straying over to Speed and Matilda. After a few minutes Speed stood up, helped Matilda pull her lush cashmere mantle over her shoulders, and escorted her out into the night.

"Where are they going?" Lincoln asked Cage in an anguished whisper when Mary had turned away to accept a cup of French coffee from one of the Hardin house servants.

"I don't know," he answered as gently as he could. "I suppose they're just going outside to talk."

They were gone for half an hour. When they slipped back into the parlor, John Hardin was in the midst of reminiscing out loud about his grandfather, who had been a hero at Saratoga and later burned down an impressive number of Indian villages all over the Ohio Territory.

"I never met the man," Hardin said. "I would very much have liked to. He died young, murdered by Shawnees. They said he had twelve Indian scalps hanging from his bookcase, just like those Christmas stockings hanging tonight from the mantelpiece."

"John, that's a dreadful story to tell on Christmas Eve," Sarah said.

"Three states named counties after him. Lincoln here knows that very well, don't you?"

"I do," Lincoln said, doing his best to stay in the conversation while monitoring the return of Speed and Matilda. Matilda looked as untroubled as ever, but Speed had a cross, confused look on his face. "I had the honor to be born in Hardin County, Kentucky."

"How's that for symmetry?" Hardin asked the group. "And not only that—you lost your grandfather to Indian perfidy just like I did."

"That's true," Lincoln said. "He was out in the fields with my father, then only a boy. An Indian sharpshooter fired at him from concealment and caught him in the heart and he went right down into the pumpkin patch. The Indian then ran out and grabbed my father and would have run off with him if my uncle Mordecai hadn't seen him from the house and took down his rifle. It was a terrible sort of shot to have to try, with that Indian hugging the boy like that, and Mordecai was still something of a boy himself. But he had to do something, and he aimed at a little shiny moon trinket on the Indian's chest, and by jings if he didn't send the ball punching right through it. That Indian fell down dead, my pa ran home to grow up and marry my mother, and here I am today telling you all about it."

Cage had heard Lincoln tell the story several times before. It was not meant to be a funny story, of course, but he had worked it over with the same consideration he brought to his extended jokes, raising the pitch of his voice in some places, pausing for dramatic effect in others, carefully gauging his audience to make sure he was following the right narrative rhythm. But tonight he told it flatly, almost disinterestedly, with a kind of rote craftsmanship that allowed his mind to be elsewhere, on what exactly was going on with Matilda Edwards and Joshua Speed. As a result the guests in the Hardin parlor did not quite know how to react, whether to be horrified by the account of the attack or amused by the droll way Lincoln credited it for his own existence. So there was not much reaction at all, just a gradual change of subject until, around midnight, the party broke up and the guests drifted upstairs to their beds.

Cage and Lincoln and Speed were all sharing an attic room with a slanted ceiling. Lincoln wasted no time in anxiously quizzing Speed as he tried to clean his teeth at the washbowl.

"What were you talking to Matilda about?"

"Nothing. It doesn't matter."

"Were you making love to her?"

"I was trying."

"What did she say?"

"Good Christ, Lincoln, let me alone. She doesn't want me. She doesn't want anybody. She's in love with Newton Strong."

"She told you that?"

"No, but she kept bringing him up. 'My good friend, Mr. Strong.' 'Mr. Strong is as good as his name.' 'Oh, you're so funny, Mr. Speed. I think you and Mr. Strong must be the funniest people in Illinois.' She knows exactly what she's doing, I'll give her credit for that. She draws you in, and draws you in, and then when you're finally close enough she looks at you as if it was the strangest idea in the world that there could possibly be anything between you. I think she's one of those women who gets satisfaction out of watching a man lay himself bare in front of her. She's got a watchmaker's curiosity about what's going on inside us."

"She's not as cold as that," Lincoln declared. "She can't be. You can see it in her eyes."

Poor naive Lincoln, Speed's look said. He'd just had his heart broken, so it was natural he would be cynical, but he'd had far more experience with women than Lincoln and was able to understand that great beauty was not necessarily the outward manifestation of a pure soul.

"Why don't you have a try at her, then?" Speed said. "Throw Mary over and go after Matilda. You won't be in my way."

"I can't throw Mary over. I tried that once. I won't do that to her again."

"Well, then, what's the point of worrying about it? You're stuck fast. Let's all get Matilda Edwards out of our minds and go to sleep."

The Christmas sky the next morning was clear. The mercury sat at just over twenty degrees, but there was no wind to draw it down farther. The stable cold did little to discourage the citizens of Jacksonville from rushing outside to celebrate Christmas. The shops were all open and the streets were crowded with rowdy wassailers and revelers. Crackers were firing everywhere and callithumpian bands assaulted the air with raucous music.

Cage had had his own bed in the Hardins' comfortable attic room but he had slept fitfully, aware of Lincoln lying awake all night in the double bed he was sharing with Speed on the other side of the room. And Lincoln's ragged mood was still glaringly obvious this morning, as the members of the Springfield contingent wove in and out of the shops, gossiping and laughing and buying trinkets for one another. Walking beside Mary, Lincoln craned his neck to keep sight of Matilda, who seemed to be everywhere at once, running from one shop window to the next and joining in the singing of the high-spirited wassailers she met along the way.

Cage broke away from the main group to slip into a bookshop, and when he came out ten minutes later he caught sight of Lincoln and Mary standing alone at the end of the street, so wrapped up in an argument that they seemed unaware of the Jacksonville Christmas crowd streaming past. Cage could not make out much of what they were saying—or, rather, what Mary was saying, because Lincoln just stood there not meeting her eyes, nodding his head in guilt-stricken agreement: "So obvious" . . . "no idea of the humiliation it causes me" . . . "well then what did you suppose you were saying?"

Mary's face was red under her bonnet and she appeared to be on the verge of lashing out with her gloved hand to strike Lincoln across the face. Afraid that one of them might look his way and draw him into an argument that ought to be private, Cage retreated back into the shop and occupied himself by browsing through a new book about Hungary.

When he went outside again they were no longer there, but they rejoined the coterie later at the Hardins' house. Judging by the stiffness they kept between themselves, they had not reconciled, but had resigned themselves to another few days of carefully orchestrated civility. By the end of the week, when the weather was beginning to set in, Cage and Speed and Lincoln saddled their horses and said goodbye to their hosts. They were anxious to get back to work before the arctic force of an Illinois winter trapped them in Jacksonville. Mary and Matilda and the others would stay with the Hardins until after the new year.

The three friends rode in silence for much of the way, a silence imposed by Lincoln's incessant brooding.

"Goddammit!" Speed blurted out at last. "You have to get yourself away from that woman somehow. Look how miserable she's making you."

"She's not the one making me miserable. It's me that's doing so, my own inconstant nature. I'm unworthy of Molly, that's the truth of the matter. Her powers of observation are very great and she sees me pining after Matilda."

"That doesn't require great powers of observation," Cage said.

"Nevertheless, it hurts her to see it. I've wronged her. I have to put thoughts of Matilda and every other woman aside and do my best not to wound Molly anymore."

Having been spurned by Matilda, Speed was not in the most resilient of moods himself, but he joined Cage in trying to convince Lincoln that he had a very confused attitude toward Mary Todd. The expectation of happiness, they argued, instead of merely the desire not to wound, should be the true foundation of a marriage.

"No," Lincoln said, "honor is the foundation of marriage, as it is the foundation of every other good thing. I've pledged myself to Molly, and the side of my character that's trying to withdraw from that pledge is a very poor fellow and I won't have him around."

Lincoln declared that he felt better now that the matter was settled for all time. He would abide by the demands of his conscience, which were completely congruent with the desires of the woman who loved him, and whom he must love in return without distraction or regret. It was a punishing sort of resolution to make, but it buoyed him nevertheless to make it, and his attitude in the saddle gradually changed from a forlorn slump to a more or less upright posture. There was some liveliness in his voice again, a fatalistic cheerfulness. He even erupted into a humorous story that neither Cage nor Speed had heard before, about a heartless lawyer who, in payment for defending a farmer in a murder charge, had demanded every piece of his client's property, from his cabin to his very chickens.

"It might have been worth it to the farmer if the lawyer had saved his life, but he was as incompetent as he was greedy, and the jury sent his man to hang. Well, that wasn't even the end of it, because the lawyer's fee included the dead man's body, which he promptly sold to a team of unscrupulous physicians. The lawyer's only request was that he be allowed to watch while they cut him up. While they were stripping the skin off the poor dead man, one of the physicians asked the lawyer why in the world he would want to witness the procedure. 'Well,' said the lawyer, 'because it's a rare thing in my profession to have the pleasure of seeing my client skinned twice.'"

Lincoln laughed as heartily as he ever had, great gusts of condensation erupting from his mouth into the cold air. Speed, thinking Lincoln was revived enough to bear the news, took the occasion to mention that he was moving to Kentucky. In an instant all of the joviality that Lincoln had been fighting to recover was gone. Under the brim of his hat his eyes went black with despair. His expression was as blank as a post.

"Why would you do that? What future can you have in Kentucky when all your friends are here?"

Speed explained about his dead father and his solemn duty to his mother to put the estate on a firm footing. Lincoln heard him out and nodded in an impatient way that of course he must leave if that was the case, if there was no other option, but it was all damned unfortunate.

"It's hard to see an intimate friend go," he said. "Very hard, especially when we've built a city together out of the wilderness."

"You'll come to visit me in Kentucky," Speed said. "You and Cage both."

"We will. We must. We can't lose touch with our friend."

His voice broke, a quick spasm of grief, and then he did his best to recover his spirits yet again. But the three men said little else as they followed the road across the empty prairie toward Springfield.

When the year ended, the skies sealed tight with snow-bearing clouds. There was an unrelenting snowfall and savage wind and cold, the kind of weather that kills livestock and kills the farmers that try to save them. It was ten degrees below on New Year's Eve as Cage sat at his desk crossing out useless lines of verse with ink that he had had to thaw by the stove. As the long day wore on he felt imprisoned, and finally put on his warmest coat and scarf and tied down the earflaps of his thick fur cap to venture out to Iles's store to see if any of the mails had made it through.

He was rewarded with a few catalogs and books he had ordered, and a single letter that had arrived on the Jacksonville stage that afternoon. The stage's drivers were still huddled over the stove drinking whiskey and expressing their awe at the weather they had just passed through, declaring that they had barely escaped losing their toes to frostbite and that if God himself ordered them back out into that howling cold they would just as soon go with the Devil to hell.

Cage was in no hurry to go back outside himself, so he read the letter he received from Mary while standing at the edge of the crowd around the raging stove:

Dear Cage,

I write in haste before the weather closes up the mails. Here is a letter I want you to deliver to Mr. Lincoln. Will you do so? It is best that a friend be with him when he reads it, as his moods of late cannot be predicted. It may be that he will be very glad to receive it; it may be that it will have a different effect. I would like you to do me the favor of reporting his reaction to me, though I will understand if your friendship to L. somehow prevents that courtesy. I am still at Jacksonville and will return in a week or so, though I don't expect to meet him in the gay world upon my return. You are an excellent friend to us both.

Mary.

He was grateful that the letter for Lincoln was sealed, which saved him the moral struggle of having to decide whether to take a peek at it. As soon as he was thoroughly warm again he went back out, meaning to walk over to Lincoln's office and hand the missive to him, and then to decide after his friend had read it whether or not he wished to comply with Mary's request that he report back on the effect it had caused. (Her manipulating hand was as always a little too visible for his comfort.) But when he went outside again the wind had picked up and darkness was precipitously spreading through the empty streets. No lamplighters would be out tonight. It would be a night of sub-zero darkness as people gathered around their fires shivering and reading and listening to the wind howling with unbroken ferocity, as if generated across a frozen sea. Cage made it home to the Palatine, but by that time his hands and feet were so throbbing and numb that he thought he could not stand walking another block to Hoffman's Row, where Lincoln might or might not be found.

1841

TWENTY-THREE

✦✦✦

H E STAYED IN BED LATE on New Year's morning. The streets were suffocatingly quiet. Normally they would have been full-on bustling on the first day of the year, people traveling to one another's houses for the customary libations. But the cold kept everyone inside and the festive seedcakes in the confectioners' windows remained unsold. Against Mrs. Hopper's admonitions, Cage ventured out again before noon to deliver his letter to Lincoln, who he assumed would be at his lodging place in Speed's store. The wind was still strong, blowing the snow with lacerating force against his exposed eyes and cheeks. It was painful to breathe, and the sun seemed not just weak but almost extinguished, leaving the planet cold and hostile and dark and dying.

He opened the door to Speed's store and slammed it shut against the wind, gasping and stamping his feet. Speed and Lincoln, by the stove in back, looked up from their books in surprise.

"It's some sort of creature," Lincoln said as Cage shuffled across the floor, unwinding his scarf and leaving behind a trail of melting snow, "but exactly what sort of creature remains a mystery."

He was doing his best to simulate his old authentic liveliness, but his voice still had a deflated edge and his good cheer was hard-won. Cage pulled off his gloves and warmed his stinging hands by the stove while Speed poured him a cup of coffee.

"You must be missing our company awful bad," Lincoln said, "to come out in weather that can turn a man's pecker into an icicle."

Cage continued thawing. He thought about saying something to Lincoln by way of an overture, but in the end he just reached into his overcoat pocket. His fingers were still so cold he could barely feel the letter as he withdrew it.

"What's this?"

"A letter to you from Mary, in Jacksonville. She sent it in care of me."

Lincoln unsealed the letter and leaned back in his chair. His temple pulsed as he read and his jaw was set tight. The letter was evidently brief. After he read it, he left it unfolded in his lap. For a moment it seemed he would toss it into the fire, but he handed it to Cage instead without a word. There was something like a smile on his face, but not very much like a smile.

Speed scooted his chair around so he and Cage could read the letter together.

Dear Mr. Lincoln,

I know you do not love me. You have said you do but it is obvious to me and to anyone observing your behavior around me that you do not. You say you love another. I do not think this is true either, though you may believe it. I am convinced you do not know what love is or how a person who pledges such an emotion to another is bound by his honor to behave. This is not your fault. You are an admirable man who has remarkably triumphed over a rude start in life, but some parts of your character are yet to be sketched. You are not yet steadfast. I hope that someday you may be, I hope that someday you may love a woman with your full heart so that she will not be confused and made to suffer by your words alone. I am disappointed as my affection for you remains constant. I will not hear a bad word said of you. You have hurt me but I judge you blameless by reason of your unusual nature and coarse upbringing. With this letter I release you from any obligations you may feel toward me. We are not engaged and I will never expect to be married to you. Please do not answer this letter. Doing so will make my present unhappiness deeper.
I would like to remain friends, after the "healing of time" has had its effect.

Mary Todd

"Well," said Cage as brightly as he thought he could get away with, "there's an end to it."

"Yes, thank God it's over," Speed said. "You can go back to the work you were born to do and not have to torture yourself anymore about this woman."

"The poor creature," Lincoln said. "What have I done to her?"

"You've done nothing to her," Cage said. "She'll be happily married within the year to someone else."

"Do you really think so?"

"Of course I do."

Lincoln folded the letter and slipped it into his coat pocket. He folded his arms tight across his narrow chest and crossed his legs.

"Are you all right?" Cage asked, to break the ponderous silence.

"Of course I'm all right," he replied. "I've secured my freedom."

But Lincoln was not all right. The next morning he was back at the legislature, and that afternoon, when Cage spotted him on the opposite side of the square talking to a group of boys who were sharpening the blades of their sleds he appeared to be in a good humor, though more subdued and preoccupied than usual. But over the next week his brooding mind would not let him rest, until he was so degraded with the hypo that Speed visited Cage once again in alarm.

"He's been lying up there in our room for two days. He won't eat and he'll barely talk to me."

Cage went to the store and found Lincoln flat on the bed staring out the window at a dead tree branch that twitched with an almost imperceptible motion against a sepulchral gray sky. It was still very cold, outside and in, and Lincoln was fully dressed, even to his brogans and the scarf around his neck. He smelled bad and two days of not eating had swiftly highlighted the despairing opacity of his eyes. His hair was greasy and lank, and the ears that were attached to the sides of his shriveled face loomed freakishly large.

"What in hell is wrong with you?" Cage said. He didn't mean to sound so harsh.

Lincoln said something but his voice was so weak Cage couldn't hear him.

"What did you say?"

Lincoln repeated himself but he was still inaudible.

"I still can't hear you."

"I said there's no reason for you to come visit me. I'm fine as I am."

"You're obviously not. What's the matter?"

Lincoln turned his head away on his sweat-soaked pillow and looked out the window again without answering. He was so profoundly enervated it seemed possible that he was actually dying.

"It's still cold out," Lincoln mumbled.

"Yes, it's still cold out."

"The clouds are so dark and heavy. They make you feel like you can't breathe."

"You may feel that way, but you're breathing just fine. Will you please tell me what's happened to you?"

He didn't answer at first, didn't seem like he was ever going to. Speed had come into the room and stood at the door with a look of deepening alarm. Finally Lincoln made some muttering response, a single unintelligible word.

"What was that?" Cage said. "Can you please speak a little more clearly?"

"Honor."

"What about honor?"

"I have none. That's what she said." He withdrew the folded letter from his coat, handed it to Cage, and pointed with a pale finger to the line in which the word appeared: "I am convinced you do not know what love is or how a person who pledges such an emotion to another is bound by his honor to behave."

"It's just a word she threw into a sentence. There's no reason to regard it as a defining statement."

"Yes, there is. She's right. I have no honor. I made a pledge and didn't stand by it, and now I'm nothing."

Cage sat back in his chair, exchanging another what-are-we-going-to-do glance with Speed. This was different and somehow more frightening than the suicidal mania that had taken hold of Lincoln a month ago when he had tried without success to break it off with Mary. They'd had to make sure he didn't really try to kill himself, but otherwise there had been more than sufficient energy in his body to keep it vital. Now that energy was entirely gone. There was no animating purpose, no will.

"He's missed two days of the session already," Speed told Cage.

"It doesn't matter," Lincoln said. He sighed in an extravagant death-rattle sort of way, releasing a cloud of rancid breath.

"It might just matter to the people of Illinois," Speed said, "if there's no Abraham Lincoln in the statehouse to save the bank and keep our state solvent and get the railroads running."

Lincoln looked at Speed with a pained smile. The idea of his own destiny was now absurd to him.

"What do you mean he can't function?" Ned Baker asked Cage as they sat at a table that night with John Hardin at the American House. "Is he truly sick or does he just have the blues?"

"It may just be the blues, but when you see him he has the look of a dying man."

"Good Lord," Baker said. "Don't tell anyone about this except his closest friends. If word got out that he's missing votes because of a woman problem—"

"It's more complicated than that."

"It might be, but it won't be seen that way, particularly by the Democrats. He's already been made to look a fool after that window business."

"Ned's right," Hardin said. "There needs to be a specific complaint he's suffering with that we can put out. He's passing gravel. No one will think twice about that, and no one will bother him. The most black-hearted Democrat will have pity on a man passing gravel."

They agreed that if they were asked about Lincoln they would say that he was writhing in pain and unable to see anyone until the stones had made their way through.

"Mary Todd is a very anxious and excitable young woman, in my opinion," Hardin said. "I saw that side of her well enough over Christmas at Jacksonville. If Lincoln is to have a wife—which I'm not sure is even a good idea—she ought to be someone like my Sarah, someone pleasant and calm who wouldn't think of meddling in the emotions of her husband."

"Our emotions are a foreign realm to women," Baker agreed. "A woman has no more business in that territory than England has in Texas."

"All this is beside the point," Cage broke in. "And it's not Lincoln's career that needs protecting now, but Lincoln himself. He can't be roused. It's no use trying to talk him out of this state he's fallen into."

"Will he kill himself?" Hardin asked.

"No. He doesn't have the energy. But he'll try his hardest to allow himself to die."

"It's hard to understand," Hardin said. "Here's a man who has made himself by force of will into one of the most indispensable men in Illinois. Meanwhile he's made a very respectable name for himself as a lawyer. He could very well be governor of this state in a few years. He knows everyone, and most of the people he knows, with a few exceptions here and there, like him a great deal, or at the very least think he's funny. A man who's that gifted and that determined to succeed wouldn't just give up because he thinks he's lost the respect of a woman—a woman he doesn't even want to marry."

"But he has, John," Ned said softly. "He's a mystery to us and to the logical mind."

They agreed Lincoln needed the help of a doctor. That night the three of them, along with Speed, arrived at Lincoln's room, somehow got him up out of his bed and into a semblance of decent dress, and walked him over to Ash Merritt's house on Jefferson Street. It was a journey of only a few blocks but Lincoln was teetering and depleted by the end of it. He displayed no more personality than a corpse as his friends got him out of his clothes and into one of Ash's nightshirts, which was comically too small for him but at least freshly laundered. Without complaint, he allowed himself to be laid down on Ash's spare bed. Ash spread a quilt over him and took his pulse.

"It's not just a duck fit," the doctor told Lincoln's friends in a whisper as they congregated in the parlor. "He's in the grip of a melancholy passion. What did Mary Todd do to him? Was it an especially brutal rejection?"

"She didn't reject him at all," Cage explained. "She released him from any obligation he felt toward her, but she did so in a way that made him feel his honor was compromised."

"Ah. So she found poor Lincoln's fatal spot. You'd better leave him with me for a while. He needs watching. The hypo can destroy a man, especially a man who wants to be destroyed. Impede the circulation of the fluids, stagnate the bile, that sort of thing. When did he last move his bowels?"

Cage turned to Speed, who said he had no idea.

"I'll give him something to loosen him up. He probably needs it, and constipation does nothing to stimulate the will to live."

Ash Merritt kept Lincoln at his house for a few days, forcing wine into his temperance-minded patient, giving him vinegar baths and mustard rubs and stroking his limbs hard with a flesh brush to move the blood along. He recovered enough to speak and to eat some bread soaked in milk and to decide that he wanted to go home, back to his room in Speed's store. The legislative session was still under way, but he did not have the strength of mind or body to return to his duties at the statehouse.

"I'm the most miserable man living," he volunteered in a faint voice when Cage stopped by with a pan of barley soup that Mrs. Hopper had made. It was still very cold and bleak and the soup had frozen on the short walk from the Palatine to Speed's store. Lincoln was out of bed, at least, warming his feet along with the soup by the stove, a blanket thrown over his shoulders and over his head, so that he looked like a medieval carving of a wizened monk in a cowl. Maybe it was a good sign that he had passed from a condition of almost utter passivity to a groaning state of self-pity. There were customers in the store below, and Cage and Lincoln could hear Speed's voice as he waited on them, his heartiness and friendliness reaching Lincoln almost as a taunt.

"What are they saying about me?" he asked. "I don't have the will to read a paper. Are they mocking me?"

"No. Everyone thinks you have gravel, and that you'll return to the assembly in a few days."

"I would rather pass a shovel-load of gravel through my pecker than feel one-tenth of what I'm feeling, Cage. Oh God, it's so horrible."

He began to cry. Maybe that was another good thing: his emotions seeping from their encapsulated gloom, like the pus from a lanced boil.

"Have you heard anything about her?" he asked. "Is she back in Springfield?"

"Yes, but it will do you no good to think about her."

"How can I not? I destroyed her life. Maybe I should write to her, beg her to marry me after all. But she wouldn't have me now, would she, after I've dishonored myself so completely?"

"You haven't dishonored yourself, and why in the world could you ever think it would be a good idea for you to take up with Mary Todd again? You're well out of it. Put that woman out of your mind, put your past with her out of your mind, and find a way to live."

"There's no way," Lincoln said. "No way for me to live."

His spoken catalog of shame and self-disgust was a painful thing to witness, but Cage thought it best to keep him speaking so that he didn't sink back into catatonic despair.

"I think the weather is having an effect on you," Cage said. "But it won't be cold forever, it won't be dark forever, and your mood will change with the weather if you give yourself a chance to let it."

Lincoln refused to acknowledge this useless bromide. He shifted the blanket so that it no longer covered his head and gave Cage a look that suggested any further comments of that sort would be painful. In the light from the stove, his forehead glistened with sweat, his eyes were still frighteningly blank. It was hard to believe there had ever been any life in them at all.

"Would you like to go to Bogotá, Colombia?" Cage asked him.

"What?"

"A diplomatic posting. Hardin said to run the idea past you, if you were up to hearing about it. The post will go to a Whig after Harrison is inaugurated. Stuart might be able to get it for you."

"I don't speak the Spanish."

"You taught yourself the law. You can learn another language."

"Is that what all my friends are arranging? To get rid of me by sending me to South America?"

"A change of scene is supposed to help in these cases."

" 'These cases!' " There was energy at last in Lincoln's voice. "I suppose by that you mean that there's nothing unusual about what I'm feeling."

"The blues are not—"

"This is not blue, Cage! This is black! Utter black! It's the blackness of a wasted life. A life that has done no one any good and that no one will ever remember, nor should. So yes, send me to Colombia! Better yet, Patagonia! Whatever remote crevice of the earth anybody wants to stuff me into will be just fine with me."

This eruption of anger lasted no longer than a powder flash, and then there was lethargy again, and intolerably morose silence. Cage gave up trying to talk Lincoln out of his malaise. His presence was only aggravating it. He went home, feeling the press of the deep gray winter sky upon his own mood, fighting against his own sense of futility. When he was in a spirited frame of mind, Abraham Lincoln was the most contagious man Cage had ever known. But now he found that his friend's inner darkness could be transmitted as well. In a less remarkable and magnetic individual the hypo would have been a private trial, but Lincoln's character was so public and powerful that it seemed capable of operating in reverse, siphoning back all the life and laughter it had once sent flooding into the world.

But over the next week he grew stronger, able to tolerate himself a little better each day, able to accept the fact that he had friends left and even to show flickering signs of gratitude for their steadfast company. He went back to the statehouse to take part in the session, back to his legal work in his and Stuart's office. He recovered his appetite to some degree, but he was still emaciated and moved with haunting slowness, as if with every step the question of whether his existence had any value was being posed anew.

On the night before Joshua Speed moved to Kentucky, there was a farewell party in the Edwards home. Lincoln could not be talked into going, though no one tried very hard, since they all knew Mary Todd and the rest of the coterie would be there. He bid a private farewell to Speed that afternoon instead.

"He sobbed like a child to see me go," Speed told Cage as they walked together up the hill toward the Edwards house. "And I'll admit I was in tears myself. It's a hard thing to part with such a good friend. You'll look out for him, of course."

"Of course."

Speed had sold his store and he could probably have insisted that Lincoln-as-resident convey to the new owner, but Lincoln himself had decided it was time to move on. There were no vacancies at the Palatine. Cage had offered to let Lincoln share his own rooms, but to his relief Lincoln said no and made arrangements to move into Butler's rooming house, where he was well known and liked and where he already took his meals.

"The best thing I can think of would be to get him to a good whorehouse," Speed said, "though I don't know that there's enough blood left in his veins to operate the pump. Maybe you should try to just keep him away from women entirely until he can string himself back together. And the two of you are required to visit me. I'll treat you both to a summer idyll in Kentucky and maybe we'll all forget about this hideous Illinois winter he's just been through."

Speed had made many friends in Springfield and the Edwards house was crowded that evening with Whigs and Democrats both. Mary was in the center of things as usual, looking perfectly intact. Stephen Douglas, who had recently been appointed a state supreme court justice after some artful judiciary packing on the part of the Democrats, seemed to have a renewed interest in her now that Lincoln was out of the race. He was in the midst of telling her a windy story. Mary kept trying to look in Cage's direction, but Douglas was standing eye to eye with her and commanding her attention. When the story was finally over she managed to break off, only to be waylaid by Bat Webb, a widowed Whig representative with two children who could always be seen hovering somewhere nervously about her at any ball or hop. He was unambiguously in love with her, though it was obvious to everyone that she found him too dull and too old. But she had done nothing that Cage knew to discourage him. Bat's transparent longing had helped to buoy her pride.

Finally she made her way over to Cage and drew him into Ninian Edwards's library just as the servants were passing out glasses of sparkling champagne for a farewell toast to Speed. They were alone in the room, the oxblood bindings of Edwards's law books arrayed behind Mary like a palisade wall.

"Is it true? Is he insane now?"

"Not insane, but your letter was a blow."

"How was it a blow? I released him! That's what he wanted, wasn't it? . . . Should I go to him?"

"No, definitely not. That would be the last thing he—"

"But does he still love me?"

"He's in torment, Mary. He's not in control of his emotions. For his sake, please don't shake him up again."

She fixed him with a skeptical look that was not far from hostility, and was about to speak again when they heard Ned Baker's booming voice calling everyone together for the toast.

"I'll stay away from him, then, if that's what you want," she said. "If you think love is the cause of torment and not its cure."

She swept past him into the parlor. They listened as Baker orated upon Speed's virtues—his steady friendship, his integrity as a man of business. Hardin raised his glass in Speed's honor next, and then a half dozen others, including Cage, who read a few humorous and heartfelt verses he had composed for the occasion.

"It was in Springfield," Speed said in reply, "that I encountered the truest friends, the warmest hearts I have ever known. It seems almost impossible that I could leave such a—"

But his emotions wouldn't let him finish. Ned Baker stood forward and patted him on the back as he gave in to teary hiccoughs. Next to Cage, Billy Herndon—ever emotional—was red-faced as he led the huzzahs that followed. Across the room Matilda Edwards stood with Mercy Levering, tears flowing like everyone else, but her face otherwise unrevealing and composed. She was unaware of all the hearts she had broken, of how her beauty had been the innocent agent of so much instability in their little Springfield circle.

Mary had found her way to Cage again now. She was clutching his arm and wiping her eyes with a handkerchief, wanting to share with him this moment of warm fellowship, and to remind him perhaps that her connection with Abraham Lincoln was not so completely severed after all.

TWENTY-FOUR

❖❖❖

ONE MORNING THREE MONTHS AFTER Lincoln's collapse, Ellie knocked loudly on Cage's door and walked unhesitatingly inside once he had opened it, a contradiction of all the arrangements they had put into place for propriety's sake when she moved into the Palatine. Something was wrong. Her lips were pressed tight and her fair skin had an angry flush.

"Read this!" she commanded, thrusting a public notice in his general direction.

"Notice is hereby given," the sheriff's handbill read, "that on the 10th day of April 1841 a Negro woman was taken up and committed to the Tazewell County jail in Tremont there to be dealt with as a Runaway Negro. She calls her name Cordelia and is about 25 years of age, of medium brown Color, slender built. Interested parties in the matter shall apply to the sheriff. She will be dealt with according to the law."

"I don't understand," Cage said. "How did she end up in jail in Tazewell County? That's sixty miles away."

"I know exactly how." Ellie snatched the public notice out of Cage's hand and replaced it with a folded-up copy of last week's *Sangamo Journal.* She pointed to one of the many advertisements for runaway slaves.

"Two hundred dollar reward!" the notice read. "Ran away from the subscriber at Frankfort June last a gingerbread complected young Negro woman named Louisa. Of tolerable good looks and build. Intelligent and well-spoken and was taught to read. Trained in the art and mystery of domestic life. Extremely skillful with her Needle. Birthmark on left shoulder in the shape of Madagascar. Some scarring on the left

257

cheek and on the back from light application of the cowhide. Will likely be well-dressed as she Stole women's clothing including a blue calico frock and a pair of red morocco-eyed slippers tied with a yellow ribbon. Signed Robert Etheridge."

Ellie sat on Cage's hard wooden chair, tapping her finger on the scattered papers on his desk. "She wasn't at work on Thursday. Her things were gone. I thought she had just decided to quit me for no reason, but she must have seen the notice in the paper and left in a panic. But she didn't get far. What will happen to her, Cage?"

"I don't know. I suppose the sheriff means to keep her in jail until her owner or his agent comes to retrieve her. She can't prove her freedom. She has no certificate."

"I need her in the shop. She's very skilled and she's not dull-witted in the least. I don't want her sent back to Kentucky to be a slave."

"We can talk to Lincoln."

"Is he back in his right mind? I don't want to waste time and money with someone who can't help us."

Cage assured her that Lincoln had managed to pull himself back into the realm of sanity, though he still had a rueful, self-punishing look and had to be reminded about mealtimes, during which he chewed his food like a man who had been talked into taking exercise. He and John Stuart had dissolved their partnership—amicably enough, one supposed, though Stuart's chronic absence in Washington and Lincoln's weeks of instability might have added to each man's thinking that it was time to move on. Lincoln was now Stephen Logan's junior partner, and the office they shared was on Fifth Street, across from Hoffman's Row.

Logan himself was on the way out when Cage and Ellie entered the office. He was, if possible, even more of a shabby dresser than Lincoln, wearing a fifty-cent hat that appeared to be made out of rat fur and a pair of brogans so cracked and peeling they might have been passed down by his great-grandfather.

"A terrible thing about Mr. Harrison," he said to Cage. "An unthinkable thing. Everyone was so excited, and now . . . Good Lord, does John Tyler think he has the right to just become the president now?"

He left the question hanging in the air as he held the door open for Cage and Ellie and then walked out onto the square. The office was much the same as Lincoln and Stuart's office had been, though even messier, with a long table for a desk and a not-long-enough settee on which they found Lincoln reclining, reading through a pile of documents. He was wearing his usual black coat, with a black mourning badge pinned to the breast. The startling news of Harrison's death had arrived only a few days earlier, and people were still trying to come to terms with the reality of it. "The President of the United States is no more!" the headline in the *Sangamo Journal* had read, but this had made no sense, because the hero of Tippecanoe had barely been inaugurated. In fact, though, they were saying it was his inauguration that had killed him, since he had spoken for two hours without a hat or overcoat in foul weather and died a month later of pneumonia.

The shock to the public was strong. There were crepe banners in the streets, salutes from minute guns and memorial addresses. A dress rehearsal, Cage would later reflect, of the national paroxysm that would follow upon the death of the man who rose to greet him and Ellie that April day in 1841.

He bid both to sit, clearing one chair of books and lifting another from the far side of the desk and setting it before Ellie. Lincoln was shy and unsettled in her presence and didn't seem able to meet her eyes. This was a legacy, Cage jealously concluded, of that night he had visited her in her room.

They talked for a moment about Harrison, the almost comically mundane manner of his death. Cage had worried that he might find Lincoln in another deep well of melancholy, after all the effort that he had gone to on Harrison's behalf, all the traveling and stumping he had done to get him elected. It was the canvass, after all, that had left him so physically and mentally fatigued and vulnerable to the confused entanglement with Mary that had almost killed him. But Harrison's death, though it was a shock and a disappointment, was nothing like the character assault that Lincoln had directed at himself from within. It seemed like something he could bear.

"My gravest concern about this whole Harrison tragedy," Lincoln was saying now, "is that John Tyler is now the president and he's the farthest thing from a true Whig."

He was starting to count off a list of Tyler's deficiencies when Ellie interrupted him. "I don't care who's a Whig and who's not. My girl has been stolen away from me and thrown in jail in Tazewell County and I want her back."

She handed Lincoln the sheriff's notice and the advertisement in the *Journal* and shifted impatiently in her chair while Lincoln read them.

"Are you sure your girl and this Louisa woman are one and the same?"

"I'm very sure," Ellie said.

"You hired a runaway slave?"

He addressed this question to Cage, who thought it might be best not to answer it directly. He just tilted his head in an ambiguous fashion.

Lincoln studied the floor for a moment in irritation or consternation, then set the documents on his desk. "Well, the timing's good," he said. "The circuit starts up in Tazewell in a few days. I'll be going there anyway. They've filed their writs of capias ad respondendum and capias ad satisfaciendum, so it remains for us to do some latinizing of our own and petition for habeas corpus. If we can get Sam Treat—he's the circuit judge—to grant the petition we can get the poor woman freed. Figure about twenty dollars ought to do it for my fee."

"It's an outrage," Ellie said.

"Well, it's the going rate, you won't find—"

"I don't mean your fee. I mean the fact that somebody could just grab Cordelia off the road. She hasn't committed a crime."

"It's crime enough to be a runaway slave."

"Isn't the point of a slave running away to Illinois the fact that when she's in a free state she's no longer a slave?"

"It's more complicated than that, Miss—"

He didn't know what to call her and she offered no lifeline. Beneath his raw complexion he was blushing. But he recovered himself and declared there was no reason to address the complexities now, as they would be adequately aired at the hearing. He would file the petition right away.

"I'll do my best to get your Negress free," he said to Ellie.

"Thank you, Abraham."

The act of her speaking his name caused the blush that had subsided to erupt again. She stood to go, and the two men rose with her.

"Would you mind," Lincoln asked Ellie, as Cage was opening the door for her, "if I detained your Mr. Weatherby here for a few minutes?"

"Why would there be any reason in the world you would have to have my permission to speak to your friend?" she asked. "Will there be a trial? Will you need me to testify?"

"Very likely."

"Then I'll be there."

When she left, Lincoln sat back down on the settee. His legs were so long that when he sat straight down his knees rose almost to his eye level. A moment of uncertain silence passed before he spoke.

"It occurred to me while you were sitting here just now that I never said much of a thank-you. One reason the hypo is so unendurable is it makes me so selfish. It cuts you off from the comfort of accepting that there are other people in the world, and that they care about your welfare. So anyway, thank you."

"From the outside, it looked like a very terrible thing to suffer through."

"I tell you, Cage, if what I felt had been equally distributed to the whole human family, there wouldn't have been a single cheerful face on earth. I didn't think I could ever get better, but I did, and I propose to stay that way."

"I'm very glad."

It seemed he should go, but Lincoln sank into a renewed silence that held Cage there a moment more.

"Why didn't you tell me?" Lincoln asked.

"Tell you what?"

"That you'd hired this girl. That you'd joined the abolitionist crusade."

"I thought it best to keep it a secret."

"Yes, but from me? Do you think I'm an enemy of Negro freedom?"

"I didn't see how it would have done you any good to know. You have some very narrow political gaps to run."

"That's true, but I hate to think that such an important friend to me as Micajah Weatherby wouldn't trust me with knowledge of any sort."

"I trust you," Cage said.

"Good. I admire what you've done to help this woman, and I'll do my best on her behalf. Were you planning to go to Tremont to hold me to account?"

"I suppose that if Ellie is going I'll go as well."

"I have an idea. Why not let her take the stage and you ride up with me? Wouldn't you like to see the marvelous workings of the circuit?"

Cage was indeed curious about the marvelous workings of the circuit, so two days later he departed with Lincoln and the rest of the judicial circuit riders to Tremont, the seat of Tazewell County where Cordelia was incarcerated and where her case would be heard.

"Now you see my real life at last," Lincoln said as he and Cage rode together on horseback across the radiant spring prairie, the smells of new grass and flowers and raw rich sod so powerfully present in the air around them that they seemed like physical bands of matter that could be reached for and touched. Lincoln had a new buggy but he had left it behind in Springfield, declaring to Cage that since the weather promised to be so fine they should travel like primitives in full unvehicularized glory. They listened to a tapestry of birdsong, the piercing notes of a bobwhite breaking through the calls of the multitudes of other species as if concluding an argument. Grouse whickered away in the distance from their approaching horses. The dark imprisoning winter that had helped to shatter Lincoln's morale was as remote from their memories now as if it had occurred in a prehistoric epoch.

By his "real life," Lincoln meant the circuit, the twice-yearly legal caravan that set out from Springfield—from Sangamon County to Tazewell County, on to McLean and Logan and half a dozen other counties before arriving again three months later where it had started. They had barely left the suburbs of Springfield this morning when Cage immediately understood the appeal: open country forever ahead, a traveling band of legal minds and raconteurs and singing companions who, upon arrival in some forsaken county seat, would partition themselves into judges and adversaries for a few days, and then when it came time for the circuit to move on they would come together again in circus fellowship. Lincoln and Cage were riding in the vanguard today, fifty yards or so ahead of the carriage bearing Judge Treat and State's Attorney David Campbell, alongside which rode a cluster of other lawyers to whom he had been given only a hasty introduction before the group set out on the Pekin Road. Treat and Campbell were Democrats—Cage didn't know about the others—but party loyalty out on the great ocean of grass was, it seemed, too puny a thought.

"We get rained on pretty regular," Lincoln explained, "and these men do their share of snoring and farting when you stop for the night and share a bed with them, but I believe the circuit works better on my spirits than one of Ash Merritt's mustard rubs."

Cage was glad to see his friend so revived. Lincoln wore his battered wide-brimmed straw hat. It shaded his eyes and made his face look less gaunt than his usual tall lawyer's hat. His duster and umbrella were strapped behind his cantle and his saddlebags were bulging with law books and legal papers. He rose high in his stirrups to take in the landscape and breathe in the air that was so fragrant with wildflowers. He was no longer stooped and slouchy. He sat his horse with the same confident bearing of the young man he had been at Kellogg's Grove almost ten years ago.

"How will you argue Cordelia's case?" Cage pressed him. Now that they were riding ahead of the others, he decided he had better try to steer the conversation toward strategy.

"Well, there's some law I can cite, though thorns have grown up around it here and there. We've got Article Six of the Northwest Ordinance on our side for a start, which says that Illinois is supposed to be a free state, though everyone knows you can keep a slave here and just call him an indentured servant. There was a case that came up a few months ago that will be pretty handy for us, since the court decided that for any person living in Illinois there's a presumption of freedom. The thorn there is that if she's a slave and they can prove it, there goes our presumption. The onus probandi as they call it lies with us."

"The onus what?"

"Burden of proof. If this Richard Etheridge Esquire shows up at the hearing to claim his property, or sends somebody to do it for him more likely, it'll make my job proving she's not a slave a little harder than I'd like it to be."

They rode all day, along a road Lincoln said he had helped lay out when he was a surveyor, across a toll bridge over Salt Creek that he had introduced a bill in the legislature to build. The very landscape seemed to belong to him, to be part of the constituency that fed his reviving sense of destiny. Beyond Salt Creek there were no groves or trees, just pure prairie and then a faint road leading through waving grass so tall it brushed against the necks of their horses. It was a road that seemed almost arbitrary in this featureless immensity, as if someone had tried to carve a route through the curving vault of heaven.

It was nearing dark when they pulled up at an inn in Delavan with fifteen miles still to go to Tremont. There were seven circuit riders, plus Cage, and they all shared the same room, dumping their baggage on the floor and then trudging into the dining room to eat greasy fried pork and stale cornbread. Cage was sore after the long ride, and when a cramp struck his leg during dinner he had to stand up to walk it off while the legal men remained at the table laughing and telling him welcome to the circuit. After dinner they played rolley-hole by torchlight, drinking and declaiming until the patient innkeeper suggested they retire to their beds. Cage shared a bed with Lincoln and Judge Treat, three others crowded together on the only other bed in the room, and the two remaining men slept on the floor on threadbare quilts. But no one really slept, partly because of the bedbugs, partly because they were all deliriously happy to be away from wives and offices and could not stop themselves from telling stories of last season's court cases, colorful suits involving marauding hogs and castration by pocketknife, bastardy and fornication and bestiality.

"This poor ignorant old farmer," Sam Treat said. "He truly believed that human beings can impregnate livestock. 'Your Honor, that man there fucked my sow and now she's gonna have some young bills on account of it, and by gum they won't be fit to sell.'"

Treat was by nature quiet and thoughtful, but after telling his story he laughed so hard he fell off the bed. Even though he was the circuit judge he was a year or two junior to most of the men in the room, who were still in their earlier thirties. They were young men in command of other people's lives, inasmuch as they were routinely charged with saving men from bankruptcy or driving them into it, arguing for their imprisonment or for their release. Cage laughed along with them, taken up by their convivial spirit. Lincoln had vouched for him when they set out from Springfield as the finest fellow in Illinois, a great poet whose book, when finished, would cause him to be recognized as the presiding genius of the prairie land. Now, at one in the morning, David Campbell declared they must drink a toast to the one true scholar in their midst, the one man not corrupted by legal arcana, who would never have to argue over whose sow got fucked by whom. Since there were no glasses to raise the toast, they passed a bottle of whiskey around. When it reached Lincoln he passed it fluidly to the next man without comment.

Why did he not drink? Surely no sense of refinement or decorum prevented it, since he was neither refined nor decorous and kept in his head an extensive archive of the filthiest stories and jests human beings had ever uttered. For all of Lincoln's instinct for hearty comradeship, his was a private mind. He was a tightly held, unrevealing man, and perhaps he was afraid of what spirituous liquors might reveal of himself, afraid of the places within himself they might lead him.

The drinking men and the lone abstainer all fell asleep within an hour of the bottle being passed around, and woke to the assault of a brilliant beam of April sun through the streaked window. Cage had slept between Lincoln and Treat on the double bed, and when he woke his head was flanked by both men's smelly stocking feet and his forehead was covered with the red scabrous bumps of bedbug bites. The men yawned and pulled on their clothes and gathered up their gear and stumbled outside to the jakes. They took turns shaving and then ate a breakfast that was as dreary and unappetizing as their supper had been the night before. None of them complained. They appeared to take a certain communal pride in enduring the hardships of the accommodations and the grimness of the food.

They set out again across the open prairie, following the road as it led to a wide gravel ford across the Mackinaw River, and in another hour they were riding through the main street of Tremont, the seat of Tazewell County. Around the county courthouse, a colonnaded building of red brick with a towering cupola, there was already a crowd of prospective litigants waiting to meet the traveling lawyers, eager to enlist them in their legal causes now that the prescribed day of judgment had arrived. Cage saw Ellie among them. The fast-moving stage had delivered her in Tremont the night before, and now she stood, patient and solitary at the edge of the crowd, wearing a striped dress of blue and white, the tight sleeves showing off the contours of her arms, the plain lace collar closed enticingly at the base of her throat, where a shell cameo was placed as if by the hand of nature. She stood with geometric composure, her hands neatly in front of her, holding the corners of the zebra shawl that framed her bodice. She nodded at Cage as he reined up beside her, but there was no smile, just a look that communicated she was glad he had arrived and that now it was time to get down to business.

Grooms were waiting to take their horses to the stable, and Lincoln and the other lawyers had hardly dismounted before they began interviewing witnesses for their upcoming cases or going over pleadings with the local attorneys. Cage realized that if he didn't pull Lincoln away at once he would be subsumed in other cases, so he and Ellie each grabbed one of his arms and walked off with him in the direction of the jail.

"I'll be back in half an hour," he called over his shoulder to his clamoring clients. "But right now I'm taken hostage and there's nothing I can do about it."

"Well, it's Mr. Lincoln!" the delighted jail keeper exclaimed as he sprung up from his chair and pumped Lincoln's hand. "We heard you were a sick man down there in Springfield for a while."

"Touch of the gravel, Bob. But I'm better now, and the circuit's always a tonic. Reckon my friends and I could talk to the Negro woman you got in here?"

The jail keeper led them upstairs, to a cell at the far end of the corridor. The jail smelled of mildew and urine and cabbage, and prisoners along the way, peering through the slots of their corroded iron doors, called out friendly greetings to the visitors. The door to Cordelia's cell shrieked on its unlubricated hinges when the jail keeper unlocked and opened it. Cordelia had heard them coming and was standing in front of her narrow cot, wearing a dress whose sleeves were torn and whose hem was caked in dried mud. She tried to suppress her tears but could not. She started to shiver—from fear, or from hope. Ellie gripped her shoulders and sat down with her on the cot, upon the single ragged blanket that Cordelia had made taut and square across the thin straw mattress in a forlorn attempt at housekeeping. She wept for a while. Ellie embraced her with a warmth that Cage did not think she would have cared to display. Watching the terrified girl, Cage rebuked himself for the exuberant comradely pleasures he had enjoyed in riding from Springfield while she had sat here in fright and isolation in this stinking cell.

"Mr. Lincoln here is your lawyer," Ellie told Cordelia. "He's here to help you."

Lincoln sat down next to them on the cot to hear her story while Cage remained standing with his back to the cell wall, upon which previous generations of male prisoners had recorded their obscene musings, either in words or in striking illustrations.

"Will you please tell me," Lincoln asked, "whether your given name is Cordelia, or Louisa, as it says in the sheriff's handbill?"

"It's Louisa. Cordelia is what I rechristened myself on my own. That's my free name."

"Well, let's continue calling you that, since our hope is that your freedom won't be interrupted for long. How did you come to find yourself in this jail, Cordelia?"

She looked at Lincoln, at his hauntingly plain face, the sad gray eyes leveled at her own. She looked only for an instant to Ellie, as if to confirm her impression that this man could be trusted, and then began telling him her story.

She was born a slave in Crittenden County, Kentucky, she said, the property of a long-widowed woman named Mrs. Etheridge. Mrs. Etheridge was a tolerant and kindly Christian woman who believed that Negroes had been made in the image of God just the same as white people had, but that the race had been degraded due to exposure to the tropical heat of Africa. She believed, however, that there were many individuals, like Louisa, in whom the spark of enterprise and intelligence had not been extinguished, and that it was her duty to improve them by giving them not just a living trade but an education sufficient to allow them to read the Bible and even suitable works of literature, such as the sonnets of Shakespeare and Milton's *Paradise Lost.*

But Mrs. Etheridge, who in her prime had been a powerful matriarch, started to become senile at a young age and before she was even fifty years old suffered from great imbecility of mind. Her son—Robert—took over her affairs. He was less kindhearted than his mother and thought that Louisa would make a better investment if he hired her out. She was highly skilled at sewing and lacework, so he contacted an agent who sent her off to Frankfort to work for a milliner. The milliner abused her with the whip and in other ways she did not want to talk about. She ran off and made her way back to the Etheridge place, where she begged Robert to take her back into the home. But he would not hear of it and told her she would go back to Frankfort or he would put her up for auction on the open market and she would see how she liked her situation then. That night she managed to go through the demented woman's desk and find the bill of sale relating to her bondage, and also a contract that her son had made with the hiring agent to send her off to Frankfort. She stole some of Mrs. Etheridge's clothes and a map of the United States and managed to talk her way into a maid's job on a steamboat that brought her down the Ohio to the Mississippi, then up the Mississippi to the Illinois, where she disembarked at Pekin in the middle of the night and made her way overland to Springfield. She had assumed that Springfield, as the capital of a free state, would be the safest place for her to settle.

"Well," Lincoln said, "going to Illinois was a bold stroke on your part. But as a general matter the top part of the state is a little freer for you Negroes than the bottom part. It's a good thing you didn't go as far south as Egypt. Springfield is where you met the gentlemen who introduced you to Mr. Weatherby here?"

"Yes sir."

"Why didn't you tell me when you saw that handbill," Ellie said, "instead of just running away?"

"A panic took hold of me, Mrs. Bicknell. That's the only reason I can say. I felt like a hunted slave and I had to run."

She cut her eyes quickly back to Lincoln.

"But I hold that I'm not a slave, sir, since I'm in Illinois."

"That's what I'll argue in court. Who seized you on the road the other day?"

"Three men. They asked me if I had a certificate of freedom and when I couldn't produce one they grabbed me and took me to the sheriff."

"Did you say anything to them about your being a runaway slave?"

"No, I kept that to myself."

"Good. What about the papers you stole?"

"I tore them up into a thousand little pieces the night I left and scattered them in the creek."

"That was well done. What do you say when people ask you how you got this scar on your cheek?"

"That it was made by an accident with a pair of shears. I don't let on that it was a stray blow from the whip."

"Are there other scars?"

"There are these." She unbuttoned her dress without shame, though she was in the presence of two men. She turned her back and lowered it six or eight inches so that they could see the scars all across her back, carved there in an irregular ladder-like pattern. Though they were not recent, they were still raised and livid and always would be so. Lincoln examined the scars with the cold scrutiny of a physician, but Cage looked away, angry at what he was seeing, ashamed at himself for thinking that because he had done a good deed in hiring Cordelia his conscience had any right to be clear.

"I would like to meet the man who did that to you," Ellie said calmly. "I would like to cut off his prick and his balls."

The remarks did not shock Cage. He knew her, and so in his own limited way did Lincoln. And no words, spoken by either a woman or a man, would have registered as obscene at that moment, where there was a far greater obscenity visible in the marks on Cordelia's flesh.

Before she raised her dress again, Lincoln pointed to another mark on her left shoulder, a reddish elongated blob. "This is the birthmark mentioned in the newspaper advertisement? The one in the shape of Madagascar?"

"Yes sir."

Lincoln stared at the birthmark for a considerable amount of time.

"Thank you. You may refasten your dress."

"What if they ask me in court if I—"

"They'll ask you nothing in court, Cordelia, because under the Black Laws Negroes aren't allowed to testify. But be assured I'll do what I can on your behalf."

They stayed that night at the Franklin House on the courthouse square, Cage and Lincoln sharing a room downstairs, Ellie in the attic room reserved for women guests. They arranged for a decent meal to be sent up to Cordelia in the jail and then the three of them met for their own dinner at a quiet tavern Lincoln knew several blocks away, removed from the hurried lawyer-and-client consultations that were taking place in the center of town before court opened the next day.

"We're on the docket in the morning," Lincoln said as he shuffled through some papers he had secured that afternoon at the courthouse. "It looks like Mr. Etheridge has sent an agent to retrieve the girl for him. Fellow named Zephaniah Tuttle. I expect he knows his business and will be a good witness. Ed Jones is the lawyer on their side—he drinks hard but he's pretty capable. I'll put you on the stand, Miss . . . Mrs. . . . ."

"Oh, for God's sake, call me Ellie."

"I'll put you on the stand if that's suitable for you. You know Cordelia the best and the jury appreciates the sight of a handsome woman. Had you ever seen those marks on her back before?"

"No."

"Did she ever say to you that she'd been whipped?"

"No."

"So you can truthfully testify that you don't know how she got those scars."

"I can. For all I know about the matter she might have wandered into a bramble patch."

"Lot of brambles in Illinois," Lincoln said. "Reminds me of the story of the old Winnebago Indian whose favorite wife ran off into the woods one night with a rival chieftain from up the river . . ."

And off he went, just like the Lincoln of old, telling the story in a winding, leisurely way, with such delight in his voice that before he reached the end of it three or four of their fellow customers in the tavern drifted over to listen. No sooner was it concluded than it reminded him of another story, and by the time he was through telling that one the quiet little out-of-the-way establishment was the liveliest place in town, everyone refilling their cups and urging Lincoln on.

Cage and Ellie left him to entertain the Tremont taverngoers. Their secret life in Springfield left them unaccustomed to walking together on the street. It was strange to be in a new town, where no one knew them and they had nothing to hide. This sense of license was intoxicating to Cage, though he knew he needed to resist it. Their business in Tazewell County was grave. If they failed in it, if Lincoln failed in presenting their case, a young woman would be enslaved and brutalized for the rest of her life.

"Is this just another case for him?" she asked. "Could he just as easily argue the opposite side?"

"What makes you say that?"

"Well, we just watched him entertaining everyone in sight while Cordelia rots in that jail cell."

"His heart isn't cold, Ellie. If that's what you mean. It's the opposite: he feels things too hard."

"All right, I believe you. I don't know him like you do."

No, she knew him in a different way. He stood firm against that familiar surge of jealousy—it was unworthy of him. And there were more important things to reckon with tonight. They had almost reached the inn where they were staying and they each instinctively stepped apart, putting a proprietary distance between them.

"I'll go in first," she said.

"All right."

But before she walked off toward the inn she turned to face him. "I want my girl back."

"I know."

Her eyes were welling in the darkness, though it was hard for Cage to understand exactly what she was feeling. The sight of those scars when Cordelia had lowered her dress had obviously triggered a deep anger, and Ellie was one of those people who was only at risk of expressing other emotions once the door of anger had been breached. Now, swamped with a kind of confused tenderness, she discreetly pressed his hand and walked into the inn.

TWENTY-FIVE

❖❖❖

T HE COURTHOUSE WAS NEW but the courtroom on its second
floor already had the hard-used feel of public spaces everywhere.
Spittoons were plentiful but the aim of the observers who crowded into
the courtroom day after day was not impressive, and so the floor was
streaked with expectorated tobacco juice. The wooden rail separating
the judge's bench and the attorneys' tables from the rest of the room
was already in need of paint, and the sconces were blackened and caked
with candle wax. In addition there was a bad smell emanating from the
unwashed bodies and garments of the citizens pressed into the courtroom, and perhaps from the rank food they carried in their pockets.

Cordelia's case was third on the docket, behind a mortgage foreclo-
sure action and a case in which the father of an unmarried daughter was
suing the man who had gotten her with child. Since the girl worked in
her father's furniture shop, he was demanding recompense for loss of
his daughter's services while she was pregnant. There was little drama
in either case, some tedious questioning of witnesses followed by whispered, friendly conversations between Lincoln and his opposing attorneys in front of the judge's bench. As the cases progressed, Cage looked
around the courtroom, trying to spot the man who was likely to be tes-
tifying against them in their own proceeding. Sitting at the end of their
bench was a fifty-year-old man with a patient-seeming face and a powerful frame who looked very much at home, well accustomed to the slow
and undramatic pace of life in a courtroom.

Just before the case was called, Cordelia was brought into the courtroom by the sheriff and seated next to Lincoln at the attorneys' table.
He poured her a glass of water and she took a series of quick, nervous

sips to reinforce her composure. Since this was merely a habeas corpus hearing there was no jury. Samuel Treat, the man who had slept in the bed with Lincoln and Cage the night before, would decide the merits of the case on his own. He moved the proceedings along briskly, listening as the lawyers made their opening remarks, Lincoln arguing his onus probandi and citing a recent case in the Illinois Supreme Court that ruled that it was "repugnant to and subversive of natural right" for a human being to have to prove his freedom, since the very concept of enslavement was conceived and founded on injustice. His courtroom manner was the same as it had been in the Truett trial: casual, direct, sociable, seemingly innocent of legal stagecraft. Edward Jones spoke next, representing the slaveholder who was making the claim that Cordelia was his escaped property. He was compact and barrel-chested. He spoke in paragraphs of symphonic perfection, spinning off into pleasing verbal variations but always returning to his main theme of the sanctity of individual property. He congratulated his learned friend Mr. Lincoln on his logical gyrations but felt it was his duty to remind His Honor that the state constitution of 1818 and law after law enacted since left no doubt as to the status of Negroes in Illinois.

Ellie was called to testify. It intoxicated Cage to see her in the witness chair, to see her in front of the public in a crowded courtroom. He was aware of the other men in the room training their attention on her, staring at her with some measure of his own unappeasable sexual hunger. She sat as naturally upright in the plain wooden chair as if it had been designed for her. Cage thought she was a little cross during Lincoln's examination, self-righteously answering questions she clearly believed were self-evident. Yes, she had employed the woman, known to her as Cordelia, seated at the attorneys' table. No, the woman had never given any indication she was anybody's slave, neither had she comported herself with any sense of wariness or fear of pursuit. She was a conscientious worker, bright-minded and skillful, clearly experienced in the domestic arts.

"Do you know where this experience was acquired?"

"No, I don't."

"Did you make assumptions about where it might have been acquired?"

"I assumed that she had been a lady's maid or perhaps the mistress of her own household."

"You did not ask her if that was the case?"

"No."

"She did not volunteer any information to the contrary?"

"No."

"During the time Cordelia was in your shop, did you notice any distinguishing scars or marks?"

"She has a scar on her cheek. I did not see any others."

"Did you ask how she came by this scar on her cheek?"

"I didn't ask her, but she volunteered that it was the result of an accident with a pair of shears."

When she was cross-examined by Jones, she was as studiously impersonal as she had been with Lincoln: a witness who projected confidence that the evidence spoke for itself and that there was no need for her to attempt to win the favor of the court in any other way.

"When you hired the woman you call Cordelia, did you ask to see her certificate of freedom?"

"No."

"You weren't aware that it's against the law to hire a Negro who fails to produce such a certificate?"

"She didn't fail to produce it. I didn't ask to see it."

"As her employer, you were obliged to ask to see it!"

"I see," Ellie said flatly, conceding the point in a way that gave Jones no other option but to change course. He asked her again where Cordelia had told her she had come from, what she had told her about how she had acquired her sewing skills, how exactly she had injured her cheek.

"You were in the shop with her day after day, week after week. Do you mean to say that you never discussed her background?"

"We have a very busy shop, especially during the legislative session. There's no time for such talk."

"Were you not curious where this woman came from?"

"No."

"Were you not curious about how in the world someone could stab herself in the cheek with a pair of shears?"

"I was not curious about that either. I was very busy. I was not her mother, or her sister, or her friend. I was her employer, and her work was very satisfactory to me."

When she was dismissed she took her seat next to Cage and allowed her arm to brush up against him. Her body was trembling, perhaps from withheld anger, perhaps from the stress of trying to reveal nothing of what she knew, yet still navigate through the narrow straits of perjury. He knew that, if need be, she would have lied as blatantly as the situation demanded. She did not consider herself particularly bound by law, but like many lawless people she had a rigid investment in justice.

After Ellie's testimony, Jones called his sole witness, the man Mr. Etheridge had hired to retrieve his human property. Zephaniah Tuttle was indeed the imposing individual Cage had noticed earlier. He brought his confident bearing to the witness chair, where he sat with excellent posture and a friendly look on his face. He had been, he testified, a drayman, a steamboatman, an overseer on several substantial properties in Crittenden and neighboring counties in Kentucky, and was presently in the business of reclaiming stolen or absconded property for a number of clients in that same area. Only a few weeks after Mr. Etheridge had placed an advertisement in a number of newspapers in central Illinois—the presumed destination of his runaway slave Louisa— he had learned that she was incarcerated in the county jail of Tazewell County and had engaged Mr. Tuttle to travel there and reclaim her.

"Did Mr. Etheridge describe Louisa to you so that you could be sure the Negress in the Tazewell County jail was indeed the same woman?"

"He did."

"What was the description he gave you?"

"Objection, Your Honor," Lincoln called out in his squeaky voice. "Hearsay. If the—"

"This is a bench trial, Mr. Lincoln," the judge interrupted. "And since I believe I have enough sense to decide about the evidence myself I will overrule your objection."

Lincoln gave a little head bow of good-natured defeat, and the testimony resumed, with the slave catcher precisely describing not just

Cordelia's height and build and shade of coloration, not just the scar on her cheek but the marks that were hidden by her dress.

"Does Louisa have a birthmark?"

"Yes, a prominent one on her left shoulder."

"Will you describe the birthmark to the court?"

"It is of a livid brownish-reddish color and is in the shape of the island of Madagascar."

"And there are scars on her back?"

"There are a multitude of scars. Owing to her intransigence, Mr. Etheridge was obliged to use the whip."

"Will you point these various marks out to the court?"

"The girl would have to stand and lower her dress a bit."

The judge ordered her to do so and Lincoln, to Cage's surprise, did not object. Perhaps he thought it was useless, perhaps he thought the spectacle of a young woman being ordered to halfway undress in a crowded courtroom would offer a stronger argument than any legal objection. Cordelia was escorted by the bailiff to the judge's bench, where she turned her back to the judge, slipped down one shoulder of her dress to display the birthmark there, then did her best to reveal the scars on her back while holding the dress up in front to cover her breasts. The courtroom was full, trials being one of the main forms of entertainment in any county seat. Tazewell County was by no means an abolitionist stronghold, but it was located far enough into the northern sphere of influence for scattered cries of "Shame!" to arise from the back of the gallery as Judge Treat dispassionately examined Cordelia's exposed back. He rapped his gavel distractedly with one hand while he signaled for Cordelia to raise her dress and sit down.

Lincoln had caught the tone of the witness's genial manner, and he engaged Mr. Tuttle during his cross-examination with a neighborly ease.

"Mr. Tuttle, you seem to know all about this Louisa and her various distinguishing marks."

"Yes sir, I do."

"Have you known her long?"

"I have studied up on her."

"That is evident, but have you had the pleasure of meeting her?"

"Before today?"

"Before today."

"I suppose not."

"Have you laid eyes on her before today?"

"No, but I've just shared a description of her with the court."

"And you got that description from Mr. Etheridge in a hearsay sort of way?"

Jones muttered an objection, Treat muttered, "Mr. Lincoln, you know better . . ." in a mildly chastening tone, and Lincoln changed course.

"Now, just to make sure we all understand why we're here today. Your position is that this woman is the slave property of this Mr. Etheridge."

"That is my position."

"Well, we should be able to dispense with the matter pretty quick then. Will you please show the court the bill of sale?"

"I don't have a bill of sale."

Lincoln pretended great surprise.

"Mr. Etheridge didn't provide you with one before sending you off all the way to Illinois?"

"That particular document has been lost, I'm afraid, Mr. Lincoln."

"Then how do you intend to prove that the slave Louisa and the woman named Cordelia are one and the same person?"

"By her marks, sir, as I have already testified."

"By the marks on her back where you say she was savagely whipped?"

"I did not say 'savagely.'"

"By the birthmark which you say is in the shape of Madagascar?"

"Yes."

"Madagascar is an island in the Indian Ocean?"

"Where it is located on the globe I don't know precisely."

Lincoln nodded in an understanding way, then—as if an idea had just come to him—he turned around and picked up a thick book from the attorneys' table.

"Well, I expect between the two of us you had more of schooling, Mr. Tuttle, so it's no wonder I didn't know where it was either. I had to consult my atlas to find out."

"Your Honor," Jones said while Lincoln opened the book to the marked page, "this case is supposed to be about personal property, not geography."

"That may be so, Mr. Jones," Treat said. "But I'm sort of interested in where Mr. Lincoln's wandering mind is going to lead us next."

"I appreciate your curiosity, Your Honor," Lincoln said as he walked over to the witness chair with his opened book.

"As you can see from this map, Mr. Tuttle, Madagascar has the honor of sharing the Indian Ocean with the island of Zanzibar. But the hand of the Creator, aided I suspect by certain influences of nature, has given them a different shape. Do you see what I mean? Would you say that one of these islands sort of strays to the left, while the other sort of strays to the right?"

"I will grant you that observation, sir."

"Thank you. And in your opinion does Madagascar stray to the left or to the right?"

"To the right."

"And what about Zanzibar?"

"Zanzibar, according to your philosophy, would be a leftward sort of island."

Lincoln took the atlas from the witness and showed it to Treat and to Jones. He said that he hoped His Honor would demonstrate the same courtesy to him as he had shown to Mr. Jones by allowing his client to once more reveal to the court her birthmark. As soon as Treat had given a weary nod, Cordelia rose and approached the bench and once again slipped down the shoulder of her dress while all three men stared at her distinguishing mark.

"Now if this birthmark island were to be said to lean one way or the other," Lincoln asked Tuttle, "which would it be?"

"Oh, for God's sake!" Jones said.

Treat had the trace of a smile on his face as he ordered the witness to answer.

"It would lean to the left," Tuttle said begrudgingly.

"Like Zanzibar?" Lincoln asked.

"They look almost the same. And they're both in the same place. Mr. Etheridge was just—"

"Would you please do me the courtesy of answering my question, Mr. Tuttle? Does this birthmark look more like Madagascar or like Zanzibar?"

"Zanzibar, but if you're going to—"

Lincoln cut off the witness with an expression of sincere thanks for his cooperation and a wish for his safe return home to Crittenden County.

His closing argument to the judge was more passionate than Cage would have predicted after the almost absurd wrangling over the shape of two islands on the other side of the world.

"It's possible, Your Honor," he said, "that you don't share my fascination with whether a birthmark might be shaped like Madagascar or like Zanzibar. You might think it pedantic of me to quibble over such a thing. But doesn't the potential loss of a fellow human being's freedom demand as close a scrutiny as can be brought to the case?

"As you know, Judge, and as some of the people in this courtroom know, I used to be a surveyor. I can assure you that in that profession the very shape of a thing has a critical bearing. Had I ever misjudged the boundaries of a claim or the location of a town site by even the smallest amount, that one mistake could have led to profound consequences, to endless legal battles or perhaps an out-and-out blood feud between warring neighbors.

"And in this case, I know that we can all agree that we're discussing something far greater than a mere property claim. Can the configuration of an island be judged a trivial detail when a woman's life is at stake, any more than when fixing a boundary a few feet one way or the other can be judged trivial? But not all the matters we've been discussing are so small. There is, for example, the looming absence of so essential a document as a bill of sale. Wouldn't a man who had taken on the awesome burden of claiming ownership of another's life at least have a receipt to show for it? Would Illinois, a free state, allow the travesty of a woman being sent into slavery without any papers whatsoever?

"The burden of proof, as you well know, Your Honor, rests squarely with the claimant. A human person in Illinois was presumed to be a free person unless proven otherwise. This was established by Article Six of the Northwest Ordinance of 1787, and it was upheld just this past December by the Illinois Supreme Court in *Kinney v. Cook.* Judge, you've seen the marks on this poor woman's back. Could it be on the basis of these scars, these hideous and inhuman scars, and on nothing else, that you are prepared to send her back across the Ohio and into the house of the man who claimed to own her and who meant to prove that he owned her not by offering a document as civilized men do, but by the insult of presenting instead the evidence of his own cruelty and indifference to her well-being?"

There was a passion in Lincoln's tone that seemed to take him by surprise even as he was speaking his summation. He had, Cage thought, meant to make a coolly logical argument, but the image of Cordelia's scarred back was in everyone's mind and it had to be in Lincoln's as well. His voice almost cracked as he concluded, and the courtroom audience was on his side; indeed, half of them were on their feet, calling out for the judge to let the girl go.

Probably as a means of putting an end to the outburst, Treat announced he would go into his chambers and mull over the evidence. In the interval, both Jones and Lincoln left the courtroom as well, to consult with other clients about other cases. Cordelia remained seated at the defendant's table, looking straight ahead, staring at the empty judge's bench. Ellie left Cage's side and walked up to sit next to her and whisper a few reassuring words. If it was a violation of court protocol, no one stopped her. In a moment she walked back and took her seat beside Cage again, this time touching and squeezing his arm.

"She's frightened," Ellie said, glancing over at the self-possessed Mr. Tuttle, who was reading the newspaper in the crowded courtroom as if he had no concern in all the world, and unaware of the hostile stares directed at his back by some of the rustling spectators in the courtroom.

Fifteen minutes later, Lincoln and Jones returned. Lincoln took his seat next to Cordelia, who was still sitting so rigidly and silently it might have appeared to a stranger that she had no real interest in the outcome. Then the judge returned and the murmuring courtroom audience grew quiet.

"I hereby grant the writ of habeas corpus," Treat said without any dramatic preamble and with a matter-of-fact inflection. He gave an equally undramatic rap of his gavel and turned to Cordelia. "You're free to go."

The courtroom broke into cheers. Lincoln and Jones stood up, cordially shook hands, and prepared to get on with the next case. Zephaniah Tuttle left the court looking perfectly unruffled but without speaking a word to anyone on his way out. Cordelia stood, wiping tears out of her eyes, quaking a little from relief. Lincoln patted her on the shoulder and the girl, forgetting for a moment all boundaries of race and propriety, leaned forward and flung her arms around his shapeless frame. Ellie, who was wiping a grudging tear or two from her own eyes, rushed forward and gripped one of his great hands in both of hers in gratitude.

"That was well done," Cage said. "Thank you, Lincoln."

He discreetly handed him his twenty dollars, and Lincoln was unembarrassed to take it. "Well, it wasn't a sure thing," he said, as he slipped the money into the pocket of his waistcoat, "but we had some law on our side—not all of it, but enough to make a meal. But listen to me, Cage. That girl is free now, but unless she's got a certificate to show to the next sheriff that takes her in, she might not slide out again."

A certificate of freedom cost a thousand dollars, not counting the legal fees that would doubtlessly be needed to acquire it. Cage pondered the limits of his magnanimity as he and Ellie and Cordelia rode home that afternoon from Tremont. The Black Laws discouraged Negroes from riding in public conveyances, and so he had already invested in hiring a roomy rockaway coach and driver to take them to Springfield. Ellie somehow managed to sleep as the coach made its lurching way back over the Mackinaw ford and across the infinity of prairie beyond. Cordelia sat upright, staring backwards, measuring off the growing distance between her and the Tazewell County jail. Though it was a warm April day she drew her shawl tighter around her shoulders as if to hold her shaken self together. Her eyes were open, almost unblinking. She looked like someone who had not slept in a long time and still did not dare to surrender consciousness. Cage did his best to reassure her that her ordeal was over, and she nodded in gratitude at his attempt, but both of them knew nothing short of a certificate of freedom could guard against its happening again.

Lincoln and the rest of the court had remained in Tazewell, where they would take care of business for a week or so before packing up and moving on again to all the seven other county seats on the circuit, not returning to Springfield until months later. A part of Cage wished he were still with them, as they rode wantonly across the landscape, singing songs and telling stories and arriving in the next county seat, where they would be welcomed by the souls whose fates they would determine. It struck Cage as a satisfying life, a consequential one, if you could bear the lice and the weary miles and the terrible food. Perhaps it was a life he should have chosen for himself, rich with companionship and authority. It would have felt good to set a slave free, rather than just pay another man to do so. It would have felt good to speak words that mattered unambiguously, rather than sit at a desk chasing down thoughts that had a way of eluding the very words used to describe them.

He left his door ajar that night, sensing that Ellie was feeling the same surge of triumphant energy as he was. Just after midnight she slipped into the room and under the covers of his bed and stayed there almost till dawn, neither of them sleeping, making love all night with an urgency born out of shared pride. It was one of those rare moments when she allowed him to glimpse that the careful, enticing distance she kept from him was as much a habit of mind as a defining boundary. But it was a habit of mind she was not likely to give up. She was a woman who couldn't allow herself to love him, or even bear to hear that he might love her. But maybe that was what he wanted too—the same enticing distance, the unclosed gap between the anticipatory present and the secured future. Cage had been observing Lincoln in this regard. Lincoln continually ran the risk of becoming a casualty of others' expectations. Look at the way he thrived on the circuit, hostage to no one's good opinion but his own, responsible to no one but the law and his clients. In Springfield society, though, he often seemed as helpless as a child, awkward and tentative. And in matters of love, or what he thought was supposed to be love, he was even more miserably confused than Cage himself.

"It's no mystery why people think he's so exceptional," she murmured sleepily in the middle of the night. Her head was buried in his chest and he could feel the breath of her words against his skin. "It's because he *is* exceptional. He wasn't uncertain or confused in that courtroom at all, was he? Not like he sometimes seems. It's fun to see a man do well what he does best."

The words were so congruent to what his own restless nighttime thoughts had been it was as if they were part of a conversation they had been having. Cage thought Lincoln had done a splendid job—and a splendid thing—in return for the twenty dollars he had been paid. But it was one thing to believe that and another to endure Ellie's uncharacteristically direct praise for a man that he could not stop thinking of as a rival.

"And I have her back," Ellie said, as she slipped out of bed to stand naked at his washstand. He watched her arrange her hair, pull on her chemise, her stockings, a petticoat and then another. She had not worn a corset but had come into his room otherwise fully dressed and would leave that way. They could hear Mrs. Hopper and Betsy setting out the things for breakfast below, they could smell cornbread baking. Ellie would have to leave right away, with exquisite stealth. Nevertheless, he felt content—what he had with her was enough. There wasn't any more, there was no point in trying to manufacture any more. In his contentment he was about to tell her he would buy Cordelia's certificate of freedom. But before he could do so she turned to him from the mirror, her face composed and business-like.

"We need to see that this doesn't happen again," she said. "I can't afford to lose that girl."

"You can afford it. The business will survive. You don't want to lose her because she means something to you."

"You say that like an accusation."

"You hear it like one."

She shrugged as she slipped on her delicate square-toed shoes. "In any case, she needs a certificate of freedom. It seems fair to me that you should pay the larger part of it. Eight hundred dollars. I'll pay the balance of two hundred."

"I don't see why I should pay more than seven hundred."

"Seven fifty."

"All right."

She frowned, but leaned over the bed to kiss him anyway, the tenderness and triumph of their night together still lingering. "You might have been a little more generous," she said.

He didn't tell her that before she started to negotiate with him he had been on the verge of announcing he would pay the whole thousand dollars himself. She wanted a deal from him, not a gift. She opened the door slightly so that she could see out into the hall, and when she saw that no one was watching she walked confidently back to her room.

TWENTY-SIX

✦✦✦

H E W O K E T O T H E M U S I C of songbirds, to the scent of lark-spur and sweet william, to the sound of children playing outside the windows, and—in the distance—the singing of slaves who were already long at work in the fields with their hemp hooks.

"Would you care for breakfast, Mr. Weatherby?" Oz said, magically appearing in the doorway at the very moment, it seemed, that Cage awoke. "It will be served presently."

"Thank you. Where's Lincoln?"

"Mr. Lincoln went into town early this morning with Rose and Morocco. His toothache was considerably worse through the night and he thought he ought to have the tooth drawn at once."

Oz was in his fifties, dignified to the point of vanity. His hair was silver and cropped close, his side-whiskers barbered to a pair of sharp darts that almost touched the sides of his mouth. His composure, vocabulary, and courtesy all seemed drawn from a play about bucolic plantation life. Cage and Lincoln were both guests in the Speed home and after two weeks neither had found a satisfactory way of relating to the captive humans who served them with such efficiency and seeming goodwill. There was no way to react to them except to do so as if they were ordinary servants. There was no point in lecturing Speed and his teeming, rambunctious family about slavery, no point in trying to take the slaves themselves aside in an attempt to win their respect by making their own discomfort known. There was nothing Cage could do other than to accept the hospitality that could not be turned away, and to silently allow this pleasant idyll to eat into his soul.

The dining room was crowded as usual when Cage came down to

breakfast, almost a dozen Speed relatives gathered around the table as slaves hurried in with hot biscuits they had just taken out of the oven in the summer kitchen. Breakfast was a casual meal, unlike dinner, which was a formidable, choreographed affair at which the Speed men took nightly turns proposing a general theme for discussion—philosophy, politics, the histories of various ancient civilizations. Side conversations were frowned upon, even from the children.

Two-year-old Eliza, the daughter of Joshua's sister Susan, reached out for Cage from her mother's lap as he approached the table. "Where Giant?" she plaintively asked.

"The Giant is getting his tooth out," Cage explained to the child. Eliza nodded her head gravely, as if she understood, but looked around for Lincoln anyway. Between the two exciting houseguests, she much preferred the Giant, who, until his painful molar had finally sent him off to his bed, had spent a good part of yesterday afternoon crouched on his back with his knees in the air balancing a squealing Eliza on the soles of his feet.

"Did the poor man sleep at all?" Susan asked Cage.

"I'd be surprised if he did. I could almost hear his tooth throbbing in the next bed."

"Well, the doctor will draw the tooth," Mrs. Speed said as she waved away an elderly house slave named Nanny who was offering her a platter of ham, "and I'm sure Mr. Lincoln will be returned to us in excellent condition." Lucy Speed was Joshua's mother. She was in her fifties and had borne many children, most of whom had gravitated as adults back to the Speed plantation, where they hovered around their widowed mother with a solicitude she had no patience for. Despite all its childbearing, her body was trim and upright, and she must have had a similar resiliency of spirit, since she spoke fondly of her late husband but showed no particular interest in mourning him. She was from aristocratic Virginia stock, her family connected somehow with Thomas Jefferson.

The other Mrs. Speed in the room, Lucy Speed's daughter-in-law Emma, took her niece from Cage's lap in time for Julia Ann, the younger house slave, to fill his coffee cup. He muttered "Thank you" reflexively, but had noticed that no one else in the household was in the habit of thanking the slaves for anything. They were well-trained, well-treated, and as placidly regarded as drifting clouds.

Cage and Lincoln had been here in the bear grass land of Kentucky, at the Speed family plantation of Farmington, for two weeks. In another week they would board a steamboat for home, but already the business and politics and feuding of Springfield felt like something that was taking place not just across the Ohio but in some frenetic kingdom far across the wide Pacific. Until his toothache, Lincoln had been as content and as calm as Cage had ever seen him. The Speeds were aswim in wealth and learning and family connections. Not only had Lucy Speed known Jefferson, but Emma Speed had astonished Cage and Lincoln the night they arrived by casually mentioning that she was the niece of John Keats! But whatever pretensions they had as a family were mostly hidden, emerging only during the high-minded conversation of the dinner hour, when lines from *The Iliad* or from the letters of Cicero might sally back and forth across the stewed mutton. Cage and Lincoln had been intimidated their first night with the Speeds, seated at the long table in formal dress in front of delicate china, their hosts' faces rosy with candlelight reflected off the faceted surfaces of crystal dinnerware. And then there had been the unsettling expertise of the slaves, as they moved silently from one diner to the next, filling wineglasses, ladling out gumbo or pudding sauce. But the intimidation quickly wore off, due to the warmth of the Speed family, the various ways in which Joshua Speed's brothers and sisters and half-siblings and in-laws made them feel welcome and enlisted them in games of whist and charades and riding expeditions and shopping trips to Louisville and tickling contests with the children.

The main house was a tasteful brick mansion with two great octagonal rooms that caused the house to flare out symmetrically on either side. From its front a broad avenue ran over a picturesque limestone bridge and out past the hemp fields to the Bardstown turnpike. There were gardens behind the house and a commodious carriage house and too many scattered outbuildings to count—any one of which, Lincoln had told Cage, was bigger than the log houses he had lived in when he was a boy in Kentucky and Indiana. An old stable had been converted into a kind of summer house, and that was where Cage had spent a good deal of his time in the last two weeks, working on his manuscript with all thoughts of business shut out of his head. Speed had in fact cleaned the place out for him for just this purpose, assuring him that his family would not think him unsocial for wanting to spend time alone with his work. The rule for guests at Farmington was that they be happy and productive, or happy and indolent if that was their preference.

Lincoln for his part was often out with Speed, watching the slaves harvest the hemp or flail the stalks for their seeds. He had a fascination with machinery and took joy in watching the fibers as they were run through hackles and ropewalks and jack screws to turn them into cordage and bagging. To Cage's mind, Lincoln had a way of ignoring the slaves as they bent over with their hemp hooks to cut down the stalks in a choking cloud of dust and pollen. Perhaps to him such back-breaking labor in the full force of the late-summer sun was nothing to be remarked upon. It was the sort of work he had grown up doing, the crushing physical and spiritual burden that had caused him to leave his luckless father's homestead and try to make his living any other way. But for Cage the problem of how much active slavery he could observe at close range without somehow speaking up about it was growing acute. He saw no good that could come out of raising the issue with his hosts. Like Joshua Speed, they had all been born into this arrangement and seemed to believe that their benign stewardship over their own slaves excused them from any moral worry about the institution itself. Once or twice he tried to share his discomfort with Lincoln, but Lincoln only said he was uncomfortable too and shrugged his narrow shoulders and went back into the house to wrestle with the children and quiz Mrs. Speed about Jefferson.

The truth was that neither Cage nor Lincoln had the will to resist the seductive force of this loving, vibrant family. The Speeds had reached out and drawn them into their circle with an openheartedness that was disorienting. It was hard for either of them to summon up a raging conscience when they had been made to feel so deeply and completely at home. Cage observed the Speed women—Mrs. Speed herself, or

Emma, or Susan, or Joshua's half sister Mary—as they bustled through the house, laughing with each other, trading recipes, arranging flowers, setting aside their needlework to speak tenderly to their children. He remembered some of that feminine brightness from his own childhood, but it had been extinguished so early by the death of his mother that it felt less like an actual memory than some hazy notion of happiness he had received from a book. His father had been a warmhearted man and had done the best he could, but a widowed father and a motherless son necessarily made up a stark household. By now he could call to mind only a dream-like approximation of his mother's face. He could recall the universal maternal timbre of her voice but not its specific sound. Being in the Speed home for two weeks had plunged him for the first time into a real awareness of what he had once had, might still have had if fortune had followed a different course.

The same hunger for what might have been was visible on Lincoln's face as he played with the children or followed the women bashfully around the house. His case was worse. He had been an even lonelier boy than Cage, more brokenhearted, more betrayed by circumstance, more confused. In most respects he was an uncommonly successful man, but his success was driven less by self-confidence than by its opposite, by a howling emotional need. Here in Kentucky, amid this throng of doting women and roughhousing children, he had seized upon the normal human joys of life as if they were something he had never known existed.

Lincoln wasn't the only one absent from the breakfast table. Speed himself had failed to appear.

"He left very early this morning on horseback," his mother said. "Even before Mr. Lincoln set out with Rose and Morocco."

"Where did he go?"

"Oh, on a very mysterious errand," Susan said. "We couldn't possibly tell you." The women smiled conspiratorially at each other. Cage could have begged them for an answer but he decided to safeguard his self-respect by finishing his breakfast and then retiring once more to his makeshift office in the summer house, where he was far too aware of writing and reading in comfort while the slaves continued their labor in the hemp fields. At four o'clock in the afternoon he looked out the

window and saw a wagon slowly cresting the little stone bridge on its
way to the main house. Morocco was driving. He was in his mid-forties
and had the most independent portfolio of any of Farmington's slaves,
entrusted with crucial postal errands and occasional matters of business. He and Rose, who was twenty years younger but similarly astute,
had taken Lincoln with them that morning when they drove into town
to sell peaches and cider from the property's orchards.

Rose rode in the back of the wagon with the leftover produce and
Lincoln swayed miserably on the seat next to Morocco. Cage walked
out of the summer house to meet them. He could see from fifty yards
away that Lincoln's jaw was swollen and packed with bloody wadding.

"I believe Mr. Lincoln here could do with a bit of a rest," Morocco
said to Cage.

"Your supposition is correct," Lincoln mumbled. "The doctor and I
had quite a wrestle over that tooth."

He nodded his thanks to Morocco and Rose and walked with Cage
toward the house. "I read somewhere," he said, "that if you breathe
exhilarating gas during the process you can have your tooth out with no
pain at all. I sure would have welcomed a taste of that gas today, Cage."

"Well, at least it's behind you."

"Not so sure. There's a piece still down in there somewhere he
couldn't get to, and if it starts hollering again I'll have to—"

He broke off when the front door opened and a group of solicitous
women came fluttering toward him in their summer dresses. He opened
his mouth in a bloody and lopsided smile and allowed them to take his
arms and lead him into the house.

The mystery of Joshua Speed's errand was revealed an hour before
dinner, when he came riding up the avenue in the still-strong summer
light in the company of a very lovely and composed young Louisville
woman named Fanny Henning. She slipped off her horse and handed
the reins to Cato, the groom, in a sustained gliding motion. She shook
hands confidently with the dozen people gathered on the porch to meet
her, and during dinner she did not shrink from fully engaging in the
one table-wide topic of conversation—the case of Joseph Smith and the
Mormons.

When asked her opinion, Miss Henning said the influence of this peculiar prophet and the power of the Nauvoo Legion rather frightened her, but quickly added she only knew what she had read in the papers and that perhaps Mr. Lincoln, who was from Illinois and served in the state assembly, would have a more informed view.

"I've read around in the Book of Mormon," Lincoln said from the unswollen side of his mouth, "and in my opinion the Bible is better written by a considerable margin."

"That's because God Himself is the author," Mrs. Speed said, "and not some angel no one has ever heard of."

Lincoln didn't bother to mention that the Whigs, just like the Democrats, had been chasing down Mormon voters for years, ever since they had arrived in Illinois. But that was politics, and the talk had now shifted to theology.

"If all other things are equal," Joshua Speed said, provoking his devout mother, "is it any stranger for God to bury golden plates for Joe Smith to find in New York than for him to present stone tablets to Moses on Mount Sinai?"

"Well, my dear son, all other things are *not* equal, as you know perfectly well. Because the Ten Commandments are the undisputed word of God and these golden plates are—well, I don't know what they are. They're plates!"

While the conversation went back and forth Lincoln spooned soup into the side of his mouth and did his best not to stare at Fanny Henning: at her radiant face and sumptuous brown hair in the candlelight, at the intoxicating way she rested her hand on Speed's forearm as she gently chided him for disagreeing with his mother. Cage monitored Lincoln's gaze as a way of not staring himself. He too was infatuated. Fanny was not as beautiful as Matilda Edwards but her poise and animation made that simple measure irrelevant. He watched her turn her head and smile at Speed, her hand still on his arm, and the way Speed winked at her in response. Once again Cage found himself craving something he was not conscious of missing in his complicated relationship with Ellie: the enclosing warmth of another human soul.

• • •

"She's not perfect, you know," Speed told the two of them later as they walked across the stone bridge in the late-summer night. Fireflies lit up the darkness around them with the rhythm of a telegraph experiment. Steadier light came from the slave cabins in the distance. They could smell cooking and hear a lonely fiddle playing.

"That's old Rheuben playing 'Balm in Gilead,'" Speed said. "When I was a little boy, I used to lie in bed with the window open and go to sleep listening to that."

"How is Fanny not perfect?" Lincoln asked.

"She's moody sometimes, and she can be a little bit self-righteous. I guess you could say that about almost anybody."

"But you're going to marry her, of course," Cage said.

"I don't know. Should I?"

"Of course you should," Lincoln said, spitting a gob of blood onto the ground. "We all should get married. Maybe I made a mistake with Molly."

"You did not," Cage firmly told him.

"I agree with Cage," Speed said. "There's no reason in the world a wife should create confusion and agitation. She should simply make a man happy."

He expelled cigar smoke into the air, where it mixed with the vaporous band of the Milky Way overhead. Cage remembered the offhand invitation Speed had extended for him to visit Ellie, the same way he might have told him to take a turn in a game of horseshoes. Growing up in a world in which so much had been provided, in which so much was assured, had freed him from any urgent need to claim possession or ownership. More than Lincoln or Cage, he was a man at ease, a man who could afford to wait for his chance to come around. He made a gesture for silence as the three of them stood there on the other side of the stone bridge, looking down the broad path that led to the big brick house. He wanted them all to listen to the purity of his slave's voice as he sang about the balm in Gilead that makes the wounded whole.

They embarked on the *Lebanon* a week later for the return journey. Speed still had a few leftover pieces of business in Springfield, so he traveled back with them, the three of them taking berths in the common room below the waterline. The water in the Ohio was low and the voyage tedious, the captain of the vessel making such careful, probing progress through the channels that Lincoln was convinced they could make better time poling a flatboat or even walking.

The *Lebanon* carried an abundance of cargo in its holds—dishware, whiskey, clothes, tools, and furniture bound for St. Louis or the merchants' shelves in the river towns it passed on the way. Every afternoon about four o'clock another sort of cargo emerged to take advantage of the open air. A dozen slaves, each attached to a chain by an iron clevis around his wrist, were ushered onto the after section of the main deck. There they would sit down and play cards or sing, though their voices were lost to the sound of the great stern wheel paddles churning the water and they occasionally had to slap at the burning sparks emanating from the twin iron chimneys above. The slaves' owner was a prosperous-looking farmer named Mr. Kelso, and he would sometimes leave them in the charge of his grown son while he joined Speed and Cage and Lincoln on the upper deck, where they sat at a table next to the bar.

"You've got to give them air," Mr. Kelso declared on the third or fourth day of the voyage. "Poor devils, you can't keep them chained up in the dark all day. Their feelings, sir, are no less acute than ours."

He said he had bought the Negroes at auction in Lexington and was taking them down the Mississippi to his place near Port Gibson. "They're a finer lot of fellows than I could have found back home," he said, "and at a cheaper price. They're a little melancholy to be leaving the scenes of their childhoods behind, and that one there—Andy, the one tuning his fiddle—I had to separate from his wife, which troubled him a great deal at first. But they're all coming along well enough, cooperating with each other, getting used to their new state in life, curious about where they're going next. Liveliness is the thing to look for when you're investing in a slave, wouldn't you say so, Mr. Speed?"

"Liveliness is a good barometer."

"You want a man with some spirit, and some common sense. If you treat them well, get them decent clothes, plentiful food, work them hard but fair, use the whip sparingly, a certain harmony sets in that's good for both master and nigger alike. And they're better off here than in Africa, by a long stretch, if you ask me. All those cannibal chieftains rounding up and eating their neighbors, and sending the ones they don't eat off to die in some Musselman's gold mine."

He stepped on the head of a turtle-shaped cuspidor at his feet. The shell lifted up and he expectorated with satisfaction into the receptacle hidden inside. He then stood up, shaking hands all around as he excused himself to help his son escort his charges back into the hold for their dinner. When he was gone, Speed snorted with suppressed laughter. "What a type he is," he whispered to Cage and Lincoln. "A real know-it-all. How are we going to endure the rest of the voyage listening to his pronouncements of the obvious?—'You've got to give them air!'—Well, yes, I rather suppose you do!"

He laughed again and rolled his eyes to heaven. But the obvious fatuity of Mr. Kelso was not the uppermost concern in Cage's mind. He was staring at the slaves on the deck. Lincoln was too. Andy, the man who had been separated from his wife, was playing some sorrowful air on his fiddle when, seeing Mr. Kelso approach, he put the instrument away into its case and stood up with the rest of the Negroes and began shuffling across the deck, out of the sunlight and back into the hold. The men were compliant, orderly. You could see the fatal resignation in their eyes as they marched forward with the chain running between them.

"A trotline," Lincoln muttered, glancing at Cage. "A human trotline."

Speed did not hear the reference, or notice the seething discomfort in his friends' attitude. He was still talking, though he had dropped Mr. Kelso and returned to the theme of marriage, whether it was possible for one man and one woman to make each other happy for life.

"Fanny comes from a splendid family," he was saying. "And God knows she's a beautiful woman, in body and in soul. Another man wouldn't hesitate for a minute. What is it about me, do you think, that makes me—"

"For God's sake, Speed, will you shut the hell up?"

The words flew out of Cage's mouth before the thought behind them had even formed. Speed's contented voice, his untroubled assumption that the slaves on this ship would receive the same benign, paternalistic stewardship that he imagined they enjoyed at Farmington, his inability even to envision the cruel servitude that would just as likely be their fate, and above all his infuriating, insulting assumption that others should applaud him and his family for their enlightened conception of human bondage—all this caused Cage to suddenly erupt. It was not all his friend's fault, and he knew it. There was the toll of his own conscience, for having spent three weeks at Farmington holding himself back from voicing his opinion about the insupportable rot that underlay the Speed family's plantation paradise. He was ashamed of himself. He had seen the whip marks on Cordelia's back, he had seen her trembling in fear at the thought of being sent back to Kentucky. How had he allowed himself to fall so far into complacency on the one subject in the world that demanded a raging denunciation?

Speed's reaction to his outburst was to laugh as if he was going along with the spirit of some joke that he didn't quite understand. Then his face tightened and he said, "What?"

"How can you go on about whether or not you'll be marrying Fanny when that man down there has just been torn from his wife?"

"I'll go on about whatever I want, Cage. *I* didn't tear that Negro from his wife. And I don't like you bringing Fanny into this argument—if an argument is what we're having—in the first place. What does she have to do with it? If you weren't such a good friend and such a formerly agreeable companion I might have to issue a challenge. Should I issue a challenge, Lincoln?"

Lincoln had been silent until now, and he was silent a moment more, his face set, watching the last of the shuffling slaves disappear beneath the overhang of the deck. "It is a troubling sight, Joshua," he finally said. "I admit that the whole thing unsettles my soul."

"Well, what exactly would you like me to do about it?"

"I don't know," Cage said. "It can't go on."

"It can and it will," Speed answered, his voice still testy and hurt. "It will go on until we have no more need of it and it simply dies away. And you might not believe me, but I hope that day comes soon. I'm not foolish like that man. I don't for a minute believe that slavery is a noble institution. But it exists, it's always existed, and the abolitionists who want to stamp it out aren't reckoning the cost to our country. Do you want a war, is that what you want? And by the way, your airy high-mindedness is really irritating, Cage, especially as it comes after you've enjoyed three weeks of slaves laundering your clothes and cooking your meals."

"I'm aware of my own hypocrisy, but there's a—"

"Oh, fuck yourself, Cage. Go write a poem about your discovery that slavery is not the finest invention in the world, and see if it changes anything!"

Speed stood so abruptly and aggressively as he said this that his chair fell to the deck behind him. Cage stood as well, in response to Speed's hostile posturing. But he felt so absurd and ashamed that he couldn't really entertain the idea of a fight, much less a duel. They glared at each other theatrically until Lincoln told them to sit down and stop making a spectacle of themselves.

"I don't like my friends to be at war," he said. When they grudgingly sat down again he got out of his own chair and turned his back on them and walked over to the railing. Cage and Speed had nothing more to say to each other, so they just contemplated Lincoln as he stared sternward, watching the great paddle wheel agitate the river. After a while he came back to them and said he believed he would have an orangeade at the bar.

"And just so you'll know," he said, "my tooth is hurting again, thanks to the two of you."

1842

TWENTY-SEVEN

◆◆◆

A YEAR PASSING. ANOTHER AUTUMN, another bitter win-
ter, the constant threat of life resolving itself into an unquiet stasis. Investment opportunities came Cage's way and he weighed liability
against opportunity with the same critical eye he brought to the composition of his verse. He was neither a heedless investor nor a careless
poet; if he were to succeed he must work with deliberation. He was past
thirty and there was no time for abandon, for following trails that could
lead him to financial ruin or to death-bound obscurity. He tried to see
beyond the moment, past the statewide financial catastrophe brought
on by the failure of the internal improvements projects. The building of
the railroads and canals had been stalled but these things would come
eventually. If a man was patient enough with his money he would benefit from holding land along a major waterway.

Veterans of the War of 1812 had been given warrants for land in
the Military Tract between the Illinois and the Mississippi. Many of
them had sold their warrants to speculators, and now the speculators
themselves were eager to sell, often at a loss, ready to move on to more
dynamic investments. Cage had been steadily investing in acreage in the
Military Tract whenever he could, but now was the time, he decided, to
increase his holdings, even at the risk of considerable debt. From several other disappointed speculators he bought land between the Rock
River and the Mississippi, the very terrain that he had helped seize from
Black Hawk and his desperate warriors. He signed the contracts and
saved his troubled conscience for the pages of his book, which he was
still composing and revising. There were new poems from his experiences in the Black Hawk War. They were angrier and more unspar-
ing than those he had previously published and which brought him his

earlier notice. These poems, together with those he had written after Cordelia's trial and his encounter with the slaves on board the *Lebanon*, laid the moral ballast of the manuscript. The love poem Ellie had spurned was part of the collection as well, though much changed and much harder. All the contents were harder, harder and crueler. He had not spared himself, or did not think he had. The persona of these poems was at heart an observer, a compromised one: a man who was righteously intolerant of slavery but a compliant guest at a slave plantation; who was disdainful of politics but drawn to the liveliness and tribal spirit of politicians; who was romantic-minded but infatuated with a woman determined not to love him. He had no wish to disguise the contradictions and flaws of his own character. The book was as honest a record as he could make of what it was like to be alive and grasping in a wild place beyond the notice of the world.

The Springfield poetry society had long since stopped meeting. Lincoln's mental collapse and Speed's move to Kentucky had taken the life from it. But Cage invited Lincoln over one night so that he could read some of the newer poems to him. He wanted Lincoln's judgment only, not the clamoring air of congratulation that had characterized the poetry society. Lincoln—his legs folded over the arms of Cage's desk chair—listened without ever stirring. The expression of absolute concentration on his face never changed.

"You're doing something very remarkable," he said after a suitable moment of silence when Cage had concluded his reading. There was deep emotion in his voice, genuine appreciation but also more than a trace of envy. "While the rest of us have been scrambling all over each other to get elected to some mere earthly position, you've been sitting here transcribing the thoughts of angels. You're making yourself immortal, Cage."

"Please don't be ridiculous."

"You'll live beyond the grave, there's no question of it."

He would not let go of the theme. He kept praising Cage's accomplishment with such fervor that it was clear that the chief thing on his mind was the ambivalence he felt about his own future. In Cage's unexpressed opinion, his friend was right to be worried. The elections were coming around again in August, a month from now, but this time Lincoln wasn't running. The Sangamon County Whigs had lost two seats in the General Assembly due to a reapportionment battle, and with too many candidates for too few seats Lincoln had been obliged to step aside so that Logan, his senior law partner, could make his own run. Lincoln was still a great man in waiting, but his path to greatness was growing hard to discern. A new bankruptcy law had recently gone into effect, and it provided a steady source of income for the Logan and Lincoln law firm. But every bankruptcy case they took on was a reminder to everyone of the role the Whigs had played in driving the state into ruin.

Lincoln stood up and took the pages from Cage's hand, pacing around the room as he leafed through them, reading back to Cage some of the lines he had just heard.

"'The shackled hand that holds the bow, draws forth the unbound song.' You're talking about that fiddle player on the steamboat?"

"In a roundabout way."

"'The unbound song,'" Lincoln repeated. He set the pages down on Cage's desk and then without asking started to sort through the letters that were scattered on the desk. He held up the invitation that had recently arrived for the September wedding of John Hardin's sister Martinette. "Are you going to this?"

"I am. We could go up to Jacksonville together."

"I'd run into Molly there."

"You've managed to avoid her somehow for a year, but I don't think you can count on doing that forever."

"Do you see her?"

"From time to time. Of course it's not like it used to be."

"She must loathe the thought of me."

"I think that one day the two of you will be friends again."

"If she can ever forgive me for what I did to her, or if I can forgive myself, perhaps we might."

This caused him to reflect on Speed, and on how content he was now in his marriage to Fanny. "He's a happy man at last. We've all dreamed dreams of Elysium but he's found his. Do you think this book will be your Elysium?"

"I don't know if Gray and Bowen will like it. And if they do, I don't know that anyone else will."

"You're superstitious of your own good fortune. I suppose I am too, though I don't know that any good fortune awaits me. It's growing harder and harder to spy Elysium from Sangamon County."

That next week there was a sprawling Fourth of July celebration on the grounds of the Edwards house. Lincoln, knowing that Mary would be much in evidence, found an excuse to be out of town on legal business. Cage had seen Mary only occasionally over the last year, sometimes encountering her on the street, sometimes at parties where the remnants of the old coterie still came together. She was sobered but not shattered by her romantic misadventure with Abraham Lincoln. There was a natural assumption around Springfield that she was the one who had spurned Lincoln, not the other way around, and that this was the reason he had gone crazy. It was an assumption that she did not bother to dispute, and probably artfully encouraged. In any case she had made sure not to appear forlorn and rejected, and the sense that she had survived some mysterious crucible only increased her attractiveness to the usual swarm of unattached men.

She listened patiently as Ninian Edwards stood on a table and orated on the founding of the Republic, on the spirit of dynamic opposition that was the genius of the United States, and that made it possible for him to invite both Whig and Democrat to his house tonight, where despite their differences they dined as friends, Americans all.

"Have you ridden the cars yet?" Mary asked Cage when her brother-in-law had finished speaking. Her skin glowed in the light of the paper lanterns. She had lost a little weight since the last time he had seen her, but she still had a robust shape that seemed to enhance her natural vivacity. Beside her was Julia Jayne, who was more slender than Mary, objectively prettier, but a notch below her companion in quick-mindedness and lethal wit. Matilda Edwards, whose beauty overrode all other considerations, was absent. She had finally gone ahead and married Newton Strong and released half the men in Illinois from their hopeless daydreams.

"We rode them to Jacksonville to see the Hardins," Mary explained. "I think the railway is the most wonderful invention in the world."

"It's like riding in a cradle, except for all the noise and the soot and the cinders," Julia said. "We looked like coal miners by the time we got to Jacksonville."

She snorted charmingly through her nose as she laughed. She and Mary were both in high spirits today, arm in arm like sisters, surveying the crowd with mischievous scrutiny, eager for gossip. As Cage was standing in front of them they both broke out into laughter at once, having seen something or someone behind him that struck them as profoundly funny.

"Don't turn around!" Mary warned. "If you do he'll know who we're laughing about."

"Who will know?"

"Jim Shields. He keeps following Julia around, trying to get her off by herself. He thinks he's irresistible to women and that she can't wait for him to lunge at her like a wolf."

"I suppose I should be flattered, a little," Julia said, "but, you see, I'm just not." She collapsed in laughter again and excused herself, heading over to a group of men that included Illinois's secretary of state, Lyman Trumbull. Trumbull greeted her with a warm grin and pulled her into his protective circle like a bull musk ox.

"She's going to marry Trumbull," Mary told Cage. "Though of course it's a secret and you mustn't tell anyone."

"I won't."

"She's almost my last unmarried friend. Who is an old spinster of twenty-three going to find to talk to?"

"You could be engaged to half of the men here before the year is out if you showed any real interest in them."

"Well, that's the problem, isn't it? Most men are so uninteresting."

She smiled glumly, knowingly, letting the thought register. She was too proud to refer to Lincoln by name, too proud to ask Cage about his whereabouts tonight. Their engagement was all in the past, in the realm of might-have-been. It could never happen now. She asked him about himself, about his book—When would it be finished? When could she read it?—and teased him about his own romantic life.

"You should definitely never get married like the rest of us mortals," she concluded. "You should live a scandalous life. You should wear an old dressing gown and have a succession of exotic women to serve as your muse. Now please forgive me. I promised Stephen Douglas I'd have some ice cream with him."

When she had left, Cage turned around looking for a familiar face to talk to and found himself instead in conversation with James Shields, the very man Mary and Julia had been helplessly ridiculing. Shields was a Democrat and a political enemy of most of Cage's legislative friends, but he was the state auditor and it was his signature on their pay warrants. He had been born in Ireland but had left as a boy and nothing much remained of his accent except a melodious softness that was at odds with his angry intensity.

"Have you heard any rumors that Miss Jayne is going to marry Lyman Trumbull?" he asked Cage. He was still staring at Julia across the picnic tables. He was in all regards a handsome man, but as far as Cage could tell his looks did him little good. They only supported a general aspect of seething resentment. He was obviously very much annoyed that Julia Jayne was paying no attention to him.

"No," Cage lied, "I haven't heard anything of the sort. The only rumor going around that I've heard is that you're about to instruct the state not to accept bank currency."

"Well, if that were true, it would only apply to the payment of taxes, and it would be the result of your friend Lincoln and his Whig associates destroying the economy in the first place. Under such conditions, it wouldn't matter who the state auditor was. He would have no choice but to rely on common sense and demand payment in specie. But of course I myself have heard no such rumor."

He laughed and took a sip of beer. They stood there talking pleasantly enough for another ten minutes, Cage doing his best to steer the conversation away from politics, since Shields was combustible on that subject. They reminisced instead about the Black Hawk War, in which Shields had also fought, and on their shipboard service—Cage as a mere deckhand on the Illinois River, Shields as a merchant seaman who had sailed all over the world and survived a fall from the topmast. An agreeable conversation between two acquaintances on a mild summer night, one of them rather pitiably lovelorn and distractedly scanning the grounds for the whereabouts of Julia Jayne. It would have been very odd even to imagine that in a few months these two men would find themselves on the opposite sides of a dueling ground, but where honor was involved—or where it could be forced into being involved—very odd things tended to happen in Illinois with great regularity.

TWENTY-EIGHT

⟨✕✕⟩

HE'S DONE IT AGAIN. That was Cage's immediate reaction as he sat in Cornelius's coffeehouse reading the incendiary letter in the *Sangamo Journal* that everyone in Springfield was talking about. The letter was purportedly written by a caustic-tongued, uneducated farm widow named Rebecca. It was the second such letter from Rebecca. The first had appeared a few weeks earlier. It was the work of another unsigned humorist and nobody had suspected Abraham Lincoln of writing it. But it must have inspired Lincoln, because this second letter was transparently his work. He had grown up among such people and the dialect—full of morsels like "kivered over" and "kungeerin" and "mought"—was precise. And funny. And cruel.

The letter took aim at James Shields's order that the state no longer take paper currency in payment of taxes. Everybody had known this was coming—Shields himself had admitted as much to Cage on that Fourth of July night two months ago. Lincoln, had he been the state auditor instead of Shields, would have had to do the same thing. But it gave the Whigs an excuse to stir up a political fuss, which Lincoln had cleverly stirred up even more in the guise of Rebecca and her disgust for the "High Comb'd Cocks" like James Shields who were now demanding that common folks somehow scare up hard silver.

The letter hewed close to acceptable political satire until it cut mercilessly deep, portraying Shields himself not just as the perpetrator of the currency directive but as a conceited romantic blowhard swanning among the maidens and widows of the Lost Township where Rebecca claimed she lived: "Dear girls, it is *distressing*, but I cannot marry you all. Too well I know how much you suffer; but do, *do* remember, it is not my fault that I am *so* handsome and *so* interesting."

It would be hard to underestimate the offense Shields would take at such a personal attack, but Cage decided it wasn't his problem. If Lincoln wanted his opinion about whether he should be continuing his self-destructive habit of character assassination through pseudonymous letters, he would be happy to offer it. But he wasn't going to track him down and lecture him. Besides, maybe it was an indication that Lincoln was recovering his confidence and his political fire, which was the only thing that made him happy.

The backfire was even worse than Cage would have predicted. A few weeks after the letter in the *Journal* appeared, Ned Baker summoned a contingent of Lincoln's friends for an emergency breakfast meeting at the American House.

"Shields is going to kill him," Ned told them. "He's really going to do it."

Shields had just returned from Quincy on state business, he said, and was storming all over town looking for Lincoln. Fortunately, Lincoln himself was out of town, up at Tremont for the start of the judicial circuit.

"What do you mean?" Cage said. "Is Shields planning to murder him?"

"No, he's going to challenge him, but Shields is hot-tempered and handy with a pistol and the result will be the same: Abraham Lincoln lying dead on the ground with a ball in his breast because of some comical letter in the newspaper."

"Shields probably just wants him to retract what he wrote," Cage said.

"Well, he can't very well retract it!" Ash Merritt said.

"Why not?"

"It's a matter of honor, of course."

"In Lincoln's case," Cage said, "honor's a dangerous virtue. It almost ended his sanity during that Mary Todd embrigglement. Now there's his mortal life to consider."

"And his political future," Ned said. "Dueling's a crime in Illinois. He could survive the duel and be convicted and barred from holding office."

"That in itself is a trifling matter," Ash pointed out. "All he'd have to do is cross the river and get out of Illinois and fight the duel in Missouri. He'll have done nothing illegal and if he kills Shields instead of Shields killing him his reputation is enhanced. Also, as the man who's been challenged he'd have his choice of weapons. That's a strong advantage."

"I thought we were here to prevent a duel," Cage said. "Not to argue how to fight one."

"Of course," Ash agreed. "But if the thing should—"

Billy Herndon interrupted them, rushing in with the morning's edition of the *Journal*.

"There's a poem in here that you all have to read right away. Oh, never mind." He picked up the paper impatiently. "I'll read it to you."

It was a new comic salvo against Shields, purportedly written by someone named "Cathleen." It took the form of a poem of mock triumph celebrating the news that Rebecca, the backwoods commentator impersonated by Lincoln, had just gotten married to none other than James Shields himself.

" 'To the widow he's bound,' " Billy read, unable to suppress a laugh, though it was a serious matter. " 'Oh! Bright be his lot!' "

"This is not going to go down with Shields, not at all," Baker said. "Really, Lincoln should know when to stop."

"It wasn't Lincoln who wrote it," Billy said. "It was Mary Todd and Julia Jayne. Sim Francis told me."

The men stared at each other in incredulity, though it made a kind of sense. Cage had, after all, witnessed the women responding with undisguised ridicule as Shields followed Julia about at the Fourth of July celebration with his mouth hanging open. And he had to admit there was a certain polish to the verses Billy had just read to them, the sort of effortless fluency that might be expected from someone like Mary who was the product of an exclusive Kentucky boarding school.

"The situation has just gotten preposterously worse," Baker said. "Something has to be done."

"And it has to be done fast," Billy said. "Because Shields just left town with John Whiteside."

"Where to?"

"Where do you think? They're heading to Tremont to entice Mr. Lincoln into a duel."

· · ·

Lincoln had to be warned. He would need the benefit of his friends' advice before he responded to a challenge for a duel. Ash said his buggy could be ready for the trip in half an hour. Cage volunteered to go with him. If Shields and Whiteside spent the night on the way, as most travelers to Tremont tended to do, they could overtake them and get to Lincoln before they arrived.

The last time Cage had made the trip to Tazewell County, to rescue Cordelia, he had ridden through the full glory of a prairie spring among the delighted wandering men of the circuit court. But today, as he sat in the seat next to Ash, the mercury easily stood at over a hundred degrees with the sun bearing down on the parched grass. The doctor's carriage was a sprightly big-wheeled device pulled by a gray gelding named Xavier. The horse snorted in the heat and shook his head and shivered the muscles of his neck to stir away the flies. There was no hint of rain, or of any other meteorological relief. Even the blue of the sky appeared to have been bleached away by the white sun. As they rode past outlying farms, hogs grunted in evaporating wallows on the side of the road. The leaves in the cornfields were so dry Cage could imagine them crackling like paper.

They stopped only to rest Xavier and to relieve themselves. Otherwise they continued at the same monotonous pace along the dry rutted road, the light carriage transmitting every bump to their sore backsides. Ash was a compulsive retailer of medical horror stories. He told Cage about famous surgeries gone wrong, of hideous cancers and deformities and curious misadventures involving the voluntary insertion of foreign objects into the urethra and the rectal canal, passageways renowned for their wonderful elasticity. It was after dark when they got to Delavan. They drove straight through, curious about whether Shields and Whiteside had put up for the night but not daring to stop for fear of being spotted by the men they were trying to overtake. They were in Tremont before midnight. They took a room at the Franklin House, where the drowsy clerk confirmed that Lincoln was also in residence.

While Ash unloaded their luggage, Cage knocked on the door of Lincoln's room. He was sharing it with two other circuit lawyers and none of them were asleep. All were still working by candlelight on pleas and continuances and other legal business that would be taken up in the court the next day.

"I'm astonished to see you," Lincoln said when he opened the door. "Has something terrible happened?"

"Not as yet." Cage glanced into the room at the two other lawyers, one of whom he recognized from his previous trip to Tazewell County, the other a stranger. They were both looking up from their work with frank curiosity. Cage whispered to Lincoln that it would be better if he packed his things and moved downstairs with him and Ash Merritt.

"Merritt is here too?"

"Yes, but I'd rather not explain everything while standing in your doorway."

Twenty minutes later, having moved in with Cage and Ash and heard the reason for their errand to Tazewell County, Lincoln paced restlessly back and forth from one wall. He kept laughing, but in a calculated, nervous way. "Who knew Shields had such a thin skin?"

"Everybody knew."

"Well, that's true enough, Cage. But if we had a rule against poking at a man's vanity there'd be no more fun left in the world."

He stopped pacing and stood against the wall, pounding it softly with the back of his head. He bent his left arm behind his back in one of his speechmaking gestures, but no speech came. He just stood there thinking.

"How do you know Whiteside?" he finally asked Ash. "He's a fellow doctor, isn't he?"

"Yes, but no fellow of mine," Ash said. "He's a blustery son of a bitch. Adjutant general in the state militia, but as far as I know he's never fought in any war. He may be goading Shields just for the excitement of it."

"Maybe Shields will have forgotten the whole thing by tomorrow and just go on home to Springfield."

"Not likely," Cage said. He handed him the cutting from that morning's paper. "There's this to remind him."

Lincoln read the poem about Rebecca marrying Shields and laughed out loud. He laughed even harder when they told him that Mary Todd and Julia Jayne had written it.

"So now we have Molly jumping into the fracas. I think she and I make a good team when it comes to giving Jim Shields a purple face."

"One member of the team may be dead in the next few days if we don't find a way of resolving this," Cage said.

"Oh, it won't come to that," Lincoln decided. "The two of you are true friends to have ridden all the way up here to warn me, but human nature being what it is Shields won't want to get killed over this nonsense any more than I do."

And yet the challenge came. John Whiteside came up to Lincoln as he was walking to the Tazewell County courthouse the next morning, took off his hat, said he had the honor of addressing him on behalf of Mr. James Shields. Whiteside was tall and slender, well-dressed, well-barbered, outwardly serene and peaceable. He had a fine nose and a pale complexion. He handed Lincoln a letter which that same Mr. Shields asked to be delivered with his compliments.

"You may thank Mr. Shields for his great kindness in initiating a correspondence with me," Lincoln said to Whiteside as Cage and Ash stood behind him, observing this charade of civility. "Have you had your breakfast, General Whiteside?"

"I have, sir, thank you."

"Well, I wish you a happy digestion, then." Whiteside stood there awkwardly waiting for Lincoln to read the letter, but instead Lincoln slipped it into the pocket of his coat. "If you'll excuse me, I have a full day inside the courthouse."

"Mr. Lincoln, you need to know that Mr. Shields is anxious for an immediate reply."

"I hate to think of your friend in a state of anxiety, General. Please tell him I'll read his letter at my first opportunity and consider its contents and my answer carefully. I'm sure he'd prefer that to a half-cocked reply when my mind is elsewhere. Why don't you call on me at the inn at, say, eight o'clock tonight?"

Whiteside had no option but to retreat. As soon as he was gone, Cage was sure Lincoln was going to take the letter out of his pocket again, but he did not.

"No," Lincoln said. "I've got people waiting on me in court and more pleas to write. I'll read Shields's letter when I've done my duty by my clients and not before."

That evening, in their room at the Franklin House, he finally pulled the letter out of his pocket and read it aloud. It referred to "articles of the most personal nature." It was almost dark outside, but the insufferably humid heat was unabating. It seemed to feed off the waning sunlight like a night-blooming plant. Cage had thrown the window open but the air was too weighty and sodden to stir from one place to another. Lincoln lay on his back on the bed, his feet planted on the wall a few inches from its end. His coat was off and a thin ring of grimy sweat was visible around his neck.

"Shields says my articles were 'calculated to degrade me,'" Lincoln said, looking up from the letter. "That couldn't be farther from the truth. I have no interest in degrading anybody."

"Read the rest of it," Ash said.

" 'I will take the liberty of requiring a full, positive and absolute retraction of all offensive allusions used by you in these communications, in relation to my private character' . . . and cetera and cetera . . . 'This may prevent consequences which no one will regret more than myself. Your obedient servant, James Shields.' "

He handed the letter to Cage, who went over it in silence with Ash as Lincoln continued to talk.

"He starts with a false inference. He says that I wrote 'articles of the most personal nature.' Well, I didn't write that first letter, I only wrote the second letter, so 'articles' plural doesn't apply."

"That's a way out," Cage said. "Though an extremely legalistic one."

"I'm an extremely legalistic critter, especially when my hide is at stake. And also shouldn't I be offended that this man jumped to the assumption that I'm the author of such a scurrilous assault on his character?"

"You *are* the author."

"Only of *one* scurrilous assault. It deeply offends me—it wounds *my* character and damages *my* reputation—to have Shields accuse me of doing it more than once."

"This is serious," Ash said. "It may feel like a comical situation, but it's not. Think carefully how you respond."

"I'm thinking very carefully, Ash. You can be sure I don't care to be shot. It would do my political career real harm to be killed by such an ass as James Shields. I think the thing to do is write an answer that will puzzle his mind a little. The more time he has to spend thinking, the better the chance he'll cool off."

He opened his portable desk, took out pen and paper, and scribbled hastily as the light disappeared. When he was finished he read his letter aloud to his friends with the same exaggerated precision Cage had seen him use in the courtroom.

"'Your note of today was handed me by General Whiteside. In that note you say you have been informed that I am the author of certain articles which you deem personally abusive of you; and without stopping to inquire whether I really am the author, or to point out what is offensive in them, you demand an unqualified retraction of all that is offensive; and then proceed to hint at consequences. Now, sir, there is in this so much of assumption of facts, and so much of menace as to consequences, that I cannot submit to answer that note any further than I have, and to add, that the consequences to which I suppose you allude, would be a matter of as great regret to me as it possibly could be to you.'"

He stared placidly at his two friends for a reaction.

"I have no idea what you're saying," Cage told him.

"I'm saying there cannot be any talk of me retracting what I said about him until he retracts his note accusing me of doing so."

"You've caused my brain to seize up," Ash said.

"Good," Lincoln said, folding the letter. "That's the intended effect."

Whiteside and Shields were eating whortleberry pudding in the dining room of their hotel when Cage and Merritt entered the establishment with Lincoln's note. At the sight of them, Shields abruptly stood, wiped his chin with his napkin, gave his visitors a curt nod, and disappeared upstairs. The elaborate protocols of the code duello forbade him from speaking directly to the representatives of the party to whom he was intending to issue a challenge.

Whiteside made a show of scraping up the last of his pudding before reading the note. He frowned and read it again.

"What kind of reply is this?" he said.

"It's the only possible reply to such an offensive insinuation," Ash said.

"This is the worst sort of humbug! All we're doing here is going around in circles!"

"Keep your voice down," Cage said, noticing that the other diners in the room had shifted their attention to Whiteside's table.

"What, sir?"

"I said please keep your voice down, General. We don't want this to be a public discussion."

"Who is this man?" Whiteside said to Ash. "Is he Lincoln's second, or are you?" He was no longer bothering with a civil, agreeable facade. His pale face had turned red with the lightning rapidity of a chameleon.

"There are no seconds," Ash said. "As yet, no challenge has been made."

"Well, that's because of the obfuscatory tactics of your—"

Cage interrupted him before his choleric voice could rise again. "Look," he said, "this is very simple. The three of us can solve this without a fight. Have Mr. Shields write to Lincoln, saying he withdraws his former note. Then all he has to do is inquire in a more civil tone if Lincoln was the author of the offensive article."

"What happens then?"

"Tempers cool."

"Shields doesn't want his temper cooled. He wants satisfaction from a man who has grievously offended him and is offending him further with his ridiculous theatricality. Tell your man to speak plain, and decide whether he is a gentleman or not!"

TWENTY-NINE

◆ ◆ ◆

LINCOLN'S DEMAND THAT SHIELDS WITHDRAW his
original accusatory note was a rhetorical trap, and Shields knew
it. He had understood that to take part in Lincoln's dance about who
had insulted whom first would lead to an ever more finely calibrated
correspondence that would, in the end, make his quest for justice nothing more than an eccentric and even laughable demand. The prickly
state auditor had had enough. The next time Whiteside appeared at the
Franklin House it was with a formal challenge in hand.

"Well, shit," Lincoln said when Whiteside left.

"Don't accept the challenge," Cage told him.

"He can't do that," Ash said.

"Of course he can. Just walk away, and—"

"No, I can't walk away," Lincoln said. "I don't live in a world where I
can get away with doing that, as much as I'd like to."

"You've got the choice of weapons," Ash said.

"I know I do. And I need something that'll give me a chance with that
little piece of shit. Broadswords."

"Broadswords?" Ash said. "You mean to fight this duel like a medieval knight?"

"I mean to fight this duel with a weapon I can kill Jim Shields with if
I need to. I've got a friend from the war days at the armory over in Jacksonville. I reckon he can spare a few broadswords."

He went to his writing desk again and made a quick sketch: two rect-
angles facing each other.

"We'll have it so the two of us both have to stay in our own little
boxes—say, ten feet across. I've got the longer arms by a considerable
margin, and I've got a lot of practice swinging an axe."

317

"Shields will see that as an unfair advantage," Ash said.

"Well, fine, if he doesn't like it, he doesn't have to fight me."

But Shields wasn't going to back out, and they all knew it. Lincoln wrote another letter, specifying the weapons and the fighting boxes, offering Shields one more chance to withdraw his offensive note so that a civil reconciliation could be undertaken between the parties. When Ash set off to deliver the note to Whiteside, Cage remained with Lincoln at the hotel.

"I've gotten you mixed up in something all over again," Lincoln said.

"You certainly have."

"Go home to Springfield. You don't have to be one of my seconds. I can find somebody else here in Tremont."

"You won't find somebody else who wants to put a stop to this as much as I do."

"That's true. Ash has a fighting streak in him. I don't know what it is about doctors but as a species they don't seem as peaceable as you might think. I could use a calm-natured friend on my side, but it's a lot to ask, particularly of a calm-natured friend. You sure about this?"

"I'm sure that fighting a duel with Shields is dangerous and ridiculous. But if you insist it has to happen, I'll stand by you."

Shields made no protest to Lincoln's terms. Whiteside told Merritt that Shields was determined to fight and would arrive at the dueling ground across the Mississippi from Alton on Thursday at eleven a.m. with broadsword in hand.

The next day Lincoln and his seconds traveled to Jacksonville. They arrived at night and took a room at the Lafayette, where just before midnight a man appeared at their door carrying a blanket-wrapped bundle. Lincoln introduced him as Colonel Nail. He was the commandant of the armory, though he was dressed as a civilian and spoke in a soft voice like someone on a secret errand. He unrolled the blanket onto the bed to reveal two long, heavy, broad-bladed swords. They were well cared for, no rust, no pitting on their lethal blades.

"I had them sharpened for you," Colonel Nail said, as Lincoln wrapped his fingers around the grip of one of the swords and lifted the weapon up in the lamplight. "Both of them the same. You could knock off a pig's head with either."

"It's a weighty weapon, Charley," Lincoln said to the colonel. "I got my hands on one of these a time or two during the war, but we drilled mostly with wooden swords."

"Well, you're welcome to borrow them," Nail said, "but I want them back. And I don't want to interfere in your business, but if somebody gets killed with one of these I don't want it known they came from the armory. I have troubles enough as it is. I won't go into them but they involve my poor wife, who is now paying the price for her habit of using scotch snuff as tooth powder."

"A puzzling addiction," Ash told him. "I treated a young woman just last month who was sick from eating snuff. I gave her a puke and up from her stomach came almost a full pint of it."

Ash and Colonel Nail discussed his wife's symptoms while Lincoln continued to inspect the swords, picking up one and then the other, gauging their weight as he seemed to ponder the gravity of their use.

In the morning, Cage woke to the sound of Lincoln and Merritt sparring with the swords outside the window while the hotel's kitchen staff watched. He got up and dressed hurriedly, left the Lafayette and walked to John Hardin's house on State Street, which almost two years ago had been the site of the fateful Christmas excursion that had led to the unraveling of Lincoln's engagement to Mary. Once John Hardin heard about the duel, Cage was sure, he would find a way to use his influence to stop it. The servant who opened the door recognized him and showed him to the parlor. The last time Cage had seen this room, it had been extravagantly decorated for Christmas, with stockings hanging from the mantel and wreaths on the windows. Now it was almost bare, the carpet taken up, the curtains down, scaffolding on the walls where paint was being stripped and reapplied.

Sarah Hardin greeted him with the same warmth he remembered from that Christmas visit and apologized for the destruction. Everything was chaos, she said. Martinette's wedding was to take place here in less than a week. But of course Cage knew that, because he had written that he was coming.

"But you're here today," she said. "I hope you didn't mistake the date. If you did, we insist that you be our guest until the wedding."

"Thank you, but I'm only here because of some urgent business I need to discuss with your husband."

"But John's not here. He's out of town on court business."

Cage trusted Sarah Hardin enough to tell her what was going on. She gasped in horror and told him she would get word to her husband at once. He would certainly want to intervene in any way he could. Why, the very idea of Mr. Lincoln taking part in such a barbaric custom as a duel! And with swords!

When he got back to the hotel, Cage didn't tell Lincoln of his talk with Sarah Hardin, or of the fact that he had spent an hour in her husband's study writing letters to Baker and other friends of Lincoln who might possibly be able to intervene in time. If only Speed were not in Kentucky. He was sure that between the two of them they could talk Lincoln into making a simple apology to Shields for his incendiary parody and doing so in a way that would not compromise his standing.

But Speed was not here and the duel that had once seemed hypothetical was taking on the force of inexorability. They started out for Alton that afternoon and put up for the night in a third-rate hotel in Carrolton. They would rise early in the morning in order to reach Alton and cross the Mississippi to the dueling ground on the Missouri side by midmorning.

It would have been difficult for Cage to sleep in any case, but the night was miserably hot and still, the atmosphere weighing so heavily upon the earth that it was an exertion just to draw breath. He lay on the sweat-soaked mattress next to Lincoln staring at the two broadswords lying on the table, their blades like the sheen of a lake upon which the moonlight shone and shifted.

Ash Merritt was asleep on the room's other bed, a narrow mattress resting on a frame built into the wall. Above it hung a faded portrait of George Washington. Ash was deep into an apparently untroubled sleep, snoring in a progressive sequence that made Cage think of a man climbing an endless stairway. It seemed impossible that there could actually be a duel tomorrow, impossible and insane.

In the middle of this endless, oppressive night, Cage wrestled with his own complicity. There was the paralyzing dread of what was to come tomorrow, but there were also bright unbidden flashes of expectation. It was a feeling he remembered from the Black Hawk War, from the day he had ridden out on that scouting mission from Kellogg's Grove—a watery knowledge that something horrible was likely to happen, but that to survive would mean a life transformed. His logical mind had convinced him that there was little likelihood of anything good resulting from tomorrow's event. But if Lincoln escaped getting killed, and escaped killing Shields in the process, there might be scraps of political advantage. Dueling was a gentlemen's ritual. Defending an obscure point of honor at peril of his life might reinforce the point that Abraham Lincoln was not satisfied with his origins, that he meant to keep rising. If Cage managed to avoid arrest, if he was spared the sight of his friend being cleaved in two by a broadsword, he might come out of the affair with a sense of public honor that would help mask the private shame he felt at having agreed to be part of a humiliating and lethal charade.

Merritt's snoring kept growing in volume, searching for a crescendo. There was a clock in the hall ticking away, but Cage didn't know what time it was. Three in the morning, maybe.

"Are you awake?" Lincoln whispered next to him. "Have you been awake all this time?"

"Yes."

"Well, why didn't you say anything? I've only been lying here pretending to sleep because I didn't want to wake you."

They got out of bed and dressed and crept out of the room, closing the door carefully behind them and then leaving the hotel. They walked without speaking until they came to a rotting pier at the edge of a creek. They sat down and stared at the unmoving surface of the water.

"I believe there's a piece of cornbread in my pocket," Lincoln said. "Want some?"

Cage shook his head. He knew Lincoln had barely eaten all day and maybe if he could get something down now it might clear his head enough to call off the fight.

"I miss my flatboat days a little," Lincoln said, chewing and looking out at the river. "Not enough to go back to them. A river looks pretty at night but the snags and perils are legion."

He threw some crumbs out onto the surface of the water but no fish rose to claim them.

"The thing that plagues my mind the most," he said, "is that I might accidentally split Shields's head in two. I wish I had never written that damned letter in the paper. He had every right to be agitated about it."

"Why can't you just tell him that?"

"Because the machine I've caught myself up in doesn't seem to go in reverse."

Lincoln decided to take off his boots and his socks and lower his great pale feet into the water. He stared at them in fascination, as though he had never noticed them before and now realized he might see them no longer. "It's funny that Molly got herself mixed up in all this. I wonder why."

"I don't know, but her poem made the situation much worse. The last thing Shields needed was a fresh humiliation."

"Well, she's got high spirits and she likes to be in the middle of things. I suppose she'd fight a duel with Shields if she could. She'd be formidable with a broadsword in her hand."

"An artfully worded apology," Cage said, not wanting to think about Mary Todd just now. "A simple retraction—I still don't see what in God's name is wrong with that. Let me write a letter and you can—"

"No, it's gone too far. There's too fine a line between apologizing and backing down. It won't matter who I'm asking to vote for me next, some ruffle-shirted grandee or a poor sucker slopping hogs all day, once they know I walked away from a fight they won't need to ask any more questions. The thing to do is for me to go through with it and do my best to disarm him somehow."

"While he's doing his best to kill you."

Lincoln seemed to concede the truth of this point as he stared down at his feet. In the center of the creek, there was a splash as a big fish of some kind slapped the surface and disappeared below. Then the creek was so silent again, and once more so still, that it seemed it had been a thousand years since it was disturbed.

"If I'm killed," he said, "you keep Ash from jumping into the fight and making things worse. I don't want the two of you drawn into my troubles any deeper than you already have been. My father will be annoyed to hear how I died and my poor stepmother'll be torn in two. Old Tom Lincoln never thought I'd amount to much but his wife believed in me like I was somebody special.

"You know what agitates my soul just now? The thought of dying without ever accomplishing a fucking thing. If anybody remembers me at all, I'll be that tall fellow whose clothes didn't fit right, the one who helped bankrupt the state of Illinois and got a sword through his gut for making fun of some conceited ass that nobody took seriously anyway."

He withdrew his feet from the water and wiped them dry with one of his socks.

"Your hands are shaking," Cage said.

"That's all right. They'll steady up when I need them to."

There was a strange sound—gasping, gurgling. If it hadn't come directly from Lincoln, Cage would have supposed it was the noise of some great fish rising from the water of the creek. It was not weeping, just a sudden strangled eruption of fear and loneliness. Lincoln hid his face behind his hand and waited for it to pass.

"Maybe at least you'll remember me," he said in a quaking voice to Cage. "Maybe you'll find room for a mention of some sad, pathetic mortal named Abraham Lincoln in one of your lesser poems."

THIRTY

◆ ◆ ◆

T HEY STOOD WATCHING THE BOAT approach across the
Mississippi. Shields sat in the stern, staring straight ahead at the
muddy shoreline, while two men labored at the oars. Although they
were facing in the other direction, Cage recognized one of them as
Whiteside.

"You'd better stand over there by yourself a ways," Ash said to Lincoln. "You and Shields should not see each other or talk to each other."

"Like the bride and groom before a wedding," Lincoln replied in a
grim voice. He picked up his sword and walked downstream twenty
yards or so, whacking at willow branches overhead, maybe consciously
trying to impress Shields and his party with his great height and
reach. As soon as the boat pulled up at the sagging dock Shields himself stepped off and walked in the other direction without looking at
either Cage or Ash or the several dozen spectators scattered along the
shore. Some of the onlookers were Negroes, slaves of the Missouri man
who owned this island and who was apparently giving them a holiday
to watch the duel. Others were curious citizens who had come over in
boats from Alton, including a couple of newspaper writers. And across
the river there were even more people gathered on the high bluffs of the
city, from which they had an excellent view of the dueling ground.

Whiteside and the other man who had rowed Shields across the river
stepped out of the boat. The other man, much to Cage's annoyance, was
Nimmo Rhodes, whom Cage had not seen since the scuffle in front of
the church where Reverend Porter had dared to speak about abolition.
The two of them walked up to Cage and Ash and shook hands.

"I remember you," Rhodes said to Cage, his eyes burning with agitation in his round face. His hair was cut close in a way that showcased his protruding ears.

"I remember you as well."

"What are all these people doing here?" he demanded to know. "Who owns these gawking niggers?"

"Let's not worry about that right now, Nimmo," Whiteside said. He was breathing heavily, winded from rowing the boat across the river. "Let's have a look at the arrangements and make sure they're satisfactory."

The four men walked past hardwood stumps and a screen of brush to a clearing exposed to the punishing noonday sun. There stood a ten-foot-long plank, set on end, with a confining box traced in the soil on either side. Whiteside stared down at it with surly intensity.

"You may measure it," Ash said. "The dimensions are exact, as laid out in Mr. Lincoln's letter."

"There's no need. It's a lethal space your friend has specified."

"Dueling's a lethal business."

"Let's not make the mistake of thinking this can't be prevented," Cage said. "In fact, as you well know we're honor-bound as seconds to attempt a reconciliation before the duel starts."

"What do you propose?"

"The same as yesterday and the day before," Ash said. "Have Shields withdraw the accusatory note and Lincoln will then be free to offer an explanation concerning the article that offended him in the first place."

"An apology is required, not an explanation."

"That's a semantic difference we can surely overcome. Shall we speak to our friends and try one last time to prevent them from splitting each other's head open?"

Whiteside gave an annoyed sigh, but agreed with Cage that the dueling code required at least one more attempt. He said he would speak to Mr. Shields once more if Dr. Merritt agreed to speak to Mr. Lincoln.

Cage and Rhodes remained in place while their associates went to confer with their principals. Rhodes was stonily silent, and Cage saw no reason to initiate a conversation with him. Instead he kept his eyes trained on Whiteside, who was speaking now to Shields. But Shields clearly wasn't listening. He had taken his coat off and was standing in his shirtsleeves and green silk waistcoat, swiping at the air with the broadsword he had brought. He had a savage, concentrated aspect, but waving the great sword made him look alarmingly small. And when he moved he had a detectable limp from his youthful fall on a ship. He was lithe and trim and might be quick even with the limp. His lack of height put him at a significant disadvantage but the murderous concentration in his eyes did not settle Cage's mind.

"Shame on your friend," Rhodes said to Cage, breaking the silence. He was staring at the dueling box that had been sketched into the ground.

"What?"

"This is a death trap for Shields and you all know it. If Lincoln had any sense of honor—"

"You just got here and I'm already tired of your righteous histrionics," Cage said. "Please shut up."

Rhodes reared his spherical head like an actor in a comic play who has just been insulted.

"'Shut up'? Don't use such intolerable language with me, sir, or you'll have a challenge of your own."

"If my language is intolerable to you, you opened the door to it by accusing my friend of having no honor."

"Well, he has no honor, sir, and you don't either!"

Rhodes stiffened, bracing himself for the challenge this charge must surely bring. But Cage was too incredulous at the man's blustery behavior to do anything other than laugh in his face.

"What are you laughing at? Didn't you hear me? Didn't you hear what I said to you?"

"Mr. Rhodes, I think we should have one duel at a time."

"Fine. When the business here is settled, I'll expect to hear from you."

"Expect all you want. Your insults mean nothing to me, and I have no interest in discussing your behavior further, and certainly no interest in fighting you over it."

He walked back to the ground where Lincoln and Ash were standing, leaving the aggrieved and sputtering Rhodes behind. He was aware of how enraged he was, how in fact he would very much enjoy some-how grinding this ill-tempered associate of Shields into atoms. But he knew he had to hold his flaring temper in check, both because it would endanger Lincoln even further if war broke out between men who were supposed to be supporting players and because Cage had no wish to be killed in a duel with Nimmo Rhodes.

"What do you think, Cage?" Lincoln asked. He had his own coat off now, his sleeves rolled up, exposing his forearms—the tensile and powerful forearms of the rail-splitter he had been. He had the same taut look in his face as when he played fives, but there was an aspect of danger that Cage had never seen before. "If Shields agrees to withdraw his note, what's my next step?"

"You should admit to the truth, that you wrote the letter he found so insulting."

"It's not a matter of 'admitting,'" Ash said. "To admit implies culpability, which implies—"

"Well, then just *proclaim* it!" Cage said. "Style it any way you want. State it any way you want. This whole matter is becoming so obscure I can't even remember what the issue between the two of you is."

"I remember it very well," Ash said. "And it's not an obscure matter at all, it's . . . Christ on the mountain, here comes Hardin!"

Before the boat he was riding in could reach the dock, John Hardin leapt out and strode impatiently through the water to the muddy shore-line. Cage's message had evidently gotten through.

"Where's Lincoln?" Hardin demanded of the onlookers gathered there. "Where's Shields? I mean to put a stop to this insanity right now!"

"Is this your doing?" Lincoln asked Cage.

"It is."

"Well, it might be a good lick. I can't talk to him myself, though. You two go and see if maybe John can help us negotiate our way out of this."

They left Lincoln to practice slicing off more willow branches and walked over to the dock to talk to Hardin. Whiteside and Rhodes did the same from their position. The two potential duelists were now alone, separated by a hundred yards and by the fighting space that had been sketched into the earth. They didn't look at each other and did not suffer anyone to approach them. The gawkers on the island looked even more nervous than the principals, starting to worry that the duel they had come to see might very well not come off.

"Gentlemen," Hardin said to the four men in the voice of a man who was used to assuming he was in charge, "Let us do our duty and find a way to extract these two men from this situation with their honor and careers intact."

"It's too late for that, John," Whiteside said.

"I reject that statement, I reject it thoroughly." Hardin locked his dark brown eyes on Whiteside with the fury and fixity of a bird of prey. "It won't be too late until one of these men is lying dead."

He demanded to be led, step by step, over the perilous rhetorical ground that had brought Lincoln and Shields to the present situation. It took twenty minutes, and many demands for clarification from Hardin, for the byzantine matter to finally be explained. He then suggested a commission of four or more fair-minded men to look into the matter and make a recommendation for resolving the misunderstanding. This was declined by Whiteside, who said he had been given clear instructions by Shields that only his friends on the field and no outsiders had the power to negotiate any sort of agreement on his behalf. From that impasse the conversation grew ever more knotty and tedious, the men moving from the shoreline in the full glare of the sun to the shade of the trees a little farther inland.

"Let me see if I have this," Hardin finally said. There was a sheen of sweat on his face which reappeared almost as soon as he wiped it away with his monogrammed handkerchief. "Lincoln must retract the article that offended Shields, but Lincoln will not answer Shields's question about whether or not he wrote it unless Shields retracts the question and asks it in a different tone."

"What goddam difference does the tone make if the offense is the same in either case?" Rhodes said.

"The goddam difference is this," Hardin replied with a smile, putting his hand on Rhodes's shoulder as if he was a comrade. "We don't know for sure if any offense was committed by Lincoln, since by the nature of Shields's inquiry Lincoln feels himself prevented from responding.

Don't you think it would be a good idea to find that out before these two men try to kill each other?"

For another half hour they argued over potential fine calibrations of phrasing. They were aided in their negotiations by the fact that the heat was growing more unbearable each minute closer to noon, by swarms of biting horseflies, and by an awareness that Lincoln had managed to distort Shields's original vivid grievance into something totally abstract. Hardin was patient; he wanted to forge a compromise that would hold, that these volatile men could accept.

Cage's memories of John Hardin would always center on this moment, on his dramaturgical intervention in the hoary old chivalric play they had all convinced themselves they must helplessly enact. They were standing on a sun-ravaged spit of land across the Mississippi from Alton, the same city from which four years later Hardin would embark at the head of his Illinois regiment for the war in Mexico. Though he would die in a surge of wanton heroism, killed by Mexican lancers at Buena Vista, he was on this day the embodiment of calm judgment, slowly diluting the tension between the warring parties by proposing exquisite legalistic remedies. All standing papers and letters between the principals would be regarded as not having existed. Lincoln would acknowledge his authorship of the September 2 article and, while not apologizing for it, state that he had had no intention of injuring the personal or private character or standing of Mr. Shields as a gentleman or a man; that if he had thought the article could produce such an effect, he would have forborne to write it.

"Those terms will suit me well enough," Lincoln said when Cage and Ash left the consultation to relay Hardin's proposal. "Let's write out the statement right now, though it ought not to come directly from me."

Lincoln, thinking ahead, had brought his portable writing desk along with his broadswords. The three men verbally crafted the document as Cage wrote it out. Then he and Ash presented it to Hardin, who presented it to Whiteside and Rhodes. From the two friends of Shields came grudging assent. Disappointed assent, Cage was sure. Rhodes, in particular, had wanted to witness a fight.

"I suppose you think the business between you and me has come to an end as well," Rhodes said to Cage, before he could even join Ash in delivering the final news to Lincoln.

"There's no business between you and me, Rhodes. As I recall we had an exchange of insults. Would you like me to apologize for mine? I do so—with whatever degree of abjectitude you think is owed to you. As far as your insults to me, I don't care about them and won't bother myself with ever thinking of them again. Or of you."

"I'll see to it that you'll have occasion to think of me," Rhodes sputtered. And then, because he could apparently think of nothing else to do, he poked Cage in the shoulder with his stubby forefinger—hard enough, it was later apparent, to cause a bruise. Then he pivoted on the ball of one of his muddy boots and walked back to his corner.

Hardin had witnessed this, and strode over to Cage to shake his hand. "You handled that well. It's important for at least somebody in a dueling party to keep his temper, otherwise you can end up with all sorts of disorganized mayhem. And I thank you for alerting me in the first place. Sometimes I wonder if Lincoln has any sense at all."

"You may have saved my life today," Lincoln said to Cage as he slipped his coat back on and they carried the unbloodied broadswords to the boat. "I don't know what I would have done if I'd stepped into that box with him, or what he would have done to me. I'm spent, Cage. I'm grateful and I'm spent."

"Well, sit in the boat and ponder how close you came to disaster and Ash and I will row you back across to Illinois."

Shields and Whiteside and Rhodes had already left the shore, and Lincoln watched them pull away with a drained, disappointed expression. "I was hoping Jim would wait around to shake hands with me."

Cage and Ash were about to take their seats at the oars when Lincoln abruptly shooed them away. "If I'm not going to slice Jim Shields in two I need to do something with my arms. Let me do the rowing. The least I owe you gentlemen is a little sweat."

The disappointed spectators on the island had all drifted back to their farms, or embarked in their own boats toward Alton. Cage pushed their vessel off as Lincoln grabbed the oars and stroked forward, joining the ragged flotilla headed across the Mississippi. Shields's boat was only a few hundred feet ahead, Whiteside and Rhodes at the oars, Shields hunched gloomily in the stern.

"Watch this," Lincoln said. "I'm going to pass them."

He rowed harder, his hands gripping the handles of the oars and his great arms drawing them back in a powerful rhythmic stroke. Cage felt the boat accelerate, saw the sudden wake behind them in the muddy, swirling water. Up ahead, Whiteside and Rhodes saw the boat coming and pulled harder at their own oars, but the two of them combined could not match Lincoln's physical strength nor even comprehend the obsessive determination that was now propelling him. He drove the blades of the oars deep into the water, pulling them through with a force and mechanical will that reminded Cage of the churning paddle wheel of the *Lebanon*. Sweat was pouring down from the brim of his hat and he had to shake his head to fling it out of his eyes, but he did so without missing a stroke.

Up ahead, Shields was watching Lincoln come on, staring at the back of his head with glowering confusion. Lincoln glanced over his shoulder, but only to gauge how much he was gaining, not yet to meet Shields's eyes. He dug deep for four or five strokes and when finally the two vessels were alongside each other he stopped rowing and did his best to regulate his breath and compose his expression. He smiled at Shields and casually said, as if they were passing on the street and there had never been any unpleasantness between them, "Afternoon, Jim."

Shields recognized that he must hold on to his self-possession or he would be humiliated beyond endurance yet again. He had no choice but to return Lincoln's greeting. He responded with a determinedly neutral nod. Lincoln nodded back and plunged the oars again. He kept driving for the Illinois side of the river, where crowds of onlookers were still waiting to find out what the result of the duel had been.

THIRTY-ONE

IF IT WERE NOT FOR THE . . . for the *gift* of marriage,"
John Hardin mused as he stood in front of Martinette Hardin's wedding guests, a glass of champagne in his hand, "what would I be? What
would any of us be?"

As he spoke, he rested his hand on the shoulder of Alex McKee, the
young lawyer who had just married his sister. Bride and groom sat at the
head of one of four long tables set up in the yard next to the Hardins'
house, tables lit by candelabras and decorated by bouquets of chrysan-
themums, set with gleaming china plates and decanters and bottles,
presided over by vigilant waiters in livery, some of them free black men
hired for the occasion, others the indentured servants of the Hardin
household.

Hardin reminisced about his first term in the assembly, back when
the legislature was still meeting in Vandalia. The road from his home
here in Jacksonville to the capital was little more than a buffalo track, the
lodging in Vandalia was miserable, the food inedible, the winter storms
so wild and biting that he could not even get to the post office to receive
a desperately anticipated letter from his wife.

"Party spirit ran high in Vandalia, as Mr. Lincoln and some of the
rest of you can attest." He tilted his glass in the direction of Lincoln,
seated at the next table over. Lincoln nodded in nostalgic confirmation. He looked almost serene, almost handsome, in the candlelight of
a still September night, only five days removed from his near duel with
James Shields. "We were not wanting in passion, in the fervent belief
that we could make our beloved state of Illinois a paradise on earth for
its citizens. But, for me, beneath the passion and the excitement there

was a deep dark pit. It was the pit of loneliness. I had the hypo, ladies and gentlemen. I had the blues. I missed my wife. I had the crushing sense that to be separated from her was not just an inconvenience, but a betrayal of all that was natural and all that was ordained by God. I realized during that season in Vandalia that a day spent apart from my Sarah was a day subtracted from life itself."

He went on, eloquently, a little tiresomely, praising the institution of marriage, its essential role in taming the wild individual beasts that we all are in danger of reverting to. Without marriage the world would still be populated, but only by the careless, loveless, undisciplined offspring of isolated men and women. It would be a wilderness, every man at his own fire, fearing the dark, shivering from the cold.

"So let us drink in thanksgiving," he said, finally holding up his glass, "that Martinette and Alex have found, in each other, a warm hearth to sit beside, a new life to share. May their love light the way as they walk hand in hand into the future they have begun to make."

The guests drank to the bride and groom. The women were in tears from Hardin's speech, some of the men too. Mary Todd was there, warm tears running unabashedly down her cheeks as she applauded Hardin's sentiments. The Hardins had been careful not to seat her at the same table as Lincoln, whom she had not seen in over a year. However, Cage had found his own place card next to hers. As moving as Hardin's toast had been, she was desperate for the testimonials to be over so that she could find out about the duel firsthand from Cage.

After Hardin's toast, soup bowls were set before them in a fluid, coordinated rush by the servants. Mary absentmindedly stirred the clear broth with her spoon and ignored the people around her as she bore in on Cage with her questions. Had it been for real or was Lincoln merely toying with Shields's pomposity? Had he really chosen swords? How close a thing had it been?

"Closer than I would have liked," Cage said. "And I hope closer than you would have liked as well."

"What do you mean?"

"Well, you were provoking Shields too, weren't you? With that poem in the paper?"

"Julia and I were just having fun!"

"That may be, but the result was to send Shields further over the edge. You almost got Lincoln killed."

Now her eyes were welling again. She dabbed at them with her dinner napkin and looked around at her neighbors, smiling at them in a way to leave the impression she was still emotionally affected by John Hardin's charming remarks on marriage. But Cage knew that they were tears of remorse and confusion.

"Am I really such a horrid person?" she whispered when she turned to face him again. She was a woman of appealing appearance who on this night looked stunning, her skin as luminous as marble in the candlelight, a silver necklace fastened at her throat in a way whose suggestiveness he could not logically interpret. It was as if she had put it there only to signal that it should be removed, that everything she wore was only for the purpose of making you understand that there was bare skin beneath it. Though she carried extra weight throughout the area of her bodice and her shoulders, it only added to the overall impression of lightness conveyed by her correct posture. Her neck was slender, her face full, with as yet only the teasing suggestion of a double chin.

"You're not horrid," Cage of course had to say. "But what you did was serious business, even if it seemed like fun at the time."

She nodded as she looked down at her soup, admitting he was right, willing to be chastened. She looked again in Lincoln's direction. Someone on her opposite side opened his mouth to talk to her but she pretended she didn't notice and turned back to Cage.

"He looks different. Not as sad and spindly as the last time I saw him. Having me out of his life must agree with him."

"It agrees with you too. You look splendid."

"Thank you, but I'm miserable."

"Why?"

She shrugged as if it were a matter of no importance. "What do you think he'll do next? Run for Stuart's seat in Congress? Run for governor? People are talking about that."

"Maybe he'll just content himself with practicing law with Logan."

"You don't believe that. Lincoln's not the sort to 'content himself' with anything. Neither are you. Neither am I."

The servants swept in once more to remove their soup bowls. The groom was standing now at the head of the main table, offering his own toast in the pause before the delivery of the main course. He was thanking the Hardins for their generosity, thanking the guests for their friendship, thanking God for creating the woman who was now—unbelievable as it seemed to him, undeserving as he was of such good fortune—his bride forevermore.

He was almost sobbing with happiness when he finished. As Cage applauded along with the other guests, his eyes were on the bride and groom but he could feel, at his side, the directed intensity of Mary Todd's emotions. At twenty-three, she was half a dozen years older than Martinette, half a dozen years overdue in discovering her own happiness, her own destiny. There had been other suitors besides Lincoln but no one else, apparently, who had captured her imagination with comparable strength. The fact that he was awkward, that he was uncultured and half-educated, unstoppable and ungovernable, bursting like a spring out of the rocky ground of his beginnings—all this had spoken to a young woman who had been reared among, and bored by, young men of unsurprising polish and promise. It made sense that she would have heedlessly joined in the attacks on James Shields by writing her own satiric verse. Like Abraham Lincoln, she had a nervous need to be at the center of whatever was happening.

After dinner the reception drifted back into the Hardins' main parlor, where the ceremony had taken place and where all the chairs that had been set down were now taken up for dancing. There were new window drapes of sea-foam green, the same shade as the bride's wedding dress, and the color scheme was repeated—subtly but detectably—in the bouquets of artificial flowers and in the pastoral painting on the fireboard.

"Well, you last saw the house in utter disarray," Sarah Hardin told Cage as they stood in front of the mantel. "I hope you weren't horrified. But as you see, we did manage to put it back together somewhat."

"It's a beautiful house, and a magnificent setting for this occasion," Cage told her. "It's a perfect wedding."

"It wouldn't have been, if you hadn't come here to warn John. We would either have been mourning Mr. Lincoln or pretending to mourn Mr. Shields."

As he talked to Mrs. Hardin, Cage faced the reflection in the pier glass behind her. Across the room he saw Mary Todd glide up to Lincoln and smile hello, the first communication that had passed between them since he had read her note releasing him from the obligation to love her. His face was frozen for a moment in uncertainty, and then at something she said he relaxed. Another moment and they were laughing—no doubt at James Shields and his inflated self-regard. When Mrs. Hardin was called away to deal with some emergency involving the wedding cake, Cage turned away from the pier glass and started to walk across the room to where Lincoln and Mary were standing. He felt a pressing sense of urgency that was not so different from the need to intercede in the duel with Shields. If they got back together, if Lincoln fell into the same black sea of despair as he had before, he might well end up just as dead as if his neck had been sliced through with a broadsword.

But he stopped before he reached them. What was he planning to do, separate them with his own hands? He would offer Abraham Lincoln his advice if he asked for it but by God he would not be his guardian. He watched Lincoln staring down at Mary with the same look on his face that had been there before. Cage thought his friend was partly afraid of Mary but hopelessly intrigued by her—drawn to her greater knowledge and guile, to the radiant beauty that she seemed capable of turning on and off like the pulsing bioluminescence of a sea creature. Cage watched them with all the clinical distance he could muster, then turned away, and saw their reflection again as they left the party behind and walked together out the front door of the Hardin mansion.

"You might have told me you were part of this dueling nonsense," Ellie said to Cage when he came back to Springfield. They were once again in his rooms, but she was fully and prohibitively dressed, armored in her whalebone corset and tightly coiffed hair. She had come not for lovemaking but to deliver a grievance. "It might have occurred to you to consider my situation."

"I don't know what situation you're talking about."

"I'm your business partner! If you'd been killed, there might have been probate, there might have been all sorts of complications that would have been very bad for my livelihood."

"I was never going to be killed, Ellie. I was only his second—his third, really."

"Well, don't seconds and thirds shoot each other in duels all the time? It's no more unthinkable than the principals killing each other over some stupid point of honor that nobody even cares about."

"Things were moving in a hurry. There wasn't time to tell you."

"There was time. You didn't want to tell me. You didn't care to hear my opinion."

"You're right. I didn't care to and I wasn't obliged to. After all, you aren't my wife. We have our own spheres and we do as we like—isn't that what we've been so careful to arrange?"

He stared at her from his chair, confident that he had made a point, feeling satisfaction in his momentary dominance of the argument, though still wishing an argument had not taken place. After his absence of more than a week, his lodgings appeared subtly unfamiliar to him: the bed and bookcases and pictures all in the same place, but changed in size or alignment or something by perhaps one degree, the way his house had looked to him as a child once when he had returned after a summer's absence and had grown perhaps an inch—everything the same but his perspective unsettlingly altered. Now he realized that that crucial one degree of difference applied as well to the woman standing before him in her salmon-colored dress, a striped ribbon at her neckline, a cameo bracelet on her wrist. Who was she? Even at moments like this, when they were at a defiant impasse over an imagined breach of their loveless contract, he was still faint with desire for her. But he was still picturing Martinette Hardin's wedding, the tears of joy on the faces of the bride and groom and guests. A contract was not the same as a union, the hunger he felt for Ellie was a different thing than love.

"I don't like to be uninformed," she was saying, the words calculated as a parting statement as she headed to the door.

"I think they're back together," he said.

"Who?"

"Lincoln and Mary Todd."

"Your friend is an interesting case," she said, finally lightening enough to give him a smile. "He doesn't seem to tire of finding new ways to destroy himself."

THIRTY-TWO

◆ ◆ ◆

IT WAS FINISHED. Cage leaned forward in his chair and squared the loose papers on his desk into a neat stack. The fair copy of his manuscript—endlessly revised, boldly reconceived more than once— was in the end only a physical object, of less discernible value than the pot of glue resting beside it. But to him it was a living thing, as breathing and brooding as its author. He had titled it *The Prairie Road.* Those three words, written in as elegant a hand as he could command on the top sheet of the manuscript, seemed to rise from the page with startling clarity and rightness, as if there could never have been any other title. It was the record of a trackless journey, of one soul's progression toward an invisible destination, through a wilderness without landmarks. Everything was in it, he thought: everything he was, everything he had seen or sensed in himself or others. It was partly a record of his own longing, a portrait of an orphaned soul afraid of being shut out of the normal congress of human life, yet almost as afraid of fitting into it. But it was also the chronicle of a city struggling to rise from the wilderness, and of other men and women with their own towering dreams. Some of these people—like Lincoln—had come from nothing, and yet had some-how developed a conviction that they could not allow themselves to be simply mortal, that they had to strive and achieve and advance and write themselves into the pages of history.

He had been awake until four in the morning writing out the fair copy, and after that he tried to go to sleep but could not. He was too excited about the finished manuscript on his desk, too full of thoughts about what it might portend. So now he was in a sleepless and exhilarated state. He washed and cleaned his teeth and changed out of yesterday's clothes, and heard the breakfast bell ringing downstairs. He was thrillingly hungry and almost quaking with joy and bewilderment that the great task had really been completed.

He couldn't be alone. He needed to tell someone. He could already picture the blank look on Ellie's face, her refusal to understand why he would be in such an emotional churn over the completion of a manuscript that was only 136 pages long, and in which the writing did not even extend margin to margin. Her own creative instincts—her eye for color and material, her almost visionary sense of the kind of things women would want to wear in one year and look back upon with horror in the next—were to her mere tools for a larger strategy of business success.

Lincoln would understand. Lincoln would celebrate with him, would be openly and flatteringly envious. Cage ran downstairs, meaning only to say good morning to his boarders as he downed a cup of coffee and took a biscuit with him to eat on the way to Lincoln's office. But he ran into Ellie in the parlor. She was fully dressed, a warm shawl around her shoulders and a bonnet tied tight to her chin, and on her way out the door.

"Well, this is a thunderbolt," she declared.

"Yes, it is," he said, thinking somehow that she knew he had finished his book. "It took me a little by surprise. But how did you know? I don't remember telling you it was about to happen."

"You didn't have to. *She* did."

"What do you mean? Who are you talking about?"

"Well, Mary Todd, of course. She left a note for me with Mrs. Hopper at seven this morning. No time to wait until the shop opens. She needs her dress altered by tonight or there'll be no wedding."

"Mary Todd is getting married? To whom?"

"I don't understand. You mean you don't know? She's getting married to Lincoln. Tonight! What did you think I meant?"

So the thunderbolt Ellie had been talking about wasn't Cage's completion of his book. It was a genuine thunderbolt, a perplexing out-of-nowhere development that made no sense. Cage hadn't talked to Lincoln for weeks—he had been out on the autumn circuit—but surely he would have written him if, in the two months since he had reconnected with Mary, he had decided to throw himself headlong into that particular swamp again.

He walked over to Lincoln's office. It was a Friday in early November, a clear sky, a cold wind coming in off the prairie agitating the leaves remaining on the trees. Stray dogs shivered in doorways and below porches, business signs swung and creaked on their chains.

"He's across the street at that new jewelry store," Stephen Logan said from his desk when Cage entered the office. "Buying a ring. Have you heard he's getting married?"

Lincoln was on his way out of the jewelry store just as Cage walked up to it. He was holding a small velvet bag and was looking just as sleep-starved and weirdly alert as Cage felt himself to be. He wore a beaver hat and his most-abused suit of clothes, wrinkled and road-worn from his circuit travels. The bow of his tie was so haphazardly made it was almost perpendicular.

"There you are!" he said to Cage. "I was on my way to find you. I'm getting married tonight and I need a best man. Will you do it?"

"Where did this idea come from?"

"Well, it came up quick, I admit. Molly and I have been sending letters back and forth while I was on the circuit and got sort of friendly through the mails again. So when I got back to Springfield we just figured why not?"

"That doesn't make any sense. Why does it have to happen tonight? Why are you just now asking me to be your best man?"

"People get married on a whim all the time, don't they? Of course there's some feathers that'll need smoothing. Mary's sister Elizabeth's a little agitated about it, and Ninian's always looked down on me, but they're turning their house over to us for the wedding and rustling up some gingerbread to feed the guests. Reverend Dresser said he'd do the honors, and I got this jeweler in there to engrave this ring overnight so we're all set for the particulars except I don't have a best man."

He opened the bag and held the gold ring out to Cage. "It'll take me another half dozen bankruptcy cases to pay it off. Take a look inside the band. I had him write 'Love is Eternal.' I hope it is."

Cage took the ring, inspected the writing inside it, then handed it back to Lincoln without commenting on it. The shops were all open now, and despite the cold the streets were crowded with people going about their morning business.

"Don't marry her," Cage blurted out.

"What? Why?"

"She's bad for you. You know that. Look what happened to you before."

"That was almost two years ago. I didn't have the sense then to know how right she is for me."

"She's *not* right for you!"

He had been speaking above the noise of the wind, but it had died down an instant before and his exasperated voice suddenly erupted with a clarion intensity he didn't intend. It startled him for a moment, but the people in the busy square went on about their errands as if they hadn't heard. Cage lowered his voice. "She'll make you miserable."

"Oh, I doubt that she will too much." He nodded hello to several men walking across the street to the capitol, then lowered his voice as he spoke to Cage again. "Anyway, the thing is done."

"Why is the thing done? Where is the harm in backing out of a rash decision? The Edwardses will be relieved, and if you and Mary decide you want to get married you can take your time and—"

"We can't take our time, Cage. If we do, there's the matter of running the risk of consequences."

"Do you mean—"

"Let's go over here."

He led Cage to the back of Hoffman's Row where they used to play fives, a time that seemed suddenly as remote to Cage as childhood. Lincoln craned his neck up and around, making sure the windows looking down on them were all closed. Still, he kept his voice almost to a whisper.

"When I got back home the other night, I wanted to see her, and I knew the Edwardses wouldn't want the two of us at their house after all the confusion that had happened between Molly and me. And they didn't think so highly of her getting involved in that Shields business, either. So I asked Sim Francis if we could meet at his house. Well, we did, and Sim and Eliza went up to bed and they left us down there in the parlor alone and told us to stay and talk as long as we wanted. So we stayed and we talked and then we started kissing and that led us on to other endeavors."

"Such as?"

"Christ, Cage! Do you have an imagination or not?" He looked up at the windows again, just to make doubly sure.

"So you see I've got to marry her."

"I don't see that at all. Plenty of men and women have had sexual relations without getting instantly married."

"There might be a baby coming."

"There's probably not!"

"But if there is, and we wait any longer to get married how would it look when the baby was born? Molly would be cast down pretty low, don't you reckon? And I wouldn't be raised up too high, either. It's a dilemma with an elegantly simple remedy. I've already got a room for us at the Globe to live in. Anyway, getting married is something I should have done a long time ago. I might be entering hell but I think not. Mary's smart and good-looking and I have the feeling she'll help take the slack out of me and improve my character and my prospects along with it. Look at Speed. Look at how happy he turned out to be with Fanny."

Cage felt all at once that he was sitting in the jury box, listening to Lincoln deliver a closing argument in a trial, an argument whose coils of logic were woven so tight that doubt could not breach them. But this time Lincoln was also trying to convince himself. His voice was higher-pitched than it would have been in a courtroom, and his gray eyes were desperate and pleading.

"I'm sorry I didn't give you more notice," he said. "But everything sort of had to happen at once. I'd like you to be my best man, as I said. I'd be honored if you would do so. All it would require is for you to take this ring and put it in your pocket and hand it to me when the reverend says it's time."

Cage had no choice but to nod. Lincoln handed him the velvet bag again and he slipped it into his waistcoat pocket, charging himself with remembering it was there when he changed clothes for the wedding.

"Don't look so solemn," Lincoln said, looking solemn himself. "I'm the happiest I've ever been."

They were back in the parlor of the Edwards house, the site of so many festivities in the past and now the scene of a strange and ambiguous marriage. The light had fallen, the candles in the chandeliers were lit, a buffet table at the far end held a wedding cake Elizabeth Edwards had somehow come up with at a day's notice, along with stacks of gingerbread and a bowl of punch. Mrs. Edwards and her husband stood behind the bride and groom as they faced the Episcopal minister who was droning his way through *The Book of Common Prayer*. Ninian Edwards looked annoyed, but that was his usual expression. Elizabeth looked worried, no doubt wondering about her sister's future with a man who had no money and no breeding and who had already rejected her once and had a tendency to embarrass himself in public. Now, if he embarrassed himself again, he would be dragging the Todd family into the center of his troubles. But even Elizabeth had to know that Abraham Lincoln was the furthest thing possible from an inconsequential man. Here he was, after all, in the Edwards house on Aristocracy Hill, marrying the sometimes beautiful, temperamental, and hard-to-interest young woman who had grown up gossiping about politics with Henry Clay and was not likely to choose a husband who did not appear to her to wear the mantle of destiny.

In any case, Mary Todd's eyes were on the preacher, not on her disapproving sister and brother-in-law. The dress Ellie had altered for her that day—perhaps taken in, since she had lost a little of the weight she had gained—was a subtle yellow, with a chain of equally subtle embroidered flowers at the neckline. The pale silk set off Mary to great advantage. Her face was a mask of triumph. From time to time she looked from Reverend Dresser to the tall, rangy man standing beside her. From time to time their eyes met, but for the most part Lincoln was looking over the head of the man who was marrying them, staring at the pattern in the wallpaper as if it held an infinity of wonders. From all appearances, he had tamed his uncertainty and was confident next to his bride. He was fashionably clothed for once, the coat tight in the sleeves, the waistcoat cut low, his cravat in a cramped bow beneath his chin. His hair was neither too short nor too wild, and weeks on the circuit had exposed his skin to the sun, so that his face was hale and ruddy, bearing no traces of the parchment-like pall that crept over it when he was worried and overworked. He was not in the least peculiar-looking on his wedding day, just a tall, gangly, rugged man, maybe handsome, maybe not, but with an evident ascetic strength of body and character, a man willingly following the course before him, hoping but not counting on it to lead to happiness.

Cage had scratched out the outlines of a best man speech during the hectic afternoon, and after the ceremony he lifted his glass and praised the heroic host and hostess, and predicted for the bride and groom a lifetime of laughter and shared confidences and interests. We could only now begin to envision, he said, the extraordinary children they would have, the bright and happy home they would create, the vaulting leaps they would make together in forging the future of Illinois, and perhaps—if Lincoln were to follow the Whig road blazed by John Stuart to the United States Congress—the future of the nation itself.

There were more toasts—by Sim Francis, by Ned Baker, by Ash Merritt, by Billy Herndon, even a not-so-grudging welcome-to-the-family from Ninian Edwards. But there was no music and no dancing and by nine o'clock the guests were standing outside the steps of the mansion with handfuls of rice. Before she entered the carriage with her new husband, Mary turned and kissed Cage on the cheek.

"You are such a friend of Mr. Lincoln," she said, her pronunciation of the word "mister" somehow driving home the fact that he was now in her possession and would remain so. "And you are of course a great friend to me. I hope you always will be."

"Of course I will," he said.

Lincoln was beside her. He saw her into the carriage and then grabbed Cage's hand and squeezed it hard and gave him a relieved smile.

"Well, Cage," he said. "I am married, after all."

"Yes, you are. And God bless you."

Lincoln kept his grip on Cage's hand for a moment more.

"I feel pretty good about it," he said. "I really do."

1843

◆ ◆ ◆

THIRTY-THREE

◆◆◆

SOMETHING WAS WRONG. Nothing specific, nothing tragic, just a needling sense that the world and everyone in it were moving forward without him. It had started with Lincoln's marriage in November. Maybe the foundation of Cage's mortal caution about the arrangement had been nothing but simple envy—or annoyance. Lincoln had all but disappeared from Cage's life these last few months. He was reportedly happy, happier than anyone had expected him to be after such a tormented courtship and thrown-together wedding, but Cage had learned nothing from Lincoln himself. He understood that a newly married man would necessarily divest himself of old habits and, to one degree or another, old friends. Still, the fact that Lincoln had not called on him or written to him, had not chosen to share the impressions and emotions of his new state, was an unexpected wound.

Equally unexpected was the parcel that arrived from Gray and Bowen just after the new year. The manuscript of *The Prairie Road* had gone out to them in early November. He had waited anxiously since for the letter confirming that they had read it and were eager to publish it. Instead they had returned the book with only a brief note:

Thank you for the submission to our house of the enclosed manuscript, bearing the title The Prairie Road. We have read it and believe the poetical work does its author much credit, in both topic and execution. We note particularly your feel for the landscape of the western regions and for the inhabitants therein. But we fear that it may be only of provincial interest, as several of our readers here have found. We regret the necessity of returning it to you without an offer of publication.

. . .

At moments of profound disappointment a man ought to turn to his wife or his closest friend. But Cage had no wife—only Ellie, who by nature would be unable to comprehend how a letter such as this could devastate his soul. As for his closest friend, he was married and living with his new wife in a room at the Globe, and except for a few chance encounters on the street, had mysteriously removed himself from Cage's orbit.

None of it made any sense. Gray and Bowen's original interest in the manuscript, once Mary Todd had managed to alert them to it, had been keen. His belief in the quality of the work itself, which had been wrought from his own heart, and perfected over a period of many years, was secure. The perfunctory rejection was as confusing as it was disheartening. He was of course too proud to approach Mary Todd—now Mrs. Abraham Lincoln—to get her opinion of what had gone wrong or whether some kind of mistake had been made. He was likewise too proud to search out Lincoln himself, to present himself to his preoccupied friend as someone in need of consolation and encouragement. He would have to suffer the blow in solitude.

He could not bear to even look at the manuscript, fearing that if he did so he might share the opinion of Gray and Bowen's office readers that it was a provincial mediocrity and no more. He locked it away in a desk drawer and resolved not to think about it until his disappointment and anger had cooled. At that point he would read it over again and, if necessary, admit that the identity he had created for himself as a man of letters had been an illusion all along.

Just when he had decided that his friendship with Abraham Lincoln had been an illusion as well, an invitation arrived, signed "Mary Lincoln," soliciting Cage's attendance at a thirty-fourth birthday celebration for her husband to be held that next week in the sitting room of the Globe Hotel.

There was no personal inscription from Mary, no "We are so looking forward to seeing you again after such an inexplicably long time apart." The note was rather formal, hinting at a formal occasion, and so Cage polished his boots and dressed in his best coat and best silk tie before striding off to the Globe in the dark and sleety cold of a February evening.

The sitting room was already crowded when he got there. All of the members of the old coterie and of the poetry society and of course the politicos and lawyers with whom Lincoln's life intersected at every turn. There was a table in the middle of the room with a great frosted sponge cake with gilded leaves around the edge and the initials "A.L." in the center. There were ham and turkey and free drinks at the bar. Who was paying for all this? Perhaps Mary's father, or one of her uncles. Or maybe the celebration was a function of the Whig Party, which was becoming more structured, taking on a clear hierarchy and meeting in conventions to choose its candidates. The other possibility was a simple levy among Lincoln's friends, though if that were the case why hadn't Cage been asked to contribute?

Lincoln spotted him almost as soon as he entered the door, immediately detached himself from the well-wishers he was talking to, and rushed over to pump his hand up and down.

"For God's sake, Cage, where have you been? Do you have any idea how much I've missed talking to you?"

"I've been where I've always been. You're the one who's fallen off the rim of the earth."

"Well, it's my fault then, I guess. Once you get married, your life starts to move on rails and you're miles off from where you started before you know it. There's a lot of fuss involved when you move to a new place with a woman. Did you know it's not just desirable but essential to have ormolu tiebacks for your window drapes?"

"Are you happy?"

"It's a marvel to me, Cage—being married. Some would say we're in a tight space, since we only have one room. And Molly—Mrs. Lincoln, as we call her now—has to do all the cleaning and housekeeping herself, which she's not used to, being a Kentucky Todd. But she's got a smile on her face most of the time and when she doesn't I've learned the art of staying out of her way. By the bye, I'm holding on to a secret that's about to—"

But Logan was calling out Lincoln's name, ordering him to by God come over by the fireplace and let the workies of the party serenade him on his birthday. They sang one rousing Whig song and then another, and would have kept going all night if Mary Lincoln, knife in hand, had not called out for silence and said it was time to cut her husband's birthday cake.

Cage had not yet had the chance to speak to her. The room was crowded, the conversation chaotic. Everyone was talking about Joseph Smith and whether the Mormon prophet had really conspired to kill the former governor of Missouri. They were gossiping about the upcoming race for U.S. Congress and whether Lincoln, Baker, and Hardin would, as seemed likely, all join in the scramble for the Whig nomination for the Seventh District.

Ned Baker did not look like a man who was preparing to challenge his good friend Abraham Lincoln. He was heaving with laughter at one of Lincoln's stories as if he hadn't heard it a dozen times before. He laughed so hard he started to choke on his cake, crumbs flying out of his mouth as Lincoln pounded him on the back. For just a moment it looked as if Ned was in real trouble, but he soon recovered himself enough to set down his empty cake plate and pick up another.

Baker and Lincoln and Ash Merritt and Logan and Billy Herndon were all standing in front of the fireplace, where big oak logs were fiercely aflame, filling that portion of the room with a surging light that made the men, with their animated, illuminated gesturing, look like actors before the footlights. The chair Jacob Early had been sitting in before Truett shot him was no longer there, and the carpet that had soaked up his blood had been replaced, but to Cage this room would forever bring to his mind nothing but the shocking crime he had witnessed with Jim Reed.

Billy Herndon was drunk and getting drunker. He had arrived without the temporizing presence of his wife, who was at home with one child and expecting another.

"Let me tell you a little something about John Hardin," Billy said when he had left the group by the fire and cornered Cage. He seemed to be under the impression they were taking up a conversation that had just been interrupted. "Yes, he's loyal to the party but he's loyal to himself first. His ambition is celestial, and he has not much more regard for the truth than Munchausen himself."

"Why are you going on about John Hardin?"

"Because it's Mr. Lincoln who should represent this district in Washington, and not anybody else. Hardin and Ned Baker should both have the decency to get out of the way."

Billy had begun studying law with Lincoln last year. Since he was the sort of man who was driven to take sides on things, it was natural he would be outraged at any threat to his patron's interests. Cage had no illusions that either Hardin or Baker would step aside for Lincoln, or that Lincoln would do the same for them. All three were friends of his, and he knew them well enough to understand that each was jealously convinced of his own destiny and more than willing to fight for it.

"She's looking at me again," Billy said. He had changed the subject so rapidly that Cage had no idea what he was talking about.

"Who's looking at you?"

Billy was staring abashedly down at his feet now but he made a slight gesture with his beer glass toward the other side of the room. Cage looked up and caught Mary Lincoln's disapproving stare an instant before she realized it had been noticed. Her countenance shifted so fast—she was laughing now about something with her friend Mercy— that Cage wasn't sure if the angry flash in her eyes had not been an illusion.

"She doesn't like me," Billy said. "She doesn't like me and she doesn't trust me around her noble husband."

"She told you that?"

"She won't tell me that or anything else. She won't look at me except to stare a hole through me. I drink with too much robustity—I'm pretty sure that's her problem. Her husband's a temperance man but he doesn't make himself the judge of the world when it comes to other people's enjoyments."

He leaned closer to Cage and whispered sloppily into his ear. "I liked things better when Mr. Lincoln wasn't married. He thinks he's happy with her but he is caged with her now and there's an awful long term ahead."

Billy was tiresomely drunk and Cage was disposed to ignore his indictment of Mary Lincoln. She was right to glare at him as much as she wished if she felt his conduct showed any risk of undermining her husband's hard-won stature in Illinois. But when he finally made it across the room to have a conversation with Mary for the first time that evening he faced something unexpected. She held out her hand and she smiled and greeted him by name but there was a strange hardness behind her eyes and a flatness in her voice.

"So glad you could come," she said as if to a stranger, "to help us celebrate Mr. Lincoln's birthday."

He laughed, assuming her distant tone was some sort of private interplay between two friends who knew each other very well. But her formal smile lingered and there was no warmth in her eyes. He asked her, stumblingly, how she enjoyed her new life at the Globe.

"Very well, thank you. We only have one room, of course, and no one to help with housekeeping. So I'm afraid my domestic skills are constantly being put to the test, but we're very happy indeed. How are you, Cage?"

How are you, Cage? At least she was still using his first name, but she deployed it with such an emotional remove that it could almost have been a taunt. He was thoroughly confused. Yes, he had been cautious about her, especially when it came to her paralyzing effects on Lincoln, but their conversations in the past had never lacked in frankness or warmth.

She looked well, a little stouter than she had been at her wedding, her face full but the skin taut across her cheekbones, flush with health and—he supposed—contentment. But it was a private contentment she had no interest in sharing with him, the man she had more than once singled out as a confidant.

"And your book?" she said. "Is it finished?"

"Finished, yes. Finished and forgotten, I'm afraid."

"Certainly not."

"Gray and Bowen found it wanting."

She drew back her head in surprise, though her surprise did not seem very great.

"Oh, what a disappointment. I'm sorry to hear that. But no doubt there's another publisher who'll be very happy to take it on."

She said this with such a disturbing lack of inflection that Cage wondered if he had imagined the enthusiasm with which she had championed his work, and how through her family connections she had elicited the interest of the publisher who had just rejected it. He withdrew from her company, after the exchange of only a few more words, feeling less like a friend than a stranger who had just been granted a formal audience.

It was about ten o'clock by then, and soon afterwards he heard her announcing that she was going upstairs to bed, saying good night to other people in the room with a comradely affection that she had unmistakably withheld from him. The rest of the guests—all men—lingered by the great fireplace, talking about Joseph Smith and the tariff and whether England's claims on Oregon had any legitimacy at all. Baker was holding forth on this issue when Lincoln put a hand on Cage's shoulder and whispered in his ear, "Stay till the bitter end, won't you? I've missed talking to you."

So he stayed, and by one in the morning he and Lincoln were alone in the room, Cage holding a glass of brandy, Lincoln holding nothing, just gripping the arms of his chair while the firelight danced across his great knuckles and he prodded a log that was not yet aflame with the toe of his boot. There was something new in his appearance—an aura of consistency. Mary no doubt enforced his grooming and made sure his clothes fit, and a slight fullness in his face testified to the fact that he had been introduced to regular mealtimes. But his ever-calculating political mind showed no sign of being at ease. Perhaps the locomotive of his ambition was running even faster, since he now had a partner who was as restless for success as he was.

"It'll be an unholy muddle, that's for sure," he was saying. "Me and Hardin and Baker all with our claws out for the same seat. The thing will have to be done carefully or we'll end up with our tidy little Whig house divided."

"Why don't you take turns?"

"It's worth thinking about, but no matter how much you'd like politics to be a cotillion it just naturally wants to be a dirt fight. Reminds me of those Clary's Grove boys over in New Salem."

He veered off into a reminiscence of first coming to live in New Salem as a young man, having to prove himself fit for habitation there by wrestling one of the town toughs while his companions hooted and spit.

"I was a scientific wrestler. It was my understanding there was supposed to be rules, but this was a tussle-and-scuffle crowd if I ever saw one. The Clary's Grove fellow I was fighting didn't waste any time in legging me and taking me down. But I decided to spring up from the ground and smile and shake his hand just like he'd never cheated. Which he hadn't, because as I had just learned there were no rules to begin with."

He smiled at the memory, kicked the fire again and studied the spray of sparks that erupted. "It hurt to lose, though. I had a high opinion of my strength back then. I could lift a barrel of whiskey by the chimes and drink out of the bunghole if I wanted to. By God I bet I could still do it today, though I'd have to forgo the drinking part because of my temperance leanings. Want to wrestle me on the carpet right now?"

"No."

"And now it's—what? Ten years later? Twelve?—and I'm thirty-four years old and married and sitting by the fire and thinking about my breakfast. And here's the strangest news of all." He lowered his voice and looked around the room, just to make sure it was empty. "She's going to have a baby."

"That's good news. I'm glad."

"So it turns out we were right to get married when we did. It was a near-run thing. Nobody knows about it yet. Haven't even written Speed. She told me not to tell anybody but I've just done so, haven't I? One thing I've experienced about being married so far is the dangerous thrill of defying your wife."

"She was pointedly unfriendly to me tonight, by the way. Is there a reason?"

"Oh, that's just because her humors are all fluctuous because of the—"

"That's not the reason and I don't believe you think it is. What has happened?"

Lincoln retreated into a careful silence. The clock above the mantelpiece, its circular dial flanked by miniature bronze maidens, beat out the passing moments like a blacksmith striking an anvil.

"Well," Lincoln said, "I told you about the satisfaction I take in defying Molly from time to time. And that's why you're here tonight."

"What do you mean?"

"The day of the wedding, when we were standing outside the jeweler's and you were trying to argue me out of going through with it? Julia Jayne happened to be walking by and overheard what you said. She made it her business to tell Molly, of course, but at least she waited until a week or so after the wedding. When Molly finally heard about it I experienced some weather out of the Old Testament. The skies parted in anger and there was thunder and lightning."

"Christ."

"You know Molly, she keeps a list in her head of who's her friend and who's her enemy and she doesn't like anybody wandering from one column to the other. But I didn't intend to celebrate my birthday without you being invited. She shouted at me about it some, but I wasn't going to hang my harp on the willow, and so here you are."

They tried to talk about other things, but there was no use. There the matter stood, as it must stand forever. Cage could not plead to Mary that he had been misunderstood, because he had not. He would not beg for her forgiveness, both because he did not care to and because in her rigid mind he had committed an unforgivable crime.

At three in the morning he walked home and went to bed, though he knew it was hopeless to try to sleep. His mind kept searching for a solution, and when it could not find one it insisted on going back in time to the improvident moment when he had told Lincoln not to marry Mary Todd. A part of his imagination seemed to think it could erase that moment. Once or twice, as he drifted off to sleep despite his gnawing restlessness, he thought he actually had. But then he would be startled awake again by the sure knowledge of a mistake that had actually happened and could never be made right.

Usually when he was too agitated for sleep, the solution was to light a candle and sit at his desk, scrawling out words and phrases, doing his best to outpace his conscious thoughts and provide a trail to follow for the next day's writing. But this habit of wild creativity was no longer of any relevance. His book was finished, locked in a drawer, rejected. The very thought of it humiliated him—all the wasted years he had given over to its composition, all the dreams he had naively allowed himself to cultivate.

A bolt of clarity shot through his thoughts: this was her work, a vengeful counterstrike at the man who had declared on a Springfield street that Mary Todd would ruin Abraham Lincoln. Perhaps she had written her father, asking him to inform his friends at Gray and Bowen that while the decision to publish Mr. Weatherby was of course one they would independently make, he himself regretted—upon further consideration of the work—that he could not support it with the same degree of enthusiasm it had once inspired. He would be very sorry if because of his recommendation they had felt their time had been wasted.

There were other ways the thing could have played out, but however it happened it would not have taken much. The publishers were busy men in a risky and unpredictable business, and any note of caution or indifference would in effect be a killing blow.

He didn't hate her, and he couldn't fault her. She was looking to her interests, striking the man she had decided was her enemy in his most vulnerable part. But from now on, he understood, being a friend of Mr. Lincoln would be a much trickier thing for Cage than it had been in the past.

1844–1846

◆ ◆ ◆

THIRTY-FOUR

◆ ◆ ◆

H E   W A S   S H A V I N G   when he caught sight of something out of the corner of his eye: a folded piece of paper slipped through the bottom of his door with the snap of an unseen wrist, enough velocity to propel it to the middle of the room. It was a note from Ellie. "Will you see me at the shop this morning on a matter of business?"

Why wouldn't she just knock on his door, or simply open it and walk inside? Their personal relationship had to be an open secret by now, and the habitual subterfuge they employed had begun to strike Cage as not only unnecessary but almost comical. They both made their home at the Palatine, but precisely because they were so intimate they could not enjoy the easy familiarity that naturally arose among people sharing meals and residing in the same house. When they were not alone, engaged in their twice-weekly sweaty lovemaking in the back of their dress shop, they could not break out of a stiff—and probably transparent—politeness.

"Here I am, I've answered your summons," he told her when he arrived at the shop a few hours later. It was only midmorning, but business was already lively. Cordelia was in the back of the store supervising two other young needlewomen. Her habitual air of nervous watchfulness no longer held her quite so tight. She was at ease and in charge. The new girls were daughters of Irish railway workers. Since they were white, there was no danger they would require the colossal expense of a certificate of freedom, though he rather doubted their diligence and skill would ever rise to Cordelia's standard. Ellie had also hired a new clerk, who was spreading out several rolls of spring fabrics on the counter for two young married women who were shopping together.

"It wasn't a summons," Ellie said as she led him past Cordelia and the two new girls to her office in the back. Cordelia paused in her work as he walked by and said good morning to her. She returned the greeting with a bow and the hint of a smile, a servile gratitude that made him feel uncomfortably satisfied with himself.

Ellie closed the office door behind them. She pulled out the chair for him and hitched herself up onto the desk, crossing her ankles beneath the hem of her deep blue silk dress. The room would have been dark if not for the window above her head, open to the cloudless blue of a late spring sky.

"What is your matter of business?" he asked.

"I want to buy you out."

She left the statement hanging there for him to contemplate, busying herself by pretending to straighten her whitework cuffs.

"You have the money to buy me out?"

"Yes. The shop has done well and I've managed it very carefully, as you know."

He did know. He had made back his initial investment almost a year ago and was now in regular receipt of a small profit.

"But I like being in business with you," he said.

"Why?"

He shrugged.

"Are you confused?" She had dropped her voice to almost a whisper. "Do you think if you're not in business with me you can't be in bed with me?"

"That's putting it a little too succinctly."

"If you think that, if you ever thought that . . . then you were wrong."

"All right." He studied her face as she looked at him, waiting for what he would say next. What did she see? A man of strength who had helped to elevate her into her present respectability, or a weak and infatuated man she had taken pleasure in manipulating? He didn't know which she saw—he didn't know which he was. All he knew was that they fit together somehow, answered some need in each other for both closeness and distance.

"What's the reason you want to buy me out?"

"I want a free hand."

"Have I told you what to buy or sell, or how to buy or sell it?"

"No, but I feel your presence."

"Sorry, but you'll have to tell me why my 'presence' is so terrible."

She pointed through the closed door to the unseen shop. "Because it keeps this from being mine. From feeling like mine. I want that feeling, I've never had it. I want to know what it's like to own something."

He believed her, was moved by her uncomplicated ambition. It made no sense to deny her request on emotional grounds. If all that was binding them to each other was indeed a business partnership, then it was better to have done with it. And accepting her offer made economic sense for him. He was low on money. Since Cordelia's trial he had bought not just her certificate of freedom but those of two other Negroes whose plights he had learned about from his abolitionist contacts Benbrook and Westridge.

Aside from that, he had leveraged himself heavily to become part of a partnership with two other men, a prosperous Whig Party operative named Rascoe and a Black Hawk War veteran named Dillon whom Cage had known casually ever since the march through the Trembling Lands. The three had signed a note with a merchant named Jacob Bunn, who in those years after the Democrats had killed off the state bank managed most of the moneylending in Springfield. The object of the partnership was to buy up even more land in the Western Military Tract, land that would be leased to farmers who would have more markets for their products if the Whigs won this year's presidential election and managed to pass a protective tariff against English goods. The Whigs were running Henry Clay, though Cage questioned whether the great man was past his prime and out of tune with the spirit of the country, which had taken on an alarming enthusiasm for the annexation of Texas and the expansion of slavery that must follow it. Whether Clay won or not, Cage had been in a mood lately to risk his assets. He had written nothing since the failure of his book and the reckless, speculative impulse that had once driven him to poetry had seamlessly transferred itself to his investments.

So he said yes to Ellie. They agreed on a price. The next day they went to Lincoln's office to have him draw up the contract. It had been almost a year and a half since the birthday party at the Globe. During that time Cage had seen Lincoln only in passing, Mary not at all. The Lincolns had moved out of the Globe and had bought a house on the corner of Eighth and Jackson. They had had their baby.

When Cage and Ellie arrived at Lincoln's office they were surprised to discover the baby there with him. He was sitting on the table his father used as a desk and teething on the knob of an ink blotter.

"Mrs. Lincoln has the headache today," he explained, "so Bobbie has fallen into my care. What do you think of him? Does he look cross-eyed to you?"

"Not at all," Ellie said. The baby by now had crawled across the baize tabletop and was reaching out his arms for her. She picked him up and in a business-like way stroked the still-downy hair on his head as he played with the strings of her bonnet. She appeared captivated and distracted in the same measure.

"Good," Lincoln said. "My wife thinks there's something wrong with his eye, but I don't see it and I'm not going to worry about it."

He stared at the baby sitting in Ellie's lap with such a transparent expression of tenderness that Cage almost felt he ought to look away. Lincoln, for all his guile and comical shape-shifting, was the most open man Cage had ever known. Having a son had evidently unleashed in him a raw paternal love he did not know how to hide or contain.

The boy was strategically named Robert Todd Lincoln, after Mary's father, whose wealth had no doubt been a factor in the family's upward move from their one-room dwelling in the Globe to their spacious new house. The law office was its usual mess but Lincoln himself looked well tended, his face shaved and hair crisply cut by Billy Florville, his collar wings starched and unstraying, the wide revers of his new broadcloth coat shiny and free of dandruff.

Ellie was warming to the baby. She had taken the watch chain from her neck so that Bobbie could examine it, and she regarded him with much the same level of curiosity as he regarded the watch chain. Maybe there was a maternal impulse beneath the curiosity, or maybe Cage just wanted there to be. If it existed, it was not as strong as her determination to keep it hidden.

While she kept Bobbie occupied, Lincoln prepared the documents for their signature and talked with Cage about the terrible disaster on board the new naval frigate *Princeton,* which had been cruising the Potomac a few months earlier to show off its massive naval gun to distinguished government visitors. But when the cannon was fired it exploded, killing eight men including the secretary of state and grievously wounding many others. President Tyler had been belowdecks—romancing a young girl, it was said—and was spared. The hero of the affair had been none other than John Hardin, the new congressman from Illinois. He had been on board as well, had survived, and had swiftly taken charge after the disaster.

"Well," Lincoln reflected, "Hardin's a heroic sort of creature. Always in the right place at the right time—stopping a duel from happening here, saving a damsel on an exploding vessel there."

The edge of bitterness in his voice was probably warranted. After all the maneuvering for the Congressional seat for the Seventh District during the last election, Lincoln and Baker and Hardin had arrived at some sort of agreement to keep peace among themselves and within the party. Hardin would get the Whig nomination first, then Baker, then Lincoln's turn would come third. It was a long time to wait, and of course there was human nature to take into account. All three men believed themselves to be in the hands of destiny, and Hardin especially might think it a disservice to the country for him to follow through with the deal and relinquish power after only one term.

And everyone's political future was hostage to the Texas question. It had been less than ten years ago when there had been such a great commotion in town about the fall of the Alamo, a minor battle that had occurred at some vague locale in Mexico few of them could have found on a map, assuming there had even been a map of Mexico in all of Springfield. The vast Texas territory seized in that conflict had become its own country, but a shaky and bankrupt country whose seat of government was a mere cluster of log houses somewhere on the southern prairie. It wanted to join the United States, and the Democrats vociferously wanted it to do so.

"All annexation would mean is a clear field for the expansion of slavery," Cage said as he signed the contract that Lincoln slid across the table toward him. "That, and probably a war with Mexico into the bargain."

Ellie handed Bobbie over to Cage so that she could countersign. The child flexed his legs against Cage's thighs and stared into his eyes with an infant's unembarrassed fixity. The probing gaze, the earnest desire to understand exactly what was going on and why—this seemed to Cage a legacy from his mother. Maybe one eye was indeed a little off. It was hard to tell.

Lincoln was still talking politics as he gathered up the signed papers.

"This fever for Texas is intolerable high," he said. "It's possible the Democrats will turn their backs on Van Buren and nominate a fire-breathing expansionist like Polk instead. And where would that leave Henry Clay?"

"It would leave him where he was to begin with," Cage said, "against the spread of slavery and therefore on the moral high ground."

"Well, the moral high ground is a mighty crumbly place."

They talked for a few minutes longer: Henry Clay, annexation, the tariff, the joy of lying on the floor bouncing Bobbie on his stomach. It was the sort of discussion that might have taken place between any lawyer and his client after business had been concluded. The civility of their conversation was awkward to them both. Their old intimacy was missing. It was forbidden, thanks to Lincoln's unforgiving wife.

Ellie noticed it as well. As they emerged from the office she slipped her hand into the crook of his arm, a natural enough thing for a woman to do while walking along the street with a male friend. But she had never taken his arm before, so the gesture rather startled him.

"Thank you," she whispered.

"No thanks are required. You paid me handsomely enough, and now you have your shop."

In answer she squeezed the inside of his arm. They passed the state-house, where the Lone Star flag was being erected behind a speaking platform in preparation for a big pro-annexation rally the Democrats were planning the next day.

"The thought of Texas is making me ill," he said.

"I know what's making you ill, and it's not Texas. It's Lincoln."

"What about him?"

"He's no longer your particular friend. How can he be, with that wife of his? Is he afraid of her, do you think?"

"Wouldn't you be?"

"Poor Cage. You're very lonely."

He made a chuffing sound, pretending that she was joking.

"That's one thing we've accomplished," Ellie said. "We're not married, and we're not afraid of each other."

They were walking down Washington Street, passing the City Hotel. Still aware of the odd companionable pressure of her hand on his arm, Cage turned to her.

"Let's celebrate your new status as an independent businesswoman. I'll buy you a dinner."

"Here? Out in the open?"

"Out in the open."

The hotel's dining room had recently been refurbished, with a new maitre d' stand of polished wood, and chandeliers and booths set between ornamental colonnades topped with heroic plaster busts representing the vanquished Indian tribes of Illinois. Cage and Ellie were shown to one of these private alcoves. They ordered a Hungarian wine recommended by the waiter, macaroni soup, and wild duck pie. The place had pretensions of formality but Ellie appeared at ease, smiling and unguarded for once, tapping the side of her foot against his beneath the table. She was a beautiful woman in a beautifully fitted dress, her lush hair pulled back into a chignon and fixed with an almost transparent tortoiseshell comb rising like the rays of the sun from the crown of her head.

The dining room was populated mostly by men. They slurped down their soup or puffed away on after-dinner cigars, laughing and lobbing bombastic observations back and forth. The City Hotel was not one of Cage's normal watering holes and most of the men were strangers to him, though with their thumbs tucked into their waistcoats and their hair puffed out at the sides from the constant squeeze of their hats he felt like he knew them all, since they looked like the opinion-spouting denizens of every tavern and dining room everywhere.

As Ellie talked about her plans for the shop—a new location, with more retail space, another clerk, another seamstress or two, an expanded inventory of accessories—Cage was aware of these male diners looking in her direction with lingering glances or outright stares. She lived mostly outside the normal currents of Springfield society, seldom venturing out from her residence and place of business. So to them she must have seemed an intoxicating stranger—new to town, unaccounted for and unexpected.

"Of course Texas belongs in the United States!" somebody was declaring across the room in a loud, familiar voice. "It's absurd to think otherwise, after all the American blood that's been spilled prying it away from Mexico."

Cage shifted his eyes in the direction of the pontificator. It was Nimmo Rhodes, leaning forward in his chair as he lectured his companion on the opposite side of the table, slapping the back of one hand into his open palm for emphasis. "And if we don't take Texas, don't you think England would like to have it? Or Mexico would like to have it back? Why Mexico would be delighted for the chance to—"

Rhodes sensed something, swiveled his head with the fluidity of an owl. Suddenly he and Cage were staring at each other across the dining room. There was movement at the corners of Rhodes's mouth, an instinctive half smile of sarcastic pleasure, then an adversarial tilt of his head that was not a greeting but some kind of statement about where the two of them stood. Cage held the man's stare, saw him move his eyes toward Ellie. He regarded her with such curious scrutiny that Cage was nearly at the point of rising and confronting him. But by then Rhodes had turned back to his own companion and was finishing his observation about Mexico and Texas as if he had never interrupted himself.

Cage saw him again the next day, standing with his fellow Democrats at the edge of the speaker's platform during the annexation rally at the statehouse. A doom-ridden sense of curiosity led Cage to attend the rally. He could almost see the train of events that the admission of Texas into the Union would bring about—slavery's vast expansion, an idiotic conflict with Mexico, a growing ideological gulf between North and South that might very easily culminate in a civil war and the end of the United States of America. He took no satisfaction in his prognosticating, or at least didn't think he did. One by one the Democratic speakers brought out their arguments. One man said that if we did not receive Texas into our national bosom, then England—aided by the abolitionists—would take it into hers. Another made a hard-to-follow argument, something to do with where the explorer La Salle had landed, that the Texas country had been part of the territory that conveyed to the United States when it purchased Louisiana from France. After him someone else declared that it would be an unconscionable waste not to annex Texas, since it was the fairest, fondest, most Edenic land on earth.

"Now that is horseshit," Cage heard someone muttering. He turned and found that he was standing next to Jim Reed, though it had not been Reed who had offered his opinion but the older man on the other side of him, who stood with his arms crossed on his chest, his sun-burned, blunt-fingered farmer's hands protruding from the white cuffs of his special-occasion shirt. Cage shook hands with Reed, who introduced him to George Donner.

"I only say it's horseshit because that's the truth," Donner explained with a friendly smile, keeping his voice low out of courtesy to the speaker, who was still droning on about the Texas paradise. He was a man almost sixty but with no slackening in his lined face and little gray yet in his black hair.

"George has tried his luck in Texas already," Reed explained.

"Tried my luck in '38 on the Brazos," Donner said. "And one year was enough, sir. A land of gallinippers and alligators and skulking Kronk Indians—that's what I would say if I were up there giving a speech about it."

"Yes, forget about Texas," Reed agreed. "Poor Davy Crockett died liberating the wrong part of Mexico. He should have gone to California instead. We should all go to California."

"I would not mind a peaceful Pacific breeze in place of an Illinois blizzard," Donner said.

Reed was dressed in an expensive-looking suit and a wide-brimmed straw hat with a sumptuously tight weave. He looked more prosperous and less agitated than he had that night in the Globe when they had witnessed Jacob Early shot and killed. He had not gotten into the tallow business after all, he told Cage, but had had some good fortune in the furniture manufacturing line and had won a contract to supply seats for the railways, which had been gratifyingly lucrative.

"My wife tells me I should be content and stay in place," he said, "but I'm like George here. Cursed with itchy feet."

Donner admitted that he was the sort of man for whom far horizons beckoned, even though he was of an age at which a man should sit on his gallery playing checkers with his grandchildren.

The three men stood at the edge of the rally, talking about the allure of distant unknown places, the speakers on the platform nattering on about the bounty of Texas in the background. Cage nodded his head as Reed and Donner spoke. He recalled the youthful wanderlust that had taken him to Europe, commiserated with them on feeling marooned in the center of the continent. Then the conversation flagged and they shook hands and went off on their separate errands. It was an encounter he might have vaguely recalled in later life, or more likely completely forgotten, had the future not seared it into his memory instead.

When the presidential election came that October, Cage was tempted to vote for James Birney, the candidate of the forthrightly abolitionist Liberty Party. But he knew it would mean throwing his vote away. The Democrats had the advantage of a bold, clear message: annex Texas, Mexico be damned if it interfered; let slavery take root where it will as the United States filled out the continent. Clay's stance on every issue was muted, murky, sophisticated. But Cage marked his ballot for the distinguished old candidate anyway, doing his part to shore up a frail barricade against the Slave Power.

He was not surprised when Polk and the Democrats won, nor as downcast as he felt he should be. Though the question of slavery loomed over everything, the election had also been about whether the country should be big or small, whether it should be restless or content. Maybe in his heart he was more of a Polk man than a Clay man, beginning to feel confined and frustrated, aware of an expansive need in his own nature that mirrored the mood of the nation.

What was holding him in Springfield, after all? The certainty that he once felt that Illinois would provide the foundation of a great personal accomplishment had degraded into a wistful dream. His work had come to nothing. He could send his book out to other publishers, but he held out no hope that they would be any more intrigued by a voice from the West than Gray and Bowen had been. Whatever it was he had with Ellie was something he had allowed her to define and control, a settled fondness beyond the risk of love. As for his friendship with Lincoln, that too was a diminished thing.

Or so he thought, until Lincoln hailed him in the street one afternoon a week or so after the elections.

"Thank God," Lincoln said. "There you are. I have something in my pocket you have to read. I haven't shown it to anybody else. I don't trust anybody's judgment but yours. It's the best thing I've ever written, Cage. Can we go to your place?"

They walked to the Palatine. All the way there, Cage couldn't stifle an instinct to keep a watchful eye out for Mary.

"Don't worry about her," Lincoln said, reading his mind.

"Why? Has she gotten over me being her enemy?"

"No, she never gets over anything. But the wrathier a wife a man has, the more he needs a friend."

The parlor was empty, and Mrs. Hopper was out on errands. They helped themselves from a tray of doughnuts left over from that morning's breakfast, and then walked upstairs to Cage's room. Lincoln sat on the bed and drew his feet up without taking off his muddy boots. Some of the domestic polish had worn off. He was still well-clothed but haggard and underfed, weary from months of futile campaigning for Henry Clay.

"The shadows will be gathering now," he said. "Did you know that Molly's stepmother was with Clay when he got the news he'd been defeated? She wrote Molly that he turned blue—the actual color blue—when he read the letter. Then he raised his wineglass and said, 'I drink to the health and happiness of all assembled here.' As fine a man as exists, and the country casts him off in favor of that humorless entity Polk."

He shoved a whole doughnut into his mouth. At least Baker had won his election, he said while he masticated it. He would be going to Congress next year, and after his term was up—assuming the agreement between Lincoln and Baker and Hardin held up—it would be Lincoln's turn to run for the seat.

"You see how I plot and plan even as I mourn Clay's loss," he said. "I'm like a character from Shakespeare. Richard the Third, or maybe Iago."

"You said you wanted me to read something."

"Yes!" Lincoln sprang out of the bed, picked up his hat from the floor where he had carelessly tossed it, and pulled a folded piece of paper out of the interior band. He thrust the paper at Cage and indicated with a swipe of his hand that he was to read it then and there. As Cage read, Lincoln stood with his arms folded and his face lowered in suspense.

It was a new poem, titled "My Childhood Home I See Again," so fluidly and feelingly written that Cage read it through with disconcerting ease, registering its emotion before its meaning. It ought to have been nothing very special, a nostalgic poem about a man revisiting the scene of his boyhood, but like everything Lincoln wrote it was so death-haunted—"Every sound appears a knell," it declared, "and every spot a grave"—that by the time Cage had read it through silently a second time he was almost shivering with gloomy admiration.

"I know there's too much of Wordsworth in it," Lincoln said.

"You're right."

"But am I right in thinking it's any good? It's not nearly what you could have pulled off with the subject, but—"

"Oh, stop it. It's good, and you know very well it is. For what it's worth, it's better than anything I've ever done."

Lincoln made a show of dismissing this idea as preposterous, but Cage hadn't meant it as flattery. The poem was to him alarmingly effective, with more gravity, more control, more heart than anything Lincoln had written before. It was steeped in fatalism, like most of his poetry, but the dark tone was honestly encountered and had nothing to do with literary effect.

"It needs work, I know. I'm not in any hurry with it, but it landed on me like a fever. I heard the first lines in my head and there was no way to keep the others from coming."

Inspiration had arrived, he explained, when he had crossed into Indiana toward the end of the campaign to rouse the people for Clay. While there, he had driven to the place they had lived when his father moved them from Kentucky.

"I was seven years old when we came to Indiana. For the first few weeks we were living in a half-faced camp. When you're seven years old and you hear panthers screaming at night and you see wolf eyes shining at you through the chinks in the logs your imagination can turn on you pretty quick. You've got your mother to calm your fears but then along comes the milk sick and it's time to help your father build her coffin, him yelling at you to stop daydreaming and get to work. I wasn't daydreaming, Cage. I was just stupefied. She died pretty wild, you see, thrashing on her bed, her tongue all swollen up and . . ."

He looked down at the floor, his face set as he did his best to drive the memory out of his head. He looked up again and fixed Cage with a look of solemn directness.

"You remember your mother?"

"Of course." But he didn't really. She'd had some nameless, endless wasting disease and she was taken from him in increments of suffering, so that each blighted day served to obscure the memory of what she had been like in those ancient days of full health. There were no portraits that he knew of. If there had been one, perhaps his father in his grief had locked it away or destroyed it.

"My mother had bluish-greenish eyes," Lincoln said. "At least as I recall. Spare-built like me. Family talk said she had some knightly Virginia blood in her, but she came by it in a sideways bastardly sort of way, since her own mother got knocked up by some fancy planter. What would you think of that, if my mother was illegitimate?"

"I wouldn't think anything of it."

"Gives you a feeling that you're not that legitimate either, and never was. I've always felt like that boy from the half-faced camp who has no right to be around regular people."

Cage didn't bother to contradict him. Lincoln was enjoying his nostalgic self-deprecation, and now that he was a husband and father and likely going to Washington to represent Illinois in Congress in the next few years, melancholy was no longer a mortal danger for him, just a mood.

"I've got a copy of that at home," Lincoln told him, indicating the poem that Cage was still holding. "Would you keep that one and do me the honor of suggesting how I can get some of the Wordsworth out of it? I miss talking to you about poetry."

"I do as well."

"And it mystifies me and bedevils me that that publishing company turned down your book. You'll send it out to someone else, of course."

"Of course, but not for a while."

"I can't fathom anyone passing up a chance to publish your work, when there are so many inferior things being brought out every day."

If Cage's theory was correct, that Mary was responsible for Gray and Bowen's sudden disinterest in his book, Lincoln surely didn't know about it. Cage was touched by his friend's honest perplexity, and of course would not breathe a word of his suspicions about Mary.

"We should meet more regular," Lincoln said. "Like we used to. I'd like you to come to the house for our conversations, but we might have to meet on neutral ground. Someplace like Cornelius's coffeehouse, or that island in the Mississippi. When Molly gets hold of a grievance she won't let go any more than a snapping turtle will."

"I understand that very well."

"I wish to God it was not so," Lincoln said.

THIRTY-FIVE

◆ ◆ ◆

EAR SIR, IT BEING A WHILE since I took my buzzard quill
in hand allow me to say that here is that same Rebecca that was
last heard from in the pages of the *Sangamo Journal* but now has the
honor of addressin the editor of the *Illinois State Register,* which is a
fine Democrat paper and the only one I read now that I seen the mighty
light of God's truth and am all for Polk and Texas and for stretchin the
country out as far as it can git. I wished I had never wrote that letter
about the Hon. Jas. Shields because it near got him into a Duel with that
awfullest Mr. Linkhorn and his associates. Well now that I am come to
be redeemed my eyes are popped open wide as a strangled possum.
That was my ocular state when I was at table at a fine dining establishment of this city and seen one of Mr. Linkhorn's friends. Jeff I said to
my dear husband, who was buyin me oysters on account of I aint never
seen one yet to that day, aint that the very same man we saw on the
duelin ground tellin Mr. Linkhorn he better open Mr. Shields with
that broadsword? And are we sure that fancy lady sittin with him is as
fancy as she thinks? Why is she not the same lady who sells dresses and
fooferaw but used to sell another Commodity that did not involve the
wearin of near as much Material?"

It went on for another two paragraphs, obliquely accusing the couple of living openly in an establishment named "for some Roman hill,"
never naming them openly, careful not to use an incendiary word like
"fornication," and to filter its accusations through the same guileless
character and voice—the farm wife named Rebecca—that Lincoln had
invented to attack Shields. Cage folded the newspaper and pushed it
back across the table to Lincoln. They had planned to meet at the cof-

feehouse to discuss edits Cage had made in "My Childhood Home," but then Lincoln had sat down with a closed-up face and handed him the piece in that morning's *Register*.

"What do you want to do?" he said when Cage had finished reading.

"What *can* I do?"

"We could sue for slander. But even in Illinois, which has a wider definition of slander than most other states, it's a hard notion to prove. About all we've got here is innuendo. It helps if the charge is direct—'I saw so-and-so fucking so-and-so,' that kind of thing."

Lincoln hesitated before he spoke again. "And then there's the matter of what might come out in a trial, about Ellie and—"

"No," Cage said. "I understand. No lawsuit."

He picked up the newspaper and walked over to the fireplace. It was a starkly cold winter day and the fire was well built up. He slipped the paper into the flames and walked back to his seat. In his imagination—perhaps in reality—every other patron in the coffeehouse was aware of what had just been written about him in the newspaper and was observing him with clinical curiosity.

"It has to be Nimmo Rhodes who wrote this," he said.

"That's my thinking too. It's all my fault. You wouldn't have made an enemy of him if it wasn't for me."

He thought there was more pain in Lincoln's expression than there must be in his own. Lincoln should very well be sorry. He had all but invented the weapon—the anonymous letter to the editor—that Rhodes had now deployed.

"If there's to be a duel," Lincoln said, "you can count on me to—"

"Oh, for Christ's sake, Lincoln, there's not going to be another duel."

He needed to talk to Ellie, but knew that if he was seen walking to her shop it would only help combust the bonfire of gossip that Nimmo Rhodes had so carefully kindled. He went home instead to the Palatine, climbed the stairs without greeting Mrs. Hopper or any of the people gathering at the table for supper. There was usually lively conversation emanating from the dining room but all he heard was an unnaturally careful discourse as the residents of the Palatine did their best to avoid speaking of the topic they must have all read about or heard about by now. Hours passed as they lingered in the parlor. He finally heard them saying good night to one another and going upstairs to their rooms.

It was long after midnight when Ellie came home. He was in bed by then, though far from sleep. He heard her footsteps on the carpeted stair runner, the sound of her door closing at the end of the hall. Twenty minutes later his own door opened and she slipped into his room on bare feet and let her robe drop to the floor. She wore nothing underneath, and wore no particular expression on her face. She shivered with cold when she joined him in bed, and continued shivering, or perhaps trembling, as they made love. He knew without having to ask that she had read Nimmo Rhodes's letter, that she understood that the boundary shielding their private lives from the world had been torn down and that there was no reason to pretend it still existed. That was why she had come so openly into his room, and why she was giving him a glimpse of what they might have had if there had not been a boundary between them as well. It was not until they were still, lying on their backs in his narrow bed, watching the down quilt move subtly up and down with their respiring, that he understood this had been the last time, and that her undisguised wanting of him tonight was an act of grieving finality that was still not quite, never would be, love.

"Not very many people on Aristocracy Hill," she finally whispered, "are going to want to buy their dresses from a whore."

"What are you going to do?"

"Fill whatever orders aren't canceled in the next few days, take a good inventory, then take the stage to Chicago to find a place to lease. Cordelia will go with me. She's already said yes and I can't manage without her. I don't know about the other girls, but I can find help when I get there."

"People might forget about it. They might not care about it in the first place."

"They'll care about it. Do you think Mary Lincoln and all the other almighty Todds won't care about it?"

She pulled back the quilt and stood up, her naked body silhouetted against the window, her breasts swaying as she clasped her arms and rocked back and forth against the cold. She bent down and picked up her robe and slipped it on quickly, hiding herself from him. She stood over his bed, looking down at him, tears streaking her face even though her expression was resolute and her voice firm.

"It would matter very much to me if you told me you understood."

THIRTY-SIX

ELLIE HAD BEEN GONE from Springfield for a year. Her letters to Cage were predictably few, carefully worded, offering very little in terms of private information about herself. There were occasional wistful recollections of their time together—"I have not forgotten and will not ever forget how kind you were to me"—but he guessed such passages were written late at night, in a low mood, and did not really reflect a spirit of looking back or regretting what she had lost. She had lost nothing, she had simply moved on. She was the same Mrs. Bicknell in a new place, in a new thriving shop. Writing back to her, Cage concealed himself as he had grown used to doing when she lived in Springfield. In his letters, he was not someone who had ever been uselessly in love with her, but only a friend and former business associate, someone who took a proportional personal interest in how she was getting on and what she would do next. He wanted to settle her mind, and in doing so perhaps settle his: he would not be coming in pursuit of her, he was through trying to claim her.

Ned Baker had won his congressional seat the previous August, and in November of 1845 the Whigs threw a party at the American House to see him off to Washington. At the event, Cage tested the waters with Mary Lincoln once again and found that her frostiness toward him had not abated. "Good evening, Cage," she said. He had just watched her hugging Ned Baker like a brother but when she turned to him her bearing was so rigid he was forced into greeting her with an awkward bow. He was angry and couldn't stop himself from emitting a little snort of exasperation, to which she raised a quizzical eyebrow.

"Is something the matter?" she asked.

"Of course something's the matter, Mary. What can we do to put a stop to this charade between us?"

"I don't know what you mean. There's nothing between us and nothing to put a stop to."

Her expression was cruelly indifferent but her face was almost ravishing, her skin warmly aglow from the lamplight spreading from a nearby sconce, but also from the surging blood within. He was pretty sure she was carrying another child.

"All right," he said. "That's where we'll leave it. I'm glad to see you looking so well."

She said she was glad to see him looking so well too, and turned away so swiftly it was almost a pirouette. Cage was eager to leave, to spare them the discomfort of being in each other's company, but he stayed long enough to say goodbye to Ned and wish him the best of fortune in Washington City. He was going to Congress at a momentous time. Texas had not yet been officially annexed but Baker would be arriving in time to vote on the resolution. Meanwhile Polk had sent an army to the border region claimed by both Texas and Mexico, with the transparent purpose of provoking an all-out war.

"Yes, there are great questions to be decided," Ned said. He had a tendency toward grandiosity and could be forgiven for not holding it in check tonight, when he had a secure grip on the next rung of his destiny. He looked even more resplendent and imposing than usual. Even his thinning hair presented an advantage, since partial baldness made the swept-forward eagle's wings on the sides of his head appear as dramatically ruffled as if he were standing with his back to a hurricane. He was a loyal Whig and a faultless Clay man, but it would be hard for an individual with such a measure of personal expansiveness not to want to apply it to the whole nation, to do his part in acquiring Oregon and Texas and any other territory that would make the map complete.

At the moment, he was careful not to be drawn into stating too firm a position on any particular issue. "One thing I'm sure of is that Washington will be a different place than Springfield. I'm told that for all its supposed excitement the house is very dull, and that nobody will listen to anyone except John Quincy Adams. A surprising number of its great men are really pigmies."

He set a conspiratorial arm on Cage's shoulder, drawing him closer and away from the general conversation.

"*He's* not a pigmy," Ned said, glancing at Lincoln, who stood in the center of the room talking to Sim Francis and Ash Merritt and a half dozen other Whig party men. "And he needs to be on a bigger stage where he can prove it. I've promised him that I'll only serve one term, but he's going to have a hard time getting the nomination over Hardin. Do what you can to keep his spirits up, won't you? I'm afraid if he can't get himself elected to Congress he'll slip into the hypo again."

On the surface, Lincoln's spirits seemed fine. He was laughing and conniving and betraying none of the envy he must have been feeling as he prepared to usher his friend off to take the congressional seat he himself very much coveted. He was even crossing the room just now to shake hands with John Hardin, who had arrived accompanied by a dramatic flurry of snow. Cage hadn't seen Hardin since he had lost the sight in his right eye in a shooting accident, not long after his heroics on board the *Princeton.* The eye was now a grayish-white field with an unmoving brown eyeball hovering near the top, though it was intact enough that it still appeared somewhat functional and made it difficult to know from which eye he was observing you. It was disconcerting, but maybe for a man like Hardin there was a sliver of an advantage, since much of politics was about hidden angles of sight.

Otherwise, Hardin was out in the open. He had just announced his candidacy for the same Seventh District congressional seat he had already held once, and which Baker was now heading off to Washington to claim. Any agreement he had made not to contest Lincoln for the nomination had been destined to fall apart, especially after Hardin's latest heroics. Affairs had been deadly between the Mormons and the rest of the population of Illinois ever since Joseph Smith and his brother had been murdered last year by a mob in Nauvoo. Anarchy had finally broken out over the summer and Hardin had been appointed by the governor to lead an expedition to put down a Mormon uprising in Carthage, which he had done with his usual decisiveness. Now, dangerously fueled by the acclaim of a grateful gentile populace, Hardin saw no reason why he shouldn't reoccupy his old congressional seat, whether or not a deal with Lincoln had been in place.

"It's a great annoyance to poor Lincoln that Hardin can't seem to do anything wrong," Ned told Cage. They stood there watching Lincoln and Hardin greeting each other, pretending still to be friends, when in fact they were each actively and covertly lining up pledges for the 1846 nomination.

"If I weren't a political creature myself I'd be sorely offended," Ned said good-naturedly. "This is supposed to be my going-away party, and they're fighting to replace me before they've even seen me off. Will you at least wish me an honest goodbye?"

"Goodbye, Ned, and good luck. And may you find your waveless shore."

"What are you talking about?"

"That poem you wrote. Don't you remember? When we were all amusing ourselves in the poetry society."

"Yes, of course I do, now that you remind me. 'For the land I seek is a waveless shore / And they who reach it shall wander no more.' Not so terribly bad, is it? God, it seems like a thousand years ago that we all sat around reading our poetry to each other. The time for poetry has passed, I suppose. Time for us all to get out of Springfield and take hold of the world."

Lincoln got the nomination after all. Despite Hardin's popularity among the electorate, Lincoln had played a closer and more strategic game among the party men, visiting and re-visiting, promising and re-promising, never taking any pledge for granted. He had managed to convince these men, and to hold them to the conviction, that Hardin and Baker had had their turns and that if Whig loyalty meant anything then turnabout was fair play. Cage heard all this not from Lincoln himself, as he would have in the old days, but from William Florville as his hair was being cut.

"Mr. Francis left this chair not five minutes ago," Florville said. "He was on his way to his newspaper office to put out the afternoon edition. He said Mr. Hardin was agitated about losing to Mr. Lincoln, but the two men are old friends and I expect they'll shake hands again soon enough."

They may shake hands, Cage thought, but it won't be the same, at least not if Mary Lincoln brings her own resentments into the matter.

Cage went over to Lincoln's office to congratulate him in person, even if he had only learned about the victory secondhand. Lincoln and Logan had dissolved their association the year before, and Lincoln had taken on Billy Herndon as his junior law partner and set up a new office with him on a different floor in the same building. Cage found the door of the new office closed, neither Lincoln nor Herndon in evidence. No doubt they were out celebrating the nomination somewhere with their intimate political associates, all the Whig men Lincoln had so carefully been lining up for years to support him against Hardin. Cage was not a party workie, he was just a friend—or at least had been—so he merely slipped a note of congratulations under the door and went by the post office to collect his mail.

There was a letter from Speed, writing from Kentucky, declaring himself happy and productive, bound up more than ever in family business but wonderfully content with his ever-supportive and even-tempered wife. He was desperate for Illinois news and for Illinois gossip. Cage hadn't written him about his rupture with Mary—or about the abandonment of his poetical career, or the abrupt departure of Ellie from his life—so every detail about old friends and old times that Speed inquired about seemed to probe at an old wound. There was no letter from Ellie, none really expected. Until he read the letter from Jacob Bunn, the creditor who held the note to the partnership he had entered into for the purchase of lands in the Western Military Tract, he had no suspicion that there was any threat to the continuance of his benumbed state of existence.

Dear Sir,

Please do me the favor of appearing at my office immediately upon receipt of this missive to present your solution to the satisfactory settlement of your current debt to me. Yours sincerely, Jacob Bunn.

Cage had no clear idea what Bunn was talking about. Yes, with his partners Rascoe and Dillon he had arranged a loan from Bunn to buy land in the Military Tract, but the note was not due for another year and the urgent tone of this letter made no sense.

"Are you serious?" Bunn said when Cage presented himself that afternoon in his office on the second floor of his sprawling store. He was younger than Cage, barely over thirty, with slick sandy hair and blandly regular features. He sat behind a polished desk he had designed himself, with carved scrollwork on its edges and cunningly recessed inkwells and letter slots. "Your associates have told you nothing?"

"I'm sorry, I don't know what you're talking about, Jacob. Nothing about what?"

"Well, turns out your Mr. Rascoe is a bankrupt and your Mr. Dillon saw a meteor in the sky and in a fit of delusion concluded his fate was to follow it to Texas. Which he apparently did day before yesterday, after selling off everything he had of value and taking the money with him."

"He said nothing to me."

"He said nothing to me, either. Nor did your other partner, Mr. Rascoe, who among other irregularities signed over as security for the note a farm in Indiana whose title has turned out to be a forgery and a mill in Morgan County that apparently doesn't exist at all. The man is a reckless gambler and he has gambled away your money."

"My money?"

Bunn opened a hinged door on the surface of his desk, withdrew a document and slid it across to Cage.

"You have joint and several liability. You signed a note together with your partners. They cannot pay, and you are liable for the whole debt. Can you pay me, and when?"

Cage sat there in Bunn's storeroom office, looking up from the document at the barrels and sacks and hogsheads stacked against the walls—coffee and molasses and New Orleans sugar. His body felt as light and agitated as a bird's.

"You have the property I signed over as security, the—"

"Joint and several," Bunn repeated, the words coming out now in a threatening hiss. "Joint and several. Your security is good as far as it goes, but you have assumed the liability of these other two men and I want to know, can you pay me, and when?"

He could not pay him, of course. Most of his ready cash had gone to buy certificates of freedom. Even if he could find an immediate buyer for the Palatine, his last unencumbered asset, it would not be nearly enough for the whole note. The hole into which he had just plummeted was very deep. If he was to have a chance of climbing out, he needed a lawyer.

THIRTY-SEVEN

◆◆◆

L INCOLN WAS IN A DISTRACTED good temper and did not notice Cage's distress when he walked into the office.

"Sit down by the stove and warm yourself," he said. "Let me just scrawl a line or two at the bottom of this letter."

He scrawled more than a line or two, sitting at his table wearing his somehow still-extant buffalo robe, a garment from which Cage could actually see the dust rising whenever Lincoln shifted in his seat. It was just the two of them in the office. Herndon, Lincoln explained, had gone to take the deposition of a defrauded widow whose case they had just taken on.

"Done!" he said, blotting the letter and sealing it. "That was to the editor of the Athens paper. They took my part against Hardin, came out for me early and strong. You have no idea how many thank-you letters I have to write, including one to you, for the kind note you slipped under my door. Of course, it's just the nomination. I still have to beat Peter Cartwright in the election. That aged gentleman has preached to every Methodist congregation between here and Cairo and he's sure to come after me for being an infidel. I'm going to have to be careful to appear as if I really believe in God and don't just like the sound of the Bible."

He stood and walked around the table to lie down on the sofa across the room from where Cage was sitting. He was in his shirtsleeves and waistcoat. He contemplatively stretched out his arms like a man getting ready for a nap. But energy was coursing through him. He suddenly leapt up again and paced around the room, oblivious to Cage except as an audience for his racing thoughts.

"Yes, of course, there's a lot of hard work ahead. Nothing is guaranteed. I have to get hold of that preacher by the balls and not let go. But it feels like things are moving at last. It's like when I was young, chopping ice on the Sangamon. Chop, chop, chop, and at long last a little channel starts to open up and your boat's under way. It's not just me alone in my little vessel now, though. There's Mrs. Lincoln and Bobbie and another baby almost to term. Let me tell you this, Cage, because I know you of all people will understand. Mary Lincoln has a temper, and when her feet are swollen to the size of—"

Finally happening to glance in Cage's direction he suddenly broke off his monologue.

"For God's sake, what's wrong? You look very pale."

"It seems I might be ruined."

"Ruined? What are you talking about?"

"I signed a note with two other men. One has fled to Texas, the other's assets have turned out to be largely fictitious."

"Joint and several?"

Cage nodded.

"You would have done well," Lincoln said, "to have consulted me before signing your name to any note at all. But don't look so defeated. There are things I can do. We're old friends and I won't let a friend fall on his sword. I haven't forgotten everything you've done for me, Cage. I might have very well killed myself over that confusion with Mary. I wanted to, you know. I might have been killed by Jim Shields, or killed him instead, in a foolish duel. Instead I'm alive, and about to fight a preacher, and have another baby coming."

He sat down at his desk again, and began scribbling a memorandum on a sheet of paper. "Bunn holds the note, I suppose?"

"Yes."

"First thing I'll do is pay him a visit. He can be reasonable if you find him in a good temper. Who are your erstwhile partners?"

"Joseph Dillon and Walter Rascoe."

Lincoln abruptly stopped writing.

"Rascoe?"

"Do you know him? Well, of course you know everybody. As it turns out, he has a forged title to—"

Lincoln held up both his hands, the gesture of a man trying to ward off unwelcome knowledge.

"Cage, I represent Walter Rascoe."

"You do? In this matter?"

"In this matter."

"Are you sure?"

"He stopped me on the street yesterday and asked for my help in resolving a financial issue. I agreed at once, though I haven't yet heard the details. We were going to meet this afternoon. Surely his matter and yours are one and the same."

"Surely they are. But *I* need your help."

"Cage, I can't give it, not under the circumstances. Rascoe contacted me first, and as a result I now represent him."

"You'll represent a stranger against a friend?"

"He's not a stranger, for one thing. He's a Whig stalwart who helped pass a resolution in Athens endorsing me against Hardin. But that's beside the point. I *would* represent a stranger against a friend—I'd *have* to—if I'd agreed to take his case first. It's a matter of professional ethics."

He stared in disbelief at Lincoln, angered by the impassive reasonableness in his lawyerly expression. Here was a man who would happily fill every newspaper in Illinois with anonymous attacks upon political enemies, who had nimbly avoided time and again taking any sort of meaningful stand on slavery, whose moral self-evidence made his endless partisan fights over internal improvements and specie payments and tariffs nothing but puzzling distractions.

Cage had been in a hollow, doom-ridden frame of mind ever since his interview with Jacob Bunn. Once again he felt as he had that night long ago at Kellogg's Grove, crowded into a dark cabin with no air to breathe, aware of a silent, besieging presence drawing closer every moment. He managed to suppress a display of open panic, but could not keep himself from sputtering in anger.

"Your idea of ethics is confounding to me," he said. "You won't reach out your hand to a drowning friend because you already have some sort of polite professional understanding with the man who threw him into the river?"

"There are other lawyers in Springfield."

"There are nothing *but* lawyers in Springfield!"

He had risen so angrily, so abruptly from his chair that he was momentarily dizzy and had to set a hand on the corner of Lincoln's table to steady himself until his blood was properly distributed again. He heard himself speaking to Lincoln in a cold-blooded tone.

"I'm sure you'll represent your client ably, and the more ably you represent him the deeper the pit you'll dig for me."

Lincoln's head drooped in sadness—or impatience. He stared for a moment at his gnarled workingman's fingers spread out root-like upon the grass-colored baize cloth covering his working space. When he looked up at Cage again, his face was composed and his voice infuriatingly even.

"I'm sorry, Cage. I can't talk to you about this any further."

He walked for hours, trying to settle himself, past the city center and outlying neighborhoods along Town Branch, past tanyards and horse treading mills, wandering through knolls and ravines that had once held groves of mature timber and were now tangles of brush and grapevines. A lightless February afternoon, a cold wind singing through the cracks of an open quarry from which the stones for wells and hearths had been dug and hewn. Springfield seemed to him now a tawdry and impure dream of a place, an impermanent human monument made from sawn-down ancient trees and from stones stolen from the ripped-open, clawed-apart earth.

He was not someone habituated to solitary drinking. Perhaps Lincoln's temperance influence had played a role in that, but to hell with Lincoln. He walked back into town holding down his hat in the freezing wind and walked through the door of a quiet hideaway off Jefferson Street called Zimri's Tavern. He took a seat at a table beneath a painting of a lovely drowned woman floating in greenish water, the sea surge gently separating her from her garments and a blunt-nosed shark swimming implacably toward her. The colors in the painting had been queasily muted over the years by the smoke-filled, lightless atmosphere of the tavern, and its sense of grimy hopelessness matched his mood exactly. He was cold from his walk and was glad for the raging fire, with its glowing loggerheads for making rum flips. He ordered a flip and drummed his numb fingers on the tabletop to bring back the circulation. There was conversation going on all around him but he heard none of it, just sat there making an inventory of all the things he thought had been within his grasp but that he saw were only baseless aspirations. He knew he could add them up in any configuration he wanted—love, friendship, security, fame, self-respect—and the sum would still be the same, a zero at the base of his soul.

He glanced up when his drink came and through a shifting veil of smoke he saw Billy Herndon sitting alone two tables over, a glass of beer between his hands, staring just as glumly as he himself was at the play of flames in the fireplace. Billy saw Cage at almost the same moment and picked up his beer and his hat and walked over to join him.

"I don't recall ever seeing you here before, and certainly not looking so alone and downcast. May I be your companion in misery tonight?"

He pulled out the heavy wooden chair with a great squeaking noise and sat down and drained half his beer.

"I will just finish this fine strong beer," he declared, "and then go home to my wife and children. I belong there, and I'm ashamed not to be there. The winds of temperance don't blow in me and there's nothing I can do about it. What has come over you, Cage?"

"Some unexpected financial difficulties."

"Well, go see Mr. Lincoln at once!"

"I did. But I seem to be on the opposite side of the case from the esteemed and professionally very ethical Mr. Lincoln."

Billy nodded along with grave sympathy as Cage told him about the conversation he had that afternoon with Lincoln.

"I'm very sorry for your trouble, Cage. Very sorry indeed. Even if your debt is as great as you say, there are things you can do. The goddam Democrats have unraveled the bankruptcy statute in an unholy manner, but the common law remedy still applies. It would require you to turn over your assets to a trustee and—"

"It's all right, Billy," Cage said. "I don't want to think about it right now anyway." He ordered himself another flip and Billy another beer. Billy protested that he ought to go home, but did not protest with much force, arguing with conviction that he could not let a despairing friend drink alone.

"Mr. Lincoln hews to a strict legal sense of things," Billy said. "I would not say this to another soul, but yours is not the only case in which it could be said his duty to the law blinds him to the right."

"What do you mean?"

"It's why I'm sitting here wrestling with my poor beleaguered conscience. He's agreed to defend a slave owner."

"He's what?"

Billy said he shouldn't talk about it, but didn't bother to wait for Cage to press him for more information before disclosing the particulars. A man named Wilford had a big farm in Illinois and an even bigger plantation in the slave state of Kentucky. He had imported one of his slaves to serve as overseer for his Illinois operation, and allowed the man to bring his wife and children along. Abolitionists had gotten wind of the arrangement, arguing that because the slave family were residing in Illinois they were now free. But Wilford still considered them his property and they had been detained in the sheriff's jail until pending the outcome of a *habeas corpus* hearing, in which Lincoln had agreed to represent Wilford.

Cage stared at Billy Herndon as he tried to comprehend what he had just been told. His mind raced back to Cordelia, trembling in that Tazewell County courtroom, slipping down her dress to reveal the whipping scars on her back. He remembered her heedlessly throwing her arms around Lincoln in gratitude when he had freed her. Could it be that Lincoln had been so untouched, so unmoved, that he was now ready to take the other side in a strikingly similar case and send a family back to bondage in Kentucky?

"I don't believe it," he told Herndon. "Why would he do that?"

"I don't know. I suppose in one sense the reason is very simple. Wilford approached him and offered him a fee. If he were a simple man, that reason might suffice. But he's an unknowable man, and there the problem of our understanding lies. I owe very much to Mr. Lincoln. Without him I would never have been at the bar, I wouldn't be his partner in his firm. But I told him I wouldn't take part in this, and so I won't. He speaks well enough of slavery as evil, but where is the proof he believes that in his core? What will he ever dare to do about it?"

Billy asked this last question imploringly, as if Cage had it in his power to provide an answer. But Cage had no insight to offer, especially since his mind was stunned with the realization he had been betrayed by Abraham Lincoln twice in the same day.

As they drank together in puzzled, angry fellowship for another hour, Cage felt the smoky atmosphere of the tavern as a crushing force, a relentless deep-ocean squeeze. He felt there was no air to breathe in his world anymore, no path of escape anywhere. He had not thought at all of his father today, but now all at once he was standing with him on the shoreline, watching him walk out into the water not with the grief and confusion of a child but with the clinical understanding of a man who shared the same dilemma and was perhaps destined to share the same fate.

He was rescued from his suicidal reverie by an eruption of laughter from the other end of the room, where a group of three men had just entered, belching more cigar smoke into the hazy tavern and intruding upon the scattered, murmuring conversations of the clients already there. The loudest offender of his solitude, Cage saw at once, was Nimmo Rhodes.

He hadn't seen him since that encounter at the City Hotel. He had not confronted him after he had written the pseudonymous newspaper letter that had driven Ellie out of town, knowing that if he did so it would only add to his enemy's pleasure in having agitated him, and would accomplish nothing. But clarity and dispassion were the tools of an untroubled mind, and Cage's mind tonight was a cyclonic brew of fear and outrage. He was delighted to discover he was filled with hate, with a heedless impulse to settle the nearest account.

"Wait here," he told Billy. He stood, paused to steady himself, and walked over to Nimmo Rhodes.

"I accept your challenge," he said.

"All right. I assume you're referring to our previous disagreement? Please have your friends communicate at their convenience the—"

Cage aimed squarely for his open mouth, relishing the prospect of shutting him up.

THIRTY-EIGHT

◆ ◆ ◆

BILLY HERNDON KEPT REPEATING he had given a good accounting of himself, but for long minutes Cage had no idea what he was talking about. He was lying on his bed in his room at the Palatine, Billy and Ash Merritt grinning encouragingly at him, Mrs. Hopper hovering solicitously at his open door.

"You gave him at the least a split lip," Billy said. "And I don't doubt he'll awaken tomorrow with two black eyes. Until he slammed your head against the bar you were Leonidas himself."

"Do you remember being in a fight with Nimmo Rhodes?" Ash asked him.

Cage nodded, the simple motion causing all sorts of turmoil inside his head, which felt like it was filled with something as thick and static as swamp water.

"Lie still and let your brain recover itself," Ash said. "It may take a few days. There's a tremendous knot on your forehead and the right side of your face is greatly bruised and swollen."

He held up a looking glass as if these deformities were marvels he ought to see. The lump protruding from his head was indeed a thing of wonder. It looked like the first knobby growth of a deer's antler. Below it his face was unrecognizable, a ballooning mass of purple and black skin.

"What time is it?" he asked.

"Midnight," Billy said. He turned to Ash. "If he's going to be all right, I ought to get home to my wife and children."

"Oh, he'll be all right," Ash said. "We've bound his hero's wounds and now all he needs to do is sleep and take the juice of lemons, which Mrs. Hopper here has agreed to administer."

His head had cleared enough by the next day for him to remember most of the details of his encounter with Nimmo Rhodes and the events of the day leading up to it. He had been beaten into unconsciousness in the fight, but even if he had knocked Rhodes out he doubted he would have felt any particular sense of triumph, or even the clarifying benefits of finally having taken action. All he had done was get drunk and lose control of himself, and the result was that his spirits and prospects were lower than ever.

He drank the astringent, barely sweetened lemonade that Ash had prescribed and that Mrs. Hopper delivered to him every few hours. He dragged himself from his bed to his chair and tried to read a book on the fall of Constantinople, but it was strangely laborious work trying to follow a simple narrative and he surrendered and picked up the newspaper instead. There was a long report about the activities of Zachary Taylor's army on the Mexican border, and the Mormon exodus that Brigham Young was leading out of Illinois beyond the Missouri. But the densely packed columns of print assaulted his brain with information, and for relief he turned to the advertisements, which had the virtue of being short and relieved by white space—notices of new city ordinances on hogs and wild dogs, advertisements from dentists and bootmakers, stage schedules and announcements for lectures and musical performances and alerts for runaway slaves. There was another circus coming into town, a "mammoth menagerie" that promised to fill the streets of Springfield with another caravan of shuffling elephants. Yet it was a reference not to something coming but to something leaving that caught his eye.

"Westward Ho! Who wants to go to California without costing them anything? As many as eight young men, of good character, who can drive an ox team, will be accommodated by gentlemen who will leave this vicinity about the first of April. You can have as much land as you want without costing you anything. The government of California gives large tracts of land to persons who move there."

It was signed George Donner and James Reed. Even in Cage's foggy state of mind, there was a bright beacon of skepticism. Wasn't the "government of California" Mexico, with whom the United States was surely about to go to war? Wouldn't they be having second thoughts about giving away "large tracts of land" to the same American adventurers who had populated Texas before revolting against Mexico and seizing the province for themselves?

But for a penniless man such as he was about to become, for a restless spirit with nothing to hold him in place, the idea of going to California with Reed and Donner and their expedition carried with it a surging sense of purpose. He sat at his desk with his pencil, account books, lists of soon-to-be-former assets. He was ruined, yes, but perhaps if he acted quickly and decisively in appealing to Jacob Bunn to agree to appoint a trustee who would sell off his holdings, he could negotiate the retention of, say, a thousand dollars, enough to buy a new horse and outfit, to lease space for his few goods in one of the wagons leaving for California, to have something left over for living expenses once he got there and provide him with the means to make some kind of a living.

He thought the knock on the door was just Mrs. Hopper bringing him more lemonade and as he stared down at his figuring he called out distractedly for her to come in. But in the window glass he caught a glancing reflection of someone filling up the doorway and turned his chair around to face Lincoln.

"You're a horrible-looking sight, Cage," he said.

"You wouldn't have liked to see me yesterday, then. The swelling has come down a good amount."

Lincoln hesitated about taking a seat, until Cage nodded in the direction of a chair. His visitor took off his hat and sat down and stretched out his legs. Cage was in no particular mood to speak to him and was happy to say nothing as Lincoln searched for the right words.

"Billy told me about the fight. You wouldn't have made an enemy like that if you hadn't acted as my friend in that ridiculous duel. I look back on that event and a few others like it and don't exactly recognize myself.

"On the other hand," he said, gesturing toward Cage's misshapen face, "I'm not sure I recognize you either."

It was an invitation for Cage to respond with a grudging laugh, but his silence drove Lincoln back into awkward self-reflection.

"Billy also said he told you about the Wilford case."

"He did."

"The duty of a lawyer—"

"Oh, shut the hell up, Lincoln."

"Are we not to be friends anymore?"

"I suppose not, since it seems there are things I hold sacred that you care very little about."

"I think that it's very easy to hold a thing sacred," Lincoln said, revealing a full anger that Cage had rarely seen. "To stand back and write poetry and be a private man."

"Whereas a public man like you, who flatters himself for his effectiveness in the material world, is sending a family back into slavery."

"The case is weak, so probably not. But I'll do my best for my client."

"Can't you see the case is not just weak, it's wrong?"

"It's not wrong for me to take it. If a man comes to me for help, no matter how despised or degraded he is, it's my duty to help him. In that respect I have the same duty as a physician."

"That's fatuous."

"It may be so to you, but I happen to believe it. I believed that when I represented Truett, and I hold to the principle even more today. What if I and other lawyers only represented clients we agreed with? The law wouldn't be the law, it would just be theater, a spectacle of shifting passions. The whole edifice of society would crumble, you can bet on that. We have a republic, but what is our republic if it can't function? If it can't hold itself together? You argue that me taking this case is a great wrong. I argue back that it's a small right."

Cage shook his head in annoyance—a mistake, since his head was still thick and concussed and the movement brought on a swirling headache. He looked at the prosperous lawyer and lawmaker sitting across the room from him. Lincoln's narrow face had been taut with worry and defiance, but now he was relaxing a bit, relieved to think that maybe this meeting wasn't going to turn out to be a grave reckoning but just a case of two old friends having a vigorous argument about the meaning of a civil society, the sort of argument they had had before Lincoln's speech to the Young Men's Lyceum on—what was it?—the nature of democratic institutions.

"Now listen, Cage," Lincoln said. "I'm going to beat Peter Cartwright and I'm going to go to Washington. And when I'm there you can judge me on my works. I reckon you won't find me as a member of Congress to be a particular friend of the Slave Power. But for now, my duty as a private man is to—"

"I'm going to California."

"What?"

He tossed the newspaper across the room with an aggressive flourish. It landed in Lincoln's lap. He held it out away from his face—maybe he was growing farsighted—and scanned it until he found the advertisement.

"With Reed and Donner?"

"Yes."

"Why?"

"Because I'm broke, and because I'm mortally tired."

"Of what?" Lincoln asked, and then, "Of who?"

Cage waved the question away, satisfying his pride by not answering it.

"I'd be tempted to go along with you," Lincoln said, "if I wasn't married to Molly, if I didn't already have a child and another one about to be born. But I don't expect you'd want to invite me."

He grasped his knees with his hands, looked around the room, trying to think of an excuse to stay. Cage refused to help him find one. Lincoln stood. He put on his hat and the top of it almost brushed the ceiling.

"You may not think it," he said, "but in everything I do, I listen for the voice of honor."

It was true, or at least true enough to give Cage a reason not to say what he said next. But he was too angry and desolate and disappointed to hold back the words that he knew, even as he spoke them, he could never repeal.

"If there's honor in you, I no longer see it."

Lincoln reacted to this declaration with shattering impassivity. He was already standing, his hat was already on his head, there was no gesture he could make except this final one: to turn from Cage and walk out the door, and walk down the street to the house on the corner of Eighth and Jackson where his pregnant wife—as unforgiving to Cage as Cage now was to Lincoln—waited for his return.

1860–1861

◆ ◆ ◆

THIRTY-NINE
✦ ✦ ✦

THE AMERICAN THEATER held four thousand people. Every seat was occupied. There had not been even a thousand people in the whole of San Francisco when Cage had arrived here, starved and shattered, thirteen years before. It had been an overgrown pueblo of adobes and shanties and billiard saloons, its harbor crowded with swaying masts. A place where the air was still fragrant with the smell of wild mint, and where the calls of gulls could still be heard above the noise of construction.

There was no chance of a gull or any other creature being heard tonight. There was only the commotion of four thousand souls simultaneously chanting the name of Edward Baker, who had moved briefly to Oregon to get himself elected senator from that state, and now had come home to San Francisco in triumph. Cage had chosen not to sit in the dress circle with John and Jesse Frémont, with Bret Harte and the other luminaries who had come to hear Ned give what the Republican audience had apparently decided would be the greatest speech in all of human history.

It was not that, but it was pretty good. When Ned finally took the stage, everything that could be waved—hands, arms, hats, handkerchiefs—was in frenzied motion, and it took almost twenty minutes for the preliminary acclaim to die down while Ned stood there holding out his hand from time to time in a grave appeal for calm. He looked older, of course—fleshier, balder, grayer. He still combed his remaining hair forward in a bird-wing style, which no doubt contributed to his latest nickname, the Old Gray Eagle.

When he finally was allowed to speak, his voice filled the theater with no evident strain and he stood there sweeping his eyes over the audience while remaining magnetically still, holding back his arm-waving theatrics until it was time for a strategic crescendo.

"The old man is talking like a god!" proclaimed the breathless reporter from *The Morning Call* halfway through the speech. He was sitting in the row in front of Cage's more seasoned man from his own paper, the *Yerba Buena Discoverer*. The old man: he supposed that was true, though Ned couldn't yet be fifty. Listening to him speak, Cage felt himself hurled back to those poetical society days in Springfield, when Ned Baker had seemed the man among them all who would reach the furthest. And he had, in a way—congressman, hero of the war with Mexico, a man who had built a railroad across Panama and helped create an empire in California while almost incidentally becoming one of the greatest orators and legal minds in the country. Now he was a United States senator, about to embark for Washington where he would throw himself into the effort of saving the Republic at its most crucial hour.

But the god that Ned Baker had become was not speaking about himself. He was speaking about Abraham Lincoln, the Republican candidate for president of the United States. (The Whigs now just a wistful memory, having broken apart over the question of slavery.)

"We don't propose to dissolve the Union," he said, his voice swelling with melodious force, "and don't propose to let anybody else dissolve it. And if Abraham Lincoln gets your vote—the vote of the people!—you can rest in the assurance that our beloved Union will be safe!"

He spoke for an hour and a half, and must have spent three hours afterwards greeting his admirers before finally being allowed to go off to bed. But when Cage met him for breakfast the next morning in Ned's suite at the City Hotel his voice was still strong, his mood ebullient. He flung open the door himself to greet Cage, grabbed him by the shoulder and drew him in and sat down at a window overlooking the bay, a shimmering satiny blue in the early-morning light.

"Thank you for your generous donation to my candidacy," he said as he poured syrup over a stack of six pancakes. "More important, thank you for seeing me. How many times have we met in the past ten years or so? Three?"

"Not more than that."

"Entirely my fault," Ned said.

"No, of course the fault is mine."

Ned looked up from his pancakes, caught Cage's eye for a moment in acknowledgment of this truth, then veered off onto another subject.

"I saw the *Discoverer* this morning. Your man did a good job of covering the speech."

"There'll be a full transcription in Wednesday's edition."

"I read it steadfastly, you know, as much for your poems as for flattering mentions of me. Your point of view, your tone, your metaphors—all first rate. You could publish that work anywhere, not just in a paper you happen to own."

"I don't think of it as anything more than a pastime."

Ned started to chastise him with a compliment, but mercifully decided to leave the topic alone. And anyway it was true. Cage was a newspaper publisher, a businessman. Like many others in San Francisco he had had the luck to be here early enough to ride the astounding wave of prosperity that had come with the discovery of gold in Coloma. His newspaper verse was expertly rendered and fairly popular. He was particularly adept at verbal seascapes that seemed to—but didn't really, he knew—create striking insights about the transient flaring of human life against the infinitude of nature. But he no longer had the soul of a poet, or any particular sort of soul at all. Every now and then he thought of the manuscript of *The Prairie Road*, accidentally thrown out with his writing desk when they had had to lighten the wagons during the Donner Party's harrowing crossing of the Great Salt Desert. He remembered that book, all of the labor it had taken to create, all the hopes he had thrown onto it, with the tolerant understanding of a man looking back upon an extinguished passion.

"I still put my hand to it, now and then," Baker was saying.

"I liked your tribute to the Fourth Illinois."

"Yes, that was good, wasn't it?" He set down his fork and recited the poem. It was about all the men under his command during the Mexican War who had died of fever or dysentery or measles beside "the rushing Rio Grande" before they had a chance to see action.

"Th' archangel's shade was slowly cast
Upon each polished brow:
But, calm and fearless to the last,
They sleep securely now."

He spoke the final lines with the unembarrassed dramatic emphasis of an actor, which was to some degree what he had become. He sniffed back tears when he was through. Just above the collar of his shirt Cage could see a raised scar on his neck from a bayonet thrust.

"Such a strange, deadly war," Ned mused. "Who would have supposed that so many of our old crowd would have found themselves fighting in Mexico, of all places? Poor Hardin dead on the field at Buena Vista, along with Henry Clay's son. And it's a miracle Jim Shields didn't die of his wounds at Cerro Gordo. Hit right through the chest and lungs with grape. I saw him in the hospital afterwards. The poor general was suffering so much I could almost forgive him for wanting to kill our friend in that duel. And I almost had to hold my nose when it came time to pin a medal on Nimmo Rhodes. I hate it when villains behave with gallantry."

Baker himself had been the great hero of Cerro Gordo, taking over the brigade from Shields after he had been wounded, seizing a Mexican battery and turning the guns upon the retreating enemy. Had he not been born in England, it could easily have been him running for president today instead of his less Mars-like friend.

"Lincoln asks about you," Ned said. "He wonders why you so rarely reply to his letters. There's no reason a falling-out has to be final. For God's sake, do you know who the regimental surgeon was in Mexico who saved Shields's life? It was Ash Merritt! Ran a silk handkerchief through his chest wound with a ramrod right there on the battlefield. There was a time when he would have very much liked to see Shields dead, as I remember."

"I never wanted to see anybody dead," Cage said, "and certainly not Lincoln. It was just all a very long time ago and things are different now."

"Different? Do you mean because of that business in the Sierra? I assure you, Cage, I've passed through some terrible trials in my life—

Chagres fever in Panama, as an instance; I would not wish any man to suffer through that. I think I know what desperation is, and it is God alone and not man who holds the right of judgment in such cases."

It was true. Most people had not been as immediately condemning as he might have expected. There had been looks of pity, and horror, and eventual admiration, since a theme of heroism had gradually attached itself to the effort he and some of the others of the Donner Party had made to get over the pass in the heart of winter and find help for the snowbound and starving emigrants left behind at Truckee Lake. But to stay alive and reach Johnson's Ranch had demanded not just the crossing of a pass but of another barrier from which there was no return. At the time, Cage's spirit had been even more winnowed than his body. They had started out already nearly dead with hunger. They staggered uphill on snowshoes they had fashioned themselves out of rawhide strips and the oxbows from their wagons, the brilliant mirror lake receding below them, the drifts of snow on which they traveled so deep their heads grazed the highest branches of the trees. Cage's conscious mind flared intermittently like heat lightning on the margins of a dark void. They had done their best at first to hold true to the protocols of human decency, though starvation had already made them as apathetic and remorseless as the wolves they imagined watching from the trees. They had prayed over the dead, and closed their eyes and covered their faces before they began to strip the flesh from their limbs. But these sacramental instincts soon subsided, and there was just the urgent question of who would die next, and how soon. There were murders. Two Indians from Sutter's Fort that had been sent to help the trapped emigrants but had starved along with them had been shot by one of the members of the snowshoe party. Cage had tried to stop it, if speaking a hoarse word of protest meant trying. His ineffectual outrage had been only a thin disguise for his own murderous rapacity.

"In any case," Ned Baker said, "that is the past, and you and I are men of the future. Lincoln men."

"Will he win?"

"Assuredly. Who else could it be? The Democrats are split between Douglas and Breckinridge. Bell may win a few states but he won't be a factor in the end. Lincoln will become president. It'll be a triumph for our nation but hell is sure to follow. If South Carolina pulls out of the Union as she threatens to do, and other states take her example, there'll be a war."

He had never stopped eating as he talked and had managed to finish off most of his pancakes. He pushed the plate with its syrup-sodden remnants away from him and poured them both more coffee. They talked for a while about Lincoln's improbable but somehow inevitable rise to his present circumstances. He had served only one term in the United States Congress and had come home in disfavor, having stood up in the House to denounce the war against Mexico at a moment when patriotic fervor was at its highest, and when martyrs like John Hardin were lying dead on Mexican battlefields.

"But I suppose you can no more separate Abraham Lincoln from politics," Ned said, "than you can separate a poet such as yourself from his pen. He was very fine in those debates with Douglas when they were running for the Senate, very firm against that goddam Kansas act. So what if he lost? He lost splendidly. 'A House Divided,' did you read that speech? And it was better for him to lose a Senate race and gain the moral advantage to win the presidency. Let no one doubt now where the man stands on slavery. He's not an abolitionist and may never be— it's not his temperament—but slavery will be abolished all the same and his hand will be on the machine. You don't doubt that he's a man of high honor and principle?"

"No. Maybe I did once, but not anymore."

"Then answer his letters, won't you? He needs his friends."

Ned reached for his coffee cup, took a scalding draught, set it down with a grimace.

"I'd like to put to you a notion," he said. "If there's going to be a war to save the Union, by God I won't stay out of it. I'll give up my Senate seat if I have to and petition the secretary of war for authority to raise a California regiment."

"But you're not the senator from California. You represent Oregon."

"No matter. I only went to Oregon because I could get elected there. It's California men I know best. Men like you."

"You want me to join your regiment?"

"You'll be a captain."

"The Black Hawk War was a long time ago, Ned."

"No matter. You're a man of standing and a man of character. Like me, you know privation. Your paper is strong for the Union and speaks with a clear voice against the spread of slavery. If it comes to a fight, will you be there?"

He was a public man but an unknown one, even to himself. He had set out for California in defeat and penury, he had crossed the Sierra and made a new life and a new fortune, but he had arrived in the Golden Land haunted and diminished.

Jim Reed, imperious and heedless, had been the cause of their arriving too late in the winter to make it over the pass. He had talked them into taking a cutoff that in the end had cost them crucial time. Along the way, one of the men had grown enraged and attacked him with a whip, and Reed had killed him with a knife. For this he had been banished from the wagon train, but he had used his banishment well—making his way to Sutter's Fort before the snow had trapped the others on the far side of the mountains and organizing the relief expeditions that finally reached the survivors at Truckee Lake. Donner and his wife had died, but Reed and his family had made it out just in time, just before they too would have had to face the ultimate necessity. When the Reeds had finally come over the pass they were alive, unlike Cage, in body and spirit both.

He might have married in California, started a family of his own, but he had fallen into an isolate stillness, deeper than the hypo, distinct from it, permanent. He functioned and even flourished outwardly, but inside there was the poison of wariness. He had many acquaintances with whom he was on excellent terms, but no intimate friends. There were several women he saw professionally, in secret, of course, out of desire and habit. Ellie had written to him after she had read the newspaper accounts of the emigrants' trials and seen his name among the list of survivors, and over the years they corresponded with as much regularity as they could, given the fact that for the letters to reach their destination they had to travel by steam packet and overland through the jungles of Panama. She was no more forthcoming or revealing than she had ever been, but there was a steadiness to her letters, an eagerness to confide all the details of the growing success of her shops and investments, that suggested something unconcluded between them. Once she sent him a carte de visite. In it she was seated in a dress of striped silk with a wide collar, her head turned away from the viewer, her hair brushed into glossy wings that covered her ears. Her face was fuller than he had known it, but—if the photographic image could be trusted—still unlined. Her mouth offered a bare hint of a smile, her gaze drifted beyond the margins of the frame, as if looking for something to settle on.

The letter Cage received from Ned Baker was postmarked April 13, 1861. He had written it the day after the firing began on Fort Sumter, just a little over a month after he had stood on the east portico of the Capitol building as Abraham Lincoln was sworn in as president of the United States.

"Will you fight in the great cause?" the letter asked. "Will you help our friend the President defend the Union? Will you accept a captaincy in the 1st California? If the answer as I hope is yes reply by mail at once, embark on the first ship headed for Panama and telegraph at the first opportunity. We are going into training at Fort Schuyler. For the country's sake join us! In haste, for I must rush to my waveless shore . . ."

He sat with the letter in his hands, rocking in a mahogany chair on his verandah looking out over the water. It was late afternoon. The marshes across the bay were crowded with shorebirds, and brown pelicans plummeted inelegantly from the sky, diving for fish whose passing schools riffled the surface. He saw the sunlight gleaming on the rolling backs of porpoises.

Cage's decision was already made. It was a matter only of arrangements. Ever since he had seen Baker at the City Hotel he had been thinking of his last meeting with Lincoln, the accusations they had thrown at each other, charges of dishonor, of moral cowardice, of opportunism. The anger and disappointment of two men who had once thought they were the same but who were different: one cautious in politics, the other cautious in life. Cage remembered all the times that he had tried to draw Lincoln back from some imagined precipice—a speech whose sentiments and theatrics he didn't think worthy of the man delivering it, a near-deadly duel that could have been avoided with a simple shift in rhetoric, a love affair that seemed capable of destroying his sanity. But what if in restraining his friend his greater, hidden motive had been merely to try to remain on safe ground himself? He had held himself apart from politics, he had allowed Ellie to hold herself apart from him. And what had Cage done about the great question of the age, except to spend a few thousand dollars so that he could maintain his righteous position that slavery was evil?

He was not naive enough to think that in joining Baker's California brigade he would be joining in a direct fight against slavery itself. The fight was for the Union, and in Lincoln's mind disunion and disorder had always been a greater menace than human bondage. But the confrontation between the North and the South would inevitably lead in the direction of slavery's outright defeat or eventual elimination. He could muster what was left of himself and step onto that field, or he could remain in his rocking chair, safe in the Golden Land.

FORTY

◆ ◆ ◆

THE BATTLE AT BALL'S BLUFF came on unexpectedly. What was meant to have been a reconnaissance across the Potomac into Virginia had provoked a full-out attack by the rebels guarding the road to Leesburg. The company that Cage commanded, along with the rest of the Federal forces at the summit of the bluff, had been caught out in the open when the fighting commenced. They were there still, finding what cover they could in an open field bordered by trees and ravines and thick growths of mountain laurel that screened the attacking Mississippians on their front. He could no longer hear the two mountain howitzers and the James Rifle that had been helping to suppress the rebel advance. Their artillery crews were probably overrun or picked off by sharpshooters. Ned Baker was in command, somewhere to Cage's right, but there were no orders coming from that direction or from anywhere else. He could not see anything through the smoke on the field and all he could hear above the firing was the screams of the wounded and the officers in their excitement boldly exhorting their men.

The thick smoke that hung in front of Cage and his men began to sway like the hide of a moving elephant, and as it dispersed it revealed the rebels clambering out of the ravine for their next charge, bayonets fixed and lowered. Cage stood up to rally his men and direct their fire onto the Mississippians, young men whose faces he could see clearly. He heard balls whipping simultaneously past either side of his head and wondered with a strange indifference how many more particles of a second it would be before one tore neatly into his brain. He felt a fatherly tenderness toward the boys under his command and even toward the boys who were trying to kill him. He hoped that they would interpret the suicidal agitation he was exhibiting as an example of courage. It was early in the war and most of the troops on both sides were armed not with rifles but with smoothbore muskets left over from other and more ancient wars. But he knew at once, from the shattering power of the projectile that struck his arm as he lifted his Colt's revolver to fire, that he had been hit by a sharpshooter's rifle firing a minie ball. He bent down to pick up his pistol with his good hand, but the motion disoriented him and he collapsed onto the ground, watching his blood pulse over the stiff winter grass. It was late afternoon and the sun was flaring between the trees and illuminating the bright arterial blood in a way that reminded him of the early-morning prairie where he and Lincoln had found the body of Bob Zanger.

He was carried off the field in a blanket and down the steep path to the river. He was evacuated only a few minutes in advance of a general rout in which the Federal troops scrambled to the base of the bluff. Many of them were picked off by seceshers shooting down at them from the summit as they tried to escape in scows and skiffs back to the safety of the Maryland shore. There was a field hospital set up on a long island in the middle of the river, where he was given chloroform and the surgeons amputated his arm above the shattered elbow. Then he was put into a canal boat and left beside the towpath to wait for an ambulance. He lay beside a dying major whose beard was stained with black blood and who emitted great groans that fouled the air with a hellish stench.

When they finally lifted Cage's stretcher and carried it to the ambulance, they passed a dead man lying in a wagon. A half dozen officers, some in tears, stood staring down at him. It was dark but there was a fire nearby and Cage could see the dead man was Ned Baker. The dramatic fringe of hair on one side of his bald head was stiffened with blood and stood upright, following the line of his staring eyes.

For a long time he was in and out of wild fevers. Once he had a dream—though it was later proved not to be—of a middle-aged Negro woman crouched over his hospital bed, instructing him that when he was better she was going to take him on the train to Chicago. Mrs. Bicknell, Cordelia said, regretted that she could not come herself but it was getting close to Christmas and there were too many orders to fill for her absence to be tolerated. She gave him the name of a ladies' hotel where she could be found if needed and told him she would be back in a few days.

On the afternoon before she returned there was a great commotion on the ward, nurses and orderlies rushing from bed to bed straightening the sheets and changing any bandages that were stained with blood or pus. Cage was still feverish but his head was clear enough to make out from the conversation that the president and his wife were coming to pay their respects to the wounded men. Cage's bed was at the end of the long room, and he watched from a distance as they came in.

He was wearing a black suit that made him look as stark as a silhouette against the whitewashed walls of the ward. His hat was off, his hair was full, the beard that Cage had seen only in newspaper illustrations and photos looked unnatural in reality. But Cage now had a beard himself, so he supposed he would have struck Lincoln in much the same way. Overall, Lincoln looked rickety, unfit, too tall, too stooped, too old—this at a time when the war was less than a year old, when there were still so many unthinkable horrors ahead. Mary was with him, passing out apples and candy as her husband joked with the bedridden soldiers. It was an amputation ward and they were all missing limbs. Some tried to push themselves up on their beds or even to stand as he stood over them, but he gently put a hand on their shoulders and asked them to do him the honor of remaining at ease. Mary looked plumper than ever, her face pinched by the flesh it had accumulated. But her eyes were steady and bright as she stared down tearfully at the men, and any hostile stories they might have read in the papers about how demanding and self-absorbed she was instantly fled from their thoughts. She was, Cage knew, the furthest thing from an unfeeling woman. She had already endured the loss of a child back in Springfield—Eddie, named for Edward Baker, the friend she and Lincoln had just lost at Ball's Bluff—and God knew there was much for her to endure yet.

They were taking their time, not wanting any of the men to feel rushed, asking their names, asking about their families, answering questions, thanking them on behalf of the nation that they had defended.

They were three-fourths of the way down the ward when Mary happened to look in Cage's direction. He doubted that she really recognized him. He was emaciated, bearded, fifteen years older than the last time she had seen him. But there was a mildly startled look in her eyes, some kind of worry, and he could sense her composing herself for an encounter she did not quite yet understand.

Cage looked away, sparing her the embarrassment of him staring at her as she tried to understand who he was. He watched Lincoln instead as he moved to the next bed, shaking hands with the soldier there whose legs were both missing. He was telling the man a story, one that Cage had heard a dozen times before in Speed's store and during the meetings of their poetical society and while crossing the spring prairies with Lincoln on the judicial circuit. It probably wasn't even Lincoln's own story, just something from an old jest book that he had modified over the years to fit his background and speaking cadence. But the soldier had never heard it and he was hiccoughing with laughter at the end of it as Lincoln rubbed the top of his head to try to make the fit subside. The whole ward was laughing, but not loud enough to shut out the sound of a young aide's boots echoing off the wooden floor as he ran through the ward. He whispered anxiously into Lincoln's ear, and the president nodded. He spoke to Mary for a second, then addressed the rest of the men whom he had not yet had the chance to meet.

"Gentlemen, I must leave you now to confer with the gods of war on some urgent business. May I come visit you again as soon as I'm free? I promise to do so."

His eyes swept up and down the length of the ward, too rapidly to linger on any one man, or to recognize a much-altered face, no longer so familiar, no longer so young.

No doubt he made good on his promise to return, but by that time Cage was already on the train to Chicago.

Acknowledgments

ALTHOUGH *A Friend of Mr. Lincoln* is a work of fiction, it is not, I hope, an act of distortion. I've done my best to hew close to the historical record of Abraham Lincoln's life during his early years in Springfield. For storytelling purposes, however, I've taken the following liberties:

Cage Weatherby is a fictional character. At certain key points in the novel, I've substituted his presence for that of real-life personages who were part of Lincoln's circle.

Ellie is an imaginary elaboration of an unknown woman William Herndon referenced in the copious—and controversial—notes he collected on Lincoln's life.

Ashbel Merritt is also fictional, though something of a composite of Lincoln's doctor friends Anson Henry and Elias Merryman.

The trial in which Lincoln defends Cordelia is my invention, though it was suggested by Lincoln's 1841 case *Bailey v. Cromwell*. Likewise, what has become known as the "Matson Slave Case" was the inspiration for a fictional legal action late in the book.

I have brazenly moved the publication date of Longfellow's *Voices of the Night* from 1839 to 1838.

Of the dozens of authors whose books I regularly consulted while researching this novel, two proved completely indispensable. *Honor's Voice: The Transformation of Abraham Lincoln,* by Douglas L. Wilson, is a definitive and eloquent assessment of Lincoln at a time when his aspiring spirit and driving ambition were often in conflict. The second and third volumes of Richard Lawrence Miller's ongoing and

413

deeply detailed biography, *Lincoln and His World,* provided me with a crucial political and social understanding of Illinois in the 1830s and 1840s.

Also important to me was Guy Fraker's *Lincoln's Ladder to the Presidency,* and I'm deeply grateful to Guy himself for his hospitality in giving me a tour of the old Eighth Judicial Circuit and for reading an early draft of this book and saving me from glaring mistakes. James Cornelius, Lincoln Curator at the Abraham Lincoln Presidential Library and Museum, also scoured the book for mistakes (thanks to him, I don't have the Kanawha River running backwards!) and was always generous with guidance and insight. Bryon Andreasen, formerly the Research Historian at the Lincoln Library, was the first person I met when I visited Springfield. He made me feel instantly at home and looked upon my nonscholarly project with confidence-building enthusiasm.

For help in many areas of research I'm also grateful to Kevin Young, Josef Kleffman, Joshua Wolf Shenk, Alan Huffines, Wayne Temple, Erika Holst, Phil Funkenbusch, Curtis Mann, Mary Ann Warmack, Don Huber, Dan Okrent, Michael Zagst, Carla Smith, Jane Haake, Mark Johnson, and Bill Miller. And I was fortunate once again to have the best copyeditor in the business, my friend Jan McInroy.

I try to keep weepy-eyed effusions out of acknowledgments pages, but I'm not sure it would have been possible for me to sustain my writing career if I hadn't had the luck to live in a place, and at a time, where my friends could include such remarkably talented writers as Lawrence Wright, William Broyles, Elizabeth Crook, H. W. Brands, Gregory Curtis, Bill Wittliff, and James Magnuson. Each of them provided moral or editorial support or both while I was writing this book. Larry Wright and Bill Broyles read early drafts and made key suggestions, and Elizabeth Crook was there with telling feedback all the way through its composition. Speaking of dear friends, I sometimes find it hard to believe my luck through the decades in being edited at Knopf by Ann Close and represented at ICM by Esther Newberg. As long as they're both at their desks, it's still the golden age of publishing.

And my wife, Sue Ellen, to whom I've been married for forty years, and our three daughters and three sons-in-law and four grandchildren, remind me every day that writing fiction does not necessarily represent a desire to escape from reality, because there's no place I'd rather be than with them.

A NOTE ABOUT THE AUTHOR

Stephen Harrigan is the author of nine previous books, including the *New York Times* best seller *The Gates of the Alamo* and *Remember Ben Clayton,* which among other awards won the James Fenimore Cooper Prize for Best Historical Novel from the Society of American Historians. He is also a writer at large for *Texas Monthly* and a screenwriter who has written many movies for television. He lives in Austin, Texas.

A NOTE ON THE TYPE

This book was set in a typeface called Bulmer. This distinguished letter is a replica of a type long famous in the history of English printing, and which was designed and cut by William Martin about 1790 for William Bulmer of the Shakespeare Press. In design, it is all but a modern face, with vertical stress, sharp differentiation between the thick and thin strokes, and nearly flat serifs. The decorative italic shows the influence of Baskerville, as Martin was a pupil of John Baskerville's.

Typeset by Scribe, Philadelphia, Pennsylvania

Printed and bound by Berryville Graphics, Berryville, Virginia

Designed by Iris Weinstein